SKIDDING
INTO
OBLIVION

FIRST EDITION
Skidding Into Oblivion © 2019 by Brian Hodge
Cover art © 2019 by Erik Mohr (Made By Emblem)
Interior & Cover design © 2019 by Jared Shapiro
Photography by Joe Gardner, on Unsplash

Distributed in Canada by
Fitzhenry & Whiteside Limited
195 Allstate Parkway
Markham, Ontario L3R 4T8
Phone: (905) 477-9700
e-mail: bookinfo@fitzhenry.ca

Distributed in the U.S. by
Consortium Book Sales & Distribution
34 Thirteenth Avenue, NE, Suite 101
Minneapolis, MN 55413
Phone: (612) 746-2600
e-mail: sales.orders@cbsd.com

Library and Archives Canada Cataloguing in Publication

Title: Skidding into oblivion / Brian Hodge.
Names: Hodge, Brian, 1960- author.
Identifiers: Canadiana (print) GBB8M7840 | Canadiana (print) 20190043938 | Canadiana (ebook)
  20190047755 | ISBN 9781771484787 (softcover) | ISBN 9781771484794 (PDF)
Classification: LCC PS3558.O34196 S55 2019 | DDC 813/.54

CHIZINE PUBLICATIONS
Peterborough, Canada
www.chizinepub.com
info@chizinepub.com

Edited by Brett Savory
Copyedited and proofread by Leigh Teetzel

Canada Council   Conseil des arts
for the Arts   du Canada

We acknowledge the support of the Canada Council for the Arts which last year invested $20.1 million in writing and publishing throughout Canada.

ONTARIO ARTS COUNCIL
CONSEIL DES ARTS DE L'ONTARIO
an Ontario government agency
un organisme du gouvernement de l'Ontario

Published with the generous assistance of the Ontario Arts Council.

Printed in Canada

BRIAN HODGE

SKIDDING INTO OBLIVION

Once more, for Doli, through time and space.

Contents

ROOTS AND ALL

The way in was almost nothing like we remembered, miles off the main road, and Gina and me with one half-decent sense of direction between us. *Do you need us to draw you a map,* our parents had asked, hers and mine both, once at the funeral home and again over the continental breakfast at the motel. *No, no, no,* we'd told them. *Of course we remember how to get to Grandma's.* Indignant, the way adults get when their parents treat them like nine-year-olds.

Three wrong turns and fifteen extra minutes of meandering later, we were in the driveway, old gravel over ancestral dirt. Gina and I looked at each other, a resurgence of some old telepathy between cousins.

"Right," I said. "We never speak of this again."

She'd insisted on driving my car, proving . . . something . . . and yanked the keys from the ignition. "I don't even want to speak about it now."

If everything had still been just the way it used to be, maybe we would've been guided by landmarks we hadn't even realized we'd internalized. But it wasn't the same, and I don't think I was just recalling some idealized version of this upstate county that had never actually existed.

I remembered the drive as a thing of excruciating boredom, an interminable landscape of fields and farmhouses, and the thing I'd dreaded most as a boy was finding ourselves behind a tractor rumbling down a road too narrow for us to pass. But once we were there, it got better, because my grandfather had never been without a couple of hunting dogs, and there were more copses of trees and tracts of deep woodland than the most determined pack of kids could explore in an entire summer.

Now, though . . .

"The way here," I said. "It wasn't always this dismal, was it?"

Gina shook her head. "Definitely not."

I was thinking of the trailers we'd passed, and the forests of junk that had grown up around them, and it seemed like there'd been a time when, if someone had a vehicle that obviously didn't run, they kept it out of sight inside a barn until it did. They didn't set it out like a trophy. I was thinking, too, of riding in my grandfather's car, meeting another going the opposite direction, his and the other driver's hands going up at the same moment in a friendly wave. Ask him who it was, and as often as not he wouldn't know. They all waved just the same. Bygone days, apparently. About all the greeting we'd gotten were sullen stares.

We stood outside the car as if we needed to reassure ourselves that we were really here. Like that maple tree next to the driveway, whose scarlet-leafed shade we parked in, like our grandfather always had—it had to have grown, but then so had I, so it no longer seemed like the beanstalk into the clouds it once was. Yet it had to be the same tree, because hanging from the lowest limbs were a couple of old dried gourds, each hollowed out, with a hole the size of a silver dollar bored into the side. There would be a bunch more hanging around behind the house. Although they couldn't have been the same gourds. It pleased me to think of Grandma Evvie doing this right up until the end. Her life measured by the generations of gourds she'd turned into birdhouses, one of many scales of time.

How long since we've been here, Gina?

Ohhh . . . gotta be . . . four or five gourds ago, at least.

Really. That long.

Yeah. Shame on us.

It was the same old clapboard farmhouse, white, always white, always peeling. I'd never seen it freshly painted, but never peeled all the way down to naked weathered wood, either, and you had to wonder if the paint didn't somehow peel straight from the can.

We let ourselves in through the side door off the kitchen—I could hardly remember ever using the front door—and it was like stepping into a time capsule, everything preserved, even the smell, a complex blend of morning coffee and delicately fried foods.

We stopped in the living room by her chair, the last place she'd ever sat. The chair was so thoroughly our grandmother's that, even as kids, we'd felt wrong sitting in it, although she'd never chased us out. It was old beyond reckoning, as upholstered chairs went, the cushions flattened by decades of gentle pressure, with armrests as wide as cutting boards. She'd done her sewing there, threaded needles always stuck along the edge.

"If you have to die, and don't we all," Gina said, "that's the way to do it."

Her chair was by the window, with a view of her nearest neighbor, who'd been the one to find her. She'd been reading, apparently. Her book lay closed on one armrest, her glasses folded and resting atop it, and she was just sitting there, her head drooping but otherwise still upright. The neighbor, Mrs. Tepovich, had thought she was asleep.

"It's like she decided it was time," I said. "You know? She waited until she'd finished her book, then decided it was time."

"It must've been a damn good book. I mean . . . if she decided nothing else was ever going to top it." Totally deadpan. That was Gina.

I spewed a time-delayed laugh. "You're going to Hell."

Then she got serious and knelt by the chair, running her hand along the knobbly old fabric. "What's going to happen to this? Nobody'd want it. There's nobody else in the world it even fits with. It was hers. But to just throw it out . . . ?"

She was right. I couldn't stand the thought of it joining a landfill.

"Maybe Mrs. Tepovich could use it." I peered through the window, toward her house. "We should go over and say hi. See if there's anything here she'd like."

This neighborly feeling seemed as natural here as it would've been foreign back home. The old woman in that distant house . . . I'd not seen her in more than a decade, but it still felt like I knew her better than any of the twenty or more people within a five-minute walk of my own door.

It was easy to forget: Really, Gina and I were just one generation out of this place, and whether directly or indirectly, it had to have left things buried in us that we didn't even suspect.

♌

If the road were a city block, we would've started at one end, and Mrs. Tepovich would've been nearly at the other. We tramped along wherever walking was easiest, a good part of it over ground that gave no hint of having been a strawberry field once, where people came from miles around to pick by the quart.

But Mrs. Tepovich, at least, hadn't changed, or not noticeably so. She'd seemed old before and was merely older now, less a shock to our systems than we were to hers. Even though she'd seen us as teenagers she still couldn't believe how we'd grown, and maybe it was just that Gina and I looked like it had been a long time since we'd had sunburns and scabs.

"Was it a good funeral?" she wanted to know.

"Nobody complained," Gina said.

"I stopped going to funerals after Dean's."

Her husband. My best memory of him was from when the strawberries came in red and ripe, and his inhuman patience as he smoked roll-your-own cigarettes and hand-cranked a shiny cylinder of homemade ice cream in a bath of rock salt and ice. The more we pleaded, the slyer he grinned and the slower he cranked.

"I've got one more funeral left in me," Mrs. Tepovich said, "and that's the one they'll have to drag me to."

It should've been sad, this little sun-cured widow with hair like white wool rambling around her house and tending her gardens alone, having just lost her neighbor and friend—a fixture in her life that had been there half a century, one of the last remaining pillars of her past now gone.

It should've been sad, but wasn't. Her eyes were too bright, too expectant, and it made me feel better than I had since I'd gotten the news days ago. *This was what Grandma Evvie was like, right up to the end. How do you justify mourning a thing like that? It should've been celebrated.*

But no, she'd gotten the usual dirge-like send-off, and I was tempted to think she would've hated it.

"So you've come to sort out the house?" Mrs. Tepovich said.

"Only before our parents do the real job," Gina told her. "They said if there was anything of Grandma's that we wanted, now would be the time to pick it out."

"So we're here for a long weekend," I said.

"Just you two? None of the others?"

More cousins, she meant. All together, we numbered nine. Ten once, but now nine, and no, none of the others would be coming, although my cousin Lindsay hadn't been shy about asking me to send her a cell phone video of a walk-through, so she could see if there was anything she wanted. I was already planning on telling her sorry, I couldn't get a signal up here.

"Well, you were her favorites, you know." Mrs. Tepovich got still, her eyes, mired in a mass of crinkles, going far away. "And Shae," she added softly. "Shae should've been here. She wouldn't have missed it."

Gina and I nodded. She was right on both counts. There were a lot of places my sister should've been over the past eight years, instead of . . . wherever. Shae should've been a lot of places, been a lot of things, instead of a riddle and a wound that had never quite healed.

"We were wondering," Gina went on, "if there was anything from over there that you would like."

"Some of that winter squash from her garden would be nice, if it's ready to pick. She always did grow the best Delicata. And you've got to eat that up quick, because it doesn't keep as long as the other kinds."

We were looking at each other on two different wavelengths.

"Well, it doesn't," she said. "The skin's too thin."

"Of course you're welcome to anything from the garden that you want," Gina said. "But that's not exactly what we meant. We thought you might like to have something from inside the house."

"Like her chair," I said, pretending to be helpful. "Would you want her chair?"

Had Mrs. Tepovich bitten into the tartest lemon ever grown, she still wouldn't have made a more sour face. "That old eyesore? What would I need with that?" She gave her head a stern shake. "No. Take that thing out back and burn it, is what you should do. I've got eyesores of my own, I don't need to take on anyone else's."

We stayed a while longer, and it was hard to leave. Harder for us than for her. She was fine with our going, unlike so many people her age I'd been around, who did everything but grab your ankle to keep you a few more minutes. I guessed that's the way it was in a place where there was always something more that needed to be done.

Just this, on our way out the door:

"I don't know if you've got anything else planned for while you're here," she said, and seemed to be directing this at me, "but don't you go poking your noses anywhere much off the roads. Those meth people that've made such a dump of the place, I hear they don't mess around."

⊌

Evening came on differently out here than it did at home, seeming to rise up from the ground and spill from the woods and overflow the ditches that ran alongside the road. I'd forgotten this. Forgotten, too, how night seemed to spread outward from the chicken coop, and creep from behind the barn, and pool in the hog wallow and gather inside the low, tin-roofed shack that had sheltered the pigs and, miraculously, was still standing after years of disuse. Night was always present here, it seemed. It just hid for a while and then slipped its leash again.

I never remembered a time when it hadn't felt better being next to somebody when night came on. We watched it from the porch, plates in our laps as we ate a supper thrown together from garden pickings and surviving leftovers from the fridge.

When she got to it, finally, Gina started in gently. "What Mrs. Tepovich said . . . about having anything else planned this weekend . . . meaning Shae, she couldn't have been talking about anything else . . . she wasn't onto something there, was she? That's not on your mind, is it, Dylan?"

"I can't come up here and not have it on my mind," I said. "But doing something, no. What's there to do that wouldn't be one kind of mistake or another?"

Not that it wasn't tempting, in concept. Find some reprobate and put the squeeze on, and if he didn't know anything, which he almost certainly wouldn't, then have him point to someone who might.

"Good," she said, then sat with it long enough to get angry. We'd never lost the anger, because it had never had a definite target. "But . . . if you did . . . you could handle yourself all right. It's what you do every day, isn't it."

"Yeah, but strength in numbers. And snipers in the towers when the cons are out in the yard."

She looked across at me and smiled, this tight, sad smile, childhood dimples replaced by curved lines. Her hair was as light as it used to get during summers, but helped by a bottle now, I suspected, and her face narrower, her cheeks thinner. When they were plump, Gina was the first girl I ever kissed, in that fumbling way of cousins ignorant of what comes next.

There was no innocence in her look now, though, like she wished it were a more lawless world, just this once, so I could put together a private army and come back up here and we'd sweep through from one side of the county to the other until we finally got to the bottom of it.

Shae was one of the ones you see headlines about, if something about their disappearance catches the news editors' eyes: MISSING GIRL LAST SEEN MONDAY NIGHT. FAMILY OF MISSING COLLEGE STUDENT MAKES TEARFUL APPEAL. Like that, until a search team gets lucky or some jogger's dog stands in a patch of weeds and won't stop barking.

Except we'd never had even that much resolution. Shae was one of the ones who never turned up. The sweetest girl you could ever hope to meet, at nineteen still visiting her grandmother, like a Red Riding Hood who trusted that all the wolves were gone, and this was all that was found: a single, bloodied scrap of a blouse hanging from the brambles about half a mile from where our mother had grown up. The rest of her, I'd always feared, was at the bottom of a mineshaft or sunk weighted into the muck of a pond or in a grave so deep in the woods there was no chance of finding her now.

I'd had three tours of duty to erode my confidence about any innate sense of decency in the human race, and if that weren't enough, signing on with the Department of Corrections had finished off the rest. For Shae, I'd always feared the worst, in too much detail, because I knew too well what people were capable of, even the good guys, even myself.

⅄

We made little progress that first evening, getting lost on a detour into some photo albums, then after an animated phone conversation with her pair of grade-schoolers, Gina went to bed early. But I stayed up with the night, listening to it a while from Grandma Evvie's chair, until listening wasn't enough, and I had to go outside to join it.

There was no cable TV out this far, and Grandma hadn't cared enough about it for a satellite dish, so she'd made do with an ancient antenna grafted to one side of the house. The rotor had always groaned in the wind, like a weather vane denied its true purpose, the sound carrying down into the house, a ghostly grinding while you tried to fall asleep on breezy nights. Now I used it as a ladder, scaling it onto the roof, and climbing the shingles to straddle the peak.

Now and again I'd see a light in the distance—the September wind parting the trees long enough to see the porch bulb of a distant neighbor, a streak of headlights on one of the farther roads—but the blackest nights I'd ever known were out here, alone with the moon and the scattershot field of stars.

So I listened, and I opened.

The memory had never left, among the clearest from those days of long summer visits—two weeks, three weeks, a month. We would sleep four and five to a room, when my cousins and sister and I were all here at once, and Grandma would settle us in and tell us bedtime stories, sometimes about animals, sometimes about Indians, sometimes about boys and girls like ourselves.

I don't remember any of them.

But there was one she returned to every now and then, and that one stuck with me. The rest were just stories, made up on the spot or reworked versions of tales she already knew, and there was nothing lingering about them. I knew that animals didn't talk; the good Indians were too foreign to me to really identify with, and I wasn't afraid the bad ones would come to get us; and as for the normal boys and girls, well, what of them when we had real adventures of our own, every day.

The stories about the Woodwalker, though . . . those were different.

That's just my name for it. My own grandmother's name for it, she admitted to us. *It's so big and old it's got no name. Like rain. The rain doesn't know it's rain. It just falls.*

It was always on the move, she told us, from one side of the county to the other. It never slept, but sometimes it settled down in the woods or the fields to rest. It could be vast, she told us, tall enough that clouds sometimes got tangled in its hair—when you saw clouds skimming along so quickly you could track their progress, that's when you knew—but it could be small, too, small enough to curl inside an acorn if the acorn needed reminding on how to grow.

You wouldn't see it even if you looked for it every day for a thousand years, she promised us, but there were times you could see evidence of its passing by. Like during a dry spell when the dust rose up from the fields—that was the Woodwalker breathing it in, seeing if it was dry enough yet to send for some rain—and in the woods, too, its true home, when the trees seemed to be swaying opposite the direction the wind was blowing.

You couldn't see it, no, but you could feel it, down deep, brushing the edges of your soul. Hardly ever during the day, not because it wasn't there, but because if you were the right sort of person, you were too busy while the sun was up. Too busy working, or learning, or visiting, or too busy playing and wilding and having fun. But at night, though, that was different. Nights were when a body slowed down. Nights were for noticing the rest.

What's the Woodwalker do? we'd ask. *What's it for?*

It loves most of what grows and hates waste and I guess you could say it pays us back, she'd tell us. *And makes sure we don't get forgetful and too full of ourselves.*

What happens then, if you do? Somebody always wanted to know that.

Awful things, she'd say. *Awful, awful things.* Which wasn't enough, because we'd beg to know more, but she'd say we were too young to hear about them, and promise to tell us when we were older, but she never did.

You're just talking about God, right? one of my cousins said once. *Aren't you?*

But Grandma never answered that, either, at least not in any way we would've understood at the time. I still remember the look, though . . . not quite a no, definitely not a yes, and the wisdom to know that we'd either understand on our own someday, or never have to.

I saw the Woodwalker once, Shae piped up, quiet and awestruck. *One weekend last fall. He was looking at two dead deer.* None of us believed her, because we believed in hunters a lot more than we believed in anything called the Woodwalker. But, little as she was, Shae wouldn't back down. Hunters, she argued, didn't stand deer on their feet again and send them on their way.

I'd never forgotten that.

And so, as the night blustered on the wings of bats and barn owls, I listened and watched and took another tiny step toward believing.

"Any time," I whispered to whatever might speak up or show itself. "Any time."

The milk had gone bad and the bacon with it, and we needed a few other things to get us through the weekend, so that next morning I volunteered to make the run back to the store near the turnoff on the main road. I decided to take the long way, setting off in the opposite direction, because it had been years and I wanted to see more of the county, and even if I made more wrong turns than right, there were worse things than getting lost on a September Saturday morning.

Mile after mile, I drove past many worse things.

You can't remember such a place from before it got this way, can't remember the people who'd proudly called it home, without wondering what they would think of it now. Would *they* have let their homes fall to ruin with such helpless apathy? Would they have sat back and watched the fields fill with weeds? Would they have ridden two wheels, three wheels, four, until they'd ripped the low hills full of gouges and scars? Not the people I remembered.

It made me feel old, not in the body but in the heart, old in a way you always say you never want to be. It was the kind of old that in a city yells at kids to get off the lawn, but here it went past annoyance and plunged into disdain. Here, they'd done real harm. They'd trampled on memories and tradition, souring so much of what I'd decided had been good about the place, and one of them, I could never forget, had snatched my sister from the face of the earth.

Who were the people who lived here now, I wondered. They couldn't all have come from somewhere else. Most, I imagined, had been raised here and never left, which made their neglect even more egregious.

But the worst of it was in the west of the county, where the coal once was. The underground mines had been tapped out when we were children, and while that's when I'd first heard the term strip-mining, I hadn't known what it meant, either as a process or its consequences.

It was plain enough now, though, all the near-surface coal gone, too, and silent wastelands left in its wake, horizon-wide lacerations of barren land pocked with mounds of topsoil, the ground still so acidic that nothing wanted to grow there.

No matter how urgently the Woodwalker might remind the seeds what to do.

It was the wrong frame of mind to have gotten in before circling back to the store. I left my sunglasses on inside, the same way I'd wear them on cloudy days while watching the inmates in the yard, and for the same reasons, too: as armor, something to protect us both, because there was no good to come from locking eyes, from letting some people see what you think of their choices and what they'd thrown away.

The place was crowded with Saturday morning shoppers, and there was no missing the sickness here. *Those meth people that've made such a dump of the place, I hear they don't mess around,* Mrs. Tepovich had said, and for that matter, neither did the meth. I knew the look—some of the inmates still had it when they transferred from local lockups to hard time—and while it wasn't on every face in the market, it was on more than enough to make me fear it was only going to get worse here. A body half-covered with leprosy doesn't have a lot of hope for the rest of it.

The worst of them had been using for years, obviously, their faces scabbed and their bones filed sharp. With teeth like crumbling gravel, they looked like they'd been sipping tonics of sulfuric acid, and it was eating through from the inside. The rest of them, as jumpy and watchful as rats, would get there. All they needed to know about tomorrow was written in the skins of their neighbors.

It had an unexpected leveling effect.

From what I remembered of when we visited as children, the men nearly always died first here, often by a wide margin. They might go along fine for decades, as tough as buzzards in a desert, but then something caught up with them and they fell hard. They'd gone into the mines and come out with black spots on their lungs, or they'd broken their backs slowly, one sunrise-to-sunset day at a time, or had stubbornly ignored some small symptom for ten years too many. The women, though, cured like leather and carried on without them. It was something you could count on.

No longer.

The race to the grave looked like anybody's to win.

When I got back to the house, I discovered we had a visitor, a surprise since there was no car in the drive. As I came in through the kitchen, Gina, over his shoulder, gave me a where-were-you-all-this-time look that she could've stolen from my ex. They were sitting at the kitchen table with empty coffee mugs, and Gina looked like the statute of limitations on her patience had expired twenty minutes earlier.

I couldn't place him, but whoever he was, he probably hadn't had the same fierce black beard, lantern jaw, and giant belly when we were kids.

"You remember Ray Sinclair," she said, then jabbed her finger at the door, and it came back in a rush: Mrs. Tepovich's great-nephew. He used to come over and play with us on those rare days that weren't already taken up with chores, and he'd been a good guide through the woods—knew where to find all the wild berries, at their peak of ripeness, and the best secluded swimming holes where the creeks widened. We shook hands, and it was like trying to grip a baseball glove.

"I was dropping some venison off at Aunt Pol's. She told me you two were over here," he said. "My condolences on Evvie. Aunt Pol thought the world of her."

I put away the milk and bacon and the rest, while Gina excused herself and slipped past, keeping an overdue appointment with some room or closet as Ray and I cleared the obligatory small talk.

"What have you got your eye on?" he asked then. "For a keepsake, I mean."

"I don't know yet," I said. "Maybe my granddad's shotgun, if it turns up."

"You do much hunting?"

"Not since he used to take me out. And after I got back from the army . . . let's just say I wasn't any too eager to aim at something alive and pull a trigger again." I'd done fine with my qualifications for the job, although that was just targets, nothing that screamed and bled and tried to belly-crawl away. "But I'm thinking if I had an old gun that I had some history with, maybe . . ." I shrugged. "I guess I could've asked for it after Granddad died, but it wouldn't have seemed right. Not that Grandma went hunting, but left alone out here, she needed it more than I did."

He nodded. "Especially after your sister."

I looked at him without being obvious about it, then realized I hadn't taken off my sunglasses yet, just like at the market. *It could've been you*, I thought. No reason to think so, but when a killing is never solved, a body never found, it can't not cross your mind when you look at some people, the ones with proximity and access and history. The ones you really don't know anything about anymore. If Ray had known where to find berries, he'd know where to bury a girl.

"Especially then," I said.

"Did I say something wrong?" he asked. "My apologies if I did."

He sounded sincere, but I'd been hearing sincere for years. *Naw, boss, I don't know who hid that shank in my bunk. Not me, boss, I didn't have nothing to do with that bag of pruno.* They were all sincere down to the rot at their core.

The other C.O.s had warned me early on: *There'll come a time when you look at everybody like they're guilty of something.*

I'd refused to believe this: *No, I know how to leave work at work.*

Now it was me telling the new C.O.s the same thing.

I took off the shades. "You didn't say anything wrong. A thing like that, you never really get over it. Time doesn't heal the wounds, it just thickens up the scars." I moved to the screen door and looked outside, smelled the autumn day, a golden scent of sun-warmed leaves. "It's not like it used to be around here, is it."

He shrugged. "Where is?"

I had him follow me outside, and turned my face to the sun, shutting my eyes and just listening, thinking that it at least sounded the way it had. That expansive, quiet sound of birds and wide-open spaces.

"When I was at the market, I would've needed at least two hands to count the people I'd be willing to bet will be dead in five years," I said. "How'd this get started?"

Ray eyed me hard. I knew it even with my eyes closed. I'd felt it as sure as if he'd poked me with two fingers. When I opened my eyes, he looked exactly like I knew he would.

"You're some kind of narc now, aren't you, Dylan?" he said.

"Corrections officer. I don't put anybody in prison, I just try to keep the peace once they're there."

He stuffed his hands in his pockets and rocked back and forth, his gaze on far distances. "Well . . . the way anything starts, I guess. A little at a time. It's a space issue, mostly. Space, privacy. We got plenty of both here. And time. Got plenty of that, too."

His great-uncle hadn't, not to my recollection. Mr. Tepovich had always had just enough time, barely, to do what needed doing. The same as my grandfather. I wondered where all that time had come from.

"How many meth labs are there around here, I wonder," I said.

"I couldn't tell you anything. All I know's what I hear, and I don't hear much."

Can't help you, boss. I don't know nothing about that.

"But if you were to get lucky and ask the right person," Ray went on, "I expect he might tell you something like it was the only thing he was ever good at. The only thing that ever worked out for him."

The trees murmured, and leaves whisked against the birdhouse gourds.

"He might even take the position that it's a blessed endeavor."

I hadn't expected this. "Blessed by who?"

His hesitation here, his uncertainty, looked like the first genuine expression since we'd started down this path. "Powers that be, I guess. Not government, not those kinds of powers. Something . . . higher." He tipped his head back, jammed his big jaw and bristly beard forward, scowling at the sky. "Say there's a place in the woods, deep, where nobody's likely to go by accident. Not big, but not well hid, either. Now say there's a team from the sheriff's department taking themselves a hike. Fifteen, twenty feet away and they don't see it. Now say the same thing happens with a group of fellows got on jackets that say 'DEA.' They all just walk on by like nothing's there."

He was after something, but I wasn't sure what. Maybe Ray didn't know, either. They say if you stick around a prison long enough, you'll see some strange things that are almost impossible to explain, and even if I hadn't, I'd heard some stories. Maybe Ray had heard that as well, and was looking for . . . what, someone who understood?

"I don't know what else you'd call that," he said, "other than blessed."

"For a man who doesn't hear much, you have some surprising insights."

His gaze returned to earth and the mask went back on. "Maybe I keep my ear to the ground a little more than I let on." He began to sidle away toward his aunt's. "You take care, Dylan. Again, sorry about Evvie."

"Hey, Ray? Silly question, but . . ." I said. "Your Aunt Polly, your own grandma, your mom, anybody . . . when you were a kid, did any of them ever tell you stories about something called the Woodwalker?"

He shook his head. "Nope. Seen my share of wood*peckers*, though." He got a few more steps away before he stopped again, something seeming to rise up that he hadn't thought of in twenty years. "Now that you mention it, I remember one from Aunt Pol about what she called Old Hickory Bones. It didn't make a lot of sense. 'Tall as the clouds, small as a nut,' that sort of nonsense. You know old women and their stories."

"Right."

He looked like he was piecing together memories from fragments. "The part that scared us most, she'd swear up and down it was true, from when she was a girl. That there was this crew of moonshiners got liquored up on their own supply and let the still fire get out of hand. Burned a few acres of woods, and some crops and a couple of homes with it. Her story went that they were found in a row with their arms and legs all smashed up and run through with hickory sticks . . . like scarecrows, kind of. And that's how Old Hickory Bones got his name. I always thought she just meant to scare us into making sure we didn't forget about our chores."

"That would do it for me," I said.

He laughed. "Those cows didn't have to wait on me for very many morning milkings, I'll tell you what." He turned serious, one big hand scrubbing at his beard. "Why do you come to ask about a thing like that?"

I gestured at the house. "You know how it is going through a place this way. Everything you turn over, there's another memory crawling out from underneath it."

∀

Later, I kept going back to what I'd said when Gina and I had first walked in and looked at Grandma's chair: that it seemed like she'd finished her book and set it aside and peacefully resolved it was a good day to die. It's the kind of invention that gives you comfort, but maybe she really had. She kept up on us, her children and grandchildren, even though we were scattered far and wide. She knew I had a vacation coming up, knew that it overlapped with Gina's.

And we were her favorites. Even Mrs. Tepovich knew that.

So I'm tempted to think Grandma trusted that, with the right timing, Gina and I would be first to go through the house. She couldn't have wanted my mother to do it. Couldn't have wanted my father to be the first up in the attic. Some things are too cruel, no matter how much love underlies them.

Maybe she'd thought we would be more likely to understand and accept. Because we were her favorites, and even though my mother had grown up here, and my aunts and uncles, too, they were so much longer out of the woods than we, her grandchildren, were.

It broke the agreeable calm of Saturday afternoon, Gina and I in different parts of the house. I was in the pantry, looking through last season's preserves and had discovered an ancient Mason jar full of coins when a warbling cry drifted down. I thought she'd come across a dead raccoon, a nest of dried-out squirrels . . . the kind of things that sometimes turn up in country attics.

But when Gina came and got me, her face was pale and her voice had been reduced to such a small thing I could barely hear it. *Shae*, she was saying, or trying to. *Shae*. Over and over, with effort and an unfocused look in her eyes. *Shae*.

I didn't believe her while climbing the folding attic ladder; still didn't while crossing the rough, creaking boards, hunched beneath the slope of the roof in the gloom and cobwebs and a smell like a century of dust. But after five or twenty minutes on my knees, I believed, all right, even if nothing made sense anymore.

There was light, a little, coming through a few small, triangular windows at the peaks. And there was air, slatted vents at either end allowing some circulation. And there was my sister's body, on a cot between a battered steamer trunk and a stack of cardboard boxes, covered by a sheet that had been drawn down as far as her chest.

The sheet wasn't dusty or discolored. It was clean, white, recently laundered. Eight years of washing her dead granddaughter's sheets—my head had trouble grasping that, and my heart just wanted to stop.

Gradually it dawned on me: With Shae eight years dead, we shouldn't have been able to recognize her. At best, she would've mummified in the dry heat, shriveled into a husk. At worst, all that was left would be scraps and bones, and the strawberry blonde silk of her hair. Instead, the most I could say was that she looked very, very thin, and when I touched her cheek, her skin was smooth and stiff but pliable, like freshly worked clay. I touched her cheek and almost expected her eyes to open.

She'd been nineteen then, was nineteen now. She'd spent the last eight years being nineteen. Nineteen and dead, only not decayed. She lay on a blanket and a bed of herbs. They were beneath her, alongside her. Sprigs and bundles had been stuffed inside the strips of another sheet that had been loosely wound around her like a shroud. The scent of them, a pungent and spicy smell of fields and trees, settled in my nose.

"Do you think Grandma did this?" Gina was behind me, pressing close. "Not *this* this, that's obvious, but . . . killed her, I mean. Not on purpose, but by accident, and she just couldn't face the rest of us."

"Right now I don't know what to think."

I shoved some junk out of the way to let more light at her. Her skin was white as a china plate, and dull, without the luster of life. Her far cheek and jaw were traced with a few pale bluish lines like scratches that had never healed. Gently, as if it were still possible to hurt her, I turned her head from side to side, feeling her neck, the back of her skull. There were no obvious wounds, although while the skin of her neck was white as well, it was a more mottled white.

"Do me a favor," I said. "Check the rest of her."

Gina's eyes popped. "Me? Why me? You're the hard-ass prison guard."

It was then I knew everything was real, because when tragedy is real, silly things cross your mind at the wrong times. *Corrections officer,* I wanted to tell her. *We don't like the G-word.*

"She's my sister. She's still a teenager," I said instead. "I shouldn't be . . . she wouldn't want me to."

Gina moved in and I moved aside and turned my back, listening to the rustle of cotton sheets and the crackle of dried herbs. My gaze roved and I spotted mousetraps, one set, one sprung, and if there were two, there were probably others. Grandma had done this, too. Set traps to keep the field mice away from her.

"She's, uh . . ." Gina's voice was shaky. "Her back, her bottom, the backs of her legs, it's all purple-black."

"That's where the blood pooled. That's normal." At least it didn't seem like she'd bled to death. "It's the only normal thing about this."

"What am I looking for, Dylan?"

"Injuries, wounds . . . is it obvious how she was hurt?"

"There's a pretty deep gash across her hipbone. And her legs are all scratched up. And her belly. There are these lines across it, like, I don't know . . . rope burns, maybe?"

Everything in me tightened. "Was she assaulted? Her privates?"

"They . . . look okay to me."

"All right. Cover her up decent again."

I inspected Shae's hands and fingertips. A few of her nails were ragged, with traces of dirt. Her toenails were mismatched, clean on one foot, the other with the same rims of dirt, as if she'd lost a shoe somewhere between life and death. Grandma had cleaned her up, that was plain to see, but hadn't scraped too deeply with the tip of the nail file. Maybe it just came down to how well she could see.

I returned to Shae's neck, the mottling there. Connect the dots and you could call it lines. If her skin weren't so ashen, it might look worse, ringed with livid bruises.

"If I had to guess, I'd say she was strangled," I told Gina. "And maybe not just her throat, but around the middle, too." Someone treating her like a python treats prey, wrapping and squeezing until it can't breathe.

We tucked her in again and covered her the rest of the way, to keep off the dust and let her return to her long, strange sleep.

"What do you want to do?" Gina said, and when I didn't answer: "The kindest thing we could do is bury her ourselves. Let it be our secret. Nobody else has to know. What good would it do if they did?"

For the first minute or two, that sounded good. Until it didn't. "You don't think Grandma knew that, too? It's not that she couldn't have. If she was strong enough to work the soil in her garden, and to get Shae up the ladder, then she was strong enough to dig a grave. And there's not one time in the last eight years I heard her say anything that made me think her mind was off track. You?"

Gina shook her head. "No."

"Then she was keeping Shae up here for a reason."

We backed off toward the ladder, because another night, another day, wasn't going to do Shae any harm.

And that's when we found the envelope that Gina must have sent flying when she first drew back the sheet.

↻

How you react to what I got to say depends on who's done the finding, our Grandma Evvie had written. *I have my hopes for who it is, and if it hasn't gone that way I won't insult the rest by spelling it out, but I think you know who you are.*

First off, I know how this looks, but how things look and how things are don't always match up.

Know this much to be true: It wasn't any man or woman that took Shae's life. The easiest thing would've been to turn her over and let folks think so and see her buried and maybe see some local boy brought up on charges because the sheriff decides he's got to put it on somebody. I won't let that happen. There's plenty to pay for around here, and maybe the place would be better off even if some of them did get sent away for something they didn't do, but I can't help put a thing like that in motion without knowing whose head it would fall on.

If I was to tell you Shae was done in by what I always called the Woodwalker, some of you might believe me and most of you probably wouldn't. Believing doesn't make a thing any more or less true, it just points you toward what you have to do next.

If I was to tell you you could have Shae back again, would you believe it enough to try?

G̱ᴿ.

In the kitchen that evening, across the red oilcloth spread over the table, Gina and I argued. We argued for a long time. It comes naturally to brothers and sisters, but cousins can be pretty good at it, too.

We argued over what was true. We argued over what couldn't possibly be real. We weren't arguing with each other so much as with ourselves, and with what fate had shoved into our faces.

Mostly, though, we argued over how far is too far, when it's for family.

〜

Living with this has been no easy task. What happened to Shae was not a just thing. Folks here once knew that whatever we called it, there really is something alive in the woods and fields, as old as time and only halfway to civilized, even if few were ever lucky or cursed enough to see it. We always trusted that if we did right by it, it would do right by us. But poor Shae paid for other folks' wrongs.

She meant well, I know. It's no secret there's a plague here and it's run through one side of this county to the other. So when Shae found a trailer in the woods where they cook up that poison, nothing would do but that she draw a map and report it.

Till the day I die I won't ever forget the one summer when all the grandchildren were here and the night little Shae spoke up to say she'd seen the Woodwalker. I don't know why she was allowed at that age to see what most folks never do in a lifetime, but not once did I think she was making it up. I believed her.

The only thing I can fathom is this: Once she decided to report that trailer and what was going on there, the Woodwalker knew her heart, and resolved to put a stop to her intentions.

⅄

I spent half of Sunday out by myself, trying to find what Shae had found, but all I had to go by was the map she'd drawn. There was no knowing how accurate it was when it was new, and like the living things they are, woods never stop changing over time. Trees grow and fall, streams divert, brambles close off paths that were once as clear as sidewalks.

And whoever had put the trailer there had had eight years to move it. What it sounded like they'd never had, though, was a reason.

I had the map, and a bundle of sticks across my back, and like any hunter I had a shotgun—not my granddad's, since that one had yet to turn up, and it's just as well I went for the one in my trunk, carried out of habit for the job—but sometimes hunters come home empty-handed.

At least I came back with a good idea of what else I needed before going out to try again.

♁

I don't want to say what I saw, but it was enough to know that it was no man using all those vines to drag her off toward the hog wallow, faster than I could chase after them. By the time I caught up, it had choked the life from her.

It didn't do this because it wanted to protect those men for their own sakes. I think it's because it wants the plague to continue until it finishes clearing away everybody who's got it, and there's nobody left in this county but folks who will treat the place right again.

These days you'll hear how the men who've brought this plague think they're beyond the reach of the law, because their hideaways can't be found. Well, I say it's only because the Woodwalker has a harsher plan than any lawman, and blinds the eyes of those who come from outside to look.

But Shae always did see those woods with different eyes.

⁜

"Remember what Grandma used to call her?" Gina asked. I was ashamed to admit I didn't. "'Our little wood-elf,'" she said, then, maybe to make me feel better, "That's not something a boy would've remembered. That's one for the girls."

"Maybe so," I said, and peeled the blanket open one more time to check my sister's face. I'd spent the last hours terrified that there had been some magic about our grandmother's attic, and that once she was carried back to the outside world again, the eight years of decay Shae had eluded would find her at last.

One more time, I wouldn't have known she wasn't just dreaming.

Instead, the magic had come with her. Or maybe the Woodwalker, spying us with the burden we'd shared through miles of woodland, knew our hearts now, too, and opened the veil for our eyes to see. Either way, I'd again followed where the old map led, and this time Shae had proven to be the key.

"Do you think it goes the other way?" Gina asked.

"What do you mean?"

"If we stood up and whoever's in there looked out, would they see us now? Or would they look straight at us and just see more trees?"

"I really don't want to put that to the test."

The trailer was small enough to hitch behind a truck, large enough for two or three people to spend a day inside without tripping over each other too badly. It sat nestled into the scooped-out hollow of a rise, painted with a fading camouflage pattern of green and brown. At one time its keepers had strung nets of nylon mesh over and around it, to weave with branches and vines, but it looked like it had been a long time since they'd bothered, and they were sagging here, collapsed there. It had a generator for electricity, propane for gas. From the trailer's roof jutted a couple of pipes that had, ever since we'd come upon it, been venting steam that had long since discouraged anything from growing too close to it.

Eventually the steam stopped, and a few minutes later came the sound of locks from the other side of the trailer door. It swung open and out stepped two men. They took a few steps away before they stripped off the gas masks they'd been wearing and let them dangle as they seemed glad to breathe the cool autumn air.

I whispered for Gina to stay put, stay low, then stepped out from our hiding place and went striding toward the clearing in-between, and maybe it did take the pair of them longer to notice than it should've. They each wore a pistol at the hip but seemed to lack the instinct to go for them.

And the trees shuddered high overhead, even though I couldn't feel or hear a breeze.

"Hi, Ray," I called, leveling the shotgun at them from the waist.

"Dylan," he said, with a tone of weary disgust. "And here I believed you when you said you weren't no narc."

For a while I'd been wondering if he'd simply dropped by while visiting his great-aunt, and Shae had suspected him for what he was and followed him here, righteous and foolhardy thing that she could be.

I glanced at the gangly, buzz-cut fellow at his side. "Who's that you're with?"

"Him? Andy Ellerby."

"Any more still inside?"

Ray's fearsome beard seemed to flare. "You probably know as well as I do, cooking is a two-man job at most." He scuffed at the ground. "Come on, Dylan, your roots are here. You don't do this. What say we see what we can work out, huh?"

I looked at his partner. Like Ray, the edges of his face and the top of his forehead were red-rimmed where the gas mask had pressed tight, and he gave me a sullen glare. "Andy Ellerby, did I know you when we were kids?"

He turned his head to spit. "What's it matter if you did or didn't, if you can't remember my name."

"Good," I said. "That makes this much a little easier."

I snapped the riot gun to my shoulder and found that, when something mattered this much, I could again aim at something alive and pull the trigger. The range was enough for the twelve-gauge load to spread out into a pattern as wide as a pie tin. Andy took it in the chest and it flung him back against the trailer so hard he left a dent.

I'd loaded it with three more of the same, but didn't need them, so I racked the slide to eject the spent shell, then the next three. Ray looked confused as the unfired shells hit the forest floor, and his hand got twitchy as he remembered the holster on his belt, but by then I was at the fifth load and put it just beneath his breastbone, where his belly started to slope.

He looked up at me from the ground, trying to breathe with a reedy wheeze, groping where I'd shot him and not comprehending his clean, unbloodied hands.

"A beanbag round," I told him. "We use them for riot control. You can't just massacre a bunch of guys with homemade knives even if they are a pack of savages."

I knelt beside him and plucked the pistol from his belt before he remembered it, tossed it aside. Behind me, Gina had crept out of hiding with her arms wrapped around herself, peering at us with the most awful combination of hope and dread I'd ever seen.

"I know you didn't mean to, and I know you don't even know you did it, but you're still the reason my little sister never got to turn twenty." I sighed, and tipped my head a moment to look at the dimming sky, and listened to the sound of every living thing, seen and unseen. "Well . . . maybe next year."

I drew the hunting knife from my belt while he gasped; called for Gina to bring me the bundle of hickory sticks that my grandmother must have sharpened years ago, and the mallet with a cast-iron head, taken down from the barn wall. It would've been easier with Granddad's chainsaw, but some things shouldn't come easy, and there are times the old ways are still the best.

I patted Ray's shoulder and remembered the stocky boy who'd taken us to the fattest tadpoles we'd ever seen, the juiciest berries we'd ever tasted. "For what it's worth, I really was hoping it wouldn't be you coming out that door."

If the family is to have Shae back again, there's some things that need doing, and I warn you, they're ugly business.

Dylan, if you're reading this, know that it was only you that I ever believed had the kind of love and fortitude in you to take care of it and not flinch from it. Whether you still had the faith in what your summers here put inside you was another matter. I figured that was a bridge we'd cross when it was time.

But then you came back from war, and whatever you'd seen and done there, you weren't right, and I knew it wasn't the time to ask. Somehow the time never did seem right. So if I was to tell you that I got used to having Shae around, even as she was, maybe you can understand that, and I hope forgive me for it.

It never seemed like all of her was gone.

The Woodwalker could've done much worse to her body, and I think it's held on to her soul. What I believe is that it didn't end her life for good, but took it to hold onto a while.

Why else would the Woodwalker have bothered to bring her back to the house?

♏

My sister saw the Woodwalker once, so she'd claimed, looking at two dead deer, and the reason she'd known it was no hunter was because hunters don't help dead deer back to their feet and send them on their way.

There's give and there's take. There's balance in everything. It was the one law none of us could hide from. Even life for life sometimes, but if Shae really did see what she thought she had, I wondered what she *hadn't* seen—what life the Woodwalker had deemed forfeit for the deer's.

As I went about the ugliest business of my life, I thought of the moonshiners from the tale Mrs. Tepovich had told Ray as a boy—how they'd burned out a stretch of woodland and fields, and the grotesque fate they'd all met. But Grandma Evvie, as it turned out, had a different take on what had happened, and why the woods and crops rebounded so quickly after the fire.

"That story about Old Hickory Bones your Aunt Pol told you?" This was the last thing I said to Ray. "It's basically true, except she was wrong about one thing. Or maybe she wanted to give you the lesson but spare you the worst. But the part about replacing the bones with hickory sticks? That's not something the Woodwalker does . . . that's the gift it expects us to give it."

Whatever else was true and wasn't, I knew this much: Grandma Evvie would never have lied about my grandfather taking part in such a grim judgment when he was a very young man, able to swing a cast-iron mallet with ease.

Just as he must've done, I cut and sliced, pounded and pushed, hurrying to get it finished before the last of the golden autumn light left the sky, until what I'd made looked something like a crucified scarecrow. It glistened and dripped, and for as terrible a sight as it was, I'd still seen worse in war. When I stood back to take it in, wrapped in the enormous roar of woodland silence, I realized that my grandmother's faith in me to do such a thing wasn't entirely a compliment.

Gina hadn't watched, hadn't even been able to listen, so she'd spent the time singing to Shae, any song she could think of, as she prepared my sister's body. She curled her among the roots of a great oak, resting on a bed of leaves and draped with a blanket of creepers and vines. How much was instruction and how much was instinct grew blurred, but it seemed right. She shivered beneath Shae's real blanket after she was done, and after I'd cleaned myself up inside the trailer, I held her a while as she cried for any of a hundred good reasons. Then I built a fire and we waited.

You let yourself hope but explain things away. No telling why that pile of leaves rustled, why that vine seemed to twitch. Anything could've done it. Flames flickered and shadows danced, while something watched us in the night—something tall enough to tangle clouds in its hair, small enough to hide in an acorn—and the forest ebbed and flowed with the magnitude of its slow, contemplative breath.

A hand first, or maybe it was a foot . . . something moved, too deliberate, too human, to explain away as anything else. Eight years since I'd heard her voice, but I recognized it instantly in the cough that came from beneath the shadows and vines. Gina and I dug, and we pulled, and scraped away leaves, and in the tangled heart of it all there was life, and now only one reason to cry. Shae coughed a long time, scrambling in a panic across the forest floor, her limbs too weak to stand, her voice too weak to scream, and I wondered if she was back at that moment eight years gone, reliving what it was like to die.

We held her until, I hoped, she thought it was just another dream.

I cupped her face, her cheeks still cold, but the fire gave them a flush of life. "Do you know me?"

Her voice was a dry rasp. "You look like my brother . . . only older."

She had so painfully much to learn. I wondered if the kindest thing wouldn't be to keep her at the house until we'd taught each other everything about where we'd been the last eight years, and the one thing I hadn't considered until now was what if she wasn't right, in ways we could never fix, in ways beyond wrong, and it seemed like the best thing for everybody would be to send her back again.

For now, though, I had too much to learn myself.

"Take her back to the house," I told Gina. "I'll catch up when I can."

They both looked at me like I was sending them out among the wolves. But somebody, somewhere, was expecting what had just been cooked up in the trailer.

"And tell them not to put the place up for sale. I'll need it myself."

It was Shae, with the wisdom of the dead, who intuited it first, with a look on her face that asked, *What did you do, Dylan, what did you do?*

I kissed them both on their cold cheeks, and turned toward the trailer before I could turn weak, and renege on the harshest terms of the trade.

Because there's give and there's take. There are balances to be kept. And there's a time in everyone's life when we realize we've become what we hate the most.

I was the bringer of plague now. There could be no other way.

And though I knew it would be a blessed endeavor, they still couldn't die fast enough.

THIS STAGNANT BREATH
OF CHANGE

Beasley had died three times within the last month alone. Each time, they'd brought him back, and each time, it got harder.

The first was a simple heart attack, which they'd fought off by jump-starting him with the defibrillator; later, balloon angioplasty.

That opened the door to human error. Beasley's vitals were normal, until, without warning, he flatlined. They'd traced that to a bag of potassium solution with too high a concentration, and got his pulse going again by shooting him up with insulin and glucose, along with intravenous calcium and inhalations of albuterol.

This last scare was the worst, a line infection that would've begun small, as they always did, then swamped him with tidal waves of bacteria before anyone realized what was happening. That was the insidious thing about line infections:. Once one line was compromised, it was all but guaranteed to spread to the rest. And he was hooked up to so many.

They got him through the worst of it, and once it looked as if Donald Beasley would survive another day, they stood down. By now, his room here at Good Sam was an ICU unto itself.

And by now, the routine was familiar enough that Bethany knew what to expect once it was over: *Hello, adrenaline crash, my old friend. Hello, relief, you seductive lie.*

As she always did, once the crisis was averted, the inevitable pushed back a little farther, she retreated to the hall in her green scrubs to shake out the stress and peer out the nearest window to search the sky for signs.

Retreating storm clouds, maybe, or a fading giant wisp of faces from years of bad dreams. There was no rational reason it had to be the sky, only that it seemed as good a source as any to unleash . . .

Well, whatever was going to happen the day they *couldn't* bring him back.

"How long can we keep this up?" Bethany asked the attending physician, who was prone to de-stressing in his own way.

Cavendish, his name, but most here just called him Doctor Richard. He puffed at a cigarette as if it were the only thing keeping him upright. He was one of those doctors who continued to smoke in spite of knowing every reason not to. It would never catch up with him. That was the problem. His, hers, and everyone else's.

"How much more can that withered old body of his take?"

"As much as we can force on it," Dr. Richard said. "I'll crack his chest open and crawl in there and stay if I have to."

"Heroics aside," she said. "Just be honest."

He'd been on staff here long enough to have treated her the summer she was eight, after she and her bicycle lost a minor altercation with a car. Today, he looked every year of it.

"If we're having this same conversation a month from now, I'll consider that a miracle." Richard chained another cig off the first. "Honest enough for you?"

A few hours later, when her shift was over, she dropped by Donald Beasley's room to reassure herself that she could leave with a clear conscience. Another post-crisis habit. Like driving past a leaky dam to make sure the cracks hadn't widened. One of the off-duty nurses was sitting in a chair by the bed, watching him. Somebody was always watching him.

The cycles of death and restoration had taken their toll. According to Beasley's charts, he was seventy-six now, but he looked at least a hundred.

He was still unconscious, but would come around again eventually, and she didn't want to be here when that happened. She'd done her time. Beasley might talk jabbering nonsense. Then again, he might be cognizant of everything, and resume begging for them to let him die. Either option was its own brand of unnervingly awful. He would tug at the restraints holding his wrists to the bed rails, feeble and mewling, and somehow, his desiccated body would find enough moisture for tears. They lived in fear of him thinking to bite through his tongue in an effort to drown in his own blood.

The watch-nurse glanced back over one heavy, rounded shoulder and nodded a dead-eyed hello. They'd gone to high school together, sort of. Janet Swain had been a senior when Bethany had come in as an undersized freshman, no boobs to speak of, and invisible.

32

They'd all gone to high school together here in Tanner Falls.

"If we can't save him, and we know it, say he's got a little time left, just not long, what would you want to do?" Janet said. "Would you give him what he deserves?"

Bethany squeezed her eyes closed. "Don't ask me something like that."

"I would. I mean, why not? Last chance, why waste the opportunity? It's only what everybody in the whole town has wanted to do to him for years. If we announced it, there'd be a line ten thousand people long. We should raffle off chances while we still can."

"Is that really what you'd want to be thinking of at the end?"

"I'd start with his eyes. Somebody going for your eyes, that's some scary business, right there. I'd leave him one, though, so he could see what I do to the rest of him."

Talk. Bethany tried to dismiss it as empty talk, no risk. They all needed to vent sometimes.

"Even old men are still attached to their ding-dongs." Janet smacked her hand on the bed rail and addressed Beasley directly. "You think that catheter was painful going in, you old buzzard? You have no idea."

If they got it out of their systems this way, maybe it would be enough, and they wouldn't lose control over the urge to act.

"And yeah, that *is* what I'll be thinking of at the end." Janet said this with a glare, almost an accusation. "That's the kind of thing you get to think of when you don't have anybody, and know you never will."

She made companionship sound like a comfort she was denied, but really, was it? Maybe Janet was the lucky one here, and would see it that way when the time came. When not dying alone meant having to watch someone you love die next to you, who really wanted that?

They could all die alone, together.

☾

Bethany walked home after her shift, because she could. All the first-stringers on the Beasley team lived close enough for a shoe-leather commute. Call it hospital policy, and plain old good sense. They wanted to be able to assemble the top tier crash team in minutes, any time of day or night, regardless of how much rain or snow or wind or ice might get in the way.

The plan had gone into effect years ago, before the old man's health started to decline. It had begun early, as soon as the first of the city fathers from a generation ago died. They would all be sick old men one day. Some of them were already old. Others were already sick middle-aged men. Over time, they'd all done what sick old men do, eventually overcoming each and every extraordinary measure to prolong their selfish lives, until Donald Beasley was the last man standing, however unsteadily.

Children used to sing about him, years ago, and maybe still would, if only there were enough kids around to pass the song down to, the way these things used to work. But after a generation, birth rates had fallen so low, by choice, that children were now a rarity in Tanner Falls, lonely and isolated. Even they knew something was wrong, in this place where their future had been taken from them before they were born.

"Old Mad Donald had a town,
iä iä oh!
And in that town he had a goat,
iä iä oh!"

Horrible little song. You had to marvel at how jubilantly children could sing of terrible things without appreciating what they were actually about. Yet she still missed the sound of it.

There was a time when Tanner Falls had been a great place to grow up. That was how she'd experienced it. You could roam all day here, under the radar of adults. Even within town, there were pockets of woodland that felt so much farther from civilization than they really were, centuries of trees grown up around ponds and laced together by streams and paths worn smooth by bicycle tires. There were fish to catch and frogs to race. There were railroad tracks to explore, wondering where they led, and hunt for treasures that might have fallen from passing trains, and if you couldn't find anything, at least there were plenty of targets daring you to throw rocks at them.

And in the city park, the concrete band shell always seemed to smell faintly of pee—a phenomenon explained by the shards of brown glass that always seemed to reappear—but it projected your voice in a most wonderful way, especially when you bunched together with your friends to see how loudly all of you could shriek together, so that even the old people who lived by the park came out on their porches to scowl.

And when you grew old enough for four wheels instead of two, you had the drive-in theater on the edge of town, and the A&W, where carhops on skates brought trays to hang on your door, loaded with burgers and onion rings and frosted mugs of root beer. And that was good for a while, as well, until it all started to seem too small, and boredom became an enemy that could only be outrun by going anywhere else but here.

Bethany didn't have to work to remember the town that way. Because it was still the same. It was all exactly the same, as immutably fixed as the old spoke-wheeled cannon on the courthouse lawn, commemorating a war no one alive had even fought in.

Like the shop on the corner over there, Stewart Drug & Sundries. *Sundries*—who even used the word anymore? Here, they did. Across the street and down the block? Where would you even expect to find something called Franklin's Dime Store today, in this, the post-Reagan years of George Bush? But here it was, unchanged from the pictures she'd seen when her parents were children. In any direction you looked where houses stood, you would see a skyline bristling with towering TV aerials, as if no one had heard of cable. They had . . . but it had never come here.

Bethany knew enough of the world beyond to realize you were meant to remember such things fondly because they were no longer around. That was how nostalgia was supposed to work—mourning defunct businesses and outmoded ways and untamed land lost to bulldozers sent by developers who called it progress. Recalling them with a golden luster because they had meant enough to your heart once to crowd out memories of all the uglier things better off forgotten.

Like that sign painted on the huge brick side of the Tanner Hotel, smack in the heart of downtown:

NIGGER, DON'T LET THE SUN SET ON YOU HERE

Nobody wanted it. Nobody liked what it had to say, or what it said now about the town. They could scarcely bring themselves to look at it. It repelled the eye, yet resisted all efforts to erase its existence. Whitewash it, paint over it, paper over it, hang a banner across it from the roof—whatever went up wouldn't last the night. Sandblasting just made a gritty mess. Even attempts at demolition were plagued by mechanical failure.

It had been more than fifteen years since they'd given up trying.

And Tanner Falls stayed just as it was in 1969.

The hotel's insistence on cleaving to the status quo was one of the first bits of evidence that something was wrong here, early proof that someone had done a terrible thing to them all.

People change. People grow. Those who can't, die off, and with luck their worst notions die with them. Nobody wanted that hateful sign anything other than gone.

Except, maybe, for Donald Beasley and the fellow town fathers from a generation ago who had beat him to the grave.

There was a time when Tanner Falls had seemed like a great place to grow up.

What an unlikely thing to have doomed it.

* * *

Matt was already home when she got there, his back-support belt hanging from its peg by the side door. His shift had an hour to go yet, and by the look of things he'd been home long enough for three cans of Iron City already. Matt was the first person she was aware of who'd figured out that once you had a job in Tanner Falls, it was impossible to lose it, a fact of life he exploited with heedless impunity. Termination was change, and hey, they couldn't have that.

So there he was, still moving the same furniture in the same warehouse that had paid him for fifteen hours a week after school in 1969, so he could save up to buy his first real guitar.

He didn't notice her, such was his focus, so for a while she watched him play. Watched him go somewhere else, the only way left to him.

He was a leftie, and so was his Les Paul. Even Bethany, who had assisted while surgeons' hands worked wonders, could never figure out how Matt could be so dexterous as to play three parts at once: rhythms on the bottom two strings, melodies on the top two, and harmony and counterpoint in the middle. The effects pedals between the guitar and amp made it even more expansive, a swirling, psychedelic storm front of thunder and squalls that climbed and plunged, that promised hope and delivered heartache.

Every generation in every town had its Matt Meadows: the guy who could've really done something, gone places, if only he'd left.

He noticed her, finally, and brought the spaceship in for a landing, the last ripple of arpeggios echoing into the sonic horizon, until the only sound left in the hush of the house was the hum of his amp.

And in every town, every girl had her own potential Matt: the guy she ended up marrying because she hadn't left, either.

"That good a day, huh?" he said.

Later they went for a walk, meandering through the neighborhood, then straying west, as she sensed he might, through neighborhoods where the houses got bigger and farther apart. He had a homing instinct, and Bethany knew where they were going to end up long before they did: a pocket of undeveloped woodland tucked alongside a tributary upstream of the falls that gave the town its name. Matt had a need to torture himself with this place, and all it had taken from them.

36

She regarded this the way she regarded the beer he brought with him, even on a stroll: didn't like it, but didn't object. Let Matt be Matt. Let him have what he needs to get by, because without it, it could be so much worse. Everything would be worse soon enough.

The trees were not packed tightly here, except for a few small, compact groves. It was mostly an open field, with thickets enclosing the sides like walls, and a stream ran through it. Matt and his friends used to put on safety goggles and thick sweatshirts and have BB gun fights here. Nobody had ever lost an eye, a tooth. Welts were as bad as it got. No wonder they'd gotten the idea they were blessed.

They were boys and, for a time, invincible.

In some other life, in some other town, she might have had a son just like that. She would've welcomed the prospect of fretting over every little injury and wound that, in the puzzling way of boys, grounded him with pride and meaning. She would've welcomed a daughter like this that just the same.

Only once had the Ortho-Novum failed. She'd kept the procedure quiet, kept Matt in the dark altogether. Nothing good could have come of him knowing. It wasn't that he would have disagreed with her decision; more that she didn't want to give him one more thing to regret.

The hoofprints. Once here, Matt always went for the hoofprints.

It was what people called them, anyway—a row of inches-deep depressions striding along the broadest clearing in the field. They hadn't filled in during the twenty-two years they'd been there, as if something about their creation had seared them in place for all time. Life shunned them. Not even the most opportunistic weeds grew in them, or anywhere close.

Honestly, Bethany didn't know if they were hoofprints or not. They were the right shape, cloven, like mirrored images of half-moons. Then again, each one was as big around as a truck tire.

She'd been a child when the event had happened, not yet ten, and although she hadn't witnessed it, she'd heard so many stories that it felt as if she had. Not that the stories were necessarily trustworthy. People were liars, even if they didn't mean to be. By now the strands of folklore had wound so inextricably around fact that it was impossible to twist them apart and get to the truth of things.

Under the black watch of a springtime new moon, the town had been lit for an instant by a flash of light. It wasn't lightning, though—no account ever mentioned a storm. It was more like reports describing the bright death of a meteorite. Nor was it white. Blue, some said. Others insisted it was green, while still others couldn't pin down a color at all, only that they didn't find it natural.

A fearsome wind had kicked up, too, and that lasted longer. Residents in the north of town swore it blew south, while those in the south swore it blew north. On the east side, they said it swept in toward the west, and here on the west side, the direction depended on how far out people were. They couldn't all be right, unless something had punched a hole in the night, like knocking out a window in an airliner, that sucked the air in from everywhere at once.

Maybe it had.

People said that something appeared through the trees that night, big enough to have appeared above even the tallest ones. Some reported a churning cloud, while others swore they witnessed vast legs striding through the woods, coarse with bristling black hair and cloven hooves. A cloud with legs? Oh, why not. Something had changed the fundamentals of reality here. Or rather, prevented change.

She couldn't recall the first time she heard someone, in a low voice, speak of the Black Goat of the Woods With a Thousand Young. It was just one of those things you grew up with, like Santa Claus and the Tooth Fairy.

"You think it'll come back, right here?" Matt said. "Is that the way it's supposed to happen?"

"I don't know," she said.

"Beasley, any of them, they've never said anything about what to expect? Not even at the end, or when they were doped out on the good meds?"

"No."

He looked at her in a way that made it feel like they were strangers. He was just thirty-two, and already his face was too lined. "You'd tell me, wouldn't you? You wouldn't keep it to yourself just to spare me?"

Briefly, she wondered if he knew about the abortion after all, how she'd D&C'd the life they'd created rather than see it born into a short, cruel existence as chattel.

"Most of those guys," she said, "I think they were in denial about what they did. They wouldn't admit they'd done anything at all, much less speculate about what the consequences were going to be like. Not to us, anyway. Why would they? They knew by the time it happened, they weren't going to be around to worry about it."

"Yeah, but . . . they had kids, grandkids."

"Denial can cover a lot of ground when you're determined."

They walked and he drank and pondered issues whose understanding would forever be denied them.

"How does something like that even get started in a town like this?" Matt said. "I bet they didn't even mean it."

"I don't know about that. Whatever happened here, it didn't happen because they were half-assed about it."

"At first, I mean, when they first started. I'll bet it was like some small town, good old boy version of the Hellfire Clubs."

"Hellfire Clubs?" This was a new one. "That sounds ominous enough to me."

"It wasn't. They were just something a bunch of upper crust English and Irish politicians and other outwardly pious types did for a lark. An excuse for them to get together to frolic with whores and feel like bad boys." Matt looked at her, and couldn't have missed her puzzled expression, how this was in his storehouse of knowledge. "I used to read up on stuff like that. When I was a kid, once I got to a certain point, all my favorites bands and musicians, they seemed like there was something dangerous about them. You'd hear how they were *into* things. Secret things. They seemed like maybe they knew stuff nobody else did. It seemed like it should be true. How else could they be so good at what they did? But eventually you realize it's just an image."

"That must've been disappointing," she said.

"I don't know what was worse." He threw his empty can to the ground, because who cared anymore. "Deciding it's all bullshit? Or realizing there's something to it after all, and these goobers here were the ones who figured it out."

Beasley remained stable over the days to come, but word of his condition had spread. There was no way of keeping a thing like that quiet. Everyone in Tanner Falls had a vested interest in his health, and its insistence on declining set off a fresh wave of subdued panic.

One would think they'd gotten it out of their systems years ago. But no.

At the sound of a daybreak ruckus on her day off, Bethany looked out to see the Hendersons, across the street and three houses down, stuffing their sedan with as much as it could hold. Middle-aged husband, middle-aged wife, twenty-something son still living with them because job prospects were dim. They loaded and argued, squabbled and hurried, and then, in a streak of taillights, they were gone.

As if nobody had ever thought of this before.

If it was happening on their block, she assumed that fear had pushed others across town into trying it, too, hopes bolstered by the mantra of the desperate: *Maybe this time will be different.*

Yeah, good luck with that.

Nearly everyone able-bodied enough to do it had attempted at least once over the last two decades to get away. Failed efforts, all. The early, unsuspecting ones were those who simply had normal, greener-pastures reasons to move along. The later refugees fled in terror, compelled by the very inability of others to leave, and the rumors that had started to spread about why the town shrugged off every attempt at modernity and change.

They'd tried everything from moving vans to impulse exits with little more than the clothes on their backs. They'd driven cars, taken buses, ridden motorcycles. The more adventurous ones had attempted it on foot, as if to steal away with no more noise than what their shoes made would let them pass beneath the notice of what waited and watched, ready to corral them like straying livestock.

Everyone, it seemed, had to prove it for themselves, and often more than once.

They would be back.

The Hendersons would be back.

⊕

While Matt slept, she made coffee and set up watch from the porch that night, all cool air and the creaking of crickets. How more normal a night could anyone ask for? Except for the first aid kit by her chair, just in case.

The moon had arced halfway across the sky before things started to happen, when the streetlights flickered and dimmed. However these entities moved, it seemed to create electromagnetic disturbances. It seemed more than a simple factor of visibility. Dimensions, some speculated. They moved in and out of different dimensions.

Bethany had no recollection of the experience herself.

One moment they weren't there, and the next they were, like full-grown trees abruptly sprouted on the Hendersons' lawn. But trees didn't scuttle from one place to another, or wield their branches like arms. They were visible only for a few moments, more shadows than details. Far too tall to fit in the house, the three of them simply smashed a pair of second-story windows with their crowns of appendages and jammed their cargo through, then scuttled away from the house and faded from view as if they'd never been there at all.

Had they been aware of her watching them? One seemed to pause and turn her way, but nothing about them remotely suggested that they had faces, much less eyes.

Surprisingly few people had seen them, even though most had been carried by them. These, the general consensus went, were but a few of the Thousand Young, left behind to enforce the pact.

She grabbed her bag and hurried for the Hendersons' house. She wondered how far they'd gotten, and where the car was, if they'd ever see it again, or the possessions they'd deemed important enough to carry. If they would even care. In maintaining the status quo, vehicles didn't seem to matter. People were paramount.

They'd locked their front door when they left this morning, but had overlooked the back, so she let herself into the house that way. It was as silent as it was dark, until she blindly slapped a light switch in the kitchen, then heard them overhead as they started to awaken. They got louder as she made her way up the stairs—the weeping, the sounds on the verge of screams, as if they hadn't yet processed what had happened. These were not cries of physical pain. She was intimately familiar with those. These were worse, in a way. Pain could be managed. Hopelessness and despair came from a deeper place than nerve endings.

She found them lying huddled in the shards of their windows. Cuts, bruises, scrapes—that was the worst of it. She could treat those. The trauma might take a lot longer to get over.

More likely, Old Mad Donald would be dead before they had a chance.

⬞

As went the Hendersons, so went the rest of Tanner Falls.

Few things were more contagious than panic, and few people were in a better position to gauge it than hospital staff. The accident rate spiked again, the way it did whenever fresh fears arose over Donald Beasley's mortality, and those prone to dulling their fears with drink did what drunks often do.

Had Beasley and the others foreseen *this*, in their selfishness?

The suicide rate spiked, too . . . or rather, attempted suicides. It never worked. They were brought in by paramedics and frantic families, and occasionally they came in under their own ghastly power—people who should've been dead, bodies broken, veins opened, brains exposed, yet somehow life had been refused exit. There was nothing worse to treat than screaming people who should've been in the morgue, and knew it; who wanted to be there, and were denied it.

Had Beasley and the rest meant for *this* to happen, in trying to preserve the town they'd claimed to love?

All along, townsfolk had continued to die of natural causes, but cheating was not allowed. Which didn't keep the desperate from trying anyway. They learned the folly of it no better than those who tried to flee, but at least the runners weren't shattering their bodies in the process. In trying to kill themselves, they had instead been slowly killing her sense of compassion, which made it all the easier for Bethany to hate them for it.

The adults, anyway.

It wasn't in her—not yet—to hate today's casualty. Allison, the girl's name. She'd hung from her back yard noose all night, and by the time her father discovered her this morning, her slim neck was stretched by inches. This soon, it was impossible to say if she would ever hold her head upright again. She was fifteen years old.

You did what you could. You made them comfortable. You tried not to contract their despair.

This was no way to live. For anyone.

And as she needed to do more and more, once a crisis was over, Bethany retreated into the hospital hall to shake it out. Soon there followed the smell of cigarette smoke. She'd come to welcome the stink of it, for these little moments of decompression with Dr. Richard.

"There's no meaning in this anymore," said the man who, two weeks ago, vowed to crawl inside Beasley's chest before letting him die.

For the first time in her life, she wished she smoked, too, because if she did, that was exactly what she would be doing now. She pointed to the fuming stick between his fingers. "Those things'll kill you, you know."

"If only." He seemed to contemplate snuffing it out, then didn't. "That's been the idea. But I don't think cancer likes me."

"The ones who die naturally . . . do you really think they've escaped what's coming?" she asked. "Or did they just get scooped up earlier than the rest of us?"

He shrugged. "A moot point for me. It was worth a try."

The hallway windows overlooked a stretch of parking lot, and beyond that stood a neighborhood of grand old houses, and beyond that the buildings of downtown, most prominently the Tanner Hotel, with that hateful sign they could never be rid of. It was the tallest thing around. They all lived under it, no matter where their homes were.

"You know, I've never believed in life at all costs. I've been called a heretic for it. Just not by anybody whose good opinion of me mattered," Richard told her. "I could never see the value of using extraordinary measures to squeeze day after day of life out of a patient when the only thing we're accomplishing is prolonging suffering. Quality of life always seemed the better benchmark to me. Somehow I got away from that."

As they stared out the window, from somewhere beyond view came the sound of another siren.

"Is this *really* quality of life?"

"Matt, my husband, says we should go out to Route Fifteen and repaint the *Welcome To Tanner Falls* sign to read *Death Row*," she said. "But of course, that would be change."

"Can't have that." Richard clucked disapproval. "Don't most patients, when it's terminal, want to be the ones to choose when they die? I think they do."

"It's the last decision they can control. At least, it should be."

"Exactly," he said. "I think I'll have a word with the mayor."

She felt the weight of responsibility bearing down from above, from Donald Beasley's room on the second floor. How nice to be rid of it.

"Are you getting at what I think you are?" she asked.

"Probably."

So it had come to this. After a moment's shock, she was surprisingly at peace with it. Then thought of her fellow nurse, Janet, sitting watch over the most hated man in the town's history. *I'd start with his eyes. . . .*

"You need to offer people more than just a choice." She couldn't believe the words coming out of her. But it had come to this. "You need to offer them catharsis."

◦

On the day of the special election, she took another turn as watch-nurse, sitting at Donald Beasley's bedside, listening to the reassuring beep of the cardiac monitor, watching the rise and fall of his chest. Machines hummed and puffed. His face and arms were a topography of wrinkles and tubes.

He was awake, even cognizant. He studiously avoided her, preferring instead to look straight ahead at the far wall, until, after an hour of being ignored, Bethany scooted her chair close enough to lean on the bed rail, and to smell the dry musty odor of him, so he couldn't pretend her away anymore.

"I get it," she told him. "I really do. How scared you all must have been. That's the last word any of you would've used with each other, or with yourselves, but that's exactly what you were. Scared. Grown men as scared as little boys when the bully shows up to take a toy truck away."

The more she had to say, the more he creaked his head away from her, toward the window and its view of the town that despised him.

"No, I get it. The whole world must've looked like it was changing all at once back then, and none of it into a place you wanted to go. Guys like my husband, they grew their hair out and started playing music you couldn't understand. Girls like me, they got birth control pills and started realizing there could be a life beyond the kitchen and the crib. We discovered drugs you shot-and-a-beer types never dreamed of."

Now that she'd started, she couldn't turn it off.

"And black people, there was no keeping them to the back of the bus anymore, was there? It didn't matter how many of their leaders that bigots like you shot, or how many dogs or firehoses you turned on them, they were going to keep coming no matter what, and that must've scared you most of all."

Under his sheet, Beasley quivered with what she hoped was impotent rage.

"You armchair patriots, you had a war the country was turning against, and deep down, maybe you even suspected that the men who wanted to keep it going were lying to you whenever it fit their agenda, only you were too dug in to admit it."

She wanted tears from him. Maybe he was finally too dried out to weep.

"The world was leaving you behind. You cowards. Everything was slipping away from you. You were probably afraid someone like Charles Manson was going to show up any day, if you didn't do something. *I get it.* So if you couldn't stop the rest of the world from moving on, you wanted to stay hunkered down here in Mayberry while it did. And I can't blame you for that, for being cowards, because that's what cowards do. It's the nature of the beast to cringe."

Under the sheet, his shallow breath had visibly quickened, and the cardiac monitor pulsed more rapidly.

"But how do you go from that to sacrificing everybody else's lives just to sustain your own illusions a little longer? That's a whole different level of greed. A bunch of goddamn sociopaths, the lot of you."

If he had a massive heart attack now, that would be the most merciful thing for him. But he didn't. Good.

"How much could you all *really* have loved your town when you bargained it away to something that shouldn't even exist? Just to keep it the way it was, until the last of your little group was dead, and then to hell with the rest of us, because we were only . . . what, bargaining chips?"

At last, with effort, Beasley rolled his head back to face her.

44

"The Goat," he whispered, slowly, with a sound like dry reeds. "The Black Goat . . . we never thought she would answer."

Maybe Matt was right. Maybe this whole unconscionable situation began as a stupid lark. Sad little men, still frolicking with whores and pretending to be bad boys, desperate to hold onto what was theirs a little longer, a little longer.

"Here's something else you never thought of." She shouldn't have been telling him, but it seemed important that he experience dread, the same as the rest of them. "Ever since people started to figure this out, the only thing that's kept you alive and whole is their fear of what will happen when you die. But even something like that runs its course. So you may not get off as easily as you thought. You know what's happening right now? The entire town is voting on what to do with you. To see if they're willing to trade these last few days, weeks, whatever we have . . . whatever *you* have . . . for the satisfaction of making you suffer."

And there—there it was. The terror in his eyes. It was what they all needed.

"I already voted before I came to work," she said. "I voted in favor of it."

☨

To the surprise of few, the special ballot initiative passed: 3658 in favor, 2077 against, and another 5100 or so who didn't bother turning out one way or another.

Judgment Day, people were calling it, and preachers argued against it with all the effectiveness of street corner lunatics. The town wanted blood now. There was no divine intervention coming, so they would take what they could get.

It happened in the town square. Thousands filled the streets, while thousands more stayed home. On the courthouse lawn, they erected the platform used for speeches on Veterans Day, Memorial Day, a half-dozen different kinds of parade days.

The mayor was there to officiate, and police officers to keep order, and when Donald Beasley was brought in an ambulance, the crowd parted like water to let it through. His care team was down to just two: one physician, Dr. Richard, and one nurse, her colleague, Janet Swain. Even though they were overseeing his death, their job was still the same:

To keep him alive as long as possible.

And Janet got her wish. She drew first blood, taking Beasley's left eye. He'd been strapped to a gurney that was propped upright, so the crowd could see it happen, and a roaring cheer went up at the sight of the emptied socket.

He may have been seventy-six years old, and looked at least a hundred, but he squealed like a feeble child.

Out in the crowd, a few rows away, Bethany averted her gaze to the ground and squirmed her hand into Matt's, to hold tight for as long as they had remaining.

"Do you want to leave?" he asked.

She shook her head no. "If you vote for something like this, you should be prepared to see it through."

Anyone who wished it got to take a turn, ushered into a line that filed up the steps on one side of the platform, descended on the other, and as far as what happened in the middle, that was up to them. Some were content to curse Beasley, others to spit on him. The rest were not so easily sated. They slapped him, sliced him, pried off nails with pliers. They took his ears. They knocked out teeth. They ground cigarettes into his forehead, and drizzled trenches into his skin with droppers full of acid.

The cheering quit long before the line was through.

People stayed, people left, people sobbed with a thousand different sorrows. Some were sick. Others wanted to get back in the line again. A few started laughing and never stopped.

Bethany reminded herself that there was a time when Tanner Falls had been a great place to grow up. Scrape the veneer away, though, and this was what you got.

The line kept advancing even after Beasley was pronounced dead, and why not. He may have cheated them out of tomorrow, but they weren't about to let him cheat them out of one last chance to take it out on his corpse.

They had an hour, give or take, before the sky pulsed with a single flash of light—green, perhaps, or blue, or maybe it was no color in the known spectrum. A fearsome wind kicked up, blowing west, pulled toward the source of the flash. They had felt this wind before.

She clutched Matt's hand so hard it had to hurt him. Had to.

All around them, their neighbors shrieked and scattered by the hundreds, and though they were buffeted from all sides, she and Matt decided not to bother. When had running *ever* worked?

"I had this dream last night," he told her, his voice starting to shake. "It felt so real. As real as life. I dreamed I was given some sort of pipe to play for God in the chaos at the heart of the universe."

Soon it became visible over distant trees and rooftops, dark and boiling, as mercurial in appearance as a storm cloud. So this was what they had summoned, called up, bargained with . . . this, the Black Goat of the Woods With a Thousand Young. It was a deity from nightmares still seeking its hold in the world, and in the east, the north, the south, wherever people had fled, they all soon found reason to shriek there, as well. Tanner Falls resounded with it. A thousand young could round up a lot of stragglers.

"So maybe we'll be okay," Matt said.

Closer, and closer still, it rent the air with a screech as if lightning could speak. It churned with mouths that opened and closed and reappeared elsewhere in the anarchy of its form.

"Why," she said, "would you ever think that?"

Three blocks away, it detoured toward the hospital, passing by it, passing *through* it, this warehouse of failed suicides, and timeless moments later the sky disgorged a furious rain of meat and blood.

"What if it could've had us all along?" Matt said. "But waited anyway?"

It was coming.

"Why would it have done that?"

Coming for the town square.

"Maybe it was curious. Maybe it wanted to see what we would do."

It was coming, as ground and pavement alike steamed beneath its pile-driver hooves.

"And maybe now, here, today," Matt said, "some of us finally became . . . worthy."

Bethany shut her eyes as tightly as her hand held Matt's, as it bore down on them with the sound and fury of a cyclone.

At last. At last. At long, elusive last. . . .

It was time to leave home.

Scars In Progress

Seeing her again after fourteen years, it was the last association I wanted to make: those ads meant to scare people away from crack and crystal meth by charting someone's downward spiral in a sequence of mug shots. A woman, always a woman. From ingénue to hag in six or eight steps.

It's always the last three where the slope of the curve takes a sharp turn and plummets toward rock bottom. But the picture just before these—this is where the real drama is, and the heartbreak. It's the fulcrum shot, the tipping point where it might've been possible for her to pull back from the brink. Except there are still those next three pictures, so you know how the story went. You get to look at her eyes in that one-way-or-the-other moment and know something she doesn't. You know the future. You know the ending.

That's what I thought of when I saw Lorelei again. That she was right at that fulcrum. I could stare as long as I needed to, with no embarrassment for either of us.

Facebook. Where else?

But that made it worse, somehow, than running into her in the grocery store on a bad day. This was the image of herself that she'd chosen to show the world. She was at a place that she wasn't trying to hide, and either she didn't know yet how badly it showed or she just didn't care.

The thing was, even then I felt certain it wasn't meth, crack, anything like that. The look was the same, that hollow look beginning to cut its way past the surface, and starting to work behind the eyes, too—eyes still bright and aware but tempered by an animal panic, a little more fight left inside.

Even so: Nothing chemical. Something else. I just knew.

The next fifteen, twenty minutes? You know the routine. I read her info, a couple of pages worth of posts, started clicking through her pictures. Saw two of myself, the Lorelei and me of fifteen or sixteen years ago. In both of them we'd found something worth smiling about, laughing at, and most of all we looked confident that the future was nothing to fear.

If you could go back in time, could you even bring yourself to tell that younger you the truth?

Back when I loved her—loved her in that self-centered, take-it-all-for-granted way you love someone in college, before you grow up—photography was a hobby of hers. It obviously still was. She'd created close to twenty albums, most of them thematically grouped, and I settled in for a while longer.

I remembered a girl who liked to shoot photos of flowers and trees, creeks and birds, sunrises and sunsets. I remembered a girl in love with brightness and saturation and vibrancy.

What there was now was a woman who'd all but succumbed to color-blindness. Check that—color apathy. The world was still a colorful place, but she'd turned her back on it. She'd spent a lot of time scuffing around sites of abandonment and desolation. Houses and hospitals, factories and farms, none of them in working order, some for years, some for decades. With no hands to paint or repair them, they'd all fallen into gray, rotting ruin, leached of color and life.

And yet . . .

They weren't without their own crumbling beauty. Lorelei had managed to capture that much, like modern versions of stone circles and barely-standing abbeys that tourists will drive half a day to find.

It started to get weird in an album shot around a vacant shopping plaza in some North Carolina town whose millwork had been outsourced years before. The place was all windows boarded over with plywood, now splintered apart to reveal the shattered glass behind it. Around it a useless perimeter of chain link fencing, sheared through until it drooped like curled paper.

In one series of shots, a figure stood on the roof, just far enough away that you couldn't make out much detail, just close enough that what you could discern left you feeling . . . how, exactly? Glad you weren't there, I guess. More silhouette than not, the figure adopted a quizzical stance as wind whipped its tattered overcoat back and forth, and it seemed to be looking straight toward the lens.

No. Straight *through* the lens. Straight into the future, and every set of eyes that would ever dare to meet its gaze.

Of all the photos I'd looked at, these had drawn the most commentary. Nobody seemed to actually like them. Variations of the word *creep* got used a lot. Even if people thought the photos were technically good, they didn't like the way the imagery made them feel.

Finally someone got curious:

 Gary Phillips Did you stage this? Is that a model or somebody you know?
Like · Reply 4

 Lorelei Swain No, I didn't stage it. I never use models. I don't even much like to take pictures of people.
Like · Reply 1

 Kelli Clifford Why the exception? You definitely took one of a people here.
Like · Reply

 Lorelei Swain That's debatable. . . .
Like · Reply 3

 Dalyn Carbajal So who (or what) are you saying that was, then? It just looks like a vagrant. Like, I hope you weren't downwind.
Like · Reply

 Lorelei Swain I could tell you. But you wouldn't believe me, so why bother?
Like · Reply 1

A chorus of begging followed. Please. Tell. Of course we'll believe you. More than a week passed before she'd answered.

 Lorelei Swain: I'm 99.9% sure it's a demon. It's not the only one in these pictures, just the most obvious one. The others, you'll have to look for them. Now let the jeers commence. But you asked, wot wot?
Like · Reply 1

This made me smile. She was still using that. Some stuffy old Britishism she'd picked up in college, or faux stuffy old Britishism. I'd never known any stuffy old Brits, so I'd never heard any end sentences with "what what?", like a suffix meaning "isn't it?" or "didn't you?"

Sample usage: *We could stay together, but that would mean you'd actually have to be there for me when I really need you, wot wot?*

Or this: *It was good of you to pay for the procedure, but it would've been great if you'd held me after it was over, wot wot?*

Or this: *You're right. There was so much more I should've been, instead of a totally typical nineteen-year-old lunkhead, wot wot?*

I went back to the photos again, and even though I knew better, clicked on the one where the figure seemed to be staring most directly, most defiantly, and dragged a copy onto my desktop. Opened it in a photo editor, and because it was mostly silhouette, I tried brightening it, enlarging it, sharpening it . . . but the bad thing about photos shrunk down for web sites is that all the fine detail is gone, especially in the shadows.

So after all your hard work, that smear of features you get, tricking you into thinking someone's face looks like it's melting, hanging off the bone—you can't trust it. It's only artifacts and illusion.

I'm 99.9% sure it's a demon.

I clicked the comment field and started to type:

Liam Dancy Ever since there have been cameras, there have been primitive people who think that taking a picture of them also takes away a piece of their soul. Maybe they're not wrong. Maybe that piece even lingers in the image. So maybe this is one very ugly soul and that's what you're all reacting to here.

Like · Reply

Or maybe I'm full of shit, wot wot?

My finger froze on the trigger for a moment.

Then I closed the browser window before clicking the Comment button and making it permanent, and the words disappeared, vanishing into the void with everything else that never gets said.

You may think you know what happened next.

You may think that I still got in touch with Lorelei, because I'd already revealed my interest by looking for her in the first place. Isn't that what guys do when they're single again? Troll around, looking up old girlfriends to see if anything's still there? You may think I got in touch because she needed it, needed something, somebody. Isn't that what you do after you've failed to keep somebody alive? Look for someone else who needs saving?

But that's not how it happened at all.

I did nothing.

Just let it go, until seven months later, when she was the one who came looking for me. That's what women do when they're single again, right? Say hi to an old boyfriend, to see if he'll bite?

Saving her, though . . . that's not why I went.

Saving her was just about the furthest thing from my mind. At first.

Maybe it was just the opposite, and I was looking for someone to finish me off, instead.

Ω

Ohio—that's where she wanted to meet. Not me going to Portland, not Lorelei coming to San Diego. Instead, she opted for neutral ground. I didn't know what the problem was with, say, San Francisco, mutually inconvenient for both of us but at least splitting the difference. Instead, she lobbied for the buckle on the Rust Belt.

So for her, obviously, it was also a field trip. If things didn't go well between us, she could fall back on shooting some more of her dismal pictures. A test for me, too, it could've been: *How much are you willing to put yourself out to see me again?*

It wasn't a nice motel, but then, there were no nice motels left in the area, because there were no nice people coming through anymore to stay in them. Maybe we were no exception. We had a look, I noticed the first time I saw our reflections in a window—a look like carnivores that hadn't eaten in a while, as we trailed after the migratory herds.

Two people reunite after more than decade, and I suppose sometimes they really do say the things everybody imagines they will:

You don't look a day older. You look better than ever. It's like no time's passed at all, like we were never apart.

I'll give us this much: Lorelei and I didn't even attempt to play that game.

Instead, almost first thing, she ran her fingertips over the scar that curled like a comma from the corner of one eye to the cheekbone, where I'd taken a heavy elbow a few months earlier. She looked at it like maybe she could peel it off like a strip of latex from a joke shop, and said, "Out of everybody I ever knew, if I'd had to guess who was going to take up cage fighting, you wouldn't've even been in the top thousand."

"Wrestling team all through high school, and you came to some of my college matches. That doesn't count?"

"I always thought that was more your dad pushing you." Her fingers found another scar, smaller, older, fainter, sneaking away from my lower lip. She had a good eye for detail and wasn't shy about staring. "And you don't even do this for money? You do this for fun?"

"It only hurts when you lose."

"Okay. How often does it hurt, then?"

"About half the time."

But you, Lorelei. It doesn't look like anybody's been taking swings at you. So what's your excuse? Because I know when we were together, you were young enough to still have some baby fat around the edges, and everybody loses that, but most of the time, that isn't a bad thing at all. I love that in a woman, when she stops looking like a girl and starts looking like what she really is. You, though. You look like something's going on like when kids play with plastic bags, stick a straw in them and suck out the air. You look like something's pulling at you from the inside.

I could've asked, had spent days of anticipation wanting to, and she seemed blunt enough that I doubted it would've bothered her. But I didn't. Because now that I was here, it didn't matter as much as I thought it would.

We spent our first couple days together wandering, and even though it felt aimless, it wasn't, because we were circling each other the whole time— not in a bad way, just seeing if and where we might fit anymore. Coming from San Diego, for me it was the coldest day of my life, November near the concrete shores of Lake Erie, wind slicing in off the water carrying a chill that cut like a hatchet. Lorelei didn't seem to notice.

She was dug in deep about one thing, and kept asking me about the fighting.

"You have to admit, it's not something most landscape designers do on the side," she said. "What's the appeal?"

"Sometimes, if you want to keep from going crazy, you just have to smash something. Might as well be a bag. Or a willing opponent. Plus there's the clarity. I like the clarity of the whole process. Everything else just falls away. It's all so . . ."

"Purifying?" she said.

Maybe it had been, once. Now it was an appealing distraction.

I was more than a year into an extended sabbatical, not even 20 percent through the lump of life insurance. From the architecture firm I worked for, there'd been a promise the job would be waiting when I was ready to go back, except I didn't want to. I *wanted* to want to. But I couldn't, because I knew it wasn't going to be enough anymore. Not enough of a distraction, and certainly not enough to make me feel an urge to see the next day. But I was lucky. I had this other thing, this thing of sweat and blood and strategies, and if I got cut, then that was easy. Everybody around me knew how to deal with that.

"It shows," she said.

"What do you mean?"

"You know that vibe you pick up on, that tells you not to mess with somebody, because it'll be the worst mistake you ever made? Well . . . you're that guy now."

I shook my head. "Fighters get challenged all the time, and a lot better ones than I am. There's always somebody who wants to see if he can take you on."

"Don't sell yourself too short, Liam." She looked around with this strangely placid expression, then patted her Nikon. "Five thousand dollars' worth of camera around my neck, and I'm not worried."

I didn't share her confidence. This was the kind of combat zone I'd never visit unless there was a very good reason, because nobody else in sight seemed to have one. Dealers and whores, users and abusers—it was an economy unto itself here, kept in motion by people whose destiny seemed to be to end up pushing their world in a shopping cart or finishing it all face-down or toes-up in a gutter.

Lorelei then, Lorelei now . . . it just didn't connect. She'd been a sorority sister, for fuck's sake.

Toward the end of the second day, the path she led us on ended in the middle of a vast parking lot that was breaking apart from below, succumbing to the patience of weeds. We faced what had been a stadium once, or what was going to be one. Either it hadn't been torn down yet, or construction had stalled. Whichever it was, the run of hard luck had started years ago and never changed.

"Does it make you think of the Colosseum, in Rome?" she asked.

I shook my head. "No."

"Me neither. It's missing something. It's missing . . . everything."

She was right. The place had no heart, no spirit. I'd toured the Colosseum once, and could feel the accumulated weight of history in every corner. This place? It was utterly vacant.

"Check in again after another two thousand years, and maybe . . ."

She cut me a sideways glance. "Do you really think anything but cockroaches and feral dogs are going to be here in two thousand years?"

I wanted there to be. Once you stop conceiving of that continuity, what does it say about you, and where does it end? You just keep dialing the cancellation date closer, until your vision is so short it doesn't even see a good reason for tomorrow.

But I didn't know. And where we were right then, everyone was already there.

Lorelei pointed toward the stadium. "Notice anything?"

Nothing out of the ordinary, no. The stadium sat on its lakefront site like a defeated castle, exuding decrepitude and neglect. The lower levels were scabbed with a patchwork of efforts to seal it up, and even from the parking lot most of the blocked entrances looked breached. Lorelei told me to look higher, but I gave up.

She peered through her lens, a telephoto as long as a tennis ball can, then handed the camera to me, still strapped around her neck. It was the closest we'd been since our first awkward hug, but prolonged now, and I smelled the last shampoo she'd used, and the soap, and underneath that the scent of her that was just purely Lorelei, until this moment forgotten, locked away in a memory, and now resurrected the way only a scent can take you back. For someone who tried not to look in reverse, I was doing a good job of wishing I were nineteen again, with a chance to do some things over.

It's how they could torture you forever, without ever touching you. Just take away something good, and only let you smell it.

"Up near the very top," she said. "Above the T on the sign."

Now I had it. And what was it, anyway, with Lorelei and unkempt figures on rooftops and other high places?

"Marcus says it's been there for four days."

"Marcus?" I said.

"You'll meet Marcus."

I lowered the camera back to her chest, and a part of me sank with it. This was not the reunion I'd believed it was going to be. "Do I even want to meet Marcus?"

"It's not what you think," she said. "And don't get sidetracked. That's the real issue, up there. I mean, four days, don't you find that fascinating? Marcus says it moves around up there, but it doesn't leave. Phoebe's got infrared, they've checked at night."

Oh. Phoebe too, now. Presumably I'd be meeting her as well.

"So you're all fascinated by an autistic wino who's good at climbing."

She nudged me with her elbow. "Come onnn. You know that's not what's going on here. You can't tell me you didn't go through my photos, and if you did that, well, I know you're capable of connecting a few dots."

Of course. I was already thinking about it. *I'm 99.9% sure it's a demon.* This was what everybody did when they started dating again after fourteen years, right?

She clicked off a few shots but grumbled they weren't going to turn out because, at this distance, using a wildlife-grade telephoto, she needed a tripod. She lowered the camera with a huff, then gave me a look like she was peering back through a doorway I hadn't gotten to yet, hopeful that I'd step through, fearful that I wouldn't. And more than ever since getting here, I saw the casualty in her, the addict, the soul on an eroding precipice, straining beneath the skin as she fought against the fall.

"Let's go in," she said. "Let's take a look around."

꡶

I recall it all now, and want to think I didn't go without a good argument—what were we, in high school, sneaking onto the football field with a six-pack late on a Saturday night? But I think I was already starting to yield to her focused madness.

"Most places they stay, it's all enclosed. Like that shopping center," she told me as we crossed the parking lot. "Places like that, there's not much light, and I don't want to get close enough to use the flash, and anyway, if they hear you coming up on them, they just hide or move away before you get there."

Funny. I'd never thought of demons as being cowardly.

"But someplace like this stadium, it's so open and airy. Maybe I'll get lucky, get a closer shot than I ever have before."

She was livelier than I'd seen so far, and that had to be good, right? At this point I was still thinking Lorelei was just delusional, but it was turning into a fun sort of delusion, a one-track delusion. The CIA wasn't after her and she knew she couldn't fly. It was like humoring somebody tone-deaf who thought she could sing.

We wriggled past crowbarred plywood and cut wire, the way in already cleared before us. But the farther in we went, and the longer we stayed, crossing concourses and tracking along sloping ramps, the more it all came down and the worse it got. The air? I don't know. Something in the air, or beside the air, weighing heavy between the molecules. Why else would it get harder to breathe?

"You feel it, don't you?" she said, not without satisfaction.

I've known a couple of people, more sensitive than most, who told me they'd visited a location where people died badly—the battlefield at Gettysburg, one of them, the other an Indian massacre at a place called Sand Creek—and it got this way for them. The weight of tragedy, of death, of inhumanity bearing down on them.

I'd always had my doubts until this moment.

This, though . . . this had to be worse. You can live with death, no matter what the numbers, because we have to. You can live with tragedy, because nobody escapes it, and then we go on. You can live with inhumanity, because you know you can be better. You *want* to be better.

But this . . . it made me want to give up. Made me want to put on three more jackets and zip them tight against the cold. It was the feeling of Lorelei's photos of the figure on the roof, multiplied a thousand times.

I took her by the elbow. "This is killing you," I said, suddenly understanding.

She looked at me, like what was left of her skin and bones was all that stood between me and the frozen black vacuum of space. "You can leave if you need to. But you do get used to it."

Dear god. Why would anyone ever want to?

I kept going anyway, our footsteps brittle on the concrete. The place seemed devoid of life, if not empty of evidence. Here and there were the sad remains of some human nest—rags and newspapers, grimy water bottles and plastic sheeting, and blackened patches of ash left by small fires. Of course the predominant color was gray—the place was mostly concrete, after all—but I'd look around and see things that should've contrasted, and didn't. Signs and lettering, conduit and cables . . . they were all fading, the color bleeding out of them. Black, red, yellow, blue, green, all of them paling into a lifeless shade of gray. On the circular decks, inside the vast empty bowl of stadium, mostly devoid of seats, just terraces with a stagnant pond at the bottom. The gray was spreading like mold, only there was nothing to scrape away, because it wasn't growing on anything. It was changing everything from the inside out.

While Lorelei took pictures, I couldn't stop looking at my hand, my shoes and sleeves and pant legs, to make sure they were still the same color.

I recall it all now, and while at the time everything was one impression flowing into another, now I know that the third level was the turning point, when I stopped trying to scapegoat my imagination and started to believe.

We'd spiraled up the stadium for the third time when we came upon a boxy structure . . . probably a snack bar. Sheer walls jutted out from the stadium's core and reached up to the angled roof.

What I saw was wrapped around either side of the corner where the snack bar's front and side walls met, but high, ten feet off the deck. At first I thought it was a trash bag or a tarp. Even a giant bat, clinging to the walls, would've made more sense. But instead, I began to see how it had splattered against the concrete, a rust-colored stain fanning out on both sides from the point of impact.

Look closer, and there were the clothes, and an old shapeless coat, flat and stuck to the walls, and beneath, the outline of a latticework of shattered bones. A head? Still there, technically.

It seemed dried out enough to have been there a while. Not the one from the roof, obviously, and now I didn't want to go any higher. If this thing had burst across level ground, fine. But it hadn't fallen. It had gone in straight at the corner, more or less horizontally. It looked like it had been launched with a catapult and struck with the force of a hundred-story fall.

Lorelei stared too, only with a little less shock. She had to feel some. She hadn't started taking pictures yet.

"Have you seen anything like this? Ever?" I asked.

"Sort of," she said. "I saw where I think one went off the roof of an abandoned mental institution. But not like this." She studied it some more, then turned around to look at the approach. "Maybe it got a running start. Ran and jumped."

"Straight at the wall? Split down the middle on a corner?" I said. "They can do that."

She shrugged and pointed at the evidence.

"*Why* would one of them do that?"

"Being creative?" She didn't know. She'd never know. "They don't have bodies of their own. They've got to borrow. Inhabit one that's weak enough to let them force their way in. Shell people, Marcus calls them. Or animals, whatever. But the bodies start falling apart on them. It's what flesh and bone does anyway, eventually. Their presence just seems to accelerate the process."

I thought of old paintings I'd seen, religion's early cautionary tales, with demons that looked like something whose origins you could almost recognize, forms corrupted along the way.

"Marcus thinks they get to a point where they've got such a hatred for the body they're in that, while there's still time, they show it as much contempt as they can." She tipped a goofy smile at me. "It's just a theory, wot wot?"

"Why do they hate the bodies that much?"

"It's not the bodies per se. It's everything. They hate existing. They *oppose* existence. They're antithetical to it all. Down to a cellular and molecular level."

Now, finally, she started taking photos. Maybe it was her way of coping. Everything looked more manageable through a lens.

"You can forget most of what religion has to say about demons," she told me. "All religion can do is try to make sense out of something that's been around for a lot longer, and try to make it fit."

"Most, you said. What does religion get right?"

"For one thing, that they dwell in the wastes and other places of desolation."

Once, that might've meant deserts and forests and high mountain crags. Now? I thought of every place Lorelei had shot her dreary photos. The dilapidated housing tracts and abandoned factories and vacant institutions fallen into ruin because the world didn't want them anymore. We'd moved on and left voids in our wake. They must've been like magnets. Demon-haunted cities, demon-haunted towns . . . maybe we'd always been living right next door to Hell.

"What demons are, when it comes down to it," Lorelei said, over her shoulder, "I've started thinking of them as the spiritual equivalent of antimatter."

♍

Those first nights in the motel it was like camp, Lorelei in the bed and me on the floor, both of us awake but neither of us in a hurry to make a move on the other. We were patient, content to let whatever might happen, happen in its own time, and maybe inclined not to rush into a mistake.

We just talked, and you'd think fourteen years would mean there'd be an endless amount of ground to cover, but the surprise was how little of it seemed to matter. So there was plenty of time and space and silence for what did.

My big one: "How in God's name did you get pulled into this?"

"It was the photography that came first," she told me. "I just started going to those kinds of places to shoot. They spoke to me more. They *reflected* me more."

Reflected how exactly, I wondered, but didn't ask. Empty? Abandoned? Gutted? It was hard to hear this without guilt. And while she was in every way a better photographer now than she'd been when I knew her before, I would've given almost anything to have her back the way she was, seeing the world the way she used to.

"Maybe it's because I've always taken photos, and that makes me observant," she said. "Or maybe I'm just wired for it. I wish I had some dramatic story for you . . . I came home one day and these things were eating my husband. I really wish I did. But I don't. I just. Started. Noticing."

It must've taken years. Years of noticing patterns, fighting disbelief, thinking she was crazy. I was getting the crash course, with an escort. Lorelei had faced this alone.

"They don't scare you?"

"I've never pushed my luck with them," she said. "But they don't seem to attack. At least I've never heard of it."

"Why don't they? It seems like something they'd do."

"I don't know."

We went quiet, then listened to some confrontation outside, in the motel parking lot or from another room. Raised voices, then genuine rage. I went tense, heart rate gone double. Before long there was only one voice, moaning, fading as the source scuttled away. No gunshots in between. A knife, maybe. Maybe soon we'd hear sirens. Or maybe we wouldn't.

"What was she like?" Lorelei asked.

Already, so many little details were starting to fuzz and fade. And what was I supposed to do, reel off a string of adjectives and specs? She was five-four and her hair looked red in bright sunlight and she was always bringing home strays and her memory never got a better workout than when we argued? Nobody asks for that.

"How long's it been now? Since she . . . ?"

"A year ago August," I said. "Fifteen months."

"So that's enough time for you to have had a few fights. Right?"

I thought a moment, counting. "Five."

"You told me that you win about half the time. What's been your record just since then?"

"I won all of them."

She didn't say anything more for a while, just let it linger as we both wondered what it implied. That I'd either poured everything into a renewed motivation to win, or I'd stopped caring whether or not I got hit, which always seems to give a fighter an edge. Probably the latter. My wife had never seen me with scars. Those came after.

"Please don't be mad at me," Lorelei finally said, "But maybe you'd like to take it all out on something that matters, for a change."

⚭

I never asked how she'd met Marcus and Phoebe. I figured it was the same with demon hunters as with UFO fanatics. That they naturally pulled toward each other by some strange form of magnetism.

Marcus and Phoebe had been camped out on the opposite side of the same shitty motel the whole time, running their own recon games on the stadium, and Lorelei took me around the next morning for introductions over coffee and donuts, the two of them looking at me like I was the newest member of the team.

I'd been wondering if they would have the same drawn, cut-down, pulled-in appearance as Lorelei. In truth, Marcus could've benefited from it. He'd been a Southern Baptist minister once, and looked like an aging Samoan who'd never turned down a chicken fried steak. Phoebe was this pixie with cropped hair and an apparent disdain for makeup. If I hadn't known better, I might've thought she was a boy, until getting close enough to see the crows-feet around her eyes.

It redoubled my curiosity—and concern—over why this seemed to be affecting Lorelei so much more. Maybe it came down to proximity. She was the one who spent the most time following those things into their lairs, encountering the residue they exuded. The same way, if you walk through enough sewers, you'll be the one breathing methane. The one contracting malaria if you spend enough time in the wrong swamp.

"I haven't agreed to this yet," I told them. "Just so you know."

"Okay. Take your time, son. They're not going anywhere," Marcus said. His voice still had the big, expansive flourishes of a preacher in the pulpit. "But then, as you have seen by that oversized flyspeck on the stadium wall, they do impose their own shelf life. I would like to do this before the other one up topside decides it's reached its expiration date."

"Here's my worry," I said. "Anything that can generate the kind of force to launch itself into a wall like that, if it takes one good swing at me, at my head . . ."

"Have you considered that to it, you may be as hard as that wall? The wall came out fine. You're both made of flesh and bone . . . you're just moved by radically different spirits within. Your distinct advantage is that you haven't spent your final days being eroded from the inside out." Marcus ripped apart a chocolate-slathered bear claw and dunked a strip in his coffee. "Anyway. I've never yet heard or witnessed anything about them that gives me reason to think they'll put up much of a fight. And they obviously have nothing but disregard for the body they squat in."

"Then why don't you take one down yourself," I said.

Marcus pushed the coffee-soaked dough into his mouth. "It's not like they just sit still for it, either. And don't let this shock you, but I don't move all that fast, and I'm not very quiet about it when I do."

Phoebe cut in. "There's something else that might be a factor." She was clearly the geek here. I figured her for the type who took a laptop with her into the toilet. "I did some research, floated Lorelei's pics of the bug-splat past some people, and . . . there's a theory that when they decide to check out like that, in a way that seems to defy physics, they may have some help. They don't just run and jump. They get *pulled*, too. They fixate on a spot of significant mass, your basic immovable object, and it's like there's a positive and a negative charge that spikes, and then—" She smacked her hands together. "Like I said, it's a theory."

The spiritual equivalent of antimatter, Lorelei had said. When particles collide, it's more than destruction. It's annihilation. Nullification.

Marcus leaned closer to me. "Didn't you ever feel like testing yourself against something more than just another man? You hit him, he hits you, one of you wins, the other loses, you hug like brothers when it's over, and what have you accomplished?" He almost looked like he envied me. "Son . . . what you have before you is an opportunity to join the rarified company of men who've wrestled angels and devils. Are you really going to pass up that chance?"

"I thought it was the devils who were supposed to be so good at temptation."

Marcus got a laugh out of that.

"What are they? Really?" I said. "I asked Lorelei, but she tells me you're the one who explains it best."

"She flatters me." Marcus looked at me with eyes gone soft-focus, his face round and serene. "I've been persuaded that what they are is remnants of the Big Bang."

I blinked at him. "That seems an unusual thing for a Southern Baptist preacher to believe in."

"Hence the former part," he said.

It was a brain-bending thing to contemplate, at least before the coffee had really kicked in. But, as he went on, I realized Marcus was right—it was difficult to conceive of a nothingness that could give sudden rise to everything, without the nothingness possessing qualities of its own beyond what we think of as mere empty space. So say the void was inclined only to remain void. Rip it apart, with the unimaginable violence of an expanding universe, blast it into primordial fragments, and down the vast gulfs of time maybe it really was possible that such debris could become self-aware, the same as matter became governed by forces that joined elements into amino acids into proteins into molecules into cells into amoebas and, finally, beings with the capacity to love and murder.

Say it happened, and call them demons. Why shouldn't they look at those of us who organize and design and build and expand as their most hated enemy?

Phoebe punched up something on her laptop and swiveled it around so I could see the screen. It was a slideshow of photos that could've been taken by Lorelei, but weren't. Mostly stark, solitary figures set against backdrops bleached of color and life. Sometimes pairs, too, and the occasional cluster, but all of them in the wastelands of our own creation.

The photos were captioned by date and location: New York. Toronto. London. Edinburg. Rio de Janeiro. Mexico City. Budapest. Copenhagen. Moscow. Jakarta. Even on the edge of Antarctica's McMurdo Station. On and on. Sometimes the lighting and telephoto stability had been good enough to show their features. Sometimes I wished it hadn't. At what point did a face stop being a face?

"Is it over? Tell me when it's over," Phoebe said. "I can hardly bring myself to look at these anymore. You know? They . . ."

I knew.

"They're being reported all over the world by people who know what to look for," Marcus said. "You know what a hockey stick looks like, don't you?" When I said sure, he nodded. "Then you know what the graph looks like that plots out the number of times they've been seen the last ten years." He moved his index finger, skimming low, then, with a whistle, shooting it sharply upward.

"And you want to have a talk with one of them," I said.

"It all means something," he said. "How are you going to find out if you never ask?"

I looked at Lorelei, and the dwindling aspects of her that remained of what I remembered. Lorelei at the brink, Lorelei on the fulcrum.

For you, I will. Not for your friends, not for the world. For you.

♓

That night in the motel, it stopped being like camp, the two of us now in the same bed. It was the first time I'd been with a woman in a year and a half, the first time with Lorelei in fourteen, and none of it seemed familiar. My body did things that felt strange and wrong, traitorous to vows that had technically ended at death-do-us-part, and I didn't know her at all anymore. Where I thought I remembered softness, her body felt hard. Where I thought there'd been smoothness, it was hollow. Where she was supposed to be hard, she just felt brittle. It was paralyzing, this fear that I'd break her. I sank into her and couldn't stop falling.

I should've felt, if not betrayed, then manipulated, that she'd lured me here under the belief it was about one thing when really it was about another. Except Lorelei only knew I was fast and good at takedowns because she'd seen flip-cam footage of one of my fights on YouTube. And she'd only discovered that because she was looking for me in the first place.

That everything somehow just fit . . . destiny, maybe.

"All this . . . was it why your husband left?" I asked.

She sighed, a deflating sound. "It's not exactly the kind of thing a guy signs on for, is it?"

Lorelei ran her hand over her belly, the flat, sunken little belly, and I knew she wasn't there anymore. Not all of her, anyway. There was a time I might've wondered how someone could've stayed haunted for so long by something she'd never seen, that had never walked or crawled or breathed, that had never made a sound, but now I understood it.

"Do you think we might've stayed together if I hadn't gotten . . ." She stopped, tried again. "If we'd been a little older, a little better equipped to deal with it?"

I had no idea. But I knew when it was a good idea to lie.

"Do you think we would've turned out much different? Like, would you have still felt the need to start fighting? Would my outlook have changed the way it did?" She turned onto her side to face me. "Would we have been any good as parents? Could we have been happy with that kind of life?"

And why did she make it sound like a one-time-only opportunity?

"Promise me something," I said. "No matter how it turns out tomorrow, whether Marcus is satisfied or not, you'll stop. You'll come back with me and you'll take a break from this. At least until it . . . loses its hold."

It took a while. But eventually she said something that sounded like okay.

⅄

The thing was still there the next morning, to everybody's relief but mine, maintaining its inhumanly patient vigil. As I looked up at it from the parking lot, knowing I'd soon be seeing and smelling it up close, I reminded myself that it was something that had mastered the art of walking around in stolen skins. The flesh and bones around it hadn't started out this way. I wondered what had happened to the previous tenant, the part of him that couldn't be seen or weighed, and must've once loved and dreamed.

I wondered what happened to them all—the dead, the evicted, the never-born.

As we entered the stadium, I'd never felt less sure of any answers.

You do get used to it, Lorelei had told me, about the emptiness and despair that emanates from these things, and it was too soon for that, but didn't matter, because if fighting teaches you one thing, it's to feel the fear and walk toward the ring anyway.

Up the ramps, up and around, and the higher we went, the fewer signs of human presence there were. There are places even urban nomads know better than to stay.

But in the end—except the takedown wasn't the end—it's hard to imagine more fear with less overt cause to feel it.

Searching, I found my way down a couple of short corridors that led to a narrow rooftop platform behind the stadium sign. And there it was. Like it had been waiting for me all along.

I rushed in and took it from the side, dropping low as I wrapped both arms around its waist and buried my head against its rib cage. The leg that ends up behind your opponent's legs, you just lift it straight out and let gravity do the work. Sit-and-spin, it's called. Finesse the landing and the roll, and you end up in mount. Simple. Textbook, even.

I cracked the thing with an elbow to the temple, then torqued my entire upper body behind a hook to the side of its chin. It was all I knew to do, because no matter what had laid claim to the body, I reasoned that it was still vulnerable to physiological trauma. Rattle its brain, scramble the circuits, and the lights would go out for a while.

Success.

Only after this was over did I register its face. And was glad I'd come at it from the side. At first glance I thought its skin had begun to slough off in layers, but on closer inspection, fascinated and appalled, I saw that its face had actually been . . . flowering. Growing new features and textures like the rippling fungus that grows on a fallen tree in the forest.

I couldn't believe it had been this easy.

Now, though, looking back, I have to wonder if it wasn't just playing along, if it experienced boredom or nostalgia, and recognized an opportunity to go back in time, revisit whatever was its version of the glory days.

Go on. Ask. They're obvious questions: Hadn't anybody who knew what they were tried this before? Hadn't anyone ever attempted to engage one of these latter-day demons in conversation? Could Marcus really have thought he'd be the first to try?

Yes, yes, and no.

Marcus' ambition was to be the first to actually get somewhere with one.

It wasn't that they couldn't talk. Or that they couldn't speak modern languages—surely they could've, and did, when it suited them. More likely, when cornered, it amused them to refuse to speak anything but languages that hardly anybody living understood. They'd been identified as issuing taunts in Old French, Old Norse, Middle English, an early form of Catalan, half a dozen Mesoamerican dialects, and others, most extinct . . . but identified only after it was too late, their borrowed bodies degenerated beyond occupancy.

Marcus was determined to prepare. Come to find out, he wasn't just any man with a mission. He was a linguistic savant.

Do you have any idea how disorienting it is to have someone talk to you and switch to a different language with every sentence? Not only failing to understand the message, but the medium itself, none of it familiar, not even in a heard-it-in-a-movie way? Marcus could do that, rattling off a string of conversational Akkadian, Aramaic, ancient Coptic. He'd spent years learning how to speak nearly thirty forgotten tongues, waiting for just this moment. While Phoebe, along with a team of geeks she worked with long-distance, had developed a language-recognition algorithm paired with an audiovisual translation engine tapping a database of a hundred more archaic languages and alphabets.

"It's kinda kludgy, still, but it works," she'd told me after a demonstration. "Even if the syntax comes out wrong, maybe there's a demon out there who'll appreciate the effort."

I'd told her that the core technology they were sitting on had to be worth millions. She didn't care, because what did that matter in a doomed world? Four years of working tech support for Hewlett-Packard had convinced her that no species this stupid could survive much longer.

Now, go on. Ask again: What about Latin? Someone had to have tried Latin.

Sure. They'd even gotten a response: *Nimium facilis. Tendo congelo.*

You are too simple. Try harder.

△

They'd set up operations a level below the one where I'd done the take-down. Captivity was simple but effective: a wrought-iron chair set before an iron railing, to which they shackled the thing's arms at the wrist and elbow. Its ankles they secured to the chair. The rest was just gear: Phoebe's turbocharged laptop, a small boom mic jacked into an audio interface feeding into the PC, a tripod-mounted camcorder.

"My god," Marcus said when the thing woke up and stared at him as if it knew exactly what was happening. He was sweating. November in northern Ohio and Marcus was sweating.

"You'll do great," I told him.

He nodded, breath loud and ragged in his nostrils, a fat man getting up there in years who looked like he needed to sit down, only nobody had thought to bring more than one chair. Then they got started, and he was steady.

It's always easier to deal with stress when there's a job to focus on. Marcus had his, and Phoebe had software to monitor, and there was no end to how many times Lorelei could make sure the camera was recording or framed just right.

But my job was over.

All I could do was stare at the malformed thing in front of me, no longer human except for its baleful eyes. The hatred behind them was a palpable force, all the worse for its utter silence as Marcus tried language after language. It was like looking into the eyes of a wolf and seeing qualities you'll never see in a mere dog: the cunning, the intelligent measuring of your worth, the primeval intelligence running back to the father of all wolves.

Its very existence was poison. The air was freighted with it, cold and vacant and despairing, as if the atmosphere I'd felt my first time here had condensed to a single point. It was leaching the warmth from my skin and the life from my blood and, for all I knew, the color from my eyes.

Maybe they were used to this, but—

"I've got to step away for a little bit," I whispered in Lorelei's ear.

She looked at me and nodded. Smiled, even. Beautifully. Radiantly. How do you smile when hurricane winds are sucking out your soul? But she did. However weakly, she did. Like the hospice smile my wife gave me a few minutes before she never woke up again.

"Take your time," Lorelei whispered back.

I didn't go down. Instead, I returned to the narrow rooftop where I'd tackled the thing behind the stadium sign. I wanted to understand what couldn't be understood, to see what it saw, what it had spent nonstop days watching. I stood where it had stood and looked out over the panorama of congestion, waste, and sprawl. The pawnshops and porn shops, the 50¢-beer bars and payday loan sharks, and the sleazy billboards hovering above it all. It boiled with sirens and honking horns, and from the other side of the stadium a breeze dragged in the smell of Lake Erie, water that no one in their right mind would drink.

And I knew that, down below, they were asking the wrong questions. *What are you watching? Why are you watching? Why do you seem to have abdicated your old roles as tempters and tormentors, and why are you so brazen about it?*

It seemed so simple from up here. What else was left for them to do?

Everything they did once, we did better, with greater efficiency, greater reach, on mass scales. The demons hadn't abdicated at all. They'd been made redundant.

And who was I to point fingers, anyway? The greatest applause, loudest cheers, most widespread approval I'd ever gotten in my life were for knocking a guy out with a flying knee to the forehead.

But I knew that, no matter how I felt about it today, I wasn't likely to change.

△

You'd think I would've heard something. But I didn't. There was only the malignant crush of silence that became too apparent on my way back down.

A toppled boom mic, an overturned tripod, a dropped computer, and in the middle of the rubble lay Marcus. There wasn't a mark on him, just a surprised, staring look in his eyes, mouth half-open with his last breath. In front of him, the chair was empty. All that remained were two forearms that hung in their shackles from the iron railing, and a pair of feet, still in their shoes, resting on the concrete floor.

Leading away from the chair were five oval blotches like coagulated blood, each about as big around a human ankle. Four steps. It had managed to take four steps. Where had it gone from there, though? Disarticulating bodies don't just vanish.

But by now, I was conditioned to the need to look high.

Eighty feet away, it was pancaked into the wall near the roof, stuck in place like a locust pulped against a windshield, the way its companion had gone out, except this time it seemed like more. More bone, more blood, more fabric, more mess. More everything.

Phoebe, too. I recognized her by the close-cropped hair, drooped over what must've been the thing's shoulder.

But of Lorelei, there was no sign.

What do you do when you lose someone in an empty stadium? Around and around and around you go.

At first I thought she'd sought shelter, and found it inside an empty custodial storage area tucked under a section of seats. It was enclosed top-to-bottom by heavy chain link fencing, and when I tried the knob of the steel-framed door, it was locked. And to think I actually felt relief at first. I really did.

Except Lorelei didn't answer me. She just sat cross-legged on the concrete floor, her back against a concrete wall. Traumatized? Catatonic? Who wouldn't be? And to think that was the best I could hope for.

Until I knew better.

It watched me scream a while. Listened to me beg and cry. I saw only Lorelei, but Lorelei never saw me. Had she been that empty, that hollowed-out already? That easy to push aside and nullify? I bloodied my fingers on the door, pounded my palms raw on the fence, beat my elbows sore and numb. It took everything in. I was grand sport.

And when I thought to try to find a scrap of metal sturdy enough to lever the door open . . . ? Only then did it move.

Lorelei's lower lip curled between her teeth, such an adorable look on her at one time; on any woman, really. But it kept going until the expression became a snarl, and then the thing wearing Lorelei bit down. Bit hard. Bit all the way through. When it had swallowed her lower lip, it started on the top one, and once that was gone too, it sucked each cheek into her gnashing teeth, until it had eaten as much of those as it could reach.

Her face. Lorelei's beautiful face. It was fraying apart and there was nothing I could do.

Her fingers dug out her eyes, popped them into her lipless mouth. Her ears were harder to tear away, but it was determined. It ripped out clumps of hair by the roots and fed them to her in fistfuls, then exploited the lacerations to start peeling away her scalp. Her jaws worked constantly. And when it tired of that, it began slamming the back of her head into the wall, idly at first, then harder, harder, until bone started to crack.

The feast continued. Harder pieces, softer pieces. Pieces it was impossible to live without. Yet still she moved . . . even as I couldn't, *wouldn't*. Because that's what you do for the people you love. You stay with them until the end. Because no one should have to go into the dark alone.

Even when it seems like nothing of what you once loved is left.

▽

There once was a man who loved grizzly bears, and went and got himself eaten by one, along with his girlfriend. His camcorder was running the whole time, although the lens cap was still on, so it only captured the sound of what happened. A filmmaker did a documentary about him, and was seen listening to the audio with a set of headphones, and the look on his face was enough.

You must never listen to this, he tells the custodian of the tape, a friend of the dead man. *I think you should not keep it. You should destroy it. Because it will be the white elephant in your room all your life.*

I have a recording like that, but it's too late for the advice. I know exactly what's on it.

Mostly, it's of a man just off-camera, his voice patient and hopeful and even, if his tone is to be believed, diplomatic, trying phrase after phrase, inquiry upon inquiry, language after language, speaking to a shabby captive who might've been mistaken for a leper, and sometimes seems to watch him, but mostly ignores him.

For eighteen minutes. Eighteen fruitless minutes.

And then? The moment Marcus had dreamed about for years.

It perks up. It answers. Like sliding a key into a lock, he'd gotten to the one language that apparently interested it. It doesn't rush, and, in the most unpleasantly lacerated voice I've ever heard, speaks for 12.6 seconds. Then, by all appearances, it loses interest again, no matter how eager Marcus is to follow up.

Three more excruciating minutes.

Until, literally, all hell breaks loose.

That was when the tripod got knocked over, but I think Lorelei did that. It's what panicked people do—knock things over. The camera was still operating, though, and in the right channel of the stereo field there are sounds that I would have no idea how to make, even if I wanted to imitate them. In the background, on the left, there's a flash of movement, Lorelei running the opposite direction. A moment later she makes a low, plaintive squeal that I wish I'd never heard.

And that's it for a while, until I return to the scene. The clatter of more running back and forth. It ends with the distant sound of some man screaming his soul out, echoing off concrete until it seems like it's coming from another dimension.

Old Persian—that was the language. It took me months to find someone who recognized it from the audio excerpt I kept sending out.

Here's what that hateful entity eventually thought was worth telling Marcus:

"The seeds were planted long ago. All but three took root, grew, and flowered. All that remains is to watch the last and greatest blooms."

When we first crawled out of the mud, our enemies had been here forever. When we first left the savannahs and our caves, they must've been ready and waiting. When we first climbed stairs of our own making, they were already at the top.

And so I think of them throughout history, terrorizing here, advising there, tempting everywhere, and forever trading in the timeless currencies of lust and envy, wrath and greed, gluttony, sloth, and pride. They could wear the robes of sages and nobility as easily as they could the rags of vagrants. But like chess masters, always thinking twenty, fifty, a hundred moves ahead.

Fighters know all about using your own strength against you.

All I do now is fight, and train, and anticipate the next one. It's all I *can* do. It's like I told Lorelei: Sometimes, if you want to keep from going crazy, you just have to smash something. So I do, and tell myself I'm more symptom than disease.

Blooms—it could mean anything.

I wonder if I'll know them when I see them.

Just Outside Our Windows, Deep Inside Our Walls

Somewhere in our early teen years it's inevitable that our parents become sources of great embarrassment to us, held accountable for everything they are and aren't, could've been or should never be. Before things can get to that stage, though, it sometimes goes the other direction. We realize, even if we can't articulate it with the same sharpness with which we sense it, that once the bloom is off the earliest years of childhood, we stand revealed as something our parents are mortified to have created.

I always knew a lot more about the latter than the former.

△

It was spring when she moved into the house next door. It must have been spring, because my window was open, and, directly across from it, so was hers, and had been for at least a day, as though the neighbors were expecting her and had to flush the stale winter air out of the room or maybe the entire uppermost floor.

Everything there was to know about life on the third floor, I understood it inside and out by this point, and had for over two years.

I knew she was there to stay because she sang. Not at first, though. At first there was just bumping and thudding, the sounds of luggage and boxes, and three voices, their words too faint to make out, but only two were familiar. I knew the sounds of my neighbors. This new female voice

sounded higher and younger than the other, entirely unfamiliar, although for all that, it seemed to me that she sounded just as tired.

She only sang later, when she thought she was alone.

Whatever the words were, it wasn't a happy-sounding song, not the kind of song you might hear sung by a group of people crowded around my parents' grand piano downstairs and someone who knew how to play it. I listened a while, then dropped to the floor and crept like a spy toward the window until I was underneath it, careful not to make any noise because she still had no way to know I was there, and I didn't want her to until I'd had a chance for a closer listen and to figure out what she was up to. In the way her voice started and stopped and started again, as though she were pausing between each line or two, the song seemed to require effort. It made me think of a song sung in tribute of someone who has died, only not in a way that sounded, in my word at the time, *churchy*.

I popped up into the window only when she seemed to have quit, not so much finishing the song as abandoning it, and called to her across the space between our houses: "What's that you were singing?"

Until now, all I'd seen of her was a silhouette, a thin shape moving around in a room and beyond the reach of the sun. But now she came to the window and smacked her elbows down onto the sill and scowled across at me. Her straight brown hair swept past both wrists as if to whisk her agitation at me, and one hand darted up to grab the bottom of the window and flexed as though she were going to slam it down, but then she kept looking at me and stopped herself, although when she spoke she sounded no less furious.

"Have you been there the whole time?"

"I was here first," I said. "I've always been here first."

"Well . . . you should *announce* yourself, is what you should do." She told me this as if she suspected she might be speaking to an idiot. She looked very much older to me, twelve or maybe as old as thirteen, and this hurt deeply, because it meant she must have been very worldly and knowledgeable when it came to idiots. "It's the *polite* thing to do."

I told her I was sorry, then asked about the song again.

"I'm sure it wouldn't mean anything to you. I'm sure you don't speak the language."

"What language?"

"The language the song's in." Now she sounded convinced beyond all doubt of my idiocy. Then her scowl lifted and she appeared to relent in her harsher appraisals. "It's not from here." After another moment, "It's not *for* here."

"Oh," I said, as if this made sense to me. "Then what are *you* doing here?"

She seemed not to have heard me even though I knew she had, and I started to feel bad for asking it at all. While at first I'd found her not very nice to look at, I began to wonder if I wasn't wrong, because now it seemed I'd only been misled by a trick of light and her annoyance. I wondered, too, if she might jump from the window, or lean forward and let herself fall. In that other world three floors down, the neighbors' house was ringed with square slabs of stone to walk on. Nobody could survive a fall like that.

"I draw," I told her, volunteering a distraction to save her life. "Want to see?"

I'd sneaked up some old ones, at least, even if I couldn't make new ones.

"Later, maybe," she said, and pulled away. Like before, her hand went to the bottom of the window, lingering a few moments, but as she moved back into the room she again left it open.

That night, after the lights were out, I lay in my bed and imagined her doing the same. I fought to stay awake as long as I could in case there were other songs to hear, or a repeat performance of the first one. Barring that, it seemed possible that she might cry instead, because that's what I'd done the first night they'd moved me up here, but just before I fell asleep I wondered if the reason I hadn't heard anything from her was because she was lying in the dark listening for some sound out of me.

σ

The distant future I imagined for myself must have been inspired by something I'd seen on TV, which helped assure me that it was possible to turn my fascinations into a life that could take me far away, where I would be loved by thousands. For what will become obvious reasons, I wanted to be a magician.

I would spend many hours planning what my stage show would be like, and soon grew bored with the idea that I would merely escape from deadly traps and make elephants disappear. This admission seemed to unlock something deep inside, an openness to possibilities that would be mine alone to explore.

While I don't believe they came while I was asleep, they were more than just flights of imagination. I began to experience long afternoons of waking dreams in which I would take stage assistants, full of smiles and trust and with no thought of doing anything other than surrendering to my will, and I would lock them into cabinets. The blades would come next, whirring and rasping through the cabinets and cutting them into four, five, even six sections, which I would separate with a flourish before moving on to

the next. It would take a while, because my audience and I could never be satisfied with my rendering just one assistant into pieces. That would only be the same old trick.

Once the assistants were in pieces and scattered around the stage, smiling and waving and tapping their feet from the separate remnants of the cabinets, I would begin to reassemble them, although never the same way they'd been. They were meant for better things. I would start simply, swapping an assistant's arms for his legs, and vice versa, or grafting her grinning head onto the middle of her body. Then, after I had basked in the applause for that trick, I would combine the parts of one assistant with those of another, and finally give one or two several more parts than they'd started with, creating human spiders, which would leave others armless and legless, to wriggle across the stage like caterpillar prey.

But the waking dreams of my performance would always end with the assistants dancing like puppets on the stage to prove to the audience how happy they were with their new bodies, and that whatever dramas had played out a few minutes earlier were just theatrics. And so everyone could go home safe and secure in the knowledge that sometimes harm was nothing more than an illusion.

∞

Her name was Roni, I found out a couple days later, which was short for Veronica, and by now short for Ronnie, too. She claimed that there had been a time, lasting for years, when she wanted to be a boy, and so *Ronnie* was how she had insisted on signing her name, writing it over and over when she was alone, just her and a pen and a piece of paper, and she didn't have to tell me why.

But while I understood the business with the paper, I didn't understand why she would need to in the first place. Why would she want to be a boy? I had to ask her this many times before she gave me any kind of an answer.

"You're a boy," she said from her window. "What have you killed?"

Bugs, I told her. And fish, because I remembered catching some once with a grandfather, and we hadn't thrown them back, so I supposed that had to count. And a couple of birds, when I had gotten to play with the pellet rifle a friend had been given for his birthday. Those were all I could remember. Except for the other times. But it seemed like those shouldn't count, because to really do something like that you have to mean it.

Roni seemed to be hoping for more, but before I could make up anything else, some stupid meaningless thing that wouldn't scare her away from the window forever, she asked me another question. "Wasn't it easier to do it because you're a boy than it would've been if you weren't?"

"I don't know," I told her, because I had no experience being a girl. Although, yes, I could imagine them being more squeamish about murderous activities. "I guess so. Probably."

"Well, there you go."

I was glad then that I wasn't a girl, because it seemed that they talked in riddles. Then again, if I *were* a girl, maybe I would have understood everything she was telling me by not coming right out and saying it.

"I heard about something in school," she said.

I nodded, and sort of remembered what that was like.

She pointed to her right, beyond the front of the houses and toward the park that our block faced. It was bright green in there now, and people were finally going there again the way they used to, little specks of color on the paths and between the trees, and every so often, when the air was just right, a laugh would carry over, and I wished I knew what was so funny.

"What I heard was that back in the winter, after Thanksgiving, three different people, on three different days, were found with their heads off," Roni said. "It wasn't any girl who did that. She wouldn't even think to do it."

"She wouldn't?" By now I was just comfortable enough with Roni to think I might be able to get away with challenging her a little. "Who says?"

"Well, she might *think* it. But she'd never *do* it."

"Why not?"

"We don't have the hands for it, for one thing." She craned her neck forward, angling to see as much of the room behind me as she could. "You've got windows in there, don't you, that look out the front? And you don't go to my school and you never seem to leave. So . . . did you see anything?"

For a moment I was suspicious. Maybe the police had sent her, and the next-door neighbors weren't really her aunt and uncle. Maybe she hadn't really come to stay with them until further notice because of . . . well, she hadn't actually said anything about why. But I didn't believe this. If the police had sent her, they would have sent her with a better lie that she could actually tell. I knew that much from TV.

"If I did see something," I said, "what would you want to know about it?"

She turned serious, thinking, as if she hadn't planned this far. Then she knew. "Most people would want to know why there wasn't any blood. But what I'd rather know is if the person who did it ran away, or just walked, like it was any other day."

This was very weird to me. "What would that matter?"

Her face became a riddle then, and she knew it, and seemed to like it that way.

"Maybe he didn't do either," I said. "Walk *or* run."

She burst out laughing. "Well, he didn't fly!"

I realized then how much more I liked her when she laughed. I never got to see anyone laugh anymore, only hear it, and not very often, only when I was lucky. After three days this was the first time she'd laughed, too, but it didn't seem likely to happen again any time soon. I remembered school, and how it could be bad enough at the start of the year, and she was getting here toward the end of a school year, and that couldn't have been easy.

So I told her maybe she wouldn't have to go to the new school if she didn't want to, that I had a governess who came most days and, if Roni wanted, she could listen at the window. The idea met with instant disdain—not because it was a bad idea, just that the offer was meaningless.

"What's she going to teach you that I don't already know?"

✳

I began to wish the spring away . . . that summer would hurry up and arrive, so the schools would lock their doors and I wouldn't have to wait for late afternoons. While the waiting didn't get any easier, at least as spring went on the days got longer, with more light filling the space between the houses. Even though we could lean in the windows and talk to each other any time of the night, it was better when I could see her, because otherwise she wouldn't seem as real. She'd tell me what they trying to teach her at school, and I'd tell her what the governess was trying to teach me, and there didn't ever seem to be much in common, and eventually I realized something was missing.

"What about art class?" I asked. "Don't you ever go to art?"

"Of course not. It's middle school."

The way she said this made it sound horrible.

"Don't you miss it? Art class?"

"I guess. I don't know." She sounded as if nobody had ever told her that she *could* miss it.

"Could you do me a favor anyway? Could you bring back some paper for me? And pencils or something?" Crayons or colored markers seemed too much to ask for at this stage, but if this first part went well, I could get to those later.

"What kind of kid doesn't have paper and pencils of his own? Everybody has those." Roni appeared not to believe me, and who could blame her.

"You say you have a governess. How do you do your lessons, then? How do you do your math problems?"

"I do them in front of her. I just don't get to keep the paper and pencils. They make her take everything away when she leaves."

Roni realized I was serious, and froze for a moment with her mouth half open and one eye half shut. No one would ever make up a thing like this. "Why?" she said, as if she'd never heard of anything so ridiculous.

"Because I draw."

"Only you and a billion other grade-school lower life-forms. So?"

I shut my eyes for a moment and sighed, and when I opened them, I think maybe, just for an instant, she saw someone else she'd never realized lived here.

"Are you going to help me or not?"

"I never said I wouldn't, did I?" She blinked a few times, startled. "I've already got all the pencils I can ever use in this lifetime. You can have a couple of those." She briefly disappeared from the window. "Knock yourself out."

She took aim and sent them flipping end-over-end, across the space and through my window. Two bright yellow pencils lying on the rug, with no one to take them away. At first I didn't dare touch them. I just wanted to look at them.

"Are you okay?" she called. "I didn't sink one in your eye, did I?"

I turned back around and remembered to thank her. Saying thank you is very important, especially when you're a prisoner.

"I've got a notebook here you can have, too. Just let me rip a few pages out first."

It was tempting. But no.

"I'd rather have blank paper. Totally blank." I'd waited this long. I could wait another day. "I hate lines."

"And speaking of lines, did you ever hear the one about beggars and choosers? That's a good one."

"I still hate lines."

She nodded, getting it. "They really don't let you have paper and writing utensils of your own. They really don't."

I shook my head no.

"What about toilet paper?" She was smirking. But she wasn't serious, although at first I thought she was, and she laughed. "Let me see what I can come up with," she said, and seemed to take a new satisfaction in it now. Something wrong to do, a law to break, and if she was lucky she might even get to steal, and it must have been then that everything

changed between us, and each of us didn't just have a neighbor to pass the time with, but maybe the closest thing either of us could find to a friend.

⚔

She came through a couple days later, way beyond anything I believed I could hope for. I'd been thinking she would bring, at best, a few dirty sheets of unwanted paper with shoe prints on them. Instead, that evening, she popped up in her window, grinning, and when I couldn't stand it anymore she held up an unopened package of copier paper.

"Five hundred sheets. I got it from a teacher's supply closet," Roni said. "Are you ever gonna owe me big time. Like maybe for the rest of eternity."

Except then we had to deal with the problem of transferring it from her room to mine. Throwing pencils was one thing. For this, she didn't trust her arm. *I* didn't trust her arm.

"Why can't I just bring it over under my clothes?" she said. "What are your parents going to do, search me?"

No, I told her. She'd never get through. I never had visitors, except for the governess, and there were locks. Besides, the paper may have come from downstairs, but it belonged to the upstairs world now. It could never go downstairs again.

But I had a dart gun, the kind with the suction cup tips. And I had string. And Roni found some rope, a little thicker than twine, that she could tie to the string I shot over. And a wicker basket her aunt no longer used in the garden, whose handle she could slip the rope through. By the time it got dark, I'd used the string to pull the rope back, first one end and then the other, and we'd looped it around our bedframes, like pulleys. I tied the ends together with one of the best knots I remembered from scouting, when they still used to let me go out, and then all we had to do was keep the handle from slipping along the rope and we could pull it back and forth, from room to room, all we wanted.

That's how she sent me the paper.

It took me even longer to touch this than it did the pencils. I knew I'd be up half the night, finding the best possible hiding place for it. Nobody could know. Nobody could *ever* know. If they found this, I'd never have a window again, just walls.

"Hey," she called over after the sky had gone dark, and she hadn't seen any sign of me for a while. "You have to tell me why. What did you do? Draw a bunch of dirty pictures once and it fried their brains?"

I leaned on the sill for a long time. In her window, she was a silhouette, a mystery lit from behind, and if I'd been a little older then, I might have wanted to draw every single strand of hair that cut the light into ribbons. She'd done the kindest thing for me that anyone ever had, and we'd never even been in the same room, or closer than twelve feet.

"Sometimes I draw things and they come true," I told her. Because she'd asked, and I had no one else to tell and couldn't imagine a day when I ever would. "Sometimes I draw things and it makes them happen. Or makes them change."

She didn't say a word. *Liar* . . . I might've expected that. Might've even hoped for it. The longer the silence, the more I wished she'd just make fun of me. My fingers hung onto the windowsill the way bird claws hold branches.

"You're not going to go away now, are you? You'll still come to the window?"

"It depends," she said.

"On what?"

"How does it work? Do you just draw anything, and whatever happens, happens? Or do you have to want it to, first?"

"I think I have to mean for it to. Even if I don't know that at the time."

And even if I *wanted* it to happen, sometimes nothing did. Otherwise, the park would've been full of T-Rexes and a brontosaurus herd. Which had made me think I was limited to working with what was there already, not making something out of nothing.

"Interesting," she said. "Listen. They tell me I'm going to have to have braces starting next year. The last thing I want is a big shiny metal mouth. If I gave you a really good look at them, do you think you could fix my teeth?"

I've always wondered what her dentist would have said if he'd ever gotten a chance to see her teeth again.

It wasn't a hard thing to do, and I was able to get a closer look at her mouth than she expected, because I had a telescope, all the better to see everything on the earth and sky I was missing. Roni stood in her window and smiled a wide, crazy smile, and I let it fill the telescope's eyepiece, and first drew her teeth the way they were, how the ones around the side tilted in and one in the front overlapped the other. Then I concentrated really hard and started changing the lines a little at a time. Twice she said it hurt, but didn't want to stop.

After we were done, it took a while before she came back from the bathroom mirror. But she said I'd done a good job.

It wasn't the first time I'd fixed something, and I was better at it by now than I was before, when I was smaller and my fingers didn't move as well, and this was all new to me, and something my parents didn't understand. All I'd done until that time was little things around the house, like switch the arms and legs on a dancing figure that spun around on top of my mother's music box. They never suspected, not until the night they had a party, for Christmas, I think, and they marched me around to all the guests, and had me show off things I'd drawn so everyone could see what a great artist they had here.

One of the guests asked me to draw his portrait.

So I did.

Except I drew him the way I wanted him, because I didn't like him. He was loud and his breath stank and he spit when he talked and it hurt my ears to be around him, so first I drew his ugly flapping mouth, and then I smeared it out, and his eyes, too, to stop him from looking at me the way he was starting to.

That changed the party in a hurry.

My parents figured things out, finally, and made me put him back together again, but I was scared by then, and didn't draw as well, and it was the first time I'd tried to make anything the way it was before. A few days later, when I was eavesdropping on my parents as they argued about what to do with me, I heard them say the man was going to be having surgeries for years.

So it was good to help Roni.

But there wasn't much else that needed changing, so the rest of the time I just drew without any other reason behind it, mostly other places I would rather be, if only I knew how to get there.

△

The school year ended for everyone but me, and summer got hotter. Whenever I wasn't having lessons and Roni wasn't somewhere else, we lived at our open windows, so our top floors got warmer, too, and we wore the windowsills smooth with our elbows.

Plus we'd never taken down the rope.

"Do you think we should?" I asked one night.

"No. Definitely not," she said. "They never paid any attention to what's going on over their heads before, so why would they start now?"

So we used the basket to pass stuff back and forth, like books and magazines and comics and music and other things we liked, plus things we made. I sent her drawings, some to keep, and she sent me some stories she was working on, not only to read but for me to draw pictures for them.

She admitted they were all set in the place where the songs came from.

Roni had never stopped singing after that first night. I was glad of it, and by now she didn't seem to mind if I heard or not. I still didn't understand the language, and she wouldn't tell me what the words meant, but I began imagining what they must've been about from the sound of them. And from her stories, which I did understand. These were mostly about girls who killed trolls and ogres, or held them captive forever, or held them captive a while and then killed them. At first I felt sorry for them, because as a fellow prisoner I knew what they were going through, but then I realized each one of them had done something terrible to the girls, so it was probably for the best when the princesses and peasants and warrior girls started by cutting off the monsters' hands.

Then, one evening, when the sky was soft and purple and fireflies flickered close to the ground, she peered at me with her head cocked at a curious tilt. "It was you, wasn't it?" she said. "Those people in the park, in the winter. You did that, didn't you?"

I'd been waiting for this for weeks. "I didn't mean to. It was an accident."

"Three different times it was an accident?" She laughed the way you laugh when you don't believe something, but didn't sound mad. She hadn't known them, so what was it to her if their heads had come off. "How did you do it without paper?"

I asked if she ever had known what it was like to want to do something so bad, only not be able to, that you thought you were going to explode. She didn't have to think about it. Well, that was me without paper. Until I'd noticed a layer of frost on the inside of the windows overlooking the park.

"All I did was look through the glass and use my fingernail to scratch an outline around them." And then flick my fingernail across their necks. "I didn't mean anything. The first time I didn't even know it would happen."

She looked confused. "When I first asked you how it worked, you told me you *did* have to mean it."

Right. I had. So maybe I was mad at the people for being able to be out while it was snowing and I had to stay inside. Maybe I'd done it the second time to make sure the first was really my fault. Maybe a third time just because I could. Mostly I remembered the way they fell, first one part and then the other, straight down into the snow without any sound.

"Is it something you'll always be able to do?"

"I guess so," I told her. "But I heard my parents talking once and they were wondering if I might grow out of it someday."

She nodded, very solemn, very serious. "I have to think about this."
"Are you mad at me?"

But she was already gone from the window. I still heard her voice, though, and it gave me hope: "I'll never tell on you, if that's what you mean."

Later that night I was awakened by the basket clunking at the window. I turned on a light, the only light burning in the whole world, and got out of bed to see what she'd sent me. It was a picture, Roni and two boys, one obviously older and one who looked younger, plus a woman and a man. Roni wasn't smiling, at least not so you could see her teeth and whether any of them were crooked or not, and I sort of remembered what it was like, having to pretend to smile that way.

Her voice was a whisper now, floating like a mist across the space between our rooms.

"If someone was going to come over, and I told you what time, and you knew who to look for, and you saw him, could you do it then?" she said. "The trick with the head?"

I rubbed my eyes and looked at the picture some more. "Who to?"

She made a sound I'd never heard. "Don't make me say it."

A little later I turned out the light because maybe it would be easier on her that way, and I listened to her breathe and leaned in the window in the moonlight so she could see I would stay there for as long as it took.

"The one in the middle," she finally said.

It was early August when I heard her crying. I didn't even know she did that, because she seemed very much older to me, twelve or maybe as old as thirteen, and I thought nothing could get to her that bad anymore.

I suppose I'd always been afraid that all of this would only be for the summer, or a year, anything but forever, that it was too good to last. I'd made a friend and so had she, and as far as I knew, no one else in the downstairs world was even aware of it, and this was just the way we liked it. But tomorrow she would be going away again. They would be coming to pick her up and take her home again.

"Nothing will change then," she told me. "They say it will this time, but I know it won't."

It was a long time before I understood what she really meant by that. At the time, all I knew was that it meant a lot to her, meant *everything* to her.

"You could come over here," I said. "I'll hide you."

She laughed through her tears. It had been a long time since I'd heard it, the you're-such-an-idiot laugh. "You don't think your parents will notice me down there looking for the keys?"

"That's not how I mean. Just come across. Like we did with the paper and everything else."

"On the rope? It'll never hold me."

It could. I was very sure of this. I told her how it could.

I didn't mean for this to make her cry even harder, but it did.

I stayed awake the rest of that night, pinching myself whenever I got sleepy, in case Roni changed her mind. It was kind of fun, because I hardly ever got to see the sunrise, and now I had a reason, something important to do for once.

"Okay," she said when the sky was first beginning to go pink and orange. "I think I trust you."

We started with her legs.

Had I ever drawn anything this carefully before? Never. Never in my whole life.

She tied each one to the rope by the ankle, and once I'd pulled them across, I unfastened them and rested them side-by-side on my bed, toes up, the way they'd be if she were lying there whole, and I never knew she had a birthmark the size of a quarter on one thigh.

Now we had to start planning more carefully, because once we did the first arm, she wouldn't be able to tie things very well with just one hand, so she had to start tying parts of herself to the line ahead of time. The last thing she did was lean over to one side with her head in the basket and wait for me to take care of the rest.

After I had all her parts laid out in place I thought of my assistants, my human spiders, and how happy we made the audience and how loudly it clapped for us. I really wanted to try it, except Roni hadn't agreed to this, and probably wouldn't like it, and I could see how impatiently her head was staring at me from the pillow.

So I just drew her back together again like normal.

"What did it feel like?" I wanted to know. "Did it hurt?"

"Not much." She thought a while longer. "Cold, though. It felt cold." She looked around at all the space I had, a whole floor to myself. "This is nice. This is really, really nice."

We cut the rope and pulled all of it over, then cut it into little pieces so she would never have to go across again. Some of the pieces we threw out the window, down to the ground and up on the roof, and the rest we hid. I knew where to hide anything.

I knew where to hide her when they brought breakfast up, and we shared it even though it wasn't enough for two of us. I knew where to hide her when the governess came, so she could listen without being heard. I just wasn't sure where to hide her if anyone really came looking. And they would, I was sure of it. It wouldn't matter that there were locks on the door at the bottom of the stairs. They'd still come looking. Because they knew there was something different about me.

But for as long as it lasted, it was the best day of my life.

In between the fun stuff, we kept watch at the window, and listened, and late in the day a car stopped in front of the house next door. People got out and I recognized them from the photo she'd sent me, including the one in the middle.

I held up paper and a pencil. "Do you still want me to? The trick with the head?"

We watched them walk closer, and I was glad all over again that I wasn't a girl, because I couldn't ever imagine myself looking that confused over a simple question.

"No," she finally whispered. "I couldn't really do that."

I sort of remembered what that was like.

It was less than an hour before they came, but before then we heard people calling outside and watched them troop over to the park and back again. Eventually the doorbell rang downstairs, big bonging chimes you could hear all the way up here.

It was time.

And I knew where to hide her now. It could work. I was very sure of this. I told her how it could, and this time she didn't cry.

I drew myself first, getting everything just right because this was the trick that mattered most of all. Then I waited while we looked at each other, because I knew now that I loved her, even if I didn't know as what, and there was nothing more to say, just listening for the voices and footsteps to get closer, until the keys began to click in the door, and Roni closed her eyes and nodded.

Back to the paper, concentrating very hard, blocking out everything else.

I drew her inside me.

And when I looked up again she was gone.

♈

That was a long time ago, in a house I hardly remember, except for every square inch of the top floor, and the views. The house isn't standing anymore.

But we'd pulled it off, waiting there innocent while they looked for her. It wasn't as if they had to tear the place apart. Even with an entire third floor to search, there are only so many places something the size of a person can hide. I think they were a little afraid of me by this time, too. There's what you know, and what you suspect, and what you don't know, and they realized what they didn't know was the biggest part of it, and so they must have decided it would be safer not to grill me too hard.

Inside, I could feel her moving, but later on she went to sleep, the way you can sleep when you're with someone you trust.

We waited a long time, weeks and then months, for the search and suspicions to die down.

"Aren't you ready to come out now?" I'd ask every so often.

"Just a little longer," she'd tell me. "This is nice. This is really, really nice."

Never in a hurry. So I asked less and less often.

Until there was no point asking anymore.

Of all the things my parents were wrong about when it came to me, why did they have to be right about this one: that the thing with the paper was something I'd grow out of someday. I don't even know when it happened. It just did, and while whatever I put down on paper looked better than ever, it just sat there doing nothing, empty and lifeless and inert.

By now I must have gone through forests of trees, trying to remember what it was like, to recapture what once seemed so easy, so I could draw her back out of me again. But the results are always the same. One more crumpled wad of paper, one more curl of ash.

Yet still, she's close, so close I can almost touch her.

But now her voice comes from so far away.

Eternal, Ever Since
Wednesday

It all sounded like fun at first, and at first, it really was.

Mom and Dad had let him stay up past his bedtime in anticipation of the late news, because, face it, one look out the window was enough to tell anyone with half a brain that it wasn't going to stop snowing any time soon. Maybe all night. The weatherman only confirmed it, while below him, names of more schools than Jakob ever realized existed slid across the bottom of the TV screen.

He only cared about one.

After he saw it, and whooped with raw, unfettered joy over tomorrow's snow day, and was told by both parents to shush, that he'd wake his sister, the weatherman sweetened the deal with the news that what they were really in for was a two-day blizzard.

His dad reacted with a defeated groan, and his mom with an indifferent shrug that implied it could be worse, things could always be worse. She could usually work from home in a pinch, as long as the power didn't go out. She turned to Jakob with a grin.

"Chocolate-chip pancakes sound about right for in the morning?"

"That's a weekend breakfast," he said.

"It sounds to me like the weekend's started early."

Four days. Assuming Friday held. *Four days.* It was practically an entire vacation, like a surprise gift someone gives you for no particular reason, only because they saw it and thought you might like it. Time stretched ahead of him like a tunnel with no end, and a part of him instantly resisted

the idea of going to bed, because if he could find a way not to sleep this entire time, it would be like squeezing an extra day out of it.

They sent him anyway, Dad telling him not to oversleep, that he'd still need Jakob to help shovel in the morning so that he could get his car out of the garage and down the driveway. That was always the way of it here—a little jubilation, then Dad was there to bring it down a notch or two.

When he got upstairs and was trudging along the second floor hallway toward his room, he saw Fiona's door open a crack, and the tip of her nose. He stopped, and she opened the door wider.

"I heard you yell," she said, her voice full of hope. "It was a good yell."

"No school tomorrow. For either of us."

She beamed at him like he was the one who had made it so. The giver of the gift.

"Probably no school Friday, either."

Her eyes popped wide and she sucked in a gasp of disbelief. He was the best brother in the world. She retreated into her room and launched herself back-first onto her bed, kicking her legs in the air, her insane mop of black curls flying. And he got the excitement, he really did, because he felt it himself . . . but Fiona was six. A first-grader. What kind of school day did she have to escape, anyway? Practicing a few letters of the alphabet on paper whose lines were so far apart you could lay a finger between them? That was no school day. That was camp.

Middle school, now that was a whole different world.

After he peed and brushed his teeth and shut himself in his room, Jakob left the light off as he stood at his window and gave thanks to the night—the white ground and the pale sky, and the warm lights still shining in the homes of the neighbors close enough to see, and best of all, the thick churning flurry showing in the orb glowing around the lawn light out front.

He unlatched his window and pushed it up, then fiddled with the screen until he could slide that up, too. The cold slapped him in the face, along with a swirl of suicidal flakes that wanted to breach the security of the house.

Jakob dragged his fingers along the windowsill, scooping a wad of snow that he left squishy enough not to hurt when he pressed it to his left eye. By the time he'd awakened this morning, it had opened up enough that he could see out of it again. While he didn't mind the bruise—in fact, the longer the bruise stuck around, the better—the skin remained swollen and pulpy and sore, and he had no use for any of that, especially now that they were on snow days and nobody he still wanted to see it was likely to.

He went to bed with one warm hand and the other one cold, pressing both of them together. For a time they seemed to even each other out, like he was something not quite alive but certainly not dead, kind of the way he figured people eventually got once they grew old enough, his parents' age for sure.

Within a few more minutes he brought himself back to life again, all the way.

Maybe it only took paying attention to keep it from happening in the first place. Maybe the ones stuck that way just weren't trying hard enough to live.

⚋

Teachers didn't assign themes like that anymore, not in middle school, but if they'd had him write one on the best snow day he could imagine, he doubted he could've improved upon the way he actually spent Thursday. It was that good.

It still started with shoveling, of course, heaving snow alongside Dad so the car could leave the garage. But once it was done, and Jakob saw his father off, Dad's Audi slaloming down to the roads that would take him to the studio for the day, everything only got better.

There was the weekend breakfast on a Thursday morning, and then there were hours of outside time. He spotted a line of tracks, like finger holes in a pie crust, that must have been made by a hare bounding along one tiring leap at a time. He followed them while he could, but by the time he got down near the Crenshaws' property at the bottom of the hill, the tracks were already filling in and nearly erased.

He built a snow fort and stocked it with an arsenal of snowballs, and although Fiona joined him, she wasn't much of an opponent, especially wrapped up so densely she looked like a ball of blue and red yarn.

"I know," she said. "Let's build a Russell Burns."

It was a good idea, even if there wasn't a lot you could do to make a snowman look like anyone in particular. Jakob worked the face, packing on extra snow to mimic Russell Burns' heavy cheeks, and the way his brow overhung his scowling eyes. Close enough. They gave him branches for arms and, after they studded his head with twigs for his spiky hair, he looked so ridiculous that Fiona collapsed to the snow in laughter so long and incapacitating that he thought he'd never get her on her feet again.

Then they bombarded him from the fort. Fiona was a terrible shot but hurled each snowball with undaunted enthusiasm while Jakob did the

damage. He snapped off an arm and blasted away a patch of twigs. If you threw at the body, their snow-Russell just ate the snow and got bigger, so Jakob went solely for headshots, bashing it to icy white pulp until he knocked it off completely.

And even though the world was better off without him, they made him a new head and did it again.

Russell deserved it, of course, on general principles all along and, as of Monday, for concrete reasons that could never be forgiven.

The schools that Jakob and Fiona attended were within walking distance of each other, and on Monday Mom was running late, so she had Jakob hoof it to the primary school and collect his sister and wait. He was running late, too.

Of all the days for Russell Burns to have been put on a similar path.

It was Fiona's backpack that set him off: My Little Pony. She was already crying beside the designated meeting tree when Jakob got there. To be honest, he didn't like the backpack, either, didn't like to be seen anywhere near the pink thing, but . . . no. Just no. She was his sister and his job was to watch out for her and he did it, even though he knew it was going to hurt.

He didn't remember who shoved whom first, but supposed it didn't matter after that. And it could have been worse—he could've come out with much more than a black eye. But while Russell may have known all there was to know about being a bully, Jakob knew a few things about actual fighting. Dad had seen to that, had sent him for lessons. Russell came out of it with a black eye of his own. Plus a bloody nose and two fat lips and a limp. By the end he was down to threats, but in some ways, those were scarier than anything his fists could do.

They gave the snow-Russell a third head and it still hadn't stopped being fun.

So that took care of the morning of this, the best snow day ever, until Mom called them in for lunch.

An hour later he was hard at it on his Xbox, deep into one more among five or six games he had that all pretty much came down to shooting his way through a bunch of monsters on another planet, or that had overrun the Earth. You couldn't overthink it, though, because how could they be smart enough to take over a planet if they were stupid enough to keep running at you when it was obvious you had all those guns. As long as you were halfway observant, you never ran out of ammunition—bullets and power cells and rockets, all this stuff lying around everywhere, waiting to be picked up, and that didn't seem very realistic, either.

But this too never stopped being fun, even if there were times when it made him wonder how he would react if Russell Burns brought a gun to school, to finish what had started on Monday. It happened sometimes. Parents tried to keep you from hearing about it when it did, but didn't have the power they thought they had to control sound.

All of which was another reason why these snow days couldn't have come at a better time.

Then the house filled with the smell of cookies, Mom and Fiona up in the kitchen going into the cookie-baking business for a few hours, and soon he had a plate of them at his elbow and hadn't even had to ask.

So that took care of the rest of the afternoon of this, the best snow day ever, until the day, as long as it had seemed, began to feel over. He was back in his room and it was barely evening, but as he stood at his window and stared out at the relentless snow and the waning light of the bone-white sky, lights winking on here and there down the road, at the Crenshaws and beyond, he still sensed the loss of the day. It made him sad somehow, because he wanted more, and he'd get it tomorrow, but it wouldn't be as fresh. It wouldn't be today.

It would never be today again.

॰

Dad came home furious, his Audi the victim of a crunched back panel. Whoever had done it hadn't even owned up to the deed, had just left it in its parking space to ruin his day once he found it.

"Is it still considered road rage if you lose it in a parking lot?" he said. "Because if I'd caught the guy, I could *not* have been held responsible."

He'd barely made it home in one piece anyway, the roads so choked after a day of nonstop snow, with more to come, that he knew he wasn't going to be able to go into the studio tomorrow, and even if he could, what would be the point, since no one else was likely to make it.

SNOWPOCALYPSE, they were calling it on that night's TV news, because they had to have a stupid name for everything big. Although if there were a video game called *Snowpocalypse*, he had no doubt that he'd want it the day it was released.

This Snowpocalypse, though, was looking not so fun now. Twenty-six hours in, it was coming down at an inch per hour. It was looking even worse than the blizzard of two years ago, when there was so much snow that the plows ran out of places to put the stuff. That first trip into the suburbs was like encountering a series of filthy new mountain ranges.

They'd managed to clear the main routes, but on the side streets the snow had gotten packed down into hard ice as dull and gray as pig iron. For weeks, they were driving on slabs of it. Like driving on a glacier, Mom said.

What he'd never seen before, though, was the evidence of where people had fallen. Using salt to de-ice the sidewalks hadn't worked. No matter how much melted, there was just more ice beneath, so it all refroze into slippery textures as jagged as a cheese grater, and here and there, you'd come across spatters and splotches of frozen blood. It was a horrible thing to contemplate. Everybody had to be wearing parkas, long pants, boots, gloves—they could only have been bleeding from above the neck.

Until seeing this, winter snow had always meant softness and quiet. You fell into it with a soft *whumph*, and as long as you were down there, you might as well make a snow angel. He'd never considered that winter could hit you in the face like a hatchet.

He'd imagined people on the ground, stunned and watching the red slush form beneath them. And *everything* hurt worse in the cold. He hoped, retroactively, that they hadn't been alone, that someone had been there to help.

If it happened to be somebody like Russell Burns, they would've just laughed.

By Friday morning the snow came up past your knees, and they were already back to a normal weekday breakfast. Fiona ate her cereal with a look like she'd been cheated in a game. Beyond the windows, the snow fort had become an indistinct mound with a dip in the middle, and the snow-Russell's toppled segments were all but buried. There would be no more justice for him.

Mom went to work in her home office, telecommuting, but while Dad had a mini-studio for himself here at the house, he didn't go in.

He was one-third owner of a real studio, although bands never recorded there and rappers never dropped by, so it wasn't like the place generated anything Jakob would've made a point to listen to. It was all music for movies and TV and commercials and games—okay, game soundtracks, that was cool—and to hear Dad talk, they were always grinding it out under some impossible deadline. Whenever Jakob had been there, only the receptionist didn't look completely stressed out.

Dad could always use a day off, but it always made the next one worse.

When he suited up and went outside with a shovel to attack the snow and clear a path to the mailbox, he didn't ask for help this time, didn't say a word at all. Jakob could watch from the windows only so long before the guilt grew too heavy. What if his dad had a heart attack out there? It would be his fault for letting it happen. Dad didn't look like the heart attack type, but you never knew.

And as much as he would rather have been doing anything else, Jakob trooped out to pitch in.

They dug and scooped, they heaved great shovelfuls to one side and the other, they leaned in hard to turn their shovels into plows, and while they eventually fought their way to the mailbox, already the path was filling in behind them. He imagined if they kept going, digging forever, making the impermanent equivalent of the vapor trail following a jet. Look back far enough, and there would no longer be any evidence of their passing.

There wasn't even any mail in the box, either.

Nobody could miss his father's weary disgust with the futility of the mission, but finally he leaned on his shovel, hair sweat-spiky around the stocking cap he wore, and grinned at him, both of them frosted top to bottom with the heavy flakes.

"Be honest. Would you rather be doing this, or sitting in school?"

No question. "This, I guess."

"You may have a bright future in ditches," Dad teased. At least Jakob hoped it was teasing. Then his father added, a little quieter, "You and me both."

Dad didn't get it. It wasn't that the schoolwork was hard. That had always come easy. Some of the time it was even interesting.

But school was a place where you had to watch everything you did, everything you said, because for the slightest wrong thing, guaranteed there was somebody ready to use it against you. Your life could fall to ruins in a single lunch hour. If somebody had a camera phone handy, the moment might live forever. It would live longer than you did.

Already it was seeming as if the Russell Burnses of the world were the ones destined to inherit it, because even though they were stupid, there was an endless supply of them, in infinite varieties, and you could look at their eyes and see how little there was behind them. They didn't feel and they didn't care. You were either their target, or in their way.

And they were just getting started.

Fiona was on the porch then, yelling across the thick white yard that Mom had made hot chocolate for everyone, and they'd better come get it before she threw it to the hogs. It was their mother's running joke. There

were no hogs. Fiona never seemed to get that. To her, the threat was real. There *were* hogs; she just hadn't seen them yet.

"Aren't you coming?" Jakob asked over his shoulder when he realized he was the only one moving.

And caught his father looking at the front door as if it were the gate of a tomb.

Dad shook his head. "I still have some things to finish up out here."

Whatever they were, he didn't seem in any hurry to get to them. Jakob watched from the window, holding his mug with his feet still chilled and his fingers tingling, sipping at the scalding cocoa while his father stood unmoving at the far edge of a yard whose boundaries had been obliterated by the snow. His father was doing some staring of his own, leaning on his shovel like it was a walking stick.

Winter made him funny, February especially. He may not have been looking in exactly the right direction, but Jakob assumed he was still staring at Finland.

Dad had come home with the tale a couple of years ago, his new favorite story of how someone had written and recorded an album. Some band in Finland had rented a big cabin out in the wilds, with its own sauna, because apparently there was no place you could go in Finland where there *wasn't* a sauna. They'd gone there at the beginning of the month with their instruments and mobile recording gear and a month's food and cases of vodka, and left at the end with a finished album.

It sounded like the perfect way to spend a February, his father had said.

Ever since, this had been Dad's gauge for perfection.

So whenever Dad was there, only not really there, that was how Jakob thought of it: He'd gone to Finland.

♫

The next morning, the snow was level with the front porch. The evergreens were burdened with it, stooped like people so feeble they could no longer hold up their heads. It was the weekend now, and the storm showed no signs of abating. On the TV news they seemed embarrassed that they had to keep using the SNOWPOCALYPSE logo, which was starting to look silly, like a kid's cartoon Band-Aid on a spouting wound, and there appeared to be some real annoyance with the weatherman, too. How could he have missed this? It was only supposed to be a two-day storm.

Disaster finally struck at home, too: They were out of coffee. It only seemed trivial if you hadn't actually seen their mom endure a morning without it.

Do something, her look at Dad said. *DO something.*

He suited up and ventured down the hill toward the Crenshaws, who by now weren't just their nearest neighbor; they were now their only visible neighbor at all, everything past that point lost behind the veil of the storm. It took Dad a long time to get there, and you could barely make him out at their door. They didn't invite him in, then it took him a long time to get back.

He walked angry, even when wading through the snow. His face was marked by the wind and cold, waxy white here and chapped red there.

"Stu says they're out of coffee, too," his father said. "I wanted to ask him then what the hell am I smelling in the house behind you? You light coffee-scented incense in the morning now, is that it? Asshole."

Fiona's eyes widened in shock, then grew consumed with worry, as if there had to be something only she could do to make everything better. *There isn't*, Jakob would have to tell her someday, although by the time she was ready to hear it, she may have figured it out for herself.

After another day of the stuff coming down, during which they all had to work harder to find something to distract themselves with—when they weren't shoveling or using brooms to knock snow off the evergreens that were getting harder and harder just to get to, or scrape it off the porch roof through the upstairs windows—he caught his mom going through the pantry with an air of solemn focus, counting on her fingers.

"This isn't the same snow, is it?" he said from the middle of the kitchen.

He had to say it again before she stopped looking at him like he was asking about, what, the weather on Mars, maybe. But this was something she herself recited every year, and it had only been a few weeks since the last time.

Every Christmas Eve she liked to read them a short little book called *A Child's Christmas In Wales*, because her own mother used to read it to her. Although the first couple of years that Fiona was old enough to pay attention, she thought it would be about kids swallowed by giant fish, so it invariably left her disappointed.

It took a few years for Jakob to get the story figured out to his own satisfaction, because the man who wrote it hardly ever came right out and clearly said what he meant. He really worked hard to dress it up, but by now it had started to seem worth the effort to try and follow what he was saying.

"But that was not the same snow," the man tells a kid who believes that the snows of then and now were identical. *"Our snow was not only shaken from white wash buckets down the sky, it came shawling out of the ground and*

swam and drifted out of the arms and hands and bodies of the trees; snow grew overnight on the roofs of the houses like a pure and grandfather moss. . . ."

This wasn't the same snow, either, he feared.

"Why would you think that?" his mom finally said.

Eternal, ever since Wednesday—the man had described it that way, too. That was the one that sounded more like it.

"It's just a story. It was just his way of blathering on about how things seem different when you're a kid. It's just a bad blizzard out there this time. Snow is snow."

Except it was obvious that she didn't believe a word of it, not for a second. Parents always seemed to tell the least convincing lies when it was most important to level with you.

⚖

And still the snow kept coming down. Or up from below, or out from within, or whatever path it took.

By Sunday night, normally a time to bemoan the inescapable fact that school would resume in a few hours, he noticed there were no lights burning at the Crenshaw house. The next morning—you couldn't call it day, because it was just a lighter version of the suffocating night—brought an urgent ringing of their doorbell.

Jakob hadn't gone downstairs yet, and peered out his window to discover a ragged trough churned up the hill, like a single fragile vein linking the houses. There was no digging a path through it now. There was only floundering on top of it, trying not to sink too deep.

He crept from his room to watch and listen from the summit of the stairs as his father opened the door to their visitor. Jakob couldn't see all of him. The angle of the doorway cut off part of him, and his dad blocked some of the rest, but what he could see looked caked in snow and bent with exhaustion. Stu Crenshaw wasn't the fit and trim man his father was.

"Looks like you guys are still okay for electricity," he wheezed.

"So far, so good."

"Ours went out yesterday. Must be a wire down right at the house."

"That would be my guess."

"The thing is, we've been burning kerosene in a couple of space heaters since then, and . . ." He let his voice trail away, sheepish. "And we've almost run through it already. You wouldn't have any to spare, would you?"

"I'm afraid not. We're out," his father said. "Sorry."

Mr. Crenshaw started to fluster and bluster. "This isn't about that coffee thing a couple days ago, is it? Come on, this is our lives we're talking about, maybe."

"It's not about anything other than being out of kerosene. That's all."

"Out. You're completely out."

"That's what I keep trying to tell you, that you don't seem to want to hear."

"But wasn't it you telling me in the middle of November how you'd laid in some cans, because of how long it took them to get around to those downed power lines last winter?" Now their neighbor was starting to sound truly angry. "I seem to remember that being you, all proud of yourself for getting that taken care of early."

"Right . . . and last month I had to run them into the studio when we had an outage there, so we could keep working under our deadlines."

This was the first Jakob had ever heard of such a thing. It hadn't happened. It couldn't have. Because if it had, they all would've had to listen to Dad gripe about it for the next two days.

"Keep working?" Mr. Crenshaw said too loudly. "How do you keep working in a place like that when the power goes out, no matter how warm and toasty you stay?"

"It's gas heat there. That's what went out. Not the electricity."

Mr. Crenshaw grumbled about a few more things, then finally ran out of them, and out of things to argue about, and stomped his way off the porch, through the drifts starting to collect there despite the overhang, while Dad slammed the door behind him.

Jakob made like a ghost back to his room, peering out his window from the very corner, not even sure why he was hiding. Just knowing that he didn't want to be seen whenever Mr. Crenshaw snapped his head around for another furious glance back at their house.

Later, when they gathered downstairs for breakfast, his father seemed proud of this one-up victory over their treacherous neighbor, yet still ate his bacon as if he were biting the heads off snakes.

"What do you want to bet Stu could find some coffee now that he didn't know they had?" Dad said. "'Well, looky here! It was hiding behind the cereal all along!'"

"We should've invited them to stay with us until this is over." It wasn't clear if Mom was saying this to Dad or to herself. "He had to be thinking it. He was just too stubborn to ask. Just like you were."

"Five more mouths to feed? Forget it. We can't," Dad said. "Because you can bet they'd find some reason to come up here empty-handed. And with the size of him, Stu eats enough for two."

Fiona stopped eating for one, unable to get her breakfast past the worried look starting to pull her face in opposite directions. She often played with the Crenshaws' younger daughter.

"What?" Dad said to her. "Alissa? Is that why you're giving me the stink-eye? She'll be fine, so stop your worrying."

He gnawed at his breakfast a while longer, then banged down his fork. "What's the exchange rate between coffee and kerosene these days, anyway? I think I'll go find out."

Mom followed him as he abandoned the table, asking what was wrong with him and telling him what a bad idea this was, a really bad idea. He brushed it off, paying attention only to the next thing he had to put on, ski pants and parka and hat and goggles and boots. Then he was out the door like he was setting off on some great vengeful adventure, and things got very quiet in the house again, but not a good quiet.

"Take your sister upstairs," Mom ordered him in a voice that he knew wouldn't tolerate any form of reply, and that left the rest implied: *And stay up there yourself.*

He escorted Fiona to her room, but she didn't want to stay there alone, and her room wasn't where he wanted to wait this out—for one thing, her window faced the wrong way—so they went to his room, instead. When he finally got her settled down, she clunked around with a guitar he'd never learned how to play, and he pulled a chair to his window to keep watch.

The snow fell as heavy as ever, but it wasn't coming in sideways, just straight down, so with no wind to fight, and the trip being downhill, Dad made okay time. Jakob eased up the window so he could listen, in case Dad called for help.

The monochrome world was without corners now, soft and rounded and under a hush so profound that all he could hear was the whisper of snow and, once his dad reached the Crenshaws', the muffled banging of his fist on their door. Someone opened it, and then came a sound of words hurled at each other to collide like sprays of ice. His father disappeared inside, and the door stayed open, even if Jakob couldn't see inside, then he heard a distant pop, and a pause, then one more.

He knew what must've happened. He knew everything there was to know right now except how to react. Knew how to do everything except leave the chair, or how to stop shivering by the window with a faceful of cold air, or how to tell his sister to stop her stupid banging on his guitar, because something important had happened.

A few minutes later, Stu Crenshaw emerged from the house with a determined swagger, returning to the rut that he and Dad had churned along the hillside.

Kerosene. He would be coming for kerosene.

Jakob was too shocked to hate the man on sight. That would come later. He only watched as Mr. Crenshaw fought the hill and the snow beneath him and the snow yet to land, as he fought gravity and the cold. Halfway to the top he began to move in starts and stops, then tried to turn around and head back down. Then he stopped getting anywhere at all, just his arms and legs moving in slower and slower motion, like he was trying to claw a hollow in the snow, until he ceased moving altogether.

Jakob knew he should report to someone what had just happened out there. It was what neighbors were supposed to do. But where could he call now that would answer? Who could he tell that would care?

Instead, he shut the window and continued to watch as the snow did the job of gravediggers, until there was nothing left to see.

♓

They didn't speak much about it afterward—at first, only as much as it took for them to coordinate an exchange of bodies between households. He supposed that the exertion worked out about even for both sides. He and his mom had a longer ordeal, uphill, but the lighter man. The Crenshaws had the heavier one, but downhill and less distance, although they had to dig him out, too.

He didn't know what the Crenshaws did with Stu, but Dad they wrapped in a blanket and put on the porch until . . . well, just until. A big, open-ended until.

The task took well into afternoon and left them exhausted, with tears frozen on their cheeks and another six or so inches of new snow to contend with. Mom, in the end, was still concerned about the family at the bottom of the hill, but when she asked Mrs. Crenshaw if she wanted to bring the kids up to ride out the rest of the storm with warmth and power, the woman only glared a moment, then spit at her.

Mom still thought this thing was going to be over.

Then they went home to settle into a cold silence. They left off the TV, because the weather report was only ever more of the same. They played no games to pass the time, because it had gotten too hard to pretend everything was normal. They didn't play music because there was no music for this.

But sound still found its way inside. Now and again would come the crack and cushioned crash as another tree toppled under the weight of the snow. And a couple days later, the entire Crenshaw home collapsed. It had been a

ranch style house, with a far flatter roof to hold the snow, and now the mound of it looked like an igloo with no way in or out.

The snow's level climbed the windows of the first floor, until it sealed them over entirely. From the second floor, they watched it rise like slow floodwaters. The weight of its accumulation packed the earliest layers tighter, tighter, and the compressed snow sought the easiest way inside. One by one the first floor's windows burst in as the snow squeezed through like crumbling dough. Besieged on all sides, the house began to creak and groan, but it was better made than the Crenshaws', and for now the walls held. Even so, it was hard not to think they were being entombed, the house like a fragile stone in a glacier forming around it. The place would be eventually crushed.

Inevitably, the snow's shifting weight sheared away a power line somewhere, and they too went dark. They had space heaters, though, and Jakob felt bad for not feeling the least bit guilty that Dad had lied about the kerosene. If they'd shared, it only would've been wasted, the rest of the Crenshaws all dead down there anyway.

If you were going to die in an avalanche, it was probably better to be cold to begin with.

Then one day it stopped. It just stopped. They woke up, sluggish as reptiles, like every morning, and each of the upstairs rooms was filled with an unfamiliar glow. He first thought it must be the light of heaven, that they'd frozen to death overnight, until he understood that it must have been so long since he'd seen actual sunlight that he now mistrusted the memory of it.

The sun was weak, but it was there, and the sky a pale blue again, streaked with the wisps of clouds in retreat. It had been an age since the veil of snow had let him see anything much past the distance to the Crenshaws' house, in any direction, but now that it had lifted, the air left clean and clear, the visual clarity was shocking. He could see for miles, it seemed.

If only there were more *to* see.

The world was all but featureless, just smooth white plains undulating to infinity from a foot or so beneath the windows. The single-story houses of their neighbors up the road were gone, buried, while the taller ones had been reduced to slivers of themselves—low shacks, or the tented shapes of roofs, or, in a couple of instances, nothing but ice-crusted chimneys to mark the spot, tombstones made of brick. The tops of a few surviving trees broke the surface like ragged bushes.

They waited a day to see if this was but a lull, after which the snow would return in fury, but it didn't. They waited, too, to see if anyone would come, not that they expected anything by ground, but they could hope for a helicopter, maybe, with a loudspeaker blaring that help was on its way.

But there was no helicopter, and no help.

"You're going to have to go out there and see what you can find," his mom told him through chattering teeth. "You and your sister both."

"Why her?" Not because he didn't want her tagging along, but because he didn't want the responsibility of a little sister he almost certainly couldn't protect if the worst happened. He could stand against bullies. This was beyond anything of the sort. "I don't think that's a good idea."

"She's smaller, she's lighter. She might be able to go places you can't."

They were both veterans of winter vacations to the mountains. He got the cross-country skis, while Fiona got the snowshoes. They sat on the edge of an open window over the front porch, putting on the skis and snowshoes with their legs dangling down the outside, then stood tentatively, terrified they would sink like stones, although with the porch roof beneath them, it wouldn't be far. But the dense snow held their distributed weight, and Fiona started looking braver by the moment.

The heavier of them, he'd gone second, and while still pressing close to the house, he leaned down to hug his mom with one arm. She strained upward to put her chill-blued lips near his ear.

"If something happens and you need to leave Fiona behind, I'll understand," Mom whispered. "She's the weakest. If it comes to that, do what you have to do."

Then she smiled, forcing it, a thing of grotesque comforts. One of her teeth had gone crooked, loose and she didn't even seem aware of it.

Maybe she was just sick, and didn't know what she was saying.

He clung to that while they shuffled away from the house, heading due west, careful to consult the compass that was a relic of his scouting days. Without it, and with every direction looking the same, they might never find their way home again. They were as far above the ground and its features as they would've been from the bottom of a lake while walking its frozen surface.

When Fiona asked how they would live now, he had no idea how to answer. So he passed the slow miles telling her everything he ever remembered learning about Ice Age cave people. The powerful but non-innovative Neanderthals who draped themselves in skins, and the far

cleverer Cro-Magnons, who learned to sew and make better and better weapons.

"We'll think of something," he said, even though he couldn't imagine what was left to hunt.

It gave him comfort to think that, somewhere, Russell Burns may have been snowpacked ten feet below. Then again, his cold heart may have rendered him an ideal survivor, made for this world, like the snowman they'd built that first day. He would swim for the surface and break through its crust and never know the difference.

This first day's trip was a failure, finding nothing but endless smooth snow and frozen ruin, and people calling across to them from frosted upstairs windows, asking if they knew any news worth telling. Others sought to coax them over—come here and get warm, come in for something to eat, we have hot chocolate here—but none of it felt right, or honest.

He supposed a ski pole would kill, if you jabbed someone in the right place.

"Why don't you want to stop?" Fiona complained after the fourth time he steered them wide. "They seemed nice. I'm hungry."

"They're *not* nice. And they don't care if you're hungry. They don't *really* want to be generous. They're what spiders would sound like in their webs, if spiders could talk."

"Oh," she said. "Wait—huh?"

"They're hungry, too. Get it?"

She almost did, but needed to hear him say it all, and he didn't have the heart to make it any plainer than he already had. It made him wonder how someday, if pressed, he would explain to her, or to someone like her, what was different about the snows of then and now.

"But that was not the same snow," he would begin, the same as the man who remembered Christmas. *"Our snow not only came roaring from out of an angry, misused sky, it came swirling out of the hearts of neighbors and dripped from the tongues and fingers of all the rest we wished were strangers. Ice grew from our window frames and eyelashes until it no longer mattered that it barred our view like prison doors."*

Something like that, at least.

Home lay at the opposite end of their tracks, not a hard path to follow, even without the compass. He wanted to get back like he'd never wanted anything in his life, except for some different decisions on Dad's part. Yet the closer they got, the more home felt like something he only wanted to look forward to, instead of actually getting there.

When they climbed through the window, the sky was soft and violet ahead of them. Mom hugged them both, then Fiona ran for the bathroom, because she'd been holding it in a long time, refusing to go in the snow. So maybe she hadn't noticed how their mother felt so cold it was like she'd been the one outside all day. The skin of her face and hands seemed so pale and thin and clear that beneath it he could see things he'd only ever seen in science books.

"We didn't find anything out there," he said, because he had to say something. "We can try another direction tomorrow."

"Maybe," she said. "It depends."

"Depends on what?" he asked, just as he heard Fiona cry out in worry from the bathroom:

What are all these teeth in the sink?

"It depends on you," Mom said, with a smile that had turned to the sharpest shards of ice.

LET MY SMILE BE YOUR UMBRELLA

Forget everything you think you know about yourself. Forget those twenty or twenty-five years of assumptions. However old you are. Instead, try looking at yourself from someone else's perspective for a change. My perspective. Empty out all those pitiful preconceptions and just look at yourself. Look at the effect you're having on the world.

What do you see then? Do you see what's really there? Can you even be that honest with yourself?

If you could, then I think you would agree that there's not much choice of what to do about it, is there? The end result? You've been claiming all along it's what you want.

What I see, it's not a question of saving, not any more. It's too late for that. Now it's come down to quarantine and eradication.

So it'll be the same with you as it's been with the others:

I'll take more pleasure in killing you than you take in being alive.

♏

Who gave you the right to not be happy, anyway? Where did you get the idea that it was okay to throw all that back in the face of a loving, benevolent universe? It's your birthright, for god's sake. It's inscribed right there in the constitution of this great land of opportunity we live in: *life, liberty, and the pursuit of happiness.* So if you squander your liberty by refusing to

pursue anything of positive worth, then really, haven't you forfeited your right to life?

And remember: According to you, that's what you've wanted for a long time.

Well, just wait, because I'm on my way.

I mean, what kind of attention whore are you, that you would do what you did? Starve yourself to death and blog about the experience so the entire world can share in your sickness—who thinks of a thing like that? If you want to be dead, you just do it, you don't throw a party and invite the world to watch.

And not to belabor the obvious, but if you want to be dead, there are a lot faster ways than starving yourself. Starvation takes a long, long time. As I'm sure you realized. As I'm sure you knew damn well before you ever decided that you'd had your last bite of food and now it was showtime.

Dehydration, now that's a lot quicker. Three or four bad days, then you're done. But obviously that didn't suit your timetable. Obviously you didn't feel inclined to call water and power, and tell them to turn off the taps, nope, won't be needing those anymore.

So I don't know whether or not you're genuinely suicidal. For sure, I believe you're miserable. You don't have to convince me on that account. But more than anything, you're an exhibitionist. You want the attention. You wanted to be found out, and then just *found*, period, before it was too late, because you picked the slowest way possible to kill yourself and gave the world plenty of time to catch up to you. Just sitting there in your apartment in Portland not eating, oh poor me, poor pitiful me, waiting for the cavalry to ride in and save you, take control of the situation and remove your choice in the matter.

Goddamn sociopath.

Photo updates, too. That was a nice touch. One a day, so the world could see your ribs and hipbones standing out a little farther each morning. Like anorexia porn. Just so you could convince the pictures-or-it-didn't-happen skeptics who were calling bullshit on your little experiment. Like, okay, maybe I'm suicidal and masochistic, but don't anyone dare call me a liar.

And they found you. Of course. Well played, applause all around. Hiding your online account behind proxy servers during those first three weeks, so they *couldn't* trace your identity . . . until you weren't. Until you mysteriously "forgot." Because all that hard work of not eating made you loopy and forgetful. Maybe it did, maybe it didn't, but you sure sounded plenty cogent in those last few blog posts.

What a difference three weeks makes, huh? You went from complete anonymity to international celebrity in three weeks. Everybody wondering what was going to happen to HungryGirl234. Everybody loves to watch a good train wreck. You turned viral in the worst sense of the word.

I said three weeks? Less time, actually. Your audience was *huge* before the plug got pulled. Or maybe it was the other way around. The plug got jacked back in. No more worries about life support for *you*. The main thing I wondered was how the hopes were split. What percentage of people was hoping that someone would get to you in time, and what percentage wanted you to follow this thing to its logical conclusion.

As to which side I came down on? Do you even have to ask?

ੳ

Wait, wait, don't tell me—you were one of those girls who spent your high school years writing poetry so embarrassingly awful that it would shame a soap opera diva. Yeah, your blog posts had that whiff about them. I bet your favorite color was black and your favorite mood was mope and your classmates voted you Most Likely To Cut Notches Up And Down Her Arms.

Please don't misunderstand. I'm not saying there's anything wrong with being sensitive. Only when you gouge out your eyes to everything on the plus side of the meter, and dramatize and catastrophize everything on the minus side. You live to suffer, and that's all, don't you? You have no interest in dining from life's rich bounty, the good along with the bad, right? All you want to do is revel in eating the shit. Just look up from your dinner table with your helpless sagging shoulders and a shit-eating sob-smile, like you're asking, "Why does this keep happening to me," except you're not the tiniest bit aware of the gigantic ladle waving around in your hand.

You know what it is that I really can't stand about people like you? It's that you're toxic and contagious and you don't even care. You're the runny-nosed moron who wanders up and sneezes on the salad bar. You're the addict who shares the dirty needles even though you know what the test results said.

Can your pathetic little pea-sized soul even begin to comprehend the magnitude of your callous indifference to the effect you're having on the world? It can be hard enough for people to keep their spirits up even when all they have to contend with is the day-to-day mundanity of seeing their dreams end up on the deferred gratification plan. Then they see you, *you*, someone who would seem to have everything to live for, see you squander

the most fundamental gifts you've been given and in the process tell them that they might as well not try, either. You apparently can't stand the idea of a world going on without you, never even noticing your absence, and now you've made it your mission to drag as many down to your level as you can.

Misery loves company, and you're living proof. You're a professional sufferer and you hung out your shingle years ago: *Abandon hope all ye who encounter me.*

Converts, that's what you want. You want followers. You want to be Queen of the Suicides, only you'll never quite manage to get around to ending the suffering for yourself, will you? No, for you, it would be enough to hear about other people following your lead, only with more commitment. Every casualty you inspire just reinforces your negative worldview that much more.

What a pity.

What a waste.

What a tragic perversion of priorities.

I'd ask if you have no shame, but I'm afraid you'd only give me a blank stare and ask what the word means.

I wish you could look up, just once, and see the sun the same way I do, and know its light rather than the shadows. I wish you could take in the first blue of the morning sky and see it as the wrapping paper around the gift of another beautiful day.

♍

And now you're at again, aren't you? HungryGirl234 rides again.

But why use that, when I know your name now. Deborah. You probably hate it, though, don't you? Such a wholesome name. Deborah. It's a cheerleader's name.

Not that you've forced the world to put you back on suicide watch. You've chosen more subtlety this time. You have to know what resorting to the same old hunger strike routine might get you, now that you're a known head case. You no longer have the luxury of anonymity, the option of teasing the world along, rationing out only as much information as you want it to have about you. You've lost control of that much.

People know who you are now. They know where to find you if they have to.

So you've taken a more measured approach. Every day, another litany of woes. Every day, another dispatch from a world that to your eyes is as colorless and gray as ashes. Every day, further confirmation that life for you really must be a tale told by an idiot, full of sound and fury, signifying nothing.

You're good at it, I'll give you that. You could do this for a living, if there was actually a paying market for it. You're the devil's propagandist, and I don't mean to flatter you when I say that you're dangerous. A person hardly has to get past the titles of your posts to fathom all they need to know about your agenda:

10 Reasons I'm A Cosmic Joke And You May Be Too.

Why Leaving Las Vegas Was Really A Comedy.

Why This? Why Me? Why Now?

I Still Resent Eating.

You, Me, And Everybody We Know = God's Chew Toys.

If your descent into nihilistic spectacle had just been that first time, I would've been willing to overlook it as a cry for help, one that finally ensured that you got what you needed, and once you were discharged, your thinking had been corrected to the point where you could see what a nutjob you really were: *Hoo weee, am I ever glad that's over!*

I would've been willing—deliriously happy, actually—to give you the benefit of the doubt that you were at least going to try. I would've been happy to wish you well, and a life of contentment, from the other side of our shared continent, and we'd each go on our way, and you would never even have to know that I exist.

So remember: You've brought this on yourself.

You have *summoned* me.

What you've been doing all along is a kind of prayer. You've been petitioning the universe, and the universe is kind, so you shouldn't be surprised when it responds via the only avenue you've left open for it. Over time, you have given it all the instructions it needs to see your final wish carried out.

Do you see the beauty of this? Are you even capable of appreciating the wonder of the grand design? You lack the courage to act on your professed convictions, so the universe employs another route to see them carried out. Once again, you're awaiting the arrival of someone who will show up and take control of the situation, and remove your choice in the matter. Only this time, you don't realize it.

It isn't all about you, you know. It's bigger than you, and always has been.

∞

I want to tell you a story, as long as I'm in transit and have nothing better to do than ignore the so-called in-flight entertainment. It's supposed to

be a comedy, but I can't say I find it particularly amusing. It's kind of mean-spirited.

But there was this boy, you see, in the neighborhood where I lived before. He was old enough that he probably should've been called a man but, for reasons of his own choosing, that label never seemed to fit. He appeared never to have graduated into manhood, or to have even considered that he should, so I call him a boy.

You remind me very much of him. He was dismal, just like you. He was self-absorbed and sour, just like you.

And every time he stepped outside the house, it was like the day suddenly got cloudy. By his demeanor alone, he could steal the sun from the sky and the moon from the night. You expected flowers to wilt in his wake, grass to die under his footsteps. His projection of negativity was so pronounced it was having an actual visceral effect on me.

He was contagious. Just like you.

I like to think I choose my neighbors carefully. The people you surround yourself with are important. I appreciate the kind of people who look forward to what each day is going to bring. I esteem the company of people who keep it cheerful and positive.

But seeing this dismal, sour boy pollute my environment . . . this disturbed me. It gnawed at me. How could I have been so wrong? How could I have missed this? How could this *weed* have sprouted in my garden? And you know that, before long, there's never just one weed. They spread.

I did try to help, I really did. I asked him why he never smiled. He had black hair that hung down over one eye, and kept flipping it out of the way, but it kept falling right back, and might as well have been stuffed in his mouth for all he managed to communicate.

I really did try to think of something I could do for him. If he would've just made an effort to stand up straight, it might've made a difference. It might've demonstrated a willingness to try and get better. Posture has an enormous effect on mood. But he seemed perfectly resigned to letting his shoulders hang as steep as a couple of ski slopes. And he completely misunderstood my intentions. There's no point in recounting what he called me.

So it became obvious there wasn't anything left to do but pull this noxious weed.

They say it takes forty-three muscles to frown, and only four to smile.

Anybody with a good knife can carve a smile into someone's face before they lose their nerve.

It takes real dedication to immortalize the frown.

But I think you'll find that keeping myself motivated is nothing I've ever had a problem with. Especially when I deeply believe in the outcome.

⸸

Can you feel my eyes on you, now that I'm finally here? They say people can, sometimes. I've heard that army scouts, observers, snipers—the ones whose success and even lives depend on not giving their position and presence away—I've heard they're trained to avoid letting their gaze linger directly on their enemy for very long. To the side is better. Because some people really can feel eyes on them, following them. The hair on the back of their neck prickles up and they just know.

But I don't think you do. You'd have to be a different kind of person. You'd have to be fully alive.

Here in your neighborhood, there must be a hundred ways to blend in and places to watch you from, and I'd be amazed if you're aware of even a handful of them. It's a busy place, full of life going on all around you, and if you'd just opened up to it and worked to make your disposition a little sunnier and meet the world halfway, we wouldn't have to have this encounter we're about to.

As I watch you, it becomes clear to me that even though I tell myself I'm doing it to learn your habits and timetables, what I'm really doing is giving you one last chance to change my mind. So show me something. Give me a reason not to follow through. Reveal to me some heretofore unsuspected capacity for joy beyond your masochistic perversion of it.

But you're giving me nothing here. *Nothing.* If anything, you're making this too easy. This shouldn't be such a cut-and-dried decision. I should wrestle with this, for god's sake. I should anguish over it.

Instead, I can't help but think it would be a kindness. When you left to go out for another coffee a few minutes ago, I almost expected you to melt under the onslaught of the rain. I've heard it can be like this in Portland. Which doesn't bother me in the least—I love a good rainy day—but even if it did, I still would refuse to let it. But maybe that's just not you. If weather has an influence on mood, and with some people it definitely does, then it may be that this goes some way toward explaining yours. So why have you never thought to just move away?

Although it can't be like this *all* the time. And you, if you're anything at all, are consistent. So let's just dismiss that right now. HungryGirl234 is not a foul-weather creation.

Really, it's unprecedented how much I'm bending over backward for you here. No one else would be giving you the kind of last-minute leeway that I am. It's not very many people who would break cover into the rain, and hurry along the sidewalk on the opposite side of the street to get ahead of you, to beat you to the coffee shop just in time to open the door for you.

And do you offer me a smile for this kindness? No. But then, neither do you act as if you're somehow owed it. You nod, okay, but it's barely perceptible, and looks to be an effort, almost painful.

In you go, just as I decide this has to be your final test. The very last chance to win your future. With the coffee house not two blocks from where you live, you're obviously a regular here. They would know you here. They have to, all of them. So, one laugh with the barista . . . come on, I'm pulling for you. I know you can do it.

Except you don't.

You just stand there encased in your green rain slicker, the hood like a monk's cowl dripping water to the floor, your head down as you count your change, then seem to decide as an aftermath to drop it all in the tip jar. A nice touch, close, but by itself it's not enough to change anything. The condemned and the terminal often give away their worldly goods, although if you don't realize that's what's actually going on here, that's the least of your problems.

And it's a shame, really, that you don't get to notice the look on the barista's face as you turn from the counter. She knows you, knows you better than you think, maybe even knows who you really are, that you're an Internet celebrity of the sickest kind. She knows what matters, and wishes better for you.

You really should've contributed more to her world, you know.

And look at this! You've at least got one surprise tucked away inside. Your stop with your to-go cup at the spice island? All along I've had you figured you for the no-frills, black coffee all the way type, but you're a cinnamon girl. Who knew?

And it's an extra-large for me, because I've got every reason to think it's going to be a long night ahead for both of us, one that I trust we'll both find purifying.

But then you're not even gone two minutes before everything goes wrong. I'm barely out the door and back on the sidewalk myself, so all I can do is watch. Watch, and can't help but think that I've failed you. If I'd been closer, maybe I could've . . .

It's not even your fault. You've got the walk light at the corner. It's yours. Anyone can see that. Even knowing you as I do, there's nothing in me that believes you have any other idea than that you're going to cross from one side of the street to the other, without incident, the same as the hundred thousand times you've done it before.

The thing is, I know what's going to happen even before it does. Look over and see the car, and the hair on the back of my neck prickles up and I just *know*, know that the car's going too fast, that it can't stop in time, and I'm running along the sidewalk, and if I'd been closer I would've pushed you or pulled you, whatever it took to get you clear. Because this isn't the way it's supposed to be.

You were meant for so much more than *this*.

The driver is aware, at least, for all the good that does, the brake lights smearing red and the car fishtailing on the wet pavement. But you don't know any of this. You never even see it coming, and I wonder that if you had, if there was time, even just a moment to react, if looking at the *genuine* prospect of your mortality would've made a difference where nothing else has.

Instead, lost inside that hood, you're blindsided. One devastating impact and there you go, tumbling into the air in the rain and the brown fan of coffee. It's not enough that you're hit the once, is it? No, you have to land on the windshield of the car passing by in the opposite lane, and bounce, spinning off that one, too.

Even I have to wince, and shut my eyes for a moment.

And does it verify your worst suspicions about the world and everyone in it, that nobody seems to want to touch you now? They'll crowd around, they'll look, but you're used to that. But I'm used to things they're not, so it doesn't bother me, not in the way it bothers them. I don't mind joining you on the pavement. I don't mind touching you. I don't mind holding you. I don't mind the parts of you that leak onto me.

Or are you even aware of anything at all?

I've never seen anybody breathe that way. This can't be good. A sharp little gulp of breath every few seconds, like a fish drowning in the air. The way your eyes are roving around, they're like a baby's, trying to find something to focus on, and it would surprise me if you have much of any idea what's happened. If you don't, that's okay, and I don't want to tell you.

"Stay with us, Deborah."

Right, that's me saying that. And I *think* it's me you're seeing now. At least your eyes don't leave me, but in a way, that's even worse, because I can see the million questions behind them and I don't know how to begin to answer them. Not here, not now, not this.

I can't even begin to answer my own.

This would've happened whether I was here or not.

I haven't changed anything. I haven't *affected* anything. I've haven't had the chance to make one single point to you.

So I was brought here to what? To witness? That's it? *That's it?*

Sometimes all you can do is kneel in the rain and ask what it is that the universe is trying to tell you. But me, I'm supposed to be way beyond that by now.

○━

You don't mind that I've let myself into your apartment, do you? It's almost like the keys crawled out of your pocket and into my hand.

I thought I'd be seeing the place under such different circumstances. Thought you'd be seeing it anew for yourself, the way it goes when we're with someone seeing something for the first time, and we imagine what it must look like through their eyes.

That's all gone now. The today that never happened.

I have to admit, never in my wildest imaginings did I expect lemon yellow walls.

Maybe you *were* trying, in your way.

I'm talking to you like you're still alive, but right now, I don't even know. I just don't know. It didn't look good, down on the street. The state you were in, it didn't look like there was much reason to hope. That's funny, coming from me, isn't it? I always find a reason to hope. I'm the quintessential hope-springs-eternal guy. So if you don't mind, I'll keep the dialogue open for now.

Lemon yellow walls. Bugger me sideways. You really had me fooled.

But it's the posters that are the illuminating part.

It takes a while to sink in. At first I wasn't grasping what it is you've really been doing here in the main room, what these posters mean together. I didn't see them as related at first. At the west end of the room, the one of some forest, either early morning or late evening, everything foggy, that one lone figure standing in the middle. And at the east end, the poster looking out on the opening of some enormous cavern, with a tiny boat sailing out into the slanted beams of sunlight coming through. At first glance, who would think these had anything to do with each other?

But it's the one in the middle of the north wall that ties them together, isn't it? That's the link. Except for the crescent moon, it's so dark and indistinct I can't even tell where the person kneeling in the middle is supposed to be. What is that? Is it a prison cell? A dungeon? A storm drain? A log fucking cabin? I'd really like to know.

The title, well, that makes sense. *The Dark Night of the Soul*. If you're going to give the thing a title, that's as good a name as any. And the quote, too, what's that for, just to rub it in? *"The mystic heart senses that suffering and sorrow can be the portal to finding the light of what is genuine. Run not from the darkness, for in time it ushers in the light."*

Look. Don't you dare talk to me about the dark night of the soul.

Honestly, this is why I'm here? What kind of joke is this?

From what garbage pit did you dredge these deceptions, anyway? Who told you you had to go through these things? They're just illusions. What garden of lies did you pick from to settle for the notion that pain and sadness are anything other than unnatural states of being that it's our duty to repel? What malfunction sent you on this detour, and convinced you that this shadow path you're on was remotely normal?

Me, I was raised better than that. I was promised better than that. I was *promised*.

That is my birthright. *That* is my due. And I *will* have the happiness I deserve.

But you? No, you fell for the worst sort of propaganda.

And look at you now.

It didn't have to be that way. It's not *supposed* to be that way. Not for you, not for me, not for anybody, and all of you who think you're going to convince me otherwise, you all find out that the light fights back, don't you? The light doesn't want to go out.

It's so clear now. I was giving you credit for being way more dangerous than you really are, when all you are is another empty puppet. You're a casualty of endless failures of imagination, and your own savage torpor. You just couldn't conceive that you live in a world so generous that everything was yours from the beginning and all you had to do was say yes. You had to make it so much harder than it really is.

If you can't deal with my exceptionalism, fine, but that doesn't mean you get to try to rob me, or drag me down to your level.

You will not rob me.

Not. Not. Not. Not. Do you hear me? *Not*.

You know, I really should leave here, because you've got nothing to teach me and this whole thing's been nothing more than a clerical error, so yes, I should just turn around and leave, but then again, you should take it as a back-handed compliment that it's so hard to turn away.

Because it's not just the posters. No, it's the fine print. My god, what kind of obsessive-compulsive are you? Until this moment I'd been wondering if you'd even seen the comments people left for you during your escapades in starvation, and now it's obvious that you did. And have, every day since.

I'll hand it to you, it's impressive, the patience it must've taken to print out every single hateful thing anyone had to say to you, and tape it to the wall around the forest poster. And then do the same thing with every kind thing someone had to say, and tape those around the cavern picture. Hundreds of them. That's patience.

You know, before, I suspected you hadn't read a word of any of it because I had you pegged for such a narcissist that you wouldn't even bother taking someone else's opinion under advisement.

And I was absolutely right, you *are* a narcissist, just a bigger one than I even dared imagine you could be. Every time your printer spit out some hate mail or a love note, and you tore off a little strip of tape, that's somebody telling you you matter, even the ones who wished you'd just die already, because at least you got a reaction.

Well, you don't. You *don't* matter. Your opinion doesn't matter. Your deluded sense of identity doesn't matter.

Really, I should leave now, but I've just got to read these first, and laugh.

Because I haven't had a laugh this good in a long time. I should be thanking you.

And I really should leave. But I need you to know that no matter what you do, now and forever, you can't rob me.

And what's the rush, anyway. I can read these and read these, up and down, across, they're all the same, empty empty empty, and it still feels like I just got here.

And I really should leave. But not until I know how you did it, how you got the walls to start changing color, from lemon yellow to . . . to . . . to whatever the opposite of that is called.

And I really. Should. Leave.

Only your windows are all covered with bars.

And the doors are nowhere to be found anymore.

WE, THE FORTUNATE BEREAVED

H e'd been relentless about it throughout the whole of October, as only a six-year-old could be, worse by the day as the month went on.

"I want it to be Daddy this year." Cody was up to what felt like a hundred times a day now that the end of the month was here, and the night at hand. "We have to do a really good job so that it's Daddy this year."

Bailey had told him nothing about this night, ever, nor had Drew when he was alive. For a few more years, at least, they'd wanted Halloween, for Cody, to be nothing more than trick-or-treating. And maybe, minus one congenital heart defect, undetected until it was too late, that's the way it would have been. Or maybe what they'd wanted wouldn't have mattered anyway. All it took was one other first-grader in the know, and soon enough they all knew. Children shared secrets even more readily than they shared bacteria and head lice.

But knowing about it was one thing. Having such an enormous personal stake in it was something else entirely.

"It's *got* to be Daddy this year."

"Then let's finish picking what we want to leave to call him," Bailey said. "Let's make it good. Have you thought really hard about what you want to pick?"

Of course he had. He'd been consumed by it all month. For Cody, the problem would be narrowing it down to just one. Because those were the rules. If he could've gotten away with it, he would've emptied his room of memories, harvested the closets clean, filled his wagon and more with them, then hauled them to the town square himself, to dump them at the

foot of the cross where the frightful thing hung, awaiting something that looked like life.

Bailey's own choice had been easier, made almost by default. Was it to be her wedding ring? No. For all it meant, it had none of Drew's essence in it. His razor, still in the bathroom even though he'd been eight months in the ground? Improbably, it had survived since the first day of his freshman year of college, and had contoured his face nearly every day of his life since. No, not that either. It was too prosaic, with none of *her* essence in it.

In prior years, she'd heard local widows joke that what they should've picked was the TV remote—if anything could call their men over from the other side, that would do the trick.

In the end, though, on this morning of the thirty-first, what she chose was Drew's favorite shirt for nights and weekends during the long months of autumn and winter. It was the king of flannel shirts, blue and white, checked like a horse blanket and thick to keep out the cold. She'd liked to wear it too, even though it swallowed her whole—adored wearing it because it smelled of him, an enveloping scent that was entirely male, entirely Drew. And he'd adored getting it back, once it smelled of her.

Just a shirt, but still, it was what love would feel like if you could wear an emotion. She couldn't imagine anything more appropriate to leave as his lure.

And Cody? She watched from the doorway of his room before he knew she was there, and saw that he'd narrowed his choices to only enough to cover his bed. It was progress. Toys and books and items of clothing and things dragged in from the yard, and it made her sad in a way she'd never been before to realize that she really had no idea what many of these things even meant to Cody in relationship to Drew. Six years old and already he lived half the time in a world of secrets, and it was only going to get worse from here.

"What's it going to be, champ?" she asked.

"This," he said, after one final deliberation that twisted him into knots, then he turned around holding his Pinewood Derby car. "We built this. We built it together. This should be right . . . right?"

One of the last great projects of the previous winter. Cody hadn't even been eligible for Cub Scouts yet, much less the race. He'd just wanted the practice, to be ready for the day he was. As he had wanted nothing else, he'd wanted to build that car. She never would've guessed how much pride and joy that a $3.99 block of wood and four wheels could bring a kindergartner and a grown man.

"It's perfect," Bailey said. "Now get your jacket and let's get going."

Dunhaven was the only town she'd ever heard of where Halloween was a school holiday, but then Dunhaven wasn't like other towns. It was the only place she knew where the night brought more than just trickery and mischief. In Dunhaven, genuine magic, dark magic, pierced the veil on All Hallows Eve.

This would come in its own time. For now, morning was bright with the golden light of a cool sun, and the streets were uncommonly busy. Everybody had business on a day like this. Along the seven-block walk from home, she saw neighbors and friends, fellow teachers from the high school, students past and students present, as well as people in from the countryside that she might not see again until next year.

Everyone had business with the dead today, or believed they did.

And she couldn't help but wonder: Who among them would die in the year to come, and who would be hoping to call them forth next October?

The town square was less crowded than she might have guessed, green and crisscrossed with sidewalks that converged at the fountain in the middle, and nearly empty now. More sunflowers than people, more shrubs than visitors, vibrant with the yellow of goldenrod and beds of sedum whose close-packed blossoms looked like bright red slashes in the earth.

One presence, at least, was a permanent fixture, and if it was an illusion of life now, no more animated than one of the benches flanking the walkways, night would change everything. Darkness would remind people why they tended not to idle about while this thing hung waiting for a soul.

It was just clothing and straw, a stuffed burlap bag for a head with buttons for eyes and stitching for a mouth and a broad-brimmed hat to hold the horsetail hair in place. Affixed to a rough-hewn field-cross in the heart of town and looking as if it had gotten lost from the corn, drawing stares instead of frightening crows . . . yet even now, it felt possible to offend it.

She held Cody's hand tighter as they approached. Usually he squirmed and pulled away when she tried that. Not today.

It seemed to wait for them, the slumped head looking down as they neared. Too light to hang there sagging like the agonized Christ of a crucifix, its pose looked casual, its weathered denim arms draped wide over the crossbar like someone stretching with a yawn across the backrest of a bench.

On the bottle-green grass, before the towering fencepost that pierced the earth, they set down their summonses: the well-worn flannel shirt and the beloved Pinewood car. These joined other items left by other hands:

a book, undoubtedly the favorite of someone's lifetime, and a baseball glove, and a folio of sheet music, and a Purple Heart medal from some war. The most unusual was a cake that looked not just frosted but frosty, as though until some time around dawn it had spent months in a freezer, never sliced and eaten, someone's happy occasion turning tragic before the plates and forks came out.

There were so many little stories here, each of them sad in its own way.

She would have to check later, though, to make sure that the shirt and car were still here. There was a strategy to this. Put your offering out too soon, and you were only prolonging temptation, increasing the odds that it might disappear. This day did not always bring out the best in people. Lonely people, bereaved people, who wouldn't mind sabotaging their neighbor's chance at a reunion if it meant improving their own.

Put your offering out too late, though, and . . . well, nobody could say for sure when was too late, when these pieces of lives left behind started being *noticed*.

By the same token, nobody could say with any certainty when this custom had even started, or how. The oldest families in town—the Ralstons and the Goslings, the Chennowics and Harringtons—all claimed some propriety in the matter, but none of their stories matched up very well with any of the others, so much so that blows had been struck over it in the past . . . at least one, ironically, fatal.

What was beyond denying, though, was that it had been going on for at least 162 years, maybe longer, from a time when the land they stood on was the town commons, bordering a cornfield whose earliest ownership would be forever disputed. The records had been lost well before the arrival of the twentieth century, in a fire that had leveled the county clerk's office.

Was it the land itself? Or something done *on* or *to* the land to forever change the spirit of the place? Was it something bound up in the people, their heritages and bloodlines, that would've followed them anywhere if they'd packed up the whole of Dunhaven and moved the town someplace else? The residents of both the town and the surrounding county, out to a distance of at least eighteen miles, had benefited from it, if *benefit* was really the proper word for such a thing, and there were many who argued that it wasn't. That it was not the blessing people thought it to be.

Which never seemed to discourage anybody from hoping to be the one whose call was answered.

The truth came down to this: Deeply ancient custom held that, on Halloween night, the cusp between summer and winter, the veil between the worlds of the living and the dead grew thin, so thin that spirits might cross over to wander for a night. Another custom—perhaps related, perhaps not, and not nearly so ancient as the other but old enough—held that scarecrows came alive on Halloween night. Dunhaven was the only place in which Bailey had ever heard of it actually happening . . . although for all she or anyone else knew, Dunhaven was the place where this legend had been born.

One night, one scarecrow, and the returned soul of one person who had died during the past year. Just one. Never none, never two or more, only the one.

The rite had inspired a deep legacy of secrecy. It had never been a thing to share with the outside world, beyond the town and surrounding farmland. Here, you grew up understanding the importance of silence even before you fully understood what it was you weren't to talk about with anyone from farther off.

In the early decades, when people journeyed by horse, and most not very far, Dunhaven had been sufficiently remote that the secret was easy enough to keep. But time brought paved roads and the vehicles that traveled them, so stronger measures were needed. Roads could be closed. Innkeepers could be persuaded to turn away potential lodgers. Lingering strangers could be made to feel unwelcome. For every threat, there was an answer.

Still, peoples' tongues were the first and last lines of defense. Most children grew up indoctrinated with tales of bogeymen who punished those who let secrets slip. By the time they were old enough to know better, they'd already seen enough each Halloween to fear that bogeymen might not necessarily be a myth. And as adults, the last thing they wanted was a tide of incomers desperately seeking assurance of life after death, driving up the property tax base in the process.

Whatever few stray whispers did manage to escape seemed to suffocate in the skepticism of the modern world, and so the sacrament remained theirs alone. It had been going on for so long they took for granted it always would . . . although people never liked to dwell on how which soul came through got decided on the other side. One preferred to believe in the concept of rest and peace, not in cutthroat competitions to seize the last second chance you might have to say goodbye.

Trinkets, things that had special meaning, seemed to sweeten the odds.

After Bailey and Cody set theirs down, they stepped back, as she took another look up at the face gazing blindly down at them, the potential of personality trying to crawl past the burlap and buttons.

"What will you say to him, if it's Daddy?" she whispered.

Cody thought for a long time. "If he'll take me with him."

Just a few simple words, worse than a dagger in the heart. Her first impulse was to tell him, *command* him, to never say such a thing. Not the best lesson to teach, that he had to censor himself around her. Hadn't she just been ruing, not half an hour ago, the fact that he already had secrets?

"Wouldn't you miss me?" she said instead. "I'd miss you. I'd miss you with all my heart." *Every minute of every day*, she almost said, but didn't want to oversell. It wasn't Cody's kind of talk. "I'd miss all the fun stuff we do."

He still didn't seem to grasp what the big deal was. Just looked at the scarecrow as if it were his escape clause, the answer to all the problems. "Then I'd come back next year."

She stiffened, thought she saw where this was going.

"Let's get you back home and into your costume," she said. "Nobody wants to be late for a party."

ŏ

In Dunhaven, Halloween ran according to a different schedule. As most of the world had come to recognize it, Halloween was a holiday for children, and a tacky one at that, all cheap scares and greed. There could be no abolishing this part of it—they were realists here—but they could at least see to it that the childish side of the day was over and done with before sunset, before things turned serious, when even the grown-ups took pause. Parties in the morning, trick-or-treating in the afternoon. It helped if the day's sky was grim, and after a bright sunrise, the clouds were starting to cooperate.

Once Cody was suited up, she took him to the gathering in the basement at St. Aidan's Episcopal and turned him loose into the clamor of his classmates and friends. She double-checked the time the party was scheduled to end, and then the next three hours were hers.

Hardly anyplace in town was more than ten minutes from anyplace else, but still, Troy's house seemed another world away. He met her at the door, and she did her best to leave her guilt about this back in that other world. It would always be waiting when she returned.

Five minutes later, she wasn't really thinking about anything at all.

She pulled and she pushed, rode and was ridden, and it was still easy to tell herself that none of this meant anything. It was just an itch that needed scratching, one she couldn't reach on her own. That was all. The first time, of all the sorry, sad clichés, had been alcohol-related, on a night six weeks ago when Cody had been on a sleepover, and in a purely unforeseen development, she'd ended up doing the same.

After Drew's funeral, she'd promised herself, and him, if he was listening, that she would wait a year, at an absolute minimum, before she'd even *think* of dating again . . . and here she had barely made it six months before skipping the pretense of dating altogether. She'd awakened that next dawn wondering how it had happened, and vowing that it wouldn't happen again . . . but it was too late. The groove had been greased, so to speak. The second time was even easier to agree to, sober, than the first had been after wine.

Troy was nothing like Drew at all, and perhaps that was what made this easier. Where Drew had been beefy, Troy was lean and hard. Where Drew had towered, Troy was compact. Where Drew's hair was black, Troy was fair all over. While Drew had been quick to laugh, Troy found the humor in subtler things. Whereas Drew had loved living in the heart of town, Troy liked it out here on the periphery, in a renovated one-time farmhouse that hadn't been attached to a farm for a generation, after Dunhaven had grown out to meet it.

To look at them, at least, she and Troy matched up much more readily than she and Drew ever had. But it would never go further than this. She couldn't imagine Troy as a father, much less a stepfather. And that, she supposed, was the safety valve here.

"Tell me the truth, would you," he said, once it was all over, one more time, and they were free to stare at the ceiling. "How are you hoping it goes tonight? Are you *really* hoping he comes through?"

How to answer without either encouraging him or sounding like a callous bitch? "If it wasn't for Cody's sake? I don't know that I'd be going through with this after all."

"Oh yeah?"

"It might be good for him," she said. "He wasn't there when Drew had his heart seizure. And I'm glad of that much, that Cody didn't have to see it. But it robbed him of his chance to say goodbye. He goes to kindergarten one morning and he's got a dad, and by the time he comes home he doesn't. So tonight would probably be good for him."

Troy traced a finger along the downy blonde fuzz at her temple, which felt better than she wanted it to. "And what about you?"

She couldn't find the words, and of course, that spoke volumes.

"If you're ambivalent, I can understand that," he said.

"Were you, with Angela?"

"Yes and no. The circumstances, they couldn't have been more different. With her, there was so much we didn't know. There were so many questions we would've liked to have answered. Obviously."

Obviously. Like, *Who took you, Angela? Who killed you? And where's the rest of you?*

She hadn't known Troy then, not in person and barely by sight. The first she'd seen of him was Halloween three years ago, Troy joining Angela Pemberton's sister Melanie, the two of them kneeling beside each other at the foot of the scarecrow, in that first row that custom reserved for the hopeful. It had been someone else's night, though, Angela apparently choosing to remain silent then and forever.

To see Melanie afterward, her crushing disappointment, was to understand the cruelty of this night. Trying not to be obvious about it, Bailey had watched Troy console her, and he'd seemed so kind and attentive that she wondered at the time if he and Melanie might become a couple in their own right. But it had never happened, and now she knew how naïve that was. Death and bereavement would always be the foundation of the relationship.

So now she saw that night for what it really was. Troy had been sowing his seeds in her heart without realizing it.

"But," he went on, "you learn what happens here, or you grow up with it, and you think it's going to be this great experience. You think, wow, who gets this chance, how lucky this place is. And some years, for some people, yeah, I'm sure it does turn out to be everything they hope it will be. But a part of me was scared. I wanted it to happen for Melanie's sake, it was her sister and all, but for me? The closer the night got, the more I didn't want it after all."

Bailey hung on every word. This was it. *This* was the thing nobody in Dunhaven ever talked about, at least not publicly, even though you could see it in their eyes every October. You could see the trepidation, the misgivings. Could recognize the look of someone who was going through with an act even though they'd begun to have second thoughts. None of which they would ever admit to. For obvious reasons: Who wanted to be first to come out and admit to being an ungrateful freak?

"What scared you about it?" she asked.

"I'd gotten to a place where I'd accepted that Angela was gone," Troy said. "That she wasn't coming back. I'd gotten to a place where I'd accepted we might never know what happened to her. And I realized I didn't *want* to know anymore. I didn't want to know how she'd suffered. And then . . ."

He seemed to have trouble, but Bailey thought she might be able to take it from here. "And then everybody expects you to put that aside for one night, and it's not as easy as it sounds?"

Troy nodded. "That's it. You'd know, wouldn't you?"

"And because you just get them back for one night, how are you supposed to deal with the pain of having to let them go all over again?"

He laughed, very quick, very soft. "You've obviously given this some thought. It's like you've got a stake in this for yourself, or something."

"But I do want it to happen for Cody," she said with resolve. "That's the bottom line. That's all that matters."

"Then I hope you get it. I hope it's him." *Him*, Troy always said. He never called Drew by name. "Who's the competition, do you know?"

She didn't, not exactly. They could only recall who'd died in the past year, and who among them might match up with the anonymous gifts lain thus far beneath the scarecrow's perch. The glove and the sheet music, the medal and the cake.

"The Purple Heart . . . I bet that was Larry Hughey's. He would've won that in Korea. He's the only veteran I can think of who's died this year."

"Oh god," she said, and imagined the man's poor widow coming out to leave the medal on the grass. "Candace Hughey's got to be in her eighties. Seems like she should be the lucky one tonight on seniority alone."

"Absolutely not," Troy said. "If you feel guilty about that, stop right now. Every time it goes to the geriatric crowd, it's a wasted year. It's like old people winning the lottery, you know? They're going to be dead in another three years anyway, so what's the point?"

She didn't want to laugh at this, but couldn't help it. "You're going to Hell for that one, I'm afraid."

"And if you're all lucky, I'll come back and tell you what it's like there."

She wasn't laughing anymore, and wondered why she had at all. It wasn't just talk, not in Dunhaven. Say a thing like that, and it could well turn out to happen.

"'Hell is other people,'" she mused, for no better reason than that it came to mind. Then again, there was always a better reason for most things. "Did you ever hear that? I don't remember who said it."

"No. But whoever it was, I'd buy him a drink."

They dawdled some more, in bed and then out, and shared a bite to eat—breakfast for him, brunch for her. They ate in the little nook before a bay window, overlooking the fading trees of autumn, bare enough and tall enough to appear to scrape the bellies of the charcoal clouds. It was almost like being outside, in the chill and unpredictable wind, on this day when the spirits gathered to roam.

And when it came time to leave, she both wanted to, and didn't.

"You going to be there tonight?" she asked.

"Should I? Do you want me to?"

Who could say what spirits understood, or were prepared to overlook? If they saw you getting on with your life, when theirs had been over a mere eight months, was that, to them, another kind of Hell?

"I don't know if that would be a good idea or not," she said.

He nodded. "I'm sure I'll hear all about it tomorrow."

When she left, every step between his door and her car felt like a few more degrees of transition between worlds—this time back to putting herself second, because that's what mothers were supposed to do. Halloween was the perfect day for this feeling, for changing masks so many times, one after another, so quickly that she could no longer be sure which of them was most real.

▫

Trick-or-treating was a supervised event in Dunhaven, the kids going out in groups overseen by at least one parent, or better yet, two. You had to love them, of course, and their excitement, all dressed up and everywhere to go, but you still didn't want them roaming at will, losing track of time. It was better for all concerned that they get in by curfew, before nightfall, when Halloween was taken over by more adult concerns.

Bailey had *wanted* to be one of the parents helping out to escort the kids around. She'd volunteered for duty again and again, but the other mothers and the few dads who pitched in wouldn't hear of it. Telling her no, of course not, you've got enough to worry about this year. Like they couldn't see that this was precisely the point—that today, of all days, was a day when she could use distractions instead of dwelling on what might or might not happen after sundown.

So after she'd collected Cody from the party at St. Aidan's, and gotten him into his costume, then dropped him off at the gradeschool gym where the candy-fueled army teamed up and set out, there could be no going home. The last thing she wanted was to sit around listening for the doorbell so she could spend the next hours throwing miniature Snickers bars at other people's children.

It was time to check on the offerings they'd left this morning anyway.

She was relieved to find them still there, right where they'd been left, along with the rest, nothing tampered with. They'd even been joined by a few more items, one a stuffed teddy bear with the nose half-chewed away, and with this one it only took a moment to figure out the likely source: the latest generation of Ralstons, Ellis and Kristen, who'd lost a baby girl to SIDS last spring.

Oh, come on, Bailey thought. *She wasn't even a year old, she wouldn't have been speaking anything more than a word at a time, so what's she got to tell you now?*

For which she felt perfectly ashamed a few moments later.

This day, this weird day—it *did* things to you, none of them good.

She'd never appreciated what a merciful thing it was that only those who'd died in the past year were able to come through. This limitation kept the incivility contained. If anyone could come back any year, the whole town would be at one another's throats each and every October. There wouldn't even be a Dunhaven by now, she was sure of it. The place would have imploded generations ago.

It wasn't just the sabotage from your fellow mourners you had to worry about, someone snitching your offering away to thin the competition for their own dearly departed. It was the sabotage you *couldn't* foresee coming that had, other years, made things interesting.

You didn't have to be old enough to remember it firsthand to have heard about the year James Gosling was caught stealing a locket and other items set out to call a woman named Meredith Hartmann, for fear of what her spirit might've had to reveal about the decade they'd kept secret from their spouses.

And beyond any living person's memory was a year that had passed into local legend. One of Dunhaven's most disreputable sons, Joseph Harrington, was alleged to have salted the earth of the entire town square, and soaked the wood of the fencepost in holy water, in an attempt to keep *anyone* from coming through. Several people had died that spring, on the same night on the eve of May, three in ways that, it was said, left their bodies so mangled they looked as though they'd gone through a combine—although no one ever needed to run a combine until harvest. Whatever had happened, Harrington had thought it better to incur the wrath of all of Dunhaven than let someone have a chance to say a word about what they'd been up to out in the woods and fields far from the heart of town.

Anywhere else, people would write that off as lore that had grown so much in the telling that by now the episode was more fable than fact. But here, given what everybody *knew* would happen each October . . . ? Here, you couldn't be so sure.

Either way, the dead had secrets, and sometimes the living had a powerful interest in making sure both stayed on the other side, unseen, unheard.

Oddly enough, the local police kept out of this part of it, stepping in only when deeds and disagreements turned violent. People complained, but Bailey got the logic behind this—it would be that much harder to keep

the peace when people started thinking you played favorites when it came to pilfering and petty theft of things left in plain sight, on public property.

If we want the privilege of speaking with the dead, she thought, *we're on our own.*

So as long as she was here and dreaded going home, she decided to do her civic duty and take a turn on unofficial watch. She hoofed it a block away, to the Jittery Bean, where she bought a hot chocolate, and brought it back here to the square and settled onto one of the benches in view of the waiting scarecrow, to make sure it all stayed on this side of fair.

She could feel it already, while dodging people on the sidewalks to and from the coffee shop, and could see it now from the bench: the eagerness of morning giving way to the nervousness of afternoon. The day was darkening too soon, it seemed, the sun gone weak in the south, the clouds sinking lower over the town, like a roof to screen them from the eye of God. A deeper chill rode in on a blustery wind that rattled leaves and windows alike.

We should've moved, she thought. *We should've moved away before Cody was born, the way we talked about. Drew would still be dead . . . but we wouldn't still be waiting to see if he's coming home.*

From here, she could see the blue-and-white of the shirt, the red lacquer of the Pinewood Derby car.

Go on, she thought. *Somebody come take them already. I'll cut you some slack, sit right here and pretend I don't see you.*

Before long, she thought she might have had a hopeful prospect, a scarf-wrapped woman walking up to the scarecrow and giving the offerings a studious look without having brought one of her own. She soon drifted toward another walkway, in no hurry to leave. In profile and from behind it was hard to tell who it was, but once she sat down on another bench, Bailey could see her clearly, and realized that it was Melanie Pemberton.

She should've guessed.

Come Halloween time, Melanie was a reliable fixture here, ever since the year of that grim business with her younger sister Angela. Came early, stayed late, would've swept the streets, probably, if they'd handed her a broom.

Melanie noticed her now, for the first time, and saw that Bailey saw her, and there came the awkward moment of being unsure whether they should go back to pretending they hadn't, or consolidate space. *Oh, why not.* Bailey pointed to the spot on the bench beside her, and Melanie came over.

She was dark-haired and the last three years had left her hard-faced bordering on severe . . . but Bailey thought she understood the ongoing need in her, and didn't judge. If Drew wasn't the one who came through tonight, she felt confident that that would be it. Free to move on. Not haunt the place year after year, seeming to hope for a replay. But, like Troy had said, with Melanie it was a whole different set of issues.

"Even as a girl, I always wondered why we leave stuff," Melanie said. "Leave *stuff*, and walk away." She was stressing the word *stuff* as though it were something unpleasant, like *hospital waste*. "*We* should be camping out here, instead. But no. We seem to accept it on faith that inanimate objects will do a better job calling back the people we're supposed to love than we can."

Bailey had never regarded it quite that way, and anyhow, who really knew what went into the founding of a tradition this old? Here, 162 years ago, if you weren't spending every waking moment of October bringing in crops and preparing for winter, you were probably going hungry and cold long before spring.

Mostly, Melanie just seemed angry. She had good reasons to be angry.

"You don't have kids, do you?" Bailey asked.

"And bring them into a world like this? Not likely. *Not* likely."

"I was just going to say," Bailey went on, "that before they get to a certain age, kids seem to see a soul in everything. Everything's alive, on some level. So who's to say they don't know something we all forgot? And maybe the ones who've died, they remember it. So they're just happy to see a familiar soul that . . . I don't know . . . loved them unconditionally, maybe?"

Melanie sat there taking this in. At least she wasn't chewing it up and spitting it back in Bailey's face.

"Unconditional," Melanie said softly. "That's hard, isn't it."

Bailey swirled her cup and drained the cocoa, now cold, to the last dribbles. "Chocolate, that's easy for unconditional love. Everything else . . . ?"

Melanie laughed a little, maybe just being polite. Then she fell back into the black hole. "The day she disappeared, Angie and I . . . we had the worst fight. We said the worst things to each other. Me, mostly. *I* said them." She bowed her head in a prayer to nothing, then snapped up again. "Of all the days, huh? Of all the days."

Bailey wanted to say something, anything, the kneejerk words that you thought nobody must have thought to tell her before now. But of course she would've heard them all, listened to them until she was sick of them, and sick of the people who kept spouting them at her like found wisdom.

Instead, Bailey kept her mouth shut and reached over to rest her hand across the back of Melanie's, until she nodded, the understanding between

them in no need of words, and it felt like time to draw her hand back again. Melanie looked at the scarecrow, and if longing alone could've done it, the thing would have come down off its cross and danced.

"That helped, actually. What you said." She sounded surprised about this. "It really did. But you know? There's only one thing that could ever make me feel like I could finally put it all behind me."

"I know."

Melanie stood and straightened her scarf. "Good luck tonight," she said, a rare wish that could assume the form of such opposing outcomes.

Evening fell, and dragged the night behind it.

The streets began to fill well before dusk, permanently now, people staking an early claim for a good view instead of having to rely on hearsay filtering back through the crowd. Everyone Bailey had seen throughout the day seemed to return fivefold, tenfold, expanding out in a circle from the center of the town square. When the span grew too great for that, the latecomers were forced to clog the streets between the low brick buildings of downtown.

Hundreds, easily. Thousands? Probably. She felt their pressure at her back, their eyes and expectations. Cody? Oblivious. Like his father, he could tune out anything he didn't want or need to hear.

She leaned close to his shoulder, thinking of his stated intention this morning to ask Drew to take him along.

"Have you thought about what *else* you're going to say to Daddy, if he comes?"

Cody nodded, looking more pensive than a six-year-old should. "Uh huh."

"Wanna tell me about the rest? Run it past me?"

Cody thought it over, then shook his head no. "That's okay."

It stung, yes, shut out again, but it was a thing to be proud of, too. *Good boy,* she thought. *This day of the year, at least, don't trust anybody.*

Here at the foot of the cross, in the alleged position of honor, they were sitting on a blanket folded quadruple to keep from hogging space and, less effectively, to shield their bottoms from the chill of the moist autumn earth. On either side, all in a tight row, were the rest of the bereaved. Candace Hughey, eighty if she was a day, eyes fixed on her husband's Purple Heart. The Ralstons, Ellis and Kristin, their true north that sad teddy bear; Kristin looked as if she'd recently finished crying and could start again if so much as a raindrop fell wrong. Others, more than a dozen by now, everybody too close for comfort in this quiet rivalry.

Cody was an hour coming down off the high of trick-or-treating, costume shed and stuffed into new clothes in a bathroom at the gradeschool rendezvous. He may not have needed it, but she poured him a hot chocolate anyway, from the Thermos she'd had filled at the Jittery Bean, to keep the inevitable sugar crash at bay a little longer.

She leaned in close again. "You know Daddy loves you very much. If it's not him tonight, that doesn't change anything. It doesn't mean any different. You know that, don't you?"

"I guess," he said.

"Where he is now, we don't know what it's like there. How they decide things. We've got our rules here, but we don't know what theirs are. Do you understand?"

Cody looked at her with, of all things, suspicion. "How come we don't know? How come nobody's asked?"

She blinked, feeling that special kind of stupid that kids could make you feel. "Asked who?"

"The dead people from before. If it's happened all these other times, then how come nobody's asked one of 'em what their rules are?"

It was a good question. Maybe it was already on his shortlist of things to discuss with Drew, or maybe he was adding it now.

"I don't know," she said. "Maybe people mean to, but then they get excited and forget."

The mayor stepped up onto a small platform and said more than a few words, as the mayors always did. It wasn't an address anyone seemed to want. This had been going on for 162 years, for god's sake, so it wasn't like there were people out there who needed a refresher on what the night was all about. This had gone on long before him and, presumably, would go on long after he became eligible to bore people from the other side.

The murmur of hundreds of conversations filled the night, a subdued sound considering the numbers. Expectant and alert, she felt electrified when something jolted her from the inside, then foolish when she realized it was just her phone, ringer off and set to vibrate. She slipped it out to find a fresh text message from Troy:

Anything yet?

No, she keyed back. *Everything quiet as a tomb. Except Mayor Bob.*

Thought I heard the wind pick up.

What r u doing now?

Movie nite. Wishing u were here to hold my hand during the scary parts.

Probably not all u wish I was holding, she keyed, and couldn't believe she'd said it, sent it. This was wrong on so many levels. Sexting, here and now,

of all times and places, like she was trying to psychically sabotage the very thing her son wanted most in the world tonight. The thing she wished she could want as much as Cody did, but couldn't.

It came down to this, she realized: She had eleven years of memories with Drew, most good, some exquisite. And she didn't want the final one, that desperate goodbye in the hospital, to be shoved aside by some new one, postmortem, the man she'd loved now wrapped inside a creepy shell of straw and old clothes and burlap, struggling to communicate whatever he felt he'd left unsaid.

Something to dream of, Troy wrote back. *Turning in early. Thought I'd be OK with this tonite but now I just want it over. Want it to be tomorrow.*

Me 2 x 1000.

"Who was that?" Cody asked after she'd put her phone away. Looking vaguely annoyed with her, as if her lapse in concentration would cost him everything. She'd lost her game face.

"Just a friend." Great—on top of everything else, guilt and lies. "She wanted to wish us good luck."

The impatience grew, thick with apprehension, everybody here in the front row appearing to feel it on some level or another. Down on the far end, a middle-aged widower was doing some breathing exercise. Five-count inhale, five-count hold, five-count exhale—she could see him ticking it off on his fingers.

The chill plunged further and the courthouse clock tower chimed nine, the mechanical crash of the hammer into the bell sharp and deep and unnerving. The echo seemed to roll for miles, still lingering in the air when something else charged the night. Was it just her, or did everyone feel it? The crowd fell silent behind her for a moment, then a groundswell of murmuring picked up again, expectant.

Bailey looked up along the cross with the same dread that guiltier souls than she was might have felt for a headsman hoisting his axe. Although she felt no wind, the fingers of one stuffed glove began to twitch. Then the arm began to stir, sliding along the crosspiece that held the thing in place, and one leg started to flex, the heel of the boot banging against the post.

You could blame everything on the wind until the head lifted.

The other arm moved, the other leg stirred, the shoulders appearing to strain as it leaned forward and weakly, so weakly, tried to push itself away from the post. The head tipped back and looked to the sky, then around at the tops of the downtown buildings, and down again, down to earth, out over the rapt and waiting throng . . . and if the thing could be said to see at all, with its black button eyes, then yes, the sight appeared to hasten its sense of urgency . . . or of agitation.

It wasn't the fact that it moved at all that most unnerved her. No, it was subtler than that. Everything breathed. Women and men, cats and cows, birds and apes. Everything breathed. But not this. Its chest and belly were as still as a corpse's. She hadn't realized how *wrong* this mimicry of life looked without breath until now.

Beside her, Cody knelt tense and wide-eyed, hands clasped at his chin as he nibbled on the tips of his thumbs. When she put her arm around his rigid shoulders, he gave no sign of noticing.

Above them, the scarecrow finally succeeded in flopping one arm free of the crosspiece, then the rest of it followed, the entire faux being tumbling to the ground, where it landed on its side with a rustle of cloth and straw. It stirred for a moment, trying to right itself with the slow, helpless squirm of an overturned turtle. Then its glove caught, and it pulled itself over onto its belly, to crawl forward on elbows and knees, toward the gifts of its summons.

It inspected them for a long time, longer than she remembered this taking in the past. Every year it was always the same—when the scarecrow took the gift, found the link, that's how you knew who it was. Up and down the row it crawled, seeming to sense that *something* was here, something it just wasn't finding.

Finally it lingered . . .

And chose.

The cake. The old cake that, this morning, looked to have come from a freezer. She hadn't known whose it was, and still didn't. Beside her, Cody gave a groan of disappointment, so she squeezed him tight to her. This time he let her, then buried his face into her side and sobbed. She glanced left, right . . . *and none of them were moving.* In fact, they looked to be growing as mystified as she was.

Then who had set it out there?

She looked again at the scarecrow. With its clumsy hands, it was now pulling the cake apart, and something about the sight triggered a wave of revulsion in her. It had no mouth, yet it was going to try to eat? No, that wasn't it—

Bailey became aware of a commotion behind her.

—it was ripping the cake apart to get to something *inside*—

She became aware of a voice trying to make itself heard above the swelling din of the crowd.

—pawing aside frosting and crumbling cake that had been packed around something inside, to pull out—

Melanie again. Melanie Pemberton, shouldering her way to the front of the crowd, past well-intended men trying to hold her back.

—a music box. Old, chipped, adorned with painted arabesques. A music box.

Angela? *This* was her sister Angela? Now, three years after she'd . . . ?

And then, apart from her own losses, maybe the most heartbreaking sight Bailey had ever seen: the scarecrow trying to wind the music box's key, to hear its song once more, but unable to, its gloved fingers not nimble enough, strong enough.

"You all gave her up for dead! Remember?" Melanie screamed at the crowd, as she broke free to take her place at the front. "All of you! That made it easier for you to stop looking, didn't it! 'Oh, Angela has to be dead by now! What can we do, life goes on!'"

Oh god, Bailey thought. *We just assumed . . .*

"Well, she's dead now! And that's on you! All of you!"

"Mom?" Cody looked up at her, his face pleading. "What's going on, I don't understand."

Nobody did, apparently. It was the noisiest Bailey had ever heard the crowd on Halloween night, confusion rippling back and forth, ricochets of resentment. It surged with unease, like an animal on the verge of being spooked.

How could this have happened? They'd found a blouse with Angela's blood; two days later, two of her fingers out by the highway. Then nothing. No word, no sign, no more evidence at all. Days passed, then weeks turning to months. The conclusion came by gradual default, spreading from person to person like a cold: The poor young woman was surely dead, the rest of her sure to be found someday.

But why the subterfuge? Why the cake, to hide something in plain sight . . . unless Melanie didn't want to set out something that she feared someone else might recognize. But if that was it . . .

No. No, the notion was too vile to entertain.

Cody tugged at her coat sleeve. "I want to go home."

By now, Melanie had managed to struggle around the end of the front row, circling to get to the scarecrow while pushing past the mayor, who must have thought he was helping by trying to stop someone he believed was making a scene. Melanie dropped beside the bundle of cloth and straw and burlap, touching it tenderly, as if anything more might drive her sister away, and it touched her back in recognition.

Bailey didn't have to hear the woman to know what was coming next. It would be the questions Melanie had been waiting years to ask.

Who took you?

Where were you kept all this time?

Who killed you?

And, you had to consider, *is he here tonight? And was there more than one?*

Though they were head to head, could Melanie even hear what her sister would say? That was why the quiet of the crowd was so important. It wasn't simply reverence or being polite; it was practical, too. Those who would know had told her that the voice of the dead sounded thin and faraway, as though it emanated from a realm within the scarecrow rather than from the thing itself.

Abruptly, then, there was no chance of hearing it, no matter how keen Melanie's ears, as somewhere close behind, in the packed and straining crowd, a string of firecrackers went off like a volley of gunshots. It was all the reason they needed to panic, a surge of bodies pressing forward from behind as people scattered from the rising cloud of smoke and flashes.

Bailey held Cody tight to her as she took a shoulder hard in the back and, along with others in the front row, went spilling into the empty space between them and the fencepost. Gifts were scattered or trampled, and she caught sight of Mrs. Hughey trying to snatch up her husband's Purple Heart, only to have her forearm snapped under an errant foot.

Worse, far worse, because it was deliberate, and like killing Angela all over again, was the second pack of firecrackers that an unseen hand lobbed toward the scarecrow. Melanie saw the fuse spitting and hissing through the air, then it landed on the effigy's back and erupted in an endless barrage of hot white pops. The first flames danced to life in seconds, then spread, feeding on shirt and straw alike. In moments it was a mass of fire, and Bailey was sure she saw the thing twist and writhe even after Melanie's hands let it go, unable to beat out the flames, forced to quit by singed palms and the shredding assault of the firecrackers.

Leaving Angela dead and gone for good, and her secrets with her.

Bailey got to both feet, pulling Cody with her, to her, and moved to the other side of the fencepost, so they wouldn't be squashed against it. Cody wanted to go home, of *course* he wanted to go home, but for now they might as well have been trapped on an island, keeping to this makeshift tree in a patch of green, surrounded by the surging sea of an unruly mob.

Close enough to spit at, the scarecrow continued to burn, its head and limbs ablaze, its back a scorched black cavity. Just as close, but out of

reach, Drew's flannel shirt and the Pinewood Derby car were crushed into the ground by lurching feet and sprawling hands.

And it seemed as if all of Dunhaven wallowed before her.

She looked out over them with growing loathing, this town that hid its secrets so well that captors and murderers could walk in confidence across the placid face of normal life. Wearing masks not just on Halloween, but every day of the year. Had she smiled at them at the market? Chatted with them in line for coffee? Let them go first in traffic? Had she taught their children in school, or driven past their homes never suspecting what may have been chained in their basements?

She hadn't known, hadn't *wanted* to know, and now felt as guilty as any of them.

I want to go home too, she thought, only now grasping the truth that home was someplace she'd never been.

From out in the street, Bailey heard a man's voice yelling above the rest, then another, and another, and realized they were shouting about Troy. Whether instigation or ignorance, it didn't matter. The thought spread effortlessly, viral: It was always the boyfriends, always the husbands. Living out there all alone . . . who knew what he got up to? They would set it right.

Good god, were they even thinking straight? Were they capable of it anymore? Troy had been looked at, investigated, cleared. She knew his home, knew his grief. But none of that mattered. Not tonight. Tonight was a night for scapegoats.

Bailey fished the phone from her pocket to call him, but after the first couple of rings, got only his voice mail. Tried again; the same.

Turning in early, he'd texted. *Thought I'd be OK with this tonite but now I just want it over.*

Yet again; the same.

Please answer, she begged. *Please. Please wake up . . .*

As she clutched her phone in one hand and her fatherless son in the other, confined by the mob to this tiny plot of earth, she remembered the adage she'd told Troy earlier in the day: *Hell is other people.* All around her, they seemed so intent on proving it.

The scarecrow was ash now, nothing left to burn.

Finally she understood what had eluded them all for 162 years: why there was only ever one. If Hell was other people, then the dead had already escaped it, and so maybe coming back through was, for them, no privilege. Maybe it was a curse.

One Possible Shape of Things to Come

Imagine this going on under your own roof. You'd think it was just you, right?

The scene was a late evening in later summer, the second day of the first visit I'd been able to pay my sister in years, trading northern Colorado for northern California. The second day of a planned six, which, yes, is a risk. That advice about company and fish going bad after three days may hold true for family even more than everyone else.

But we were grown-ups now. That whole pattern of torment and retaliation was behind us. Grown-ups. Meredith more than me, maybe, but we'd always evolved at different rates.

Here's how I knew Meredith was permanently done with glow sticks, whirling her bikini top overhead at pool parties, and yacking up Mike's Hard Lemonade into bushes: For the past five years, her life's orbit had happily revolved around a benign dictator who now stood three-foot-seven and still had to be stopped from eating from the potpourri bowl. Because he insisted it was purple cereal.

Here's how a typical discussion about that would go:

"See that water it's in? We don't pour water over cereal, do we?" *Unimpeachable logic from his dad, Ethan, my brother-in-law.*

"It's clear milk." *Declared with the unshakable conviction of a CEO.*

"But milk isn't clear." *Your puny logic is doomed to fail, dad-man.*

"Yes it is. It's from see-through cows." *You were warned.*

I loved this kid, my one and only nephew, Micah. He was everything I aspired to be, if only I could still get away with it. One thing I was looking forward to most in the world was being the cool uncle. The unsavory adult he could talk to about things he could never bring up with his parents, and who was going to turn him onto cultural touchstones that would make him a demigod among his friends.

In time. In time.

For now, my visit mostly amounted to medical missionary work with Ethan after the resident five-year-old was in bed. I'd brought along a care package of the sort of things that Ethan, poor bastard, never got to enjoy anymore. Sometimes it's all about saving your fallen brothers.

"It's a Korean revenge flick, that's all you need to know," I told him while loading the disc in the Blu-ray player. Then we reacquainted him with the simple joys of our generation's version of tuning in, turning on, dropping out. Our one concession was using a nebulizer because, if we insisted on getting quietly baked, Meredith didn't want the house smelling like smoke. It wasn't the same, until we just didn't care.

"Jesus," Ethan said a half-hour in. "The Koreans don't fuck around."

"No," I said. "They don't."

"I forgot they made movies like this." He inhaled a hit of mist and looked utterly baffled. "It's all *Lion King* and mermaid shit now. At some point you just go numb. It's either go numb, or realize there's a set number of times you can hear the same stupid cheerful song before you hear it telling you to hang yourself. And you don't want to find that number."

"Easy," I said. "Brook's here. I've got your back. I'm here to help."

He watched awhile longer. "I'm going to miss you when you're gone, brother."

None of which was the weird part. Scenes like that were no doubt going on all over, in millions of homes, everyone thinking that, a few misgivings aside, all was right with the world . . . even though, even then, it wasn't.

We had the movie down and were contemplating another when Meredith poked her head in the family room and gave us a sour look that wasn't too harsh, as if, as reprobates go, we could've been worse.

"You need to see this. Now." It was clear she was speaking to Ethan and it was obviously about Micah. "Hurry."

I followed, too, both of us adopting my sister's haste-stealth pace up the carpeted stairs, until the three of us clustered in Micah's doorway. Ethan peered over her right shoulder as I peered over her left.

"I just checked in on him, and he was like this," she whispered. "Should we be worried about this?"

Micah's room was dim, despite the nightlight burning along one baseboard and the wedge of light from the hallway's ceiling lamp behind us. His bed was empty, the covers rumpled and trailing into the floor, as if they sought to join the scattered toys.

His back was to us, as Micah stood in the far corner, facing into it with his head tipped halfway down. He was as motionless as I'd ever seen any kid out of bed.

"What's going on with him?" Meredith whispered.

Ethan slipped past, steering around the toys until he was at Micah's knobby little shoulder. "Hey. Buddy? Shouldn't you be in bed?"

No response, and by now, my sister was there, too. "Micah? Why are you standing in the corner?"

I thought he wasn't going to respond to that, either, that maybe he'd been sleepwalking and didn't hear them. Then he turned his head to look back at us, and awake or not, everything was still slowed down, dreamlike, his voice a flat monotone.

"I've been bad," he said.

Both Meredith and Ethan told him no, no, he hadn't been bad, and this was true, he hadn't really misbehaved during the entire time I'd been there. Regardless, he shook his head with great slowness and terrible weight, as if the matter were settled.

"They told me to wait here," he said.

"*Who* told you?" Meredith asked.

Back to the silent treatment. He wasn't answering that one.

"Wait for what?" Ethan said.

"To be punished."

As they steered him back to his bed, Micah went willingly, seeming to let it happen rather than under his own steam, and they tucked him in tight, cinching him down with more covers than he needed in late summer. He fell asleep immediately, if he'd even been awake at all, and they left his door open all the way.

Meredith looked genuinely weirded out. "He's never done that before."

"And he might never again." Me, just trying to be helpful.

"It's always something new," Ethan said, except I couldn't tell if that was a complaint or his way of dismissing it as nothing serious.

We dawdled around, binning the idea of a second movie, and while we talked about going to bed, too, by the time I trailed off to the guest room, Meredith was still up, finding one more thing, one more thing that needed doing. Between each, she would check to make sure Micah was still down for the long count.

And it *was* serious. A thing like that, you'd naturally assume it was a one-off, unique to your own four walls. But the same scenario was going on all over.

You feel guilty for not realizing that . . . but really, what could we have done even if we'd known?

Micah had no recollection of any of it the next day, and seemed his normal self, which is to say infused with the exuberant power of a thousand shrieking suns and ready to expend it on the nearest expanse of grass or cluster of playground equipment he could get to. He had a swimming class in there somewhere, too.

"I wouldn't worry about it," I told Meredith as, in a park a mile from their home, we watched him brachiate along a set of monkey rings, him and a couple dozen other high-decibel yard-apes. "I did a thing or two like that when we were little. I don't remember it, just Mom laughing about it."

"What did you do?" she asked.

"One night she found me sleeping on the floor at the end of my bed, on my back, butt against the bed and my legs bent at the knee so they were up on the mattress. She asked what I was doing down there, and according to her, I said: 'Oh, Mom, it's just a fad, you don't understand.'"

She shrugged, no recollection of this, either. "How old were you?"

"It was a few years ago, one weekend I was home from college," I said, and Meredith rolled her eyes and kicked me lightly in the shin. "Primary school sometime, it doesn't matter."

"That was just you being your goofy self, it's not the same," she said. "Last night, that was . . . worrisome."

It would be to her, even though I thought she was reading more into it than there really was. Kids just did creepy things sometimes.

But I understood her upset, just the same. I'd been sent to corners a few times, at home and at school. A couple times, in class, I'd also been ordered to stand with my nose pressed into a small circle drawn on the chalkboard. I could barely reach it, and had to strain. Both were unpleasant, shameful experiences, but the corner was worse. It was more isolating, the way the walls came together, closing in. And while the chalk circle was its own punishment, the corner was just a prelude, a holding cell where I had to wait for some more overt penalty that was coming.

The corner was a container that gradually filled with dread.

"Where did he even pick that up?" Meredith asked.

"You've never done it to him?" I asked. "Sent him to the corner?"

She shook her head no. "When he gets a time-out, it's usually just having to sit in a chair."

"What about pre-school last year? Do they do it there?"

"I don't think so. It's not on their list of approved disciplinary measures. I'll ask."

I couldn't help it: The list I instantly imagined included both the revocation of playground privileges and thumbscrews. I couldn't joke about it with her, though. She wouldn't have laughed, only glared. *That's not funny, Brook.* Not even a little? *No!* There was a time, though, and I rather missed that version of my sister. The current one was less coiffed, less blond, and altogether more disheveled, but wound tighter.

Then again, the prior model was the one who'd sworn she was never going to have kids, because (a) she had too much else to live for besides some parasitical offspring, and (b) kind of a crap world to bring one into anyway, wasn't it, what with rising oceans and climbing temperatures and that sense of malaise that we were all scrabbling along the downside slope of a bell curve with our parents on its apex behind us.

People change, some more drastically than others, and sometimes for reasons that aren't obvious. She hadn't even gotten pregnant by accident.

"And what does Micah think he needs to be punished for, that was the worst part," she said. "Did you seem him? He looked . . ."

Hopeless, I thought, but didn't dare utter this, either.

"Look at the way he's coming off right now. That's a boy who doesn't feel guilty for anything," I said instead. Then I pointed toward the sidelines, where one of the kids had gone sullen and tearful and bratty enough to hurl away a sandwich as soon as his mom gave it to him. "Now there's a kid who looks like he could use a little more punishment in his life."

I scanned the crop of parents, nearly all women plus one beleaguered-looking dad.

"I see you've got some hot moms here," I said. "Any hot *single* moms?"

Meredith huffed. "That's privileged information. Besides, you might want to start with hot running water at some point today."

I knocked shoulders with her. "Come on, there's got to be some MILF action you can set me up with. You don't want the sole responsibility for keeping me entertained the whole time I'm here, do you? You see how easy it is for me to have a corrupting influence on your husband."

"Let's keep that in the family, okay? I'd like to still be able to show my face here after you leave." Then she started to laugh, the thing I'd been

after all along. "What was that repulsive pick-up line you used to use in college? You swore it worked a few times just because it was so pitiful."

"'Let me lower your standards'... is that the one you're thinking about?"

"That's it." She gave me an abrupt sideways look. "Ewww, you're not still...?"

"No," I said, then gave the playground a predacious once-over. "But what better place to bring it out of retirement?"

She squared off with me, starting to loosen up. "I know you're just trying to goad me. It's like your favorite sport now or something. I know you're not half as revolting as you pretend to be."

"That's almost generous of you."

"You're actually good dad material, if you'd ever get serious and decide you want that. You really are. Every time I get to watch you with Micah, I see how true that is. You know one big reason why? You're patient. At every age he's been around you, you've been infinitely patient with him. I bet you don't even realize how important that is."

"It's probably just the weed."

"Uh huh. Probably." She sounded wholly unconvinced. I couldn't faze her anymore this morning. "Keep telling yourself that."

We quieted down and watched the kids play, but every now and then I sneaked a peek at one of the moms, imagining what life would be like with her, chaotic breakfast tables and weary dinners, never-ending laundry cycles, and overbooked calendars, and always, always, this stubborn guilt that she could've been doing better instead of recognizing that maybe she was doing a pretty terrific job with what she had. It didn't sound so bad.

Now the big question: Could I elicit as much patience as I apparently possessed?

Which steered me toward the drama with the kid who'd flung the sandwich, to see how that was coming along. Maybe my legendary patience had limits.

The boy was shaking his head no, no, no. I couldn't hear what he was saying over the cacophony of shouts and squeals, but I'd always been good at reading lips.

I don't wanna go home for a nap, he appeared to be saying. *I don't wanna have to stand in the corner again.*

He really didn't. I'd never seen a kid more adamant about anything.

They're mean to me there.

They're mean everywhere, I could've told him. But of course that just would have been another evasion, the kind I'd always been so good at, to keep from confronting the real issue until it was too late.

ю

That night Micah was at it again, up and in the corner within ninety minutes of bedtime. They had him knock back a shot of children's NyQuil in hopes it would keep him down until morning, and this worked at least as long as it took for the rest of us to drift off. But I later woke in the guest room to the sound of stressed-out crying, and knew Meredith had found him back where he didn't belong, and when I checked my phone, found it was 3:18 a.m.

I got up. Who needs more than three solid hours, anyway?

"I'll watch him," I told my sister. "Just go to sleep. I'll stay up and watch him."

In a chair in a room in the glow of a dim nightlight watching over a little boy who made no noise as he slept—it felt like I was the one with a problem.

As I watched Micah not move, watched his clock do nothing, I asked myself how it was possible to get lost in a chair. The stillness of the room, and the house beyond it, seem to deepen and grow. It was more than an absence of activity. It felt like an actual void, cut off from everything bright and warm. There were no neighbors anymore, and when a car rolled past on the street, the headlights might as well have been a flicker from another galaxy. I could no longer feel certain that Meredith and Ethan still existed anywhere I could get to from here.

And within minutes, Micah got up. One more time.

He rose with a start, as if someone had poked him awake. He pushed himself up to sit on the edge of his bed and sighed, the most bone-weary sigh I'd ever heard, then trudged over to the corner. To wait. To wait, apparently, as long as it took. I let him get there before I made a move to intercept him.

"Micah," I whispered at his ear. "What's going on?"

It took a while for the words to sink in, like they were settling into ooze. Then he put his finger to his lips. *Shhhh.*

"They'll hear you," he whispered back.

"Who will?"

The same as the night before, he didn't answer. Now I wondered if it wasn't because he hadn't heard the question, and instead was because he really had no words for the answer.

I remembered the kid from the playground. "Are they mean there?"

"Yes," he said. "They hate everybody."

"Are they the ones that tell you to come here and wait?"

He nodded.

"What if you didn't listen to them?"

He had to let that one sink in, too. Then, "They'll just make it worse."

"Let's go for a ride," I said. "Let's go camp out downstairs."

I hoisted him up against one shoulder and carried him to the family room, where I curled him onto the couch. The plan was to spoon with him and trap him in place so we both could sleep until morning. But first, I felt a need to go back upstairs to Micah's room, to stand where he'd stood, to wait where he'd waited, and just . . . see what was there to perceive, if anything.

I'd forgotten since childhood: You don't so much stand in a corner as lean into it, a shoulder on each wall. Your chest and the walls make a triangle, a connection like a closing circuit. I'd forgotten how the sound of your breathing comes back at you. At your feet, three planes coming together, wall and wall and floor. Overhead, the same. Except it was so dark, I couldn't see anything, definitely not at my feet.

Above, though . . .

Was there suddenly more light? Or were my eyes getting accustomed to what little there was? I stared at that murky, shadowed point in space where the planes met and the lines converged—x-axis, y-axis, z-axis—into the corner of a cube. It occurred to me that they didn't just stop. Each axis had to keep going on the other side of the wall and beyond the ceiling, continuing into another dimension.

Maybe that was just the weed, too.

But I could still feel it. Something more than shadows was building here. There was a sense of pressure, a warping of the space contained by the angles, the way a balloon distorts on one side when squeezed from the other.

Then I saw it, just for a moment, the convergence point bulging into a kind of circle, as if a sphere had intersected the corner of the cube, to reveal—I thought of it as an eye even before I realized it probably was one. Not because it looked like any eye I was used to seeing, and seeing with. It wasn't. Instead, it was a multifaceted network of hexagons, a compound eye. Yet before I even realized this, I was thinking of it as an eye because it gave me the impression that, whatever it belonged to, it had seen me. Then it winked out.

I backed away, stutter-stepping, until I ran into Micah's bed and dropped butt-first onto the mattress, where I sat and watched the corner for a long time. But it only stayed a corner, pretending to be normal.

Downstairs again, I found Micah where I'd left him, and tried my best to keep him safe through the rest of the night.

It must have worked. The next thing I knew, Meredith and Ethan were standing over the family room couch as daylight scratched at the windows.

"Explain . . . ?" she said.

"We're camping out," I told them. "Listen, you really should let Micah sleep in your bed tonight. There's something wrong with his room."

And twenty-four hours later, the next morning, it didn't matter what else we might have tried to get Micah past this strange phase, or what conclusions we might have come to after more clueless debate on what was going on with the poor kid. Because this time I woke to the sound of, well, not so much crying as keening.

While fumbling out into the hallway, I begged all the unseen forces that never listened to make whatever I might find something that would surprise me. Meredith had broken something and cut her foot. A bird had gotten in through the window and was panicking. Something small, something she was overreacting to. Anything but the obvious. Anything but Micah.

But, like I said, they never listened.

My nephew and my sister were both wearing pajamas, and she was cradling him in one corner of the bedroom . . . which, I had to guess, was where she found him as soon as she'd awakened a minute earlier. Ethan was a couple feet away, in a T-shirt and boxer shorts, and had dropped into a fetal squat, wrapping himself up with both arms.

To look at Micah, you wouldn't know anything was wrong. He looked like he was sleeping. But a mom would know better, wouldn't she? She'd know.

And nobody cries like that over someone who's just hard to wake up.

I stayed over, longer than I'd planned, for the funeral and another few days past that. Staying felt wrong, and I had a gaming shop that wasn't going to continue running itself for much longer, but to leave would've felt worse. Mostly I listened, because there was nothing I could say that would make anything one bit better.

Cheer up, you're not in this alone, it's on the news, this is going on all over—a lot of good that would do. But it was true. You could call it an epidemic, but it hadn't started in one place, then spread. It seemed to be going on

everywhere at once, with no center, and had been for over a week before Micah succumbed to it. It merely took some time before the pieces began coming together to make the big picture, terrible as it was. Every death is local.

So during those first few days, I listened, and hugged Meredith and Ethan, a lot, because they didn't seem to have it in them to hug each other. And when I went back to Colorado, finally, that was the last time I saw them as a couple.

Statistically, the odds are pretty grim that a couple that loses a child will split up. It's not something you ask about, but I have to wonder if it doesn't come down to two-way blame and an unwillingness to forgive.

Meredith and Ethan didn't buck those odds. And I can state definitively there was blame between them, maybe not out in the open, but I'd noticed undercurrents of it in that first week after Micah was gone, each of them wondering why the other hadn't awakened when Micah squirmed out from between them to go stand in the corner for the last time. But they blamed themselves, too, and so did I, for the things I'd noticed and didn't know how to process into something meaningful, preventative.

Within a few months, Meredith went back to live with our parents for an undetermined period of time. Ethan downsized homes for obvious reasons, but it didn't matter for long. He worked as a wind turbine technician, a dangerous job even on the most upbeat day of your life, and one day he fell 200 feet to the ground. His partner on the job said he didn't scream once on the way down.

Did he do it on purpose? I don't know. But I do remember him telling me he'd decided to make a career in renewable energy not only because it couldn't be outsourced to some third-world indentured servant, but because he cared about the world Micah would be growing up in, and about leaving it a little cleaner.

I can see how something like that would stop mattering.

The world no longer looked like a place anybody would be growing up in eventually.

In the grand scheme, they were dropping all over. It was more than local, more than regional, more than national. It was global. Everywhere, parents were waking up to find their children dead in corners, for no apparent reason. Autopsies couldn't pin it down. It was as if, one medical examiner said, they were being switched off.

The phenomenon was reminiscent of SIDS—Sudden Infant Death Syndrome—so somebody somewhere tagged it STODS, for Sudden Toddler Death Syndrome, and the label stuck, even though most of the casualties had already learned to walk just fine.

The cure sounded simple enough: *keep them out of the goddamn corner.* Easier said than done, though. I knew from talking with my sister that anyone who tries to watch a kid every moment of every day slips up eventually. What could you do? Tie them down to their beds? Lock them out to sleep in the yard as the seasons change and the nights turn cold?

They died anyway, and the ages got younger. They died in cribs and playpens; those have corners, too. They fell asleep in cars and never woke up; angles meet in cars, as well. Desperate parents left their houses and apartments to move into tents in backyards and parks, yet this only delayed the inevitable, at least in the square and rectangular tents. Soon, you couldn't find a round, domelike tent for sale anywhere—not for retail prices, anyway. If you had the money, you could turn to the enterprising people who, loath to let a disaster go to waste, had bought them all up and were letting them go online for tens, even hundreds, on the dollar.

But whatever was outside always seemed to get in eventually. We live on a spherical world, but that's one fractal that doesn't scale down well. Across the surface, it's mostly angles.

Then there were the guardians of reason, who kept insisting at increasing volume that people were being hysterical and superstitious, that corners weren't a cause, because that was impossible. Instead, this was a quirky behavioral symptom of some fatal malady, maybe a new virus, that hadn't been identified yet.

Their children died, too, no matter how thoroughly they'd been quarantined.

At least they stayed consistent after the video came out. All they had to do was call it a hoax or an optical glitch, or just hold up a contemptuously dismissive hand and say we don't know *what* it shows.

I must have seen it two hundred times. Whenever someplace ran the clip, I had to stop and see it again. It was like one of those scenes in a movie that you watch over and over, wishing for it to turn out differently. Just once.

Her name was Heather Myers, and in a matter of weeks her demise became the most viewed death since the assassination of John F. Kennedy. She was eight years old.

It was recorded with a high-definition nanny cam her parents hadn't needed to set up for years, but broke out of storage, mounted on a shelf

in her room, and connected to a laptop, so they could keep an eye on her in this new plague age. The story went that they were watching her in shifts, and then one of them zonked out. So when Heather got up around 2:30 a.m., nobody was awake to intercept her.

Looking down from slightly above, the footage has that ghostly quality common to infrared. When she stirs and sits up on the bed, her hair looks white. For a couple of moments she appears to be having a conversation with someone who can't be seen, but there was never any audio, so whatever she said was lost. Then it's off to the corner with her. You never see her face again. Just her back.

Most showings of the video fast-forward through the next twenty-two minutes, because all she does is stand there. The timestamp numbers in the corner whir, and whatever small shifts she makes look tight and jerky, like she's vibrating erratically. Then the count returns to real time and you wait for the inevitable, the way she drops to the floor like a puppet whose strings have been cut.

You suspect you must've missed something, and unless you have superhuman eyes, *Matrix*-style bullet-time vision, you probably did. The prepared video backs up for a helpful slow-motion replay, frame by frame, until it freezes and you see what was over and done with in about 1/30th of a second: a pulse of energy that seems to originate in the corner over her head and zigzags down to connect with the top of her skull, like an arc from a Tesla coil. Even then, it's hard to discern, because it isn't bright, the way you expect an energy discharge to look. Just the opposite.

Black lightning, someone called it. What other name could you give it? That's exactly what it looks like.

You hope she didn't suffer, and it doesn't appear she did. The impression you get is that someone, something, somewhere, just shut her down.

That the footage was airing throughout the world every few minutes of every hour of every day might have seemed like a good idea. It's a warning. The unexpected result was how the death rate spiked higher still, parents deciding to snuff their own children, for their own good, instead of letting this happen to them.

"*I'd rather send him to God pure than let the demons take him,*" one father said in a notorious clip. "*I'm not sorry I did it, only sorry I had to. I'd do it again.*"

And so it went, as an entire generation continued to fall, one way or another.

As for the Myers, Heather's parents . . . they didn't stay together, either. I didn't have the heart to look up what happened to either of them after that.

But I still remembered them two years later, whenever I thought of Meredith and Ethan, deep into this quiet holocaust, while wondering why now, of all times. Why did I have to pick now to fall in love, to be a stepfather?

☩

For theoretical physicists, it was the best of times, it was the worst of times.

They got to be rock stars. Not just to an audience of predisposed geeks, but to the general population, even the ones who found science somehow suspect. A few had been rock stars for years already, because they were telegenic and had a knack for teaching, making brain-twisting concepts accessible to anybody who didn't drool. Now they all had a platform and the entire world was paying attention.

Then again, in their newfound celebrity, they were presiding over what could only be called an extinction event. Bummer, there.

They spoke of higher dimensions and the theory that multiple universes existed side by side, like bubbles. They speculated that what was happening was the result of an overlap, or a spongy collision in the foam of space-time. They mused about what might happen when matter and energy occupying the same space at widely differing frequencies suddenly entrained. They went on tangents about multidimensional geometry, and explored the idea that physically defined lines in our space projected into the space of someplace else, creating pathways that could be followed back to our own. What looked to us like a corner may have been, to them, a crossroads.

Them . . . ? There had to be a them, of course, even if we had no clue who or what they were. Just that they seemed to have no interest in sharing.

Whatever the experts disagreed on, and that was most of it, they all agreed on one thing:

You don't need to kill off every individual, or even most of them, to exterminate a species. Just the youngest, the most vulnerable. Just the ones who embody the future. Eventually, millions of funerals later, everybody gets the message. All it takes is patience. All you have to do is wait for the rest to age and die off of whatever would've killed them anyway.

This was a long-term plan, obviously.

You don't even have to kill off all the young ones. If a few slip through, no matter. They'll grow up witnessing enough death and mourning that the last thing they want to do is breed. They'll see all they need to of the kind of pain they don't want any part of.

"I'm never having kids," Jodi would say.

She was seven years old and had never met Meredith, yet sounded exactly like my sister when she was in college, with one difference: I *believed* Jodi.

"Does it hurt to get your tubes tied?" she asked me one day.

"Do you even know what your tubes are?"

"Sure I know. Everybody knows that." She was bluffing. I adored the way she bluffed, the full-statured, how-dare-you-question-me conviction behind it. "Are *your* tubes tied?"

"I've got different kinds of tubes. You don't tie those, you have them snipped."

Jodi waited for more, then got impatient. "Well? Are they snipped?"

"Yep."

"Did it hurt?"

More than you could ever know, I thought, but that's not the answer you give a seven-year-old you're trying to keep alive day by day, and happy, even though she's already lost nearly every friend she ever had.

"Not for long," I told her instead.

She would come to me with things she wouldn't bring up with her mother—I guess because Jodi could read faces like a human lie detector, and could see there were conversations that caused her mom visible distress, while I was more utilitarian. I was the next best thing to a real father: I wasn't going away, didn't embarrass easily, and would tell her as much of the truth as I could.

Sometimes I would catch Elsa watching me with her daughter, content to let whatever was passing between us play out, and I could hear Meredith telling me what seemed ludicrous at the time: *"You're actually good dad material, if you'd ever get serious and decide you want that."*

And I wanted it after all.

It just wasn't supposed to be like this.

Jodi and I would often go for next-best-thing-to-father and daughter walks, straying from our neighborhood in one direction or another. Sometimes we'd head to a park with its silent playground, where I would push her on a swing set whose chains creaked like an old man's knees, as if it took them a while to remember what it was like to move. For Jodi's sake, I would miss the step-cousin she'd never get to play with, and she would grill me on topics that careened between trivial and profound.

"Why do they hate kids so much?" she asked one day. "Those people on the other side, what did we ever do to them?"

"Well, for starters, they're not people," I said. "I don't think they're anything close to people."

We were scuffing along a road a few blocks from home, on the edge of things, where vacant lots and empty land bore the scars of early construction that had started a couple years ago, then stalled and never resumed. With a population in sudden, steep decline, what use was there for new homes? Actually, this time there was—architects had started to rethink everything about what a new house was supposed to look like, and what they'd come up with resembled an amoeba more than a traditional home, and I guess the developers had decided it was cheaper to start elsewhere than retrofit the boxy basements and foundations that had already been laid here. In a few places, skeletons of two-by-fours weathered where they stood.

"If they're not people," Jodi said, "then what are they?"

"I don't have a clue." No lies. "People a lot smarter than I am have gotten into fistfights trying to sort that out."

"That's dumb," she said.

"Smart people have dumb moments."

That didn't do anything for her morale, and I regretted having said it, because I feared it would linger the rest of her life. However long that proved to be.

There's a remark I encountered once: That in little boys, there's almost no hint of the men they'll become, but in every little girl you can already see the woman she'll be. And in Jodi, I really could see her future self, if she could make it there: thoughtful and confident, like her mother, but more impatient without being cruel about it, and with a crusader's sense of justice.

The latter quality was why she enjoyed walking this particular route, past the acreage where the construction had faltered. As young as she was at the time, she'd been terribly concerned about the resident prairie dogs that were slated to be gassed for living in the wrong place, and she'd gone door-to-door collecting money for their legal defense by an ecological group that wanted time to trap and relocate them.

Now, I think, she looked at their dirt-ridged mounds and their scurrying brown forms as a personal victory, even a symbol of hope. She was clever enough to look at big rodents and see civilization on the brink.

"We're like the prairie dogs were. That's why they hate us. We're in the way," she decided. "But look, *they're* still here."

And maybe they were safe from us. But they still had to watch out for hawks.

We'd turned around and were on our way back home when Jodi picked this day to ask me the worst thing she ever had.

"Do you think the black lightning hurts?"

I certainly had a parent's impulse to tell her to not worry. To make promises I had no way of keeping, and in the process deceive myself that she couldn't see straight through that. It was a daily battle.

"It doesn't seem to," I forced myself to say. "It seems quick."

"Where do we go when it hits?"

"Nowhere, if you're lucky. Nowhere at all. If you're lucky, it's like a light being switched off."

"You're supposed to tell me someplace beautiful," she smirked. "Where my friends and my dead cat are all waiting for me."

"And if your mom asks, that's exactly what I said."

Okay, so the woman Jodi would become would have a cruel streak in her after all, just for laughs.

"Race you," she said a half-block from home, and broke into a sprint.

I let her keep the lead. We had different doors we went in: the normal front door for me, and for her, I'd rigged a little round tunnel into the back that she was still young enough to find crawling through fun.

So it took her longer, and the race was a draw.

Once inside, I went through my usual obsessive-compulsive routine, inspecting all the corners and edge lines of the baseboards and molding I'd plastered thickly over, turning right-angled rooms into cave chambers where ceilings and walls and floors flowed smoothly into each other, connected by little round hobbit-style doors for Jodi to pass through. As I did every time, I tried to look at it all with fresh eyes, asking, *What did I miss, what did I miss, what could I have missed?*

This was a daily battle, too.

⁜

Hope rekindled for a while. The excitement and tension were remarkably like in the movies, as the people with the big brains came up with their hail-Mary plan. The human race strikes back. Welcome to Planet Earth, motherfuckers. Don't let the lithosphere hit you in the ass on the way out.

Exactly what the plan entailed, we lowly civilians didn't know, apparently didn't need to know, but there was a good chance we wouldn't have understood even if they'd spelled out the details. So where was Jeff Goldblum in all this, I wondered. He'd break it down for the rest of us. About all we knew was that it was happening at the Fermilab Main Injector particle accelerator west of Chicago, with an end goal of keeping the great veil intact so everyone could get back to pretending we were the only things in the cosmos that mattered.

Elsa and Jodi and I made pancakes that morning, while streaming the live feed from outside the 6800-acre facility on my laptop at the kitchen table.

"This is boring," Jodi said after watching for a few minutes. "It's just some guy out talking in front of a building."

"It's all going on underground," Elsa told her. "Thirty feet down."

"Then why don't they show it down there?"

That one I fielded: "Because then it would just be some guy talking in front of a wall, and you'd think that was *super* boring."

"This way, at least there are birds," Elsa said.

She tried to keep it light. Elsa always tried to keep it light. But to me, the tension from her was as radiant as a heat lamp. She had a long body, long limbs, a long face, long hair yanked back into a ponytail, and now seemed like an assembly of taut cables, topped off with eyes wide with apprehension.

So she was already primed for catastrophe. There wasn't much change in her demeanor when, in the middle of the broadcast, the guy doing the live feed stopped in mid-nod and touched his earpiece, scowled downward a moment, and said, "Can you repeat that?" and then glanced up with eyes like Elsa's just before the video went blank and the sound went dead.

I couldn't move. Not a twitch. That feeling you get right before a chair tips back too far? Exactly. A thousand miles away, here I was waiting for a shockwave, with no idea what it would be like. If the fabric of our reality came ripping apart one colliding light-speed particle at a time, would we know it was happening?

Would I have time to tell them I loved them?

I said it anyway, just in case, and was glad I did, even if it wasn't the last time.

Over the next few hours, nobody came forward to announce what went wrong, although the helicopter footage started to appear. There was no smoking rubble to see, but since there was familiarity in that, what actually was visible seemed far worse precisely because it was so strange and *un*familiar.

Thirty feet underground, the Fermilab's Main Injector accelerator was a two-mile ring, but was now a two-mile trench of collapsed earth, like a giant moat surrounding a newborn island of green grass and thick trees. The soil continued to subside for the next fourteen hours, as if something wasn't yet done sucking it down from underneath. There was speculation of having created a vacuum of unimaginable power. There were rumors that most of the subterranean infrastructure was simply gone.

And I wondered if it was possible to slam a door shut so hard you only end up widening the doorway.

There are days you wake up and, despite your best hopes and greatest efforts, nothing's changed. The wrong people still die.

Here's how you know that everything arrayed against you, seen and unseen, has won: *I can live with this*, you tell yourself. *What's the big deal, anyway? It just takes a little getting used to.*

That, and the fact that tears no longer seem as wet, as long as they keep running from other people's eyes.

Then there are the days you wake up and everything has changed. The world around you and the world beyond and the world beyond that. My sister could tell you all about this.

Sometimes you see it coming, sometimes not. As for which is better, which is worse . . . probably I should have given up ranking things as better or worse a long time ago. I just knew I recognized the sound of a brand new now in Jodi's voice that moment we heard it:

"Mommy?" she said from the foot of the bed. "Brook?"

I started to sit up, get up, but then Elsa's hand was on my arm, holding tight and pulling me back down.

"No. I don't want to know," she said. "Not yet."

Instead, she held out her other arm, beckoning for Jodi to join us, that whatever it was could wait. We could defy it that much, by a minute or a morning, as long as we were together. So Jodi crawled onto the bed, and if she'd been my daughter for real, she would have squeezed in between us, but instead she went for Elsa's arms alone, and I held her by proxy in this flimsy, makeshift shelter of curved walls and rounded doorways that I'd always feared would never be enough.

While at the window, through the curtains — I was sneaking a peek back over my shoulder—the dawn came on with a strange light the likes of which I'd never seen, with a tapestry of shouts and sirens in the distance, and every so often the sound of soft thumps on the roof.

And since it was true that you could see in every girl the woman she would be, I hoped the reverse might hold, as well. That in every woman you could see the shade of the little girl she'd been. I looked across the inches at Elsa as she, in turn, nuzzled Jodi, stared past the swirls of hair and ear, and the strong line of her jaw, which I imagined softening, plumping . . . and she was there, that girl, in all her varied years and phases.

I wished I'd known her then, too, back and back and back some more. I wished I could have known her all along. I wished I could've shared every dream. I wished I could have been the kind of protector who could hold off tomorrows.

Because we all still had so much growing yet to do.

Eventually we hit the point where not knowing was worse, and followed the lure of this strangely hued morning to the front windows to see how the world had changed. It was beautiful, in its way—breathtaking, even. I assumed the sky and sun were still there, but to our eyes they'd been replaced by something like the Northern Lights, only crisper and more malevolent.

The black lightning wasn't really black after all, not when there was this much of it. The luster it gave off was more of a deep lavender. It arced from branch to branch and tree to tree, as if it had found every angle made by everything that grew. It shot between the roofs of houses, from the peaks and eaves. Throughout the neighborhood the ground was littered with the bodies of birds and squirrels, and the pets that liked to roam at night, and wilder things that crept unseen—here a raccoon, there a mule deer, over there a skunk—and every now and again there came another thud on the roof as one more bird fell from a sky it was no longer fit to soar.

I wondered if Elsa saw things differently now, but now was too late. There were no guns in the house, no pills, because still, she thought suicide was a sin.

We came and went from the windows, but made no moves yet for the door, to get it over with. Because it was obvious that everything in sight that couldn't scream and die was being chipped away, reshaped, refined, faceted like diamonds in the rough.

Compound eyes would prefer it all that way, wouldn't they?

I drew them close, my girls, and skimmed their faces with my rounded fingertips—the bumps of their noses, the curves of their cheeks, the orbits of their clear brown eyes—and wondered what could be so alien that it would find such smooth contours so abhorrent.

The issue was not whether God had been a polygon all along.

The issue was what was going to happen now that He was.

As the world around us was remade in His image.

Cures for a Sickened World

Mr. Sunshine woke up with a hangover as hard-earned as I'd ever seen. When you're a road manager for touring bands, hangovers are as much a part of the routine as sound checks and the bleary-eyed boredom of all-night drives. After twenty-three years of this, I'd witnessed people coming to and sweating out the effects of everything that could possibly come in a bottle or a small, unmarked packet. But someone who'd been out for the last thirty-plus hours and two thousand miles . . . that was new.

A scheduled cocktail of injectable benzodiazepines will do that, keep you asleep or in a stupor for the duration.

Mr. Sunshine spent a few groggy minutes rubbing his head and blinking at the sky and the trees and the nearby slopes and snow-spattered peaks in the distance. He could see the barn from here, and maybe the cottage through the trees. He was getting the idea: He was rousing in the ass-end of nowhere.

He groped one hand across the ground for purchase, then tried to push himself upright, toppling back to the spring-lush meadow three times before he figured out the reason he couldn't stand was because his ankles were laced together with zip-tie cuffs.

Tomas tossed him a bottle of water. He had to be thirsty down there. Every pull at the bottle let him speak a little more clearly—though that didn't necessarily mean he had anything worth saying.

His given name was Derrick. Derrick Yardley. Mr. Sunshine was the byline he wrote under, obviously meant to be ironic. Guys like him are all about the irony. All about the smirk.

"First off, nobody's going to believe you," Tomas told him. "Nobody. Second, that's enough out of you for now. There's only so many times you can say 'what the fuck' before it gets old."

He was focusing, finally, but it was obvious that he still had no idea who was talking to him, much less who I was. Apparently he only knew what Tomas looked like onstage, or in promo photos, the persona that Tomas Lundvall called Ghast. At the moment, in camo pants and a black sweatshirt, he looked like a particularly intense hunter. He was clean-shaven again, too, ridding himself of his beard because it was starting to gray early, and he no longer wanted to waste the time or mental energy dyeing it.

"Third," Tomas said. "Normally I have no use for stupid dichotomies about how there are two kinds of people in the world. But just this once I'm going to make an exception. There *are* two kinds. There are those who'll be missed. And there's you."

"Where am I?" Derrick Yardley croaked.

When you don't know, one range of mountains looks about the same as another. All he would know was that the Cascades of Oregon looked nothing like downtown Chicago. There was a lot of distance between him and the roofie that first put him under; the sycophant at the club who wasn't what he thought she was.

"Let's call it a hell of your own making," Tomas said.

And I didn't know what I was thinking, signing off on this. That's the thing with bands like Balrog, guys like Tomas. You spend enough time on the road with them, and the craziness starts to seem reasonable. My whole thing was organization and logistics, making sure that people and gear got from Point A to Points B through Z, on time and intact. By the end of a fifty-four-date North American tour, even a kidnapping victim stops seeming out of the ordinary. It's just a prank. He's just one more piece of cargo, who needs the right kind of van.

"Sorry about the bad review," Derrick tried, but even he looked aware of how empty that was.

"I've had bad reviews before," Tomas said. "Do I look like someone who's going to let a bad review leave a mark on my day?"

Onstage, he looked like a charred nightmare. But even without his stage wear on—without the crusted old leather, without the war paint, or more accurately, corpse paint, without the blood—he was still an imposing figure. He stood tall and lanky, ropy muscle knotted over a towering framework of bone. His eyes and demeanor could project warmth when he was feeling it. He didn't appear to be feeling it now.

"But what you do, you can't call them reviews, can you? You don't seem to ever talk about what's there. You just react to the idea of its existence."

From one pocket, Tomas pulled out a couple of quartered pages, a printout from the online magazine that Derrick Yardley wrote for, a pop culture site called *The Pipeline*. Tomas dropped them into Derrick's lap.

"Go on," he said. "Read it. Out loud."

We waited for him to unfold the pages, and Derrick's face went the color of cream cheese. Now, finally, he knew.

"Hey. It's just . . . it's not . . ."

"Go *on*." This time, Tomas punted a boot tip into Derrick's ribs for emphasis. "Read it like you mean it."

"Come on, it was supposed to be funny."

"Then make me laugh."

He was squirming now, getting a full sense of how isolated we were. "I'm not really a performer."

"Apparently I'm not much of one, either, but that's never stopped me." Tomas gave him a harder kick that sent him scuttling back with a yelp.

Go on, just read the stupid thing, I willed him, and after a couple of shaky breaths, he smoothed the pages and got started:

> *Well, fuck me with a pentagram, points and all, but that's rich. If you're going to call your new album* Cures for a Sickened World, *maybe you might first want to make sure you haven't spent your previous nine albums establishing yourself as part of the disease.*

Derrick peeked over the top of the pages, to see if any more pain was coming, but Tomas only stood there as impassive as a granite carving, so he continued.

> *Listen, dipshits, I've got your cure right here. Kill yourselves! Do it onstage, film it as a how-to video for every other lame-ass band that would stoop to follow in your wake, and take as much of your poxy audience with you as you can, because if they're supporting you, then they're part of the disease, too. Do that much, and the rest of us will all feel so much better in the morning. Because, if I haven't made myself clear enough, the prospect of performing acupuncture on my testicles with rusty needles is preferable to the idea of waking up tomorrow suffering the knowledge that this is still a world afflicted with a Balrog infestation.*

The entire band had taken exception to this broadside, but none more so than Tomas. Co-founder. Rhythm guitar. Lead vocals. Main songwriter. He wasn't a solo artist, but it was very much *his* band.

> *Balrog. See how their name has R – O – G in it? They're missing a huge opportunity here, but I'll get back to that. For now, just look at these asshats. I know it hurts, but look at them. Take a good, hard look and keep trying to remember these are grown men. Allegedly. Grown men painted up like fucking rodeo clowns that the ancient Greeks might've sent into the fucking Labyrinth to distract the fucking Minotaur, because even the Minotaur would have to possess enough of a sense of humor to fall down fucking laughing. We get it, you twats! You're evil! With a capital Eve! Or something.*

Interesting that he chose to deride them for being grown men. Because, just based on his approach to so-called journalism, I would've thought it was coming from some smarmy douchebag still in college, or not long out. But he'd obviously seen his thirtieth birthday, maybe even his thirty-fifth.

> *I don't even know where to begin. So why bother. Just this: If this pack of sheep in wolves' clothing proves anything, it's that pretend-evil can still be a lucrative career path as long as your amp knobs go to eleven and you're lucky enough to find four other hairy dudes with the same birth defect that gives them a super scary scowl. Didn't these short-bus regulars have mothers around to warn them that their faces were going to freeze like that? Sorry, my bad. They didn't have mothers! They were born of goats!*

Okay, so the guys had gotten a laugh out of that part.

> *Speaking of goats, that's how much I don't want to hear any more from these shit-mongers. I'd rather be staked out spread-eagle while Satan's most incontinent he-goat takes a steaming infernal dump on my face than listen to another minute of this. I can almost guarantee that the sound of it would be more musical. I would rather scarf up a rotting platter of serpent roadkill scraped off the Highway To Hell, end-to-end, washed down with a bucket of demon jizz.*
> *Back to that R – O – G in their name: They've got it backwards. In the world of so-called extreme metal, you can't swing a ritually sacrificed*

cat without hitting some band with G – O – R in its name. I looked it up so you don't have to. Gorgoroth. Gorguts. Gorefest. Belphegor. Cirith Gorgor. Don't make me go on. So what I humbly suggest is that the brainiacs in Balrog change their name to Gorgonzola, so they can quit dicking around and lay claim, once and for all, to the title of Cheesiest Metal Band In The World.

And that was that. Mr. Sunshine folded the papers again and, when Tomas made no move to take them back, set them on the grass, lightly, as if hoping they might vanish in a puff of fairy dust.

Tomas stood with folded arms. "You never even listened to the review copy, did you?"

Getting through the reading without another kick in the ribs seemed to have given him a little fire. "You're so fucking wise and all-seeing, what do *you* think?"

"I think it was a rhetorical question," Tomas said. "They're all like that, aren't they? Your 'reviews.' Every line trying to be more insulting than the line before. I got bored looking for anything different before I could find it."

"You'd be looking a long time."

"I'm curious," Tomas said. "Did you aspire to be a sham all along, or did that just happen? There's no other word for it. Sham. You occupy a position that implies objectivity, but your mind is made up about something before it even occurs to the creator to create it. Your hatred isn't just cowardly. It's lazy."

One corner of his mouth curled into a self-satisfied sneer. "It's consistent."

I'd already figured him for the kind that couldn't lose. The readers who lapped it up, thought his shtick was the funniest thing they'd ever seen, that was pure validation. But so were the ones who thought he was a plague, and took the time to say so. The more pique in their comments, the better. Attention was attention. He was the kind who'd find scorn just as nutritious as praise.

As long as no one was actually holding him accountable.

So when Tomas squatted next to him, Derrick began to squirm with unease again. Tomas could go a long time without blinking. Silence didn't bother him. Eye contact didn't bother him. He was a master of simmering hostility.

"The hatreds I have, I come by them honestly. They're considered," he said. "Let me tell you a few of them. I hate smug little hipsters in retro cardigans and thick black glasses. I hate disingenuousness. I hate people who say 'my bad.' I hate people who lack the courage to back up their professed convictions." He pushed his hair back out of his eyes so nothing got in the way of the glare. "All my hatreds, they're earned. I've put the time and effort into cultivating them. They're pure. But you . . . you dishonor that ethos."

Now, finally, Tomas took back the printout, although he didn't unfold it. What he needed was already in memory. "Do you get off when people quote your own words back to you? 'I'd rather be staked out spread-eagle while Satan's most incontinent he-goat takes a steaming infernal dump on my face than listen to another minute of this.' When I read that, I didn't see hyperbole. What I saw was you laying down a challenge for yourself."

Tomas stood again, as, moment by moment, Derrick started to put the pieces together.

"You may find this disappointing, but Satan is about as real to me as Saturday morning cartoons. You might've even picked up on that if you'd bothered to look into the album a little."

Still weakened by his hours of sedation, Derrick was in no condition to put up a fight as Tomas dragged him by his bound ankles halfway across the meadow, where a quartet of iron stakes was already driven into the ground.

"But I do believe in goats," he said. "We'll start there."

There wasn't much of a struggle even when Tomas lashed him, limb by limb, to the stakes, although he had plenty to say to Tomas's back as he walked away.

It was when Tomas reappeared, leading the shaggy, horned thing from the barn, that Mr. Sunshine really started to squeal.

ŏ

The band was based out of Seattle, but hardly anyone knew about this remote place that Tomas Lundvall owned high in the Cascades, across the border in Oregon. The rest of the band knew. I assumed there was a real estate agent who knew. Now I knew. And, naturally, so did Mr. Sunshine—not exactly trustworthy inner circle material.

"When you told him that nobody's going to believe him," I said to Tomas later, inside the cottage's kitchen. "I need to know you mean that. I need to know there's not going to be blowback from this once we get him back home. This is the kind of thing that the term 'federal crime' was invented for."

Tomas looked amused. "Isn't it a little late to start looking for assurances now?"

"I trusted you on faith when that's all there was time for. I never said details wouldn't matter."

"No, you didn't," Tomas said. "He can talk all he wants, if he's not too afraid to do it, and it's only going to sound like so much delirium. He'll never know where he's been, exactly. You'll drop him off outside an emergency room, and with everything in his system, it's only going to look like he's been on a bender for a few days. While he's gone, there's somebody in Chicago still using his ATM card once or twice a day. And his phone. There are pictures on the phone from a couple nights ago at the club, and he's having a good time. There'll be a few more by the end, too blurry to make out. It's all time-stamped. He'll have it all with him again by the time he lands at the ER." Tomas seesawed his upturned hands like a balance scale. "Which would you believe?"

A bit later, as the sun was starting to fade, Tomas went out to hose Derrick Yardley down and get him moved from the meadow into the barn for the night and take him a plate of food.

He was quiet now, had either screamed himself hoarse or given it up hours ago as pointless. There was no one coming, no one to hear. The nearest neighbor seemed to be at least a mile away, along winding roads, while the hills and valleys would contain almost any mortal sound.

This was land made to shield miseries from view, and keep them secret.

The place seemed as if it might have first sprung up as some long-ago settler's homestead. The barn may have even been original, minus repairs, although the cottage was clearly newer, a replacement built on the foundation of the original. Its rustic nature seemed more by design than scarcity, and it was solid through and through, built of heavy timber, with a lot of stonework, too, including a rock fireplace that would have fit right into a hunting lodge.

As a getaway home, it was an unusual choice. Retreats, for those who could afford them, usually meant luxury and ostentation, oceanside villas and penthouses thirty floors above the great unwashed. I didn't have to be Tomas Lundvall's accountant to know that, even after seventeen years of second-tier success in the music industry, he didn't have that kind of money . . . but then, he didn't have those kind of aspirations, either. He had no use for a place that others would look at and envy. Instead, I figured, he would need a place to exile himself from the stink of humanity.

He was back in the cottage after a few minutes.

"You're just going to leave him by himself all night?" I asked.

"If you're worried he's going to get away, you can join him and keep watch. As for myself, I have faith in the chain and the anvil."

I wasn't expecting that. "You've chained him to an anvil?"

"It's a very big anvil."

He looked at me then as if studying me. It was blatant. All these years of working for the band, and I'd never managed to decide if he did that with people because he was assessing what made them tick, or forever looking for some quality that he himself was missing.

"End of the tour leg and all," he said. We had a month of precious downtime before heading to Europe for the summer festival circuit. "Are you sure you don't have someplace better you'd rather be?"

"Apparently I don't. But you know that already." I'd married late, and even then, because of all the time on the road, it hadn't lasted. I wouldn't try again until I was a stationary target, if there was someone out there who would even have me by then. "You did ask for my help with this, remember."

"It wasn't part of your job description. You could have said no."

"I figured you would've gone through with it anyway. I didn't want to hear about it going wrong because somebody else fucked it up for you."

He appeared pleased by this. Although even I wasn't sure if it came out of a warped sense of loyalty or just the challenge of it, to see if I could get away with this madness. Had I really become that bored with life? That desperate to avoid going home to an empty apartment before helming the next leg of the tour got me out again?

"Having second thoughts?" Tomas asked.

"It's just a lot of trouble to go to, and a lot of risk, to get back at some douchebag who said nasty things about you."

He looked at me as if I didn't understand anything. "It's not about revenge. Punishment is only a means to an end. He needs to be educated. He needs to be corrected. If I feed his own words straight back to him, then maybe he'll realize he should use them better in the future."

"And you don't think this is a little excessive?"

"The stove has to be hot if you're ever going to learn not to touch it."

"I've only ever heard that about kids," I said. "He's not a kid."

"Exactly the point," Tomas said. "He's not a child, but he's still no better than a baby who's just learned to stand up and reach a wall so he can smear it with whatever he's managed to scoop out of his diaper. There have always been people like that, but they were ignored by most people who recognized them for what they were. Now . . . now they set the parameters of conversation. They've found each other. They try to outdo each other in pointlessness, and their last allegiance is to the truth, or even accuracy, if that means it would take three more minutes of their time to check. They set the agenda. They have a voice that drowns out whatever remains of basic intelligence and actual thought. They're the human equivalent of a car alarm that won't shut off."

"And you're educating exactly one of them."

But Tomas seemed unconcerned by the math. "Even the longest symphony starts with a single note."

���

Day two: *"I would rather scarf up a rotting platter of serpent roadkill scraped off the Highway To Hell, tail-to-head, washed down with a bucket of demon jizz."*

Tomas held him to it.

It wasn't anything I wanted to see, so I'm not sure what he had prepared, exactly. In contrast to yesterday's ordeal, this was something that required Derrick's active participation, rather than passively lying on the ground as it happened to him. Which explained the Taser that Tomas took with him to the barn. Cooperation now meant coercion.

So no, I didn't want to see it. But I could hear it.

Mr. Sunshine was in stronger voice this morning, and I could clearly make out what he was saying when he shouted that he would listen to the music, for fuck's sake, he would listen all day, it had just been figures of speech, exaggeration for laughs, just empty words, nothing any sane person would take seriously.

He still hadn't grasped that it wasn't about that at all.

From the kitchen table in the cottage, still working on morning coffee, I found it a one-sided conversation. I couldn't hear anything Tomas said. I once heard him profess that he wanted whatever he had to say to be worth straining to hear, and so it must have been in the barn. Wrath, with him, was not colored red. It was the blue of glacial ice.

All I could hear were the sounds of pain, and soon, the sounds of sickness, of gagging and retching, broken up by wails of utter despair. It came and went in cycles, as if after a certain point Derrick Yardley was too stricken to go on, and Tomas allowed him time to recover before resuming the putrefied feast where he'd left off.

It went on all morning.

You could call such things a taint on what was otherwise a glorious late spring morning in an unspoiled paradise. But they only augmented and enhanced something that was already there.

I didn't like this place.

After twenty-three years of reducing world travel to a daily grind, I'd developed a sensitivity to places. I don't know how, it just accrued, an awareness of what certain places had absorbed and what they exuded. Clubs and concert halls radiate an energy from all the performances they've hosted. Hotel rooms are mostly soulless and anonymous, but now and then I've stepped into one that's toxic, and known that something very bad happened there.

Here, though, it wasn't the cottage so much as everything else.

I could step outside and come face-to-face with it, in any direction, until it drove me back inside for the illusion of refuge. It was in the hills, and the way they seemed to leer down in curiosity and contempt. It was in the trees, and the way so many of them grew twisted even though they were sheltered from the corkscrewing gales that would have done this to them. It was in the rocks and the way they weathered, as if some truer, crueler form were trying to break through. It was in the shadows, and the way they seemed to hide something, all but its piercing and inquisitive gaze. It was in the wind, and how it fell just short of an intelligible whisper that I feared I would learn to decipher if I stayed long enough. And when a torrential shower swept through that afternoon, it was in that, too, if only because, in conspiracy, it cloaked everything else and gave me room to doubt, wondering if it wasn't just my imagination. Three months of exhaustion, jitters, and road nerves catching up with me all at once.

"What made you buy this place?" I asked Tomas that evening, as the sun went down on another terrible day in Derrick Yardley's life, and we sat before the fireplace sharing wine.

"Don't you know anything about real estate?" he said. "Location, location, location."

"You know what I mean."

Tomas nodded, studying me again. "So you're cueing into it already. I wondered. I can't say what most people are like because hardly anyone has been here and I want to keep it that way."

"Somebody had to bring you up here the first time. What about them?"

"It was just another normal transaction for both of us. I sensed it was a good fit. I sensed that very strongly, but I couldn't have explained why. I try not to be arrogant enough to think whatever's in this place might have sprung up or settled here because of me, but it's hard. That huge rock star ego, you know." I caught a strong whiff of sarcasm. "Maybe some of both. We fed each other."

I imagined him here alone, doing the things you would expect anyone in his line of work to do: recharging, decompressing after spending months meeting the demands of other people, writing new songs. Exploring, too; there was a strong undercurrent of nature worship in Balrog's music.

But I could also envision him doing the sorts of things that you might *not* expect, not if you dismissed the band as nothing but creatures of hollow image.

They and I went back far enough that I took it for granted that their look, their sound, their lyrics, everything, was more than mere theater. While theater was important, it was still a reflection of something real. Ghast wasn't just Tomas Lundvall's stage name, a character he put on along with the leather and paint. It was a part of him.

"Balrog isn't a band that's about exorcising demons," I once overheard him say in a backstage interview. *"What we're about is communicating with them."*

Sure, that could only be more myth making. Yet I believed he meant it. I was just never sure exactly where the lines were with him.

So I had to ask: "Am I even going to be taking Yardley back to Chicago?"

Tomas didn't seem surprised by the question. "Why would you still be here if you weren't?"

"To give me time to get used to the idea," I said. "You couldn't have me just drop him off and turn around, because that would be admitting upfront that he wasn't going to be leaving here alive."

Tomas swirled his wine and held it up to the fire, mesmerized by its red glow. "Would it be a problem if he didn't?"

"I didn't sign on for that."

"I know. The question is, what would you do about it?"

Could I take Tomas, if it came to that—was this the bottom-line question here? Almost certainly I could. Yes, he was imposing, and almost fifteen years younger, but I was the size of a movie Viking and still had the muscle from back when I started as a roadie, along with fifteen years more experience brawling. We could both put a hurt on each other.

"I don't know," I finally said. "Yet."

"Neither do I."

"You sure you're not just playing coy?" I almost jumped when, in the fireplace, a knot of wood went off like a rifle shot, in a shower of sparks. "I know what that review says. I know what's coming tomorrow. Go through with that, and you'd be sending him back with physical damage."

"And your point is . . . ?"

"That makes it harder to square with him losing a week to a binge. He doesn't just have a wild story now. He's got real injuries, and oh hey look, they're exactly what he wrote about in his review of *you*. You'd be stupid to send him back with actual evidence. You know that."

"You're right. So maybe I shouldn't."

When shit gets real—I'd heard this expression for years, but had never felt the full weight of it until now. Finally, I recognized the real reason why I'd gone along with Tomas's plan. I was in awe. Who would be crazy enough, committed enough, to do something like this? I could think of only two scenes. Some rappers, maybe. But it wouldn't be this elaborate. Just quick payback, all about the disrespect. And then there was the darkest fringe of extreme metal, where they thought the devil was real.

Except Tomas didn't believe in him, either.

"Why don't we name it," I said. "Sacrifice? Is that what you're thinking about?"

"That's too simplistic a concept. But for the sake of discussion . . . okay."

"Weren't you just saying yesterday that the devil is as real to you as Saturday morning cartoons?"

"That's why I called it too simplistic a concept." He lingered a moment, as if he'd never had to explain himself before. "The way I see it, there are things infinitely older than any childish conceptions of god and some adversarial devil. There's only chaos, and the manifest forms that come out of it, and the fleeting intelligences that guide them. Magnitudes of order rise and fall, and all we are are the building blocks it uses to make things and then topple them over to start again."

He stared out at the dusk, and the only sound was the fire and, beyond the open window, the dripping of the newly ended rain from the eaves.

"I can't say for certain what's going on in this place," he told me. "If it's that the membrane between chaos and order is thin here. Or if it's because, right here, the process has already reached its height on one side of the fulcrum, and now it's started to drop the other way. . . .

"I just know that, if you're willing to put in the work, you can play with the other blocks."

°₀°

Later that evening I went out to the barn to see Derrick Yardley for myself. He was a disheveled figure huddled against a rough wall under the tepid light of a dangling sixty-watt bulb. Something else dangled from another crossbeam, low enough to hang tools on, but this one I had to stare at until I comprehended that it was the ragged, meat-stripped skeleton of a snake longer than my arm. The barn interior stank of bile and decay.

Across the dirt floor, in a pen, yesterday's goat munched happily on sweet grass. No place smells bad to a goat.

Mr. Sunshine was as degraded a human being as I'd ever seen. A thick leather cuff was snug around one ankle and a ten-foot chain anchored him to a huge, honest-to-god anvil that looked like it had been around since the formation of the earth. In a radius around him, and on nearly every square inch of him, was the evidence of violent and explosive sickness.

"Fuck you, too," he croaked as I approached.

I offered him a plastic bottle with the clinical look of something that had come from behind a pharmacy counter.

He eyed it with suspicion. "What's that? Something else for me to puke up?"

"It's an antibiotic. Liquid ampicillin. He thought it would be a good idea." I looked at the chunks and splatters in the dirt. "Considering."

He grabbed it, uncapped and sniffed it, and took a sip.

"Not all at once. Just a swig or two every few hours."

"I know how antibiotics work. Jesus. Now, if I just had a clock to tell me when a few hours have gone by." He rolled his eyes. "Are we done here?"

I respected that he wasn't feigning gratitude, trying to win me over, beg. No Stockholm Syndrome for him. It was business as usual: all spite, all the time.

"You've got a style to what you do. No denying that. I'm just curious why. Why take that approach?"

He stared at me like I'd spoken gibberish. "*Why . . . ?* I don't get the question."

He really didn't, did he? "What do you get out of it?"

Again, more incredulity. That little open-mouthed, side-to-side headshake when someone can't believe he's hearing such idiocy. "I get more hits than anyone else there. More page views, more sticky-time, more link follow-throughs. I win."

Okay, I thought. Just as calm and clearheaded as could be.

Fuck this guy.

Maybe 90% of everything really was crap. I don't know. But he'd made it his life's mission to punish people for even trying, regardless of the outcome.

"Yeah," I said. "We're done here."

Then, finally, I looked up into the hayloft, because I was starting to feel gutless for avoiding it, telling myself that whatever I'd heard shifting around up there was just a rat. Or a barn owl. Or a snake the size of a fire hose. Or any of the other manifest forms allowed by chaos. In that moment it looked like all of them, all at once, at least what I could make out from filling in the gaps between the shadows . . . until even the shadows unraveled, and perhaps there had been nothing to see after all.

So maybe Derrick should've paid attention to the music. He might have learned something: that in stirring up all that hate, he should've expected to someday summon up something worse than a simple ass-kicking.

Day three: *"The prospect of performing acupuncture on my testicles with rusty needles is preferable to the idea of waking up tomorrow suffering the knowledge that this is still a world afflicted with a Balrog infestation."*

When you're in, you might as well go all the way.

The day threw another downpour at us, and I was glad of it, the sonic insulation between my ears and what was going on inside the barn. The shrieking rose and fell, sometimes cutting through lulls in the rain. But for the most part, it sounded far away, the kind of screams you're willing to dismiss as coming from a neighbor's TV.

At what point had I stopped seeing Derrick Yardley as human? At what point had this become irreversible? I had a long drive ahead to mull that over. My luggage was packed and ready to go, not that it took long. I'd been traveling light for twenty-three years . . . lighter than ever, now that I seemed to have left my conscience behind. Maybe I would find it at home. Maybe I'd lost it along some road I would never recognize if I traveled it again.

I stepped out the cottage's back door and stood beneath the awning, staring through the watery curtain at the mouth of the barn. There was no sound but the rain. I wished Mr. Sunshine a quick death. A *meaningful* death, as one of the building blocks of chaos and order.

I didn't know what Tomas's specific intentions were, and he hadn't said, maybe because he didn't want the embarrassment of committing to something he couldn't deliver. Some kind of transfiguration, maybe. Some act of will that would send ripples through what he called the noosphere . . . the sphere of human thought. The world according to Ghast.

By now I was considering that I'd been wrong all along about what Tomas's stage persona meant to him. I could see it, finally. It wasn't so much that Ghast was a part of him but, rather, something he aspired to be.

And then he came out of the barn and walked up to me, standing there looking hesitant and soaked to the skin. His hair hung to his chest in sodden tendrils and he had to blink water from his eyes. Just another wet guy in the rain.

"Are you ready to take him back?" he asked.

"If that's what you want," I said. "What changed your mind?"

He started to say something, then shook his head. Nothing he wanted to articulate, to admit to. He just pushed past me, inside the cottage.

"I need to get the BZD, put him to sleep for the trip," was all he said.

A part of me was relieved—the better part, I hoped. But another part of me was deeply disappointed. Because I was curious. I'd felt the currents churning around us, in the fabric of earth and rock and trees and sky. I'd seen *something* in the hayloft, be it manifest form or fleeting intelligence. I was ready to believe that nothing might be true, that everything might be permitted. Tomas—or Ghast—had persuaded me of that much.

So I wondered what would've happened next, if his nerve had held out a little longer.

Syringe in hand, Tomas—just Tomas—pushed past me again and returned to the barn.

And the rain hammered down.

I knew him well enough to suspect that this surrender of plans was something he'd want to handle without an audience, so I waited a couple minutes. Then a couple more. How long did it take to sedate one guy, anyway?

At least it doesn't take any special powers to know when something's not right.

So now it was my turn to get soaked to the skin.

I found Tomas on the barn floor, beneath the anvil. The enormous anvil heavy enough to anchor a captive in place for three days. His chest and ribcage were as caved in as the bones of a serpent run over on the highway. But it hadn't only hit him there. He'd taken a blow to the head, as well.

Put it this way: He no longer needed makeup to look like a nightmare.

And Derrick Yardley? He was as far away as ten feet of chain would allow, every last inch of it, wide-eyed and pressed against a support beam as if he wanted to merge with it. He was trying to talk. He just wasn't there yet.

I looked up at the hayloft.

By day, the barn's shadows retreated higher, and I followed them, drawn by movement that I sensed more than saw. But something was up there, and whether it scurried or flowed I couldn't say, this malformed collective of rat and owl and snake . . . and now goat. The pen was empty. I followed its path up the sloping underside of the roof, until it reached the peak and kept going through the angled juncture, as if squeezing through a crack in time.

With nothing more to see overhead, I looked at Tomas again, not merely killed, but demolished. If I had to ascribe motivation to something beyond understanding, I'd have to say it was disappointed in him.

"It said it didn't have much time," Derrick Yardley finally got out, in a halting voice. "It said I'm more their servant than he ever was. What did it mean?"

He looked at me, pleading yet cunning, as if I were supposed to have his answers.

"What did it mean?"

When I left, I closed the barn door behind me, and would've chained it shut, except the only chain I knew of was attached to Derrick Yardley already. I had a sense that it wouldn't matter for long, anyway.

As the rain let up, anyone could feel it in the air.

THE SAME DEEP WATERS AS YOU

A STORY OF H.P. LOVECRAFT'S INNSMOUTH

They were down to the last leg of the trip, miles of iron-gray ocean skimming three hundred feet below the helicopter, and she was regretting ever having said yes. The rocky coastline of northern Washington slid out from beneath them and there they were, suspended over a sea as forbidding as the day itself. If they crashed, the water would claim them for its own long before anyone could find them.

Kerry had never warmed to the sea—now less than ever.

Had saying no even been an option? *The Department of Homeland Security would like to enlist your help as a consultant*, was what the pitch boiled down to, and the pair who'd come to her door yesterday looked genetically incapable of processing the word no. They couldn't tell her what. They couldn't tell her where. They could only tell her to dress warm. Better be ready for rain, too.

The sole scenario Kerry could think of was that someone wanted her insights into a more intuitive way to train dogs, maybe. Or something a little more out there, something to do with birds, dolphins, apes, horses . . . a plan that some questionable genius had devised to exploit some animal ability that they wanted to know how to tap. She'd been less compelled by the appeal to patriotism than simply wanting to make whatever they were doing go as well as possible for the animals.

But this? No one could ever have imagined this.

The island began to waver into view through the film of rain that streaked and jittered along the window, a triangular patch of uninviting rocks and evergreens and secrecy. They were down there.

Since before her parents were born, they'd always been down there.

It had begun before dawn: an uncomfortably silent car ride from her ranch to the airport in Missoula, a flight across Montana and Washington, touchdown at Sea-Tac, and the helicopter the rest of the way. Just before this final leg of the journey was the point they took her phone from her and searched her bag. Straight off the plane and fresh on the tarmac, bypassing the terminal entirely, Kerry was turned over to a man who introduced himself as Colonel Daniel Escovedo and said he was in charge of the facility they were going to.

"You'll be dealing exclusively with me from now on," he told her. His brown scalp was speckled with rain. If his hair were any shorter, you wouldn't have been able to say he had hair at all. "Are you having fun yet?"

"Not really, no." So far, this had been like agreeing to her own kidnapping.

They were strapped in and back in the air in minutes, just the two of them in the passenger cabin, knee-to-knee in facing seats.

"There's been a lot of haggling about how much to tell you," Escovedo said as she watched the ground fall away again. "Anyone who gets involved with this, in any capacity, they're working on a need-to-know basis. If it's not relevant to the job they're doing, then they just don't know. Or what they think they know isn't necessarily the truth, but it's enough to satisfy them."

Kerry studied him as he spoke. He was older than she first thought, maybe in his mid-fifties, with a decade and a half on her, but he had the lightly lined face of someone who didn't smile much. He would still be a terror in his seventies. You could just tell.

"What ultimately got decided for you is full disclosure. Which is to say, you'll know as much as I do. You're not going to know what you're looking for, or whether or not it's relevant, if you've got no context for it. But here's the first thing you need to wrap your head around: What you're going to see, most of the last fifteen presidents haven't been aware of."

She felt a plunge in her stomach as distinct as if their altitude had plummeted. "How is that possible? If he's the commander-in-chief, doesn't he . . . ?"

Escovedo shook his head. "Need-to-know. There are security levels above the office of president. Politicians come and go. Career military and intelligence, we stick around."

"And I'm none of the above."

It was quickly getting frightening, this inner circle business. If she'd ever thought she would feel privileged, privy to something so hidden, now she knew better. There really were things you didn't want to know, because the privilege came with too much of a cost.

"Sometimes exceptions have to be made," he said, then didn't even blink at the next part. "And I really wish there was a nicer way to tell you this, but if you divulge any of what you see, you'll want to think very hard about that first. Do that, and it's going to ruin your life. First, nobody's going to believe you anyway. All it will do is make you a laughingstock. Before long, you'll lose your TV show. You'll lose credibility in what a lot of people see as a fringe field anyway. Beyond that . . . do I even need to go beyond that?"

Tabby—that was her first thought. Only thought, really. They would try to see that Tabitha was taken from her. The custody fight three years ago had been bruising enough, Mason doing his about-face on what he'd once found so beguiling about her, now trying to use it as a weapon, to make her seem unfit, unstable. *She talks to animals, your honor. She thinks they talk back.*

"I'm just the messenger," Colonel Escovedo said. "Okay?"

She wished she were better at conversations like this. Conversations in general. Oh, to not be intimidated by this. Oh, to look him in the eye and leave no doubt that he'd have to do better than that to scare her. To have just the right words to make him feel smaller, like the bully he was.

"I'm assuming you've heard of Guantanamo Bay in Cuba? What it's for?"

"Yes," she said in a hush. Okay, this was the ultimate threat. Say the wrong thing and she'd disappear from Montana, or Los Angeles, and reappear there, in the prison where there was no timetable for getting out. Just her and 160-odd suspected terrorists.

His eyes crinkled, almost a smile. "Try not to look so horrified. The threat part, that ended before I mentioned Gitmo."

Had it been that obvious? How nice she could amuse him this fine, rainy day.

"Where we're going is an older version of Guantanamo Bay," Escovedo went on. "It's the home of the most long-term enemy combatants ever held in U.S. custody."

"How long is long-term?"

"They've been detained since 1928."

She had to let that sink in. And was beyond guessing what she could bring to the table. Animals, that was her thing, it had always been her thing. Not P.O.W.s, least of all those whose capture dated back to the decade after the First World War.

"Are you sure you have the right person?" she asked.

"Kerry Larimer. Star of *The Animal Whisperer*, a modest but consistent hit on the Discovery Channel, currently shooting its fourth season. Which

you got after gaining a reputation as a behavioral specialist for rich people's exotic pets. You *look* like her."

"Okay, then." Surrender. They knew who they wanted. "How many prisoners?" From that long ago, it was a wonder there were any left at all.

"Sixty-three."

Everything about this kept slithering out of her grasp. "They'd be over a hundred years old by now. What possible danger could they pose? How could anyone justify—?"

The colonel raised a hand. "It sounds appalling, I agree. But what you need to understand from this point forward is that, regardless of how or when they were born, it's doubtful that they're still human."

He pulled an iPad from his valise and handed it over, and here, finally, was the tipping point when the world forever changed. One photo, that was all it took. There were more—she must've flipped through a dozen—but really, the first one had been enough. Of course it wasn't human. It was a travesty of human. All the others were just evolutionary insult upon injury.

"What you see there is what you get," he said. "Have you ever heard of a town in Massachusetts called Innsmouth?"

Kerry shook her head. "I don't think so."

"No reason you should've. It's a little pisshole seaport whose best days were already behind it by the time of the Civil War. In the winter of 1927--28, there was a series of raids there, jointly conducted by the FBI and U.S. Army, with naval support. Officially—remember, this was during Prohibition—it was to shut down bootlegging operations bringing whiskey down the coast from Canada. The truth . . ." He took back the iPad from her nerveless fingers. "Nothing explains the truth better than seeing it with your own eyes."

"You can't talk to them. That's what this is about, isn't it?" she said. "You can't communicate with them, and you think I can."

Escovedo smiled, and until now, she didn't think he had it in him. "It must be true about you, then. You're psychic after all."

"Is it that they can't talk, or won't?"

"That's never been satisfactorily determined," he said. "The ones who still looked more or less human when they were taken prisoner, they could, and did. But they didn't stay that way. Human, I mean. That's the way this mutation works." He tapped the iPad. "What you saw there is the result of decades of change. Most of them were brought in like that already. The rest eventually got there. And the changes go more than skin deep. Their throats are different now. On the inside. Maybe this keeps them from speaking in a way that you and I would find intelligible, or maybe it doesn't but they're really consistent about pretending it does, because they're all on the same page. They do communicate with each other, that's a given. They've been recorded extensively doing that, and the sounds have been analyzed to exhaustion, and the consensus is that these sounds have their own syntax. The same way bird songs do. Just not as nice to listen to."

"If they've been under your roof all this time, they've spent almost a century away from whatever culture they had where they came from. All that would be gone now, wouldn't it? The world's changed so much since then they wouldn't even recognize it," she said. "You're not doing science. You're doing national security. What I don't understand is why it's so important to communicate with them after all this time."

"All those changes you're talking about, that stops at the seashore. Drop them in the ocean and they'd feel right at home." He zipped the iPad back into his valise. "Whatever they might've had to say in 1928, that doesn't matter. Or '48, or '88. It's what we need to know *now* that's created a sense of urgency."

Once the helicopter had set down on the island, Kerry hadn't even left the cabin before thinking she'd never been to a more miserable place in her life. Rocky and rain-lashed, miles off the mainland, it was buffeted by winds that snapped from one direction and then another, so that the pines that grew here didn't know which way to go, twisted until they seemed to lean and leer with ill intent.

"It's not always like this," Escovedo assured her. "Sometimes there's sleet, too."

It was the size of a large shopping plaza, a skewed triangular shape, with a helipad and boat dock on one point, and a scattering of outbuildings clustered along another, including what she assumed were offices and barracks for those unfortunate enough to have been assigned to duty here, everything laced together by a network of roads and pathways.

It was dominated, though, by a hulking brick monstrosity that looked exactly like what it was—a vintage relic of a prison—although it could pass for other things, too: an old factory or power plant, or, more likely, a wartime fortress, a leftover outpost from an era when the west coast feared the Japanese fleet. It had been built in 1942, Escovedo told her. No one would have questioned the need for it at the time, and since then, people were simply used to it, if they even knew it was there. Boaters might be curious, but the shoreline was studded at intervals with signs, and she

imagined that whatever they said was enough to repel the inquisitive—that, and the triple rows of fencing crowned with loops of razor wire.

Inside her rain slicker, Kerry yanked the hood's drawstring tight and leaned into the needles of rain. October—it was only October. Imagine this place in January. Of course it didn't bother the colonel one bit. They were halfway along the path to the outbuildings when she turned to him and tugged the edge of her hood aside.

"I'm not psychic," she told him. "You called me that in the helicopter. That's not how I look at what I do."

"Noted," he said, noncommittal and unconcerned.

"I'm serious. If you're going to bring me out here, to this place, it's important to me that you understand what I do, and aren't snickering about it behind my back."

"You're here, aren't you? Obviously somebody high up the chain of command has faith in you."

That gave her pause to consider. This wouldn't have been a lark on their part. Bringing in a civilian on something most presidents hadn't known about would never have been done on a hunch—see if this works, and if it doesn't, no harm done. She would've been vetted, extensively, and she wondered how they'd done it. Coming up with pretenses to interview past clients, perhaps, or people who'd appeared on *The Animal Whisperer*, to ascertain that they really were the just-folks they were purported to be, and that it wasn't scripted; that she genuinely had done for them what she was supposed to.

"What about you, though? Have you seen the show?"

"I got forwarded the season one DVDs. I watched the first couple episodes." He grew more thoughtful, less official. "The polar bear at the Cleveland Zoo, that was interesting. That's 1500 pounds of apex predator you're dealing with. And you went in there without so much as a stick of wood between you and it. Just because it was having OCD issues? That takes either a big pair of balls or a serious case of stupid. And I don't think you're stupid."

"That's a start, I guess," she said. "Is that particular episode why I'm here? You figured since I did that, I wouldn't spook easily with these prisoners of yours?"

"I imagine it was factored in." The gravel that lined the path crunched underfoot for several paces before he spoke again. "If you don't think of yourself as psychic, what is it, then? How *does* it work?"

"I don't really know." Kerry had always dreaded the question, because she'd never been good at answering it. "It's been there as far back as I can remember, and I've gotten better at it, but I think that's just through the doing. It's a sense as much as anything. But not like sight or smell or taste. I compare it to balance. Can you explain how your sense of balance works?"

He cut her a sideways glance, betraying nothing, but she saw he didn't have a clue. "Mine? You're on a need-to-know basis here, remember."

Very good. Very dry. Escovedo was probably more fun than he let on.

"Right," she said. "Everybody else's, then. Most people have no idea. It's so intrinsic they take it for granted. A few may know it has to do with the inner ear. And a few of them, that it's centered in the vestibular apparatus, those three tiny loops full of fluid. One for up, one for down, one for forward and backward. But you don't need to know any of that to walk like we are now and not fall over. Well . . . that's what the animal thing is like for me. It's there, but I don't know the mechanism behind it."

He mused this over for several paces. "So that's your way of dodging the question?"

Kerry grinned at the ground. "It usually works."

"It's a good smokescreen. Really, though."

"Really? It's . . ." She drew the word out, a soft hiss while gathering her thoughts. "A combination of things. It's like receiving emotions, feelings, sensory impressions, mental imagery, either still or with motion. Any or all. Sometimes it's not even that, it's just . . . pure knowing, is the best way I know to phrase it."

"Pure knowing?" He sounded skeptical.

"Have you been in combat?"

"Yes."

"Then even if you haven't experienced it yourself, I'd be surprised if you haven't seen it or heard about it in people you trust—a strong sense that you should be very careful in that building, or approaching that next rise. They can't point to anything concrete to explain why. They just know. And they're often right."

Escovedo nodded. "Put in that context, it makes sense."

"Plus, for what it's worth, they ran a functional MRI on me, just for fun. That's on the season two DVD bonuses. Apparently the language center of my brain is very highly developed. Ninety-eighth percentile, something like that. So maybe that has something to do with it."

"Interesting," Escovedo said, and nothing more, so she decided to quit while she was ahead.

The path curved and split before them, and though they weren't taking the left-hand branch to the prison, still, the closer they drew to it, darkened by rain and contemptuous of the wind, the greater the edifice seemed to

loom over everything else on the island. It was like something grown from the sea, an iceberg of brick, with the worst of it hidden from view. When the wind blew just right, it carried with it a smell of fish, generations of them, as if left to spoil and never cleaned up.

Kerry stared past it, to the sea surging all the way to the horizon. This was an island only if you looked at it from out there. Simple, then: *Don't ever go out there.*

She'd never had a problem with swimming pools. You could see through those. Lakes, oceans, rivers . . . these were something entirely different. These were *dark* waters, full of secrets and unintended tombs. Shipwrecks, sunken airplanes, houses at the bottom of flooded valleys . . . they were sepulchers of dread, trapped in another world where they so plainly did not belong.

Not unlike the way she was feeling this very moment.

❦

As she looked around Colonel Escovedo's office in the administrative building, it seemed almost as much a cell as anything they could have over at the prison. It was without windows, so the lighting was all artificial, fluorescent and unflattering. It aged him, and she didn't want to think what it had to be doing to her own appearance. In one corner, a dehumidifier chugged away, but the air still felt heavy and damp. Day in, day out, it must have been like working in a mine.

"Here's the situation. Why now," he said. "Their behavior over there, it's been pretty much unchanged ever since they were moved to this installation. With one exception. Late summer, 1997, for about a month. I wasn't here then, but according to the records, it was like . . ." He paused, groping for the right words. "A hive mind. Like they were a single organism. They spent most of their time aligned to a precise angle to the southwest. The commanding officer at the time mentioned in his reports that it was like they were waiting for something. Inhumanly patient, just waiting. Then, eventually, they stopped and everything went back to normal."

"Until now?" she said.

"Nine days ago. They're doing it again."

"Did anybody figure out what was special about that month?"

"We think so. It took years, though. Three years before some analyst made the connection, and even then, you know, it's still a lucky accident. Maybe you've heard how it is with these agencies, they don't talk to each other, don't share notes. You've got a key here, and a lock on the other side of the world, and nobody in the middle who knows enough to put the two together. It's better now than it used to be, but it took the 9/11 attacks to get them to even *think* about correlating intel better."

"So what happened that summer?"

"Just listen," he said, and spun in his chair to the hardware behind him.

She'd been wondering about that anyway. Considering how functional his office was, it seemed not merely excessive, but out of character, that Escovedo would have an array of what looked to be high-end audio-video components, all feeding into a pair of three-way speakers and a subwoofer. He dialed in a sound file on the LCD of one of the rack modules, then thumbed the play button.

At first it was soothing, a muted drone both airy and deep, a lonely noise that some movie's sound designer might have used to suggest the desolation of outer space. But no, this wasn't about space. It had to be the sea, this all led back to the sea. It was the sound of deep waters, the black depths where sunlight never reached.

Then came a new sound, deeper than deep, a slow eruption digging its way free of the drone, climbing in pitch, rising, rising, then plummeting back to leave her once more with the sound of the void. After moments of anticipation, it happened again, like a roar from an abyss, and prickled the fine hairs on the back of her neck—a primal response, but then, what was more primal than the ocean and the threats beneath its waves?

This was why she'd never liked the sea. This never knowing what was there, until it was upon you.

"Heard enough?" Escovedo asked, and seemed amused at her mute nod. "*That* happened. Their hive mind behavior coincided with that."

"What *was* it?"

"That's the big question. It was recorded several times during the summer of 1997, then never again. Since 1960, we've had the oceans bugged for sound, basically. We've got them full of microphones that we put there to listen for Soviet submarines, when we thought it was a possibility we'd be going to war with them. They're down hundreds of feet, along an ocean layer called the sound channel. For sound conductivity, it's the Goldilocks zone—it's just right. After the Cold War was over, these mic networks were decommissioned from military use and turned over for scientific research. Whales, seismic events, underwater volcanoes, that sort of thing. Most of it, it's instantly identifiable. The people whose job it is to listen to what the mics pick up, 99.99 percent of the time they know exactly what they've got because the sounds conform to signature patterns, and they're just so familiar.

"But every so often they get one they can't identify. It doesn't fit any known pattern. So they give it a cute name and it stays a mystery. This one, they called it the 'Bloop.' Makes it sound like a kid farting in the bathtub, doesn't it?"

She pointed at the speakers. "An awfully big kid and an awfully big tub."

"Now you're getting ahead of me. The Bloop's point of origin was calculated to be in the south Pacific . . . maybe not coincidentally, not far from Polynesia, which is generally conceded as the place of origin for what eventually came to be known in Massachusetts as 'the Innsmouth look.' Some outside influence was brought home from Polynesia in the 1800s during a series of trading expeditions by a sea captain named Obed Marsh."

"Are you talking about a disease, or a genetic abnormality?"

Escovedo slapped one hand onto a sheaf of bound papers lying on one side of his desk. "You can be the judge of that. I've got a summary here for you to look over, before you get started tomorrow. It'll give you more background on the town and its history. The whole thing's a knotted-up tangle of fact and rumor and local legend and god knows what all, but it's not my job to sort out what's what. I've got enough on my plate sticking with facts, and the fact is, I'm in charge of keeping sixty-three of these proto-human monstrosities hidden from the world, and I know they're cued into something anomalous, but I don't know what. The other fact is, the last time they acted like this was fifteen years ago, while those mics were picking up one of the loudest sounds ever recorded on the planet."

"How loud was it?"

"Every time that sound went off, it wasn't just a local event. It was picked up over a span of five thousand kilometers."

The thought made her head swim. Something with that much power behind it . . . there could be nothing good about it. Something that loud was the sound of death, of cataclysm and extinction events. It was the sound of an asteroid strike, of a volcano not just erupting, but vaporizing a land mass—Krakatoa, the island of Thera. She imagined standing here, past the northwestern edge of the continental U.S., and hearing something happen in New York. Okay, sound traveled better in water than in air, but still—*three thousand miles.*

"Despite that," Escovedo said, "the analysts say it most closely matches a profile of something alive."

"A whale?" There couldn't be anything bigger, not for millions of years.

The colonel shook his head. "Keep going. Somebody who briefed me on this compared it to a blue whale plugged in and running through the amplifier stacks at every show Metallica has ever played, all at once. She also said that what they captured probably wasn't even the whole sound. That it's likely that a lot of frequencies and details got naturally filtered out along the way."

"Whatever it was . . . there have to be theories."

"Sure. Just nothing that fits with all the known pieces."

"Is the sound occurring again?"

"No. We don't know what they're cueing in on this time."

He pointed at the prison. Even though he couldn't see it, because there were no windows, and now she wondered if he didn't prefer it that way. Block it out with walls, and maybe for a few minutes at a time he could pretend he was somewhere else, assigned to some other duty.

"But *they* do," he said. "Those abominations over there know. We just need to find the key to getting them to tell us."

She was billeted in what Colonel Escovedo called the guest barracks, the only visitor in a building that could accommodate eight in privacy, sixteen if they doubled up. Visitors, Kerry figured, would be a rare occurrence here, and the place felt that way, little lived in and not much used. The rain had strengthened closer to evening and beat hard on the low roof, a lonely sound that built from room to vacant room.

When she heard the deep thump of the helicopter rotors pick up, then recede into the sky—having waited, apparently, until it was clear she would be staying—she felt unaccountably abandoned, stranded with no way off this outpost that lay beyond not just the rim of civilization, but beyond the frontiers of even her expanded sense of life, of humans and animals and what passed between them.

Every now and then she heard someone outside, crunching past on foot or on an all-terrain four-wheeler. If she looked, they were reduced to dark, indistinct smears wavering in the water that sluiced down the windows. She had the run of most of the island if she wanted, although that was mainly just a license to get soaked under the sky. The buildings were forbidden, other than her quarters and the admin office, and, of course, the prison, as long as she was being escorted. And, apart for the colonel, she was apparently expected to pretend to be the invisible woman. She and the duty personnel were off-limits to each other. She wasn't to speak to them, and they were under orders not to speak with her.

They didn't know the truth—it was the only explanation that made sense. They didn't know, because they didn't need to. They'd been fed a cover story. Maybe they believed they were guarding the maddened survivors of a disease, a genetic mutation, an industrial accident or something that had fallen from space and that did terrible things to DNA. Maybe they'd all been fed a different lie, so that if they got together to compare notes they wouldn't know which to believe.

For that matter, she wasn't sure she did, either.

First things first, though: She set up a framed photo of Tabitha on a table out in the barracks' common room, shot over the summer when they'd gone horseback riding in the Sawtooth Range. Her daughter's sixth birthday. Rarely was a picture snapped in which Tabby wasn't beaming, giddy with life, but this was one of them, her little face rapt with focus. Still in the saddle, she was leaning forward, hugging the mare's neck, her braided hair a blonde stripe along the chestnut hide, and it looked for all the world as if the two of them were sharing a secret.

The photo would be her beacon, her lighthouse shining from home.

She fixed a mug of hot cocoa in the kitchenette, then settled into one of the chairs with the summary report that Escovedo had sent with her.

Except for its cold, matter-of-fact tone, it read like bizarre fiction. If she hadn't seen the photos, she wouldn't have believed it: a series of raids in an isolated Massachusetts seaport that swept up more than two hundred residents, most of whose appearances exhibited combinations of human, ichthyoid, and amphibian traits. The Innsmouth look had been well-known to the neighboring towns for at least two generations—"an unsavory haven of inbreeding and circus folk," according to a derisive comment culled from an Ipswich newspaper of the era—but even then, Innsmouth had been careful to put forward the best face it possibly could. Which meant, in most cases, residents still on the low side of middle-age . . . at least when it came to the families that had a few decades' worth of roots in the town, rather than its more recent newcomers.

With age came change so drastic that the affected people gradually lost all resemblance to who they'd been as children and young adults, eventually reaching the point that they let themselves be seen only by each other, taking care to hide from public view in a warren of dilapidated homes, warehouses, and limestone caverns that honeycombed the area.

One page of the report displayed a sequence of photos of what was ostensibly the same person, identified as Giles Shapleigh, eighteen years old when detained in 1928. He'd been a handsome kid in the first photo, and if he had nothing to smile about when it was taken, you could at least see the potential for a roguish, cockeyed grin. By his twenty-fifth year, he'd visibly aged, his hair receded and thinning, and after seven years of captivity he had the sullen look of a convict. By thirty, he was bald as a cue ball, and his skull had seemed to narrow. By thirty-five, his jowls had widened enough to render his neck almost nonexistent, giving him a bullet-headed appearance that she found all the more unnerving for his dead-eyed stare.

By the time he was sixty, with astronauts not long on the moon, there was nothing left to connect Giles Shapleigh with who or what he'd been, neither his identity nor his species. Still, though, his transformation wasn't yet complete.

He was merely catching up to his friends, neighbors, and relatives. By the time of those Prohibition-era raids, most of the others had been this way for years—decades, some of them. Although they aged, they didn't seem to weaken and, while they could be killed, if merely left to themselves, they most certainly didn't die.

They could languish, though. As those first years went on, with the Innsmouth prisoners scattered throughout a handful of remote quarantine facilities across New England, it became obvious that they didn't do well in the kind of environment reserved for normal prisoners: barred cells, bright lights, exercise yards . . . *dryness*. Some of them developed a skin condition that resembled powdery mildew, a white, dusty crust that spread across them in patches. There was a genuine fear that, whatever it was, it might jump from captives to captors, and prove more virulent in wholly human hosts, although this never happened.

Thus it was decided: They didn't need a standard prison so much as they needed their own zoo. That they got it was something she found strangely heartening. What was missing from the report, presumably because she had no need to know, was *why*.

While she didn't want to admit it, Kerry had no illusions—the expedient thing would've been to kill them off. No one would have known, and undoubtedly there would've been those who found it an easy order to carry out. It was wartime, and if war proved anything, it proved how simple it was to dehumanize people even when they looked just like you. This was 1942, and this was already happening on an industrial scale across Europe. These people from Innsmouth would have had few advocates. To merely look at them was to feel revulsion, to sense a challenge to everything you thought you knew about the world, about what could and couldn't be. Most people would look at them and think they deserved to die. They were an insult to existence, to cherished beliefs.

Yet they lived. They'd outlived the men who'd rounded them up, and their first jailers, and most of their jailers since. They'd outlived everyone

who'd opted to keep them a secret down through the generations . . . yet for what?

Perhaps morality *had* factored into the decision to keep them alive, but she doubted morality had weighed heaviest. Maybe, paradoxically, it had been done out of fear. They may have rounded up over two hundred of Innsmouth's strangest, but many more had escaped—by most accounts, fleeing into the harbor, then the ocean beyond. To exterminate these captives because they were unnatural would be to throw away the greatest resource they might possess in case they ever faced these beings again, under worse circumstances.

Full disclosure, Escovedo had promised. She would know as much as he did. But when she finished the report along with the cocoa, she had no faith whatsoever that she was on par with the colonel, or that even he'd been told the half of it himself.

How much did a man need to know, really, to be a glorified prison warden?

Questions nagged, starting with the numbers. She slung on her coat and headed back out into the rain, even colder now, as it needled down from a dusk descending on the island like a dark gray blanket. She found the colonel still in his office, and supposed by now he was used to people dripping on his floor.

"What happened to rest of them?" she asked. "Your report says there were over two hundred to start with. And that this place was built to house up to three hundred. So I guess somebody thought more might turn up. But you're down to sixty-three. And they don't die of natural causes. So what happened to the others?"

"What does it matter? For your purposes, I mean. What you're here to do."

"Did you know that animals understand the idea of extermination? Wolves do. Dogs at the pound do. Cattle do, once they get to the slaughterhouse pens. They may not be able to articulate it, but they pick up on it. From miles away, sometimes, they can pick up on it." She felt a chilly drop of water slither down her forehead. "I don't know about fish or reptiles. But whatever humanity may still exist in these prisoners of yours, I wouldn't be surprised if it's left them just as sensitive to the concept of extermination, or worse."

He looked at her blankly, waiting for more. He didn't get it.

"For all I know, you're sending me in there as the latest interrogator who wants to find out the best way to commit genocide on the rest of their kind. *That's* why it matters. Is that how they're going to see me?"

Escovedo looked at her for a long time, his gaze fixated on her, not moving, just studying her increasing unease as she tried to divine what he was thinking. If he was angry, or disappointed, or considering sending her home before she'd even set foot in the prison. He stared so long she had no idea which it could be, until she realized that the stare *was* the point.

"They've got these eyes," he said. "They don't blink. They've got no white part to them anymore, so you don't know where they're looking, exactly. It's more like looking into a mirror than another eye. A mirror that makes you want to look away. So . . . how they'll *see* you?" he said, with a quick shake of his head and a hopeless snort of a laugh. "I have no idea *what* they see."

She wondered how long he'd been in this command. If he would ever get used to the presence of such an alien enemy. If any of them did, his predecessors, back to the beginning. That much she could see.

"Like I said, I stick with facts," he said. "I can tell you this much: When you've got a discovery like *them*, you have to expect that every so often another one or two of them are going to disappear into the system."

"The system," she said. "What does that mean?"

"You were right, we don't do science here. But they do in other places," he told her. "You can't be naïve enough to think research means spending the day watching them crawl around and writing down what they had for lunch."

Naïve? No. Kerry supposed she had suspected before she'd even slogged over here to ask. Just to make sure. You didn't have to be naïve to hope for better.

She carried the answer into dreams that night, where it became excruciatingly obvious that, while the Innsmouth prisoners may have lost the ability to speak in any known language, when properly motivated, they could still shriek.

⚨

Morning traded the rain for fog, lots of it, a chilly cloud that had settled over the island before dawn. There was no more sky and sea, no more distance, just whatever lay a few feet in front of her, and endless gray beyond. Without the gravel pathways, she was afraid she might've lost her bearings, maybe wander to the edge of the island. Tangle herself in razor wire, and hang there and die before anyone noticed.

She could feel it now, the channels open and her deepest intuition rising: This was the worst place she'd ever been, and she couldn't tell which side bore the greater blame.

With breakfast in her belly and coffee in hand, she met Escovedo at his office, so he could escort her to the corner of the island where the prison

stood facing west, looking out over the sea. There would be no more land until Asia. Immense, made of brick so saturated with wet air that its walls looked slimed, the prison emerged from the mist like a sunken ship.

What would it be like, she wondered, to enter a place and not come out for seventy years? What would that do to one's mind? Were they even sane now? Or did they merely view this as a brief interruption in their lives? Unless they were murdered outright—a possibility—their lifespans were indefinite. Maybe they knew that time was their ally. Time would kill their captors, generation by generation, while they went on. Time would bring down every wall. All terrestrial life might go extinct, while they went on.

As long as they could make it those last few dozen yards to the sea.

"Have any of them ever escaped from here?" she asked.

"No."

"Don't you find that odd? I do. Hasn't most every prison had at least one escape over seventy years?"

"Not this one. It doesn't run like a regular prison. The inmates don't work. There's no kitchen, no laundry trucks, no freedom to tunnel. They don't get visitors. So we all just spend all day looking at each other." He paused in the arched, inset doorway, his finger on the call button that would summon the guards inside to open up. "If you want my unfiltered opinion, those of us who pulled this duty are the real prisoners."

Inside, it was all gates and checkpoints, the drab institutional hallways saturated with a lingering smell of fish. *Them*, she was smelling *them*. Like people who spent their workdays around death and decay, the soldiers here would carry it home in their pores. You had to pity them that. They would be smelling it after a year of showers, whether it was there or not.

Stairs, finally, a series of flights that seemed to follow the curvature of some central core. It deposited them near the top of the building, on an observation deck. Every vantage point around the retaining wall, particularly a trio of guard posts, overlooked an enormous pit, like an abandoned rock quarry. Flat terraces and rounded pillows of stone rose here and there out of a pool of murky seawater. Along the walls, rough stairways led up to three tiers of rooms, cells without bars.

This wasn't a prison where the inmates would need to be protected from each other. They were all on the same side down there, prisoners of an undeclared war.

Above the pit, the roof was louvered, so apparently, although closed now, it could be opened. They could see the sky. They would have air and rain. Sunshine, if that still meant anything to them.

The water, she'd learned from last night's briefing paper, was no stagnant pool. It was continually refreshed, with drains along the bottom and grated pipes midway up the walls that periodically spewed a gusher like a tidal surge. Decades of this had streaked the walls with darker stains, each like a ragged brush stroke straight down from the rusty grate to the foaming surface of their makeshift sea.

Fish even lived in it, and why not? The prisoners had to eat.

Not at the moment, though. They lined the rocks in groups, as many as would fit on any given surface, sitting, squatting, facing the unseen ocean in eerily perfect alignment to one another.

"What do you make of it?" he asked.

Kerry thought of fish she'd watched in commercial aquariums, in nature documentaries, fish swimming in their thousands, singularly directed, and then, in an instantaneous response to some stimulus, changing directions in perfect unison. "I would say they're schooling."

From where they'd entered the observation deck, she could see only their backs, and began to circle the retaining wall for a better view.

Their basic shapes looked human, but the details were all wrong. Their skin ranged from dusky gray to light green, with pale bellies—dappled sometimes, an effect like sunlight through water—and rubbery looking even from here, as though it would be slick as a wetsuit to the touch, at least the areas that hadn't gone hard and scaly. Some wore the remnants of clothing, although she doubted anything would hold up long in the water and rocks, while others chose to go entirely without. They were finned and they were spiny, no two quite the same, and their hands webbed between the fingers, their feet ridiculously outsized. Their smooth heads were uncommonly narrow, all of them, but still more human than not. Their faces, though, were ghastly. These were faces for another world, with thick-lipped mouths made to gulp water, and eyes to peer through the murky gloom of the deep. Their noses were all but gone, just vestigial nubs now, flattened and slitted. The females' breasts had been similarly subsumed, down to little more than hard bumps.

She clutched the top of the wall until her fingernails began to bend. Not even photographs could truly prepare you for seeing them in the flesh.

I wish I'd never known, she thought. *I can never be the same again.*

"You want to just pick one at random, see where it goes?" Escovedo asked.

"How do you see this working? We haven't talked about that," she said. "What, you pull one of them out and put us in a room together, each of us on either side of a table?"

"Do you have any better ideas?"

"It seems so artificial. The environment of an interrogation room, I mean. I need them open, if that makes sense. Their minds, open. A room like that, it's like you're doing everything you can to close them off from the start."

"Well, I'm not sending you in down there into the middle of all sixty-three of them, if that's what you're getting at. I have no idea how they'd react, and there's no way I could guarantee your safety."

She glanced at the guard posts, only now registering why they were so perfectly triangulated. Nothing was out of reach of their rifles.

"And you don't want to set up a situation where you'd have to open fire on the group, right?"

"It would be counterproductive."

"Then you pick one," she said. "You know them better than I do."

⟨⊢

If the Innsmouth prisoners still had a sense of patriarchy, then Escovedo must have decided to start her at the top of their pecking order.

The one they brought her was named Barnabas Marsh, if he even had a use anymore for a name that none of his kind could speak. Maybe names only served the convenience of their captors now, although if any name still carried weight, it would be the name of Marsh. Barnabas was the grandson of Obed Marsh, the ship's captain who, as village legend held, had sailed to strange places above the sea and below it, and brought back both the DNA and partnerships that had altered the course of Innsmouth's history.

Barnabas had been old even when taken prisoner, and by human terms he was now beyond ancient. She tried not to think of him as monstrous, but no other word wanted to settle on him, on any of them. Marsh, though, she found all the more monstrous for the fact that she could see in him the puffed-up, barrel-chested bearing of a once-domineering man who'd never forgotten who and what he had been.

Behind the wattles of his expanded neck, gills rippled with indignation. The thick lips, wider than any human mouth she'd ever seen, stretched downward at each corner in a permanent, magisterial sneer.

He waddled when he walked, as if no longer made for the land, and when the two guards in suits of body armor deposited him in the room, he looked her up and down, then shuffled in as if resigned to tolerating her until this interruption was over. He stopped long enough to give the table and chairs in the center of the room a scornful glance, then continued to the corner, where he slid to the floor with a shoulder on each wall, the angle where they met giving room for his sharp-spined back.

She took the floor as well.

"I believe you can understand me. Every word," Kerry said. "You either can't or won't speak the way you did for the first decades of your life, but I can't think of any reason why you shouldn't still understand me. And that puts you way ahead of all the rest of God's creatures I've managed to communicate with."

He looked at her with his bulging dark eyes, and Escovedo had been right. It was a disconcertingly inhuman gaze, not even mammalian. It wasn't anthropomorphizing to say that mammals—dogs, cats, even a plethora of wilder beasts—had often looked at her with a kind of warmth. But *this*, these eyes . . . they were cold, with a remote scrutiny that she sensed regarded her as lesser in every way.

The room's air, cool to begin with, seemed to chill even more as her skin crawled with an urge to put distance between them. Could he sense that she feared him? Maybe he took this as a given. That he could be dangerous was obvious—the closer you looked, the more he seemed covered with sharp points, none more lethal than the tips of his stubby fingers. But she had to trust the prison staff to ensure her safety. While there was no guard in here to make the energy worse than it was already, they were being watched on a closed-circuit camera. If Marsh threatened her, the room would be flooded with a gas that would put them both out in seconds. She'd wake up with a headache, and Marsh would wake up back in the pit.

And nothing would be accomplished.

"I say 'God's creatures' because I don't know how else to think of you," she said. "I know how *they* think of you. They think you're all aberrations. Unnatural. Not that I'm telling you anything you probably haven't already overheard from them every day for more than eighty years."

And did that catch his interest, even a little? If the subtle tilt of his head meant anything, maybe it did.

"But if you exist, entire families of you, colonies of you, then you can't be an aberration. You're within the realm of nature's possibilities."

Until this moment, she'd had no idea what she would say to him. With animals, she was accustomed to speaking without much concern for what exactly she said. It was more how she said it. Like very young children, animals cued in on tone, not language. They nearly always seemed to favor a higher-pitched voice. They responded to touch.

None of which was going to work here.

But Barnabas Marsh was a presence, and a powerful one, radiant with a sense of age. She kept speaking to him, seeking a way through the gulf between them, the same as she always did. No matter what the species, there always seemed to be a way, always something to which she could attune—an image, a sound, a taste, some heightened sense that overwhelmed her and, once she regained her equilibrium, let her use it as the key in the door that would open the way for more.

She spoke to him of the sea, the most obvious thing, because no matter what the differences between them, they had that much in common. It flowed in each of them, water and salt, and they'd both come from it; he was just closer to returning, was all. Soon she felt the pull of tides, the tug of currents, the cold wet draw of gravity luring down, down, down to greater depths, then the equipoise of pressure, and where once it might've crushed, now it comforted, a cold cocoon that was both a blanket and a world, tingling along her skin with news coming from a thousand leagues in every direction—

And with a start she realized that the sea hadn't been her idea at all.

She'd only followed where he led. Whether Marsh meant to or not.

Kerry looked him in his cold, inhuman eyes, not knowing quite what lay behind them, until she began to get a sense that the sea was *all* that lay behind them. The sea was all he thought of, all he wanted, all that mattered, a yearning so focused that she truly doubted she could slip past it to ferret out what was so special about *now*. What they all sensed happening *now*, just as they had fifteen years ago.

It was all one and the same, of course, bound inextricably together, but first they had to reclaim the sea.

△

And so it went the rest of the day, with one after another of this sad parade of prisoners, until she'd seen nearly twenty of them. Nothing that she would've dared call progress, just inklings of impressions, snippets of sensations, none of it coalescing into a meaningful whole, and all of it subsumed beneath a churning ache to return to the sea. It was their defense against her, and she doubted they even knew it.

Whatever was different about her, whatever had enabled her to whisper with creatures that she and the rest of the world found more appealing, it wasn't made to penetrate a human-born despair that had hardened over most of a century.

There was little light remaining in the day when she left the prison in defeat, and little enough to begin with. It was now a colorless world of approaching darkness. She walked a straight line, sense of direction lost in the clammy mist that clung to her as surely as the permeating smell of the prisoners. She knew she had to come to the island's edge eventually, and if she saw another human being before tomorrow, it would be too soon.

Escovedo found her anyway, and she had to assume he'd been following all along. Just letting her get some time and distance before, what, her debriefing? Kerry stood facing the water as it slopped against a shoreline of rocks the size of piled skulls, her hand clutching the inner fence. By now it seemed that the island was less a prison than a concentration camp.

"For what it's worth," the colonel said, "I didn't expect it to go well the first day."

"What makes you think a second day is going to go any better?"

"Rapport?" He lifted a Thermos, uncapped it, and it steamed in the air. "But rapport takes time."

"Time." She rattled the fence. "Will I even be leaving here?"

"I hope that's a joke." He poured into the Thermos cup without asking and gave it to her. "Here. The cold can sneak up on you out like this."

She sipped at the cup, coffee, not the best she'd ever had but far from the worst. It warmed her, though, and that was a plus. "Let me ask you something. Have they ever bred? Either here or wherever they were held before? Have *any* of them bred?"

"No. Why do you ask?"

"It's something I was picking up on from a few of them. The urge. You know it when you feel it. Across species, it's a great common denominator."

"I don't know what to tell you, other than that they haven't."

"Don't you find that odd?"

"I find the whole situation odd."

"What I mean is, even pandas in captivity manage to get pregnant once in a while."

"I've just never really thought about it."

"You regard them as prisoners, you *have* to, I get that. And the females don't look all that different from the males. But suppose they looked more like normal men and women. What would you expect if you had a prison with a mixed-gender population that had unrestricted access to each other?"

"I get your point, but . . ." He wasn't stonewalling, she could tell. He genuinely had never considered this. Because he'd never had to. "Wouldn't it be that they're too old?"

"I thought it was already established that once they get like this, age is no longer a factor. But even if it was, Giles Shapleigh wasn't too old when they first grabbed him. He was eighteen. Out of more than two hundred, he can't have been the only young one. You remember what the urge was like when you were eighteen?"

Escovedo grunted a laugh. "Every chance I get."

"Only he's never acted on it. None of them have."

"A fact that I can't say distresses me."

"It's just . . ." she said, then shut up. She had her answer. They'd never bred. Wanted to, maybe felt driven to, but hadn't. Perhaps captivity affected their fertility, or short-circuited the urge from becoming action.

Or maybe it was just an incredible act of discipline. They had to realize what would happen to their offspring. They would never be allowed to keep them, raise them. Their children would face a future of tests and vivisection. Even monstrosities would want better for their babies.

"I have an observation to make," Kerry said. "It's not going to go any better tomorrow, or the day after that. Not if you want me to keep doing it like today. It's like they have this shell around them." She tipped the coffee to her lips and eyed him over the rim, and he was impossible to read. "Should I go on?"

"I'm listening."

"You're right, rapport takes time. But it takes more than that. Your prisoners may have something beyond human senses, but they still have human intellects. More or less. It feels overlaid with something else, and it's not anything good, but fundamentally they haven't stopped being human, and they need to be dealt with that way. Not like they're entirely animals."

She stopped a moment to gauge him, and saw that she at least hadn't lost him. Although she'd not proposed anything yet.

"If they *looked* more human to you, don't you think the way you'd be trying to establish rapport would be to treat them more like human beings?" she said. "I read the news. I watch TV. I've heard the arguments about torture. For and against. I know what they are. The main thing I took away is that when you consult the people who've been good at getting reliable information from prisoners, they'll tell you they did it by being humane. Which includes letting the prisoner have something he wants, or loves. There was a captured German officer in World War Two who loved chess. He opened up after his interrogator started playing chess with him. That's all it took."

"I don't think these things are going to be interested in board games."

"No. But there's something every one of them wants," she said. "There's something they love more than anything else in the world."

And why does it have to be the same thing I dread?

When she told him how they might be able to use that to their advantage, she expected Escovedo to say no, out of the question. Instead, he thought it over for all of five seconds and said yes.

"I don't like it, but we need to fast-track this," he said. "We don't just eyeball their alignment in the pit, you know. We measure it with a laser. That's how we know how precisely oriented they are. And since last night they've shifted. Whatever they're cued in on has moved north."

▽

The next morning, dawn came as dawn should, the sky clear and the fog blown away and the sun an actual presence over the horizon. After two days of being scarcely able to see fifty feet in front of her, it seemed as if she could see forever. There was something joyously liberating in it. After just two days.

So what was it going to feel like for Barnabas Marsh to experience the ocean for the first time in more than eighty years? The true sea, not the simulation of it siphoned off and pumped into the pit. Restrained by a makeshift leash, yes, three riflemen ready to shoot from the shore, that too, three more ready to shoot from the parapet of the prison . . . but it would still be the sea.

That it would be Marsh they would try this with was inevitable. It might not be safe and they might get only one chance at this. He was cunning, she had to assume, but he was the oldest by far, and a direct descendant of the man who'd brought this destiny to Innsmouth in the first place. He would have the deepest reservoir of knowledge.

And, maybe, the arrogance to want to share it, and gloat.

Kerry was waiting by the shallows when they brought him down, at one end of a long chain whose other end was padlocked to the frame of a four-wheel all-terrain cycle that puttered along behind him—he might have been able to throw men off balance in a tug-of-war, but not this.

Although he had plenty of slack, Marsh paused a few yards from the water's edge, stopping to stare out at the shimmering expanse of sea. The rest of them might have seen mistrust in his hesitation, or savoring the moment, but neither of these felt right. *Reacquainting*, she thought. *That's it.*

He trudged forward then, trailing chain, and as he neared the water, he cast a curious look at her, standing there in a slick blue wetsuit they'd outfitted her with, face-mask and snorkel in her hand. It gave him pause again, and in whatever bit of Marsh that was still human, she saw that he understood, realized who was responsible for this.

Gratitude, though, was not part of his nature. Once in the water, he vanished in moments, marked only by the clattering of his chain along the rocks.

She'd thought it wise to allow Marsh several minutes alone, just himself and the sea. They were midway through it when Escovedo joined her at the water's edge.

"You sure you're up for this?" he said. "It's obvious how much you don't like the idea, even if it was yours."

She glanced over at Marsh's chain, now still. "I don't like to see anything captive when it has the capacity to lament its conditions."

"That's not what I mean. If you think you've been keeping it under wraps that you've got a problem with water, you haven't. I could spot it two days ago, soon as we left the mainland behind."

She grinned down at her flippers, sheepish. Busted. "Don't worry. I'll deal."

"But you still know how to snorkel . . . ?"

"How else are you going to get over a phobia?" She laughed, needing to, and it helped. "It went great in the heated indoor pool."

She fitted the mask over her face and popped in the snorkel's mouthpiece, and went in after Marsh. Calves, knees . . . every step forward was an effort, so she thought of Tabby. *The sooner I get results, the quicker I'll get home.* Thighs, waist . . . then she was in Marsh's world, unnerved by the fear that she would find him waiting for her, tooth and claw, ready to rip through her in a final act of defiance.

But he was nowhere near her. She floated facedown, kicking lightly and visually tracking the chain down the slope of the shoreline, until she saw it disappear over a drop-off into a well that was several feet deeper. *There he is.* She hovered in place, staring down at Marsh as he luxuriated in the water. Ecstatic—there was no other word for him. Twisting, turning, undulating, the chain only a minor impediment, he would shoot up near the surface, then turn and plunge back to the bottom, rolling in the murk he stirred up, doing it again, again, again. His joyous abandon was like a child's.

He saw her and stilled, floating midway between surface and sand, a sight from a nightmare, worse than a shark because even in this world he was so utterly alien.

And it was never going to get any less unnerving. She sucked in a deep breath through the snorkel, then plunged downward, keeping a bit of distance between them as she swam to the bottom.

Two minutes and then some—that was how long she could hold her breath.

Kerry homed in on a loose rock that looked heavy enough to counter her buoyancy, then checked the dive compass strapped to her wrist like an oversized watch. She wrestled the wave-smoothed stone into her lap and sat cross-legged on the bottom, matching as precisely as she could the latest of the southwesterly alignments that had so captivated Marsh and the other sixty-two of them. Sitting on the seabed with the Pacific alive around her, muffled in her ears and receding into a blue-green haze, as she half expected something even worse than Marsh to come swimming straight at her out of the void.

Somewhere above and behind her, he was watching.

She stayed down until her lungs began to ache, then pushed free of the stone and rose to the surface, where she purged the snorkel with a gust of spent air, then flipped to return to the seabed. Closer this time, mere feet between her and Marsh as she settled again, no longer needing the compass—she found her bearing naturally, and time began to slow, and so did her heartbeat in spite of the fear, then the fear was gone, washed away in the currents that tugged at her like temptations.

Up again, down again, and it felt as if she were staying below longer each time, her capacity for breath expanding to fill the need, until she was all but on the outside of herself looking in, marveling at this creature she'd become, amphibious, neither of the land nor the water, yet belonging to both. She lived in a bubble of breath in an infinite now, lungs satiated, awareness creeping forward along this trajectory she was aligned with, as if it were a cable that spanned the seas, and if she could only follow it, she would learn the secrets it withheld from all but the initiated—

And he was there, Barnabas Marsh a looming presence drifting alongside her. If there was anything to read in his cold face, his unplumbed eyes, it was curiosity. She had become something he'd never seen before, something between his enemies and his people, and changing by the moment.

She peered at him, nothing between them now but the thin plastic window of her mask and a few nourishing inches of water.

What is it that's out there? she asked. *Tell me. I want to know. I want to understand.*

It was true—she did. She would wonder even if she hadn't been asked to. She would wonder every day for the rest of her life. Her existence would be marred by not knowing.

Tell me what it is that lies beyond. . . .

She saw it then, a thought like a whisper become an echo, as it began to build on itself, the occlusions between worlds parting in swirls of ink and oceans. And there was so *much* of it, this was something that couldn't be—who could build such a thing, and who would dream of finding it *here*, at depths that might crush a submarine—then she realized that all she was seeing was one wall, one mighty wall, built of blocks the size of boxcars, a feat that couldn't be equaled even on land. She knew without seeing the whole that it spanned miles, that if this tiny prison island could sink into it, it would be lost forever, an insignificant patch of pebbles and mud to what lived there—

And she was wholly herself again, with a desperate need to breathe.

Kerry wrestled the rock off her lap for the last time, kicking for a surface as far away as the sun. As she shot past Barnabas Marsh she was gripped by a terror that he would seize her ankle to pull her back down.

But she knew she could fight that, so what he did was worse somehow, nothing she knew that he *could* do, and maybe none of these unsuspecting men on the island did, either. It was what sound could be if sound were needles, a piercing skirl that ripped through her like an electric shock and clapped her ears as sharply as a pressure wave. She spun in the water, not knowing up from down, and when she stabilized and saw Marsh nearby, she realized he wasn't even directing this at her. She was just a bystander who got in the way. Instead, he was facing out to sea, the greater sea, unleashing this sound into the abyss.

She floundered to the surface and broke through, graceless and gasping, and heard Colonel Escovedo shout a command, and in the next instant heard the roar of an engine as the four-wheeler went racing up the rock-strewn slope of the island's western edge. The chain snapped taut, and moments later Marsh burst from the shallows in a spray of surf and foam, dragged twisting up onto the beach. Someone fired a shot, and someone else another, and of course no one heard her calling from nearly a hundred feet out, treading water now, and they were all shooting, so none of them heard her cry out that they had the wrong idea. But bullets first, questions later, she supposed.

His blood was still red. She had to admit, she'd wondered.

▽

It took the rest of the morning before she was ready to be debriefed, and Escovedo let her have it, didn't press for too much, too soon. She needed to be warm again, needed to get past the shock of seeing Barnabas Marsh shot to pieces on the beach. Repellent though he was, she'd still linked with him in her way, whispered back and forth, and he'd been alive one minute, among the oldest living beings on the earth, then dead the next.

She ached from the sound he'd made, as if every muscle and organ inside her had been snapped like a rubber band. Her head throbbed with the assault on her ears.

In the colonel's office, finally, behind closed doors, Kerry told him of the colossal ruins somewhere far beneath the sea.

"Does any of that even make sense?" she asked. "It doesn't to me. It felt real enough at the time, but now . . . it has to have been a dream of his. Or maybe Marsh was insane. How could anyone have even known if he was?"

Behind his desk, Escovedo didn't move for the longest time, leaning on his elbows and frowning at his interlaced hands. Had he heard her at all? Finally he unlocked one of the drawers and withdrew a folder; shook out some photos, then put one back and slid the rest across to her. Eight in all.

"What you saw," he said. "Did it look anything like this?"

She put them in rows, four over four, like puzzle pieces, seeing how they might fit together. And she needed them all at once, to bludgeon herself into accepting the reality of it: stretches of walls, suggestions of towers, some standing, some collapsed, all fitted together from blocks of greenish stone that could have been shaped by both hammers and razors. Everything was restricted to what spotlights could reach, limned by a cobalt haze that faded into inky blackness. Here, too, were windows and gateways and wide, irregular terraces that might have been stairs, only for nothing that walked on human feet. There was no sense of scale, nothing to measure it by, but she'd sensed it once today already, and it had the feeling of enormity and measureless age.

It was the stuff of nightmares, out of place and out of time, waiting in the cold, wet dark.

"They've been enhanced because of the low-light conditions and the distance," Escovedo said. "It's like the shots of the Titanic. The only light down that far is what you can send on a submersible. Except the Navy's lost every single one they've sent down there. They just go offline. These pictures . . . they're from the one that lasted the longest."

She looked up again. The folder they'd come from was gone. "You held one back. I can't see it?"

He shook his head. "Need to know."

"It shows something that different from the others?"

Nothing. He was as much a block of stone as the walls.

"Something living?" She remembered his description of the sound heard across three thousand miles of ocean: *The analysts say it most closely matches a profile of something alive.* "Is that it?"

"I won't tell you you're right." He appeared to be choosing his words with care. "But if that's what you'd picked up on out there with Marsh, then maybe we'd have a chance to talk about photo number nine."

She wanted to know. Needed to know as badly as she'd needed to breathe this morning, waking up to herself too far under the surface of the sea.

"What about the rest of them? We can keep trying."

He shook his head no. "We've come to the end of this experiment. I've already arranged for your transportation back home tomorrow."

Just like that. It felt as if she were being fired. She hadn't even delivered. She'd not told them anything they didn't already know about. She'd only confirmed it. What had made that unearthly noise, what the Innsmouth prisoners were waiting for—that's what they were really after.

"We're only just getting started. You can't rush something like this. There are sixty-two more of them over there, one of them is sure to—"

He cut her off with a slash of his hand. "Sixty-two of them who are in an uproar now. They didn't see what happened to Marsh, but they've got the general idea."

"Then maybe you shouldn't have been so quick to order his execution."

"That was for you. I thought we were protecting you." He held up his hands then, appeasement, time-out. "I appreciate your willingness to continue. I do. But even if they were still in what passes for a good mood with them, we've still reached an impasse here. You can't get through to them on our turf, and I can't risk sending you back out with another of them onto theirs. It doesn't matter that Marsh didn't actually attack you. I can't risk another of them doing what he did to make me think he had."

"I don't follow you." It had been uncomfortable, yes, and she had no desire to experience it again, but it was hardly fatal.

"I've been doing a lot of thinking about what that sound he made meant," Escovedo said. "What I keep coming back to is that he was sending a distress call."

She wished she could've left the island sooner. That the moment the colonel told her they were finished, he'd already had the helicopter waiting. However late they got her home again, surely by now she would be in her own bed, holding her daughter close because she needed her Tabby even more than Tabby needed her.

Awake part of the time and a toss-up the rest, asleep but dreaming she was still trying to get there. Caught between midnight and dawn, the weather turning for the worse again, the crack and boom of thunder like artillery, with bullets of rain strafing the roof.

She had to be sleeping some of the time, though, and dreaming of something other than insomnia. She knew perfectly well she was in a bed, but there were times in the night when it felt as if she were still below, deeper than she'd gone this morning, in the cold of the depths far beyond the reach of the sun, drifting beside leviathan walls lit by a phosphorescence whose source she couldn't pin down. The walls themselves were tricky to navigate, like being on the outside of a maze, yet still lost within it, finding herself turning strange corners that seemed to jut outward, only to find that they turned in. She was going to drown down here, swamped by a sudden thrashing panic over her air tank going empty, only to realize. . .

She'd never strapped on one to begin with.

She belonged here, in this place that was everything that made her recoil.

Marsh, she thought, once she could tell ceiling from sea. Although he was dead, Marsh was still with her, in an overlapping echo of whispers. Dead, but still dreaming.

When she woke for good, though, it was as abruptly as could be, jolted by the sound of a siren so loud it promised nothing less than a cataclysm. It rose and fell like the howling of a feral god. She supposed soldiers knew how to react, but she wasn't one of them. Every instinct told her to hug the mattress and melt beneath the covers and hope it all went away.

But that was a strategy for people prone to dying in their beds.

She was dressed and out the door in two minutes, and though she had to squint against the cold sting of the rain, she looked immediately to the prison. Everything on the island, alive or motorized, seemed to be moving in that direction, and for a moment she wondered if she should too —safety in numbers, and what if something was *driving* them that way, from the east end?

But the searchlights along the parapet told a different story, three beams stabbing out over the open water, shafts of brilliant white shimmering with rain and sweeping to and fro against the black of night. *A distress call*, Escovedo had said—had it been answered? Was the island under attack, an invasion by Innsmouth's cousins who'd come swarming onto the beach? No, that didn't seem right, either. The spotlights were not aimed down, but out. Straight out.

She stood rooted to the spot, pelted by rain, lashed by wind, frozen with dread that something terrible was on its way. The island had never felt so small. Even the prison looked tiny now, a vulnerable citadel standing alone against the three co-conspirators of ocean, night, and sky.

Ahead of the roving spotlights, the rain was a curtain separating the island from the sea, then it parted, silently at first, the prow of a ship spearing into view, emerging from the blackness as though born from it. No lights, no one visible on board, not even any engine noise that she could hear—just a dead ship propelled by the night or something in it. The sound came next, a tortured grinding of steel across rock so loud it made the siren seem weak and thin. The ship's prow heaved higher as it was driven up onto the island, the rest of it coming into view, the body of the shark behind the cone of its snout.

And she'd thought the thunder was loud. When the freighter plowed into the prison the ground shuddered beneath her, the building cracking apart as though riven by an axe, one of the spotlights tumbling down along with an avalanche of bricks and masonry before winking out for good. She watched men struggle, watched men fall, and at last the ship's momentum was spent. For a breathless moment it was perfectly still. Then, with another grinding protest of metal on stone, the ship began to list, like twisting a knife after sticking it in. The entire right side of the prison buckled and collapsed outward, and with it went the siren and another of the searchlights. The last of the lights reeled upward, aimed back at the building's own roofline.

Only now could she hear men shouting, only now could she hear the gunfire.

Only now could she hear men scream.

And still the ground seemed to shudder beneath her feet.

It seemed as if that should've been the end of it, accident and aftermath, but soon more of the prison began to fall, as if deliberately wrenched apart. She saw another cascade of bricks tumble to the left, light now flickering and spilling from within the prison on both sides.

Something rose into view from the other side, thick as the trunk of the tallest oak that had ever grown, but flexible, glistening in the searing light. It wrapped around another section of wall and pulled it down as easily as peeling wood from rotten wood. She thought it some kind of serpent at first, until, through the wreckage of the building, she saw the suggestion of more, coiling and uncoiling, and a body—or head—behind those.

And still the ground seemed to shudder beneath her feet.

It was nothing seismic—she understood that now. She recalled being in the majestic company of elephants once, and how the ground sometimes quivered in their vicinity as they called to one another from miles away, booming out frequencies so deep they were below the threshold of human hearing, a rumble that only their own kind could decipher.

This was the beast's voice.

And if they heard it in New York, in Barrow, Alaska, and in the Sea of Cortez, she would not have been surprised.

It filled her, reverberating through rock and earth, up past her shoes, juddering the soles of her feet, radiating through her bones and every fiber of muscle, every cell of fat, until her vision scrambled and she feared every organ would liquefy. At last it rose into the range of her feeble ears, a groan that a glacier might make. As the sound climbed higher she clapped both hands over her ears, and if she could have turtled her head into her body she would've done that too, as its voice became a roar became a bellow became a blaring onslaught like the trumpets of Judgment Day, a fanfare to split the sky for the coming of God.

Instead, *this* was what had arrived, this vast and monstrous entity, some inhuman travesty's idea of a deity. She saw it now for what it was to these loathsome creatures from Innsmouth—the god they prayed to, the Mecca that they faced—but then something whispered inside, and she wondered if she was wrong. As immense and terrifying as this thing was, what if it presaged more, and was only preparing the way, the John the Baptist for something even worse.

Shaking, she sunk to her knees, hoping only that she might pass beneath its notice as the last sixty-two prisoners from Innsmouth climbed up and over the top of the prison's ruins, and reclaimed their place in the sea.

Ω

To be honest, she had to admit to herself that the very idea of Innsmouth, and what had happened here in generations past, fascinated her as much as it appalled her.

Grow up and grow older in a world of interstate highways, cable TV, satellite surveillance, the Internet, and cameras in your pocket, and it was easy to forget how remote a place could once be, even on the continental U.S., and not all that long ago, all things considered. It was easy to forget how you might live a lifetime having no idea what was going on in a community just ten miles away, because you never had any need to go there, or much desire, either, since you'd always heard they were an unfriendly lot who didn't welcome strangers, and preferred to keep to themselves.

Innsmouth was no longer as isolated as it once was, but it still had the feeling of remoteness, of being adrift in time, a place where businesses struggled to take root, then quietly died back into vacant storefronts. It seemed to dwell under a shadow that would forever keep outsiders from finding a reason to go there, or stay long if they had.

Unlike herself. She'd been there close to a month, since two days after Christmas, and still didn't know when she would leave.

She got the sense that, for many of the town's residents, making strangers feel unwelcome was a tradition they felt honor-bound to uphold. Their greetings were taciturn, if extended at all, and they watched as if she were a shoplifter, even when crossing the street, or strolling the riverwalk along the Manuxet in the middle of the day. But her money was good, and there was no shortage of houses to rent—although her criteria were stricter than most—and a divorced mother with a six-year-old daughter could surely pose no threat.

None of them seemed to recognize her from television, although would they let on if they did? She recognized none of them, either, nothing in anyone's face or feet that hinted at the old, reviled Innsmouth look. They no longer seemed to have anything to hide here, but maybe the instinct that they did went so far back that they knew no other way.

Although what to make of that one storefront on Eliot Street, in what passed for the heart of the town? The stenciled lettering—charmingly antiquated and quaint—on the plate glass window identified the place as THE INNSMOUTH SOCIETY FOR PRESERVATION AND RESTORATION.

It seemed never to be open.

Yet it never seemed neglected.

Invariably, whenever she peered through the window Kerry would see that someone had been there since the last time she'd looked, but it always felt as if she'd missed them by five minutes or so. She would strain for a better look at the framed photos on the walls, tintypes and sepia tones, glimpses of bygone days that seemed to be someone's idea of something worth bringing back.

Or perhaps their idea of a homecoming.

It was January in New England, and most days so cold it redefined the word bitter, but she didn't miss a single one, climbing seven flights of stairs to take up her vigil for as long as she could endure it. The house was an old Victorian on Lafayette Street, four proud stories tall, peaked and gabled to within an inch of its moldering life. The only thing she cared about was that its roof had an iron-railed widow's walk with an unobstructed view of the decrepit harbor and the breakwater and, another mile out to sea, the humpbacked spine of rock called Devil Reef.

As was the custom during the height of the Age of Sail, the widow's walk had been built around the house's main chimney. Build a roaring fire down below, and the radiant bricks would keep her warm enough for a couple of hours at a time, even when the sky spit snow at her, while she brought the binoculars to her eyes every so often to check if there was anything new to see out there.

"I'm bored." This from Tabitha, nearly every day. *Booorrrrred*, the way she said it. "There's nothing to do here."

"I know, sweetie," Kerry would answer. "Just a little longer."

"When are they coming?" Tabby would ask.

"Soon," she would answer. "Pretty soon."

But in truth, she couldn't say. Their journey was a long one. Would they risk traversing the locks and dams of the Panama Canal? Or would they take the safer route, around Argentina's Cape Horn, where they would exchange Pacific for Atlantic, south for north, then head home, at long last home.

She knew only that they were on their way, more certain of this than any sane person had a right to be. The assurance was there whenever the world grew still and silent, more than a thought . . . a whisper that had never left, as if not all of Barnabas Marsh had died, the greater part of him subsumed into the hive mind of the rest of his kind. To taunt? To punish? To gloat? In the weeks after their island prison fell, there was no place she could go where its taint couldn't follow. Not Montana, not Los Angeles, not New Orleans, for the episode of *The Animal Whisperer* they'd tried to film before putting it on hiatus.

She swam with them in sleep. She awoke retching with the taste of coldest blood in her mouth. Her belly skimmed through mud and silt in quiet moments; her shoulders and flanks brushed through shivery forests of weeds; her fingers tricked her into thinking that her daughter's precious cheek felt cool and slimy. The dark of night could bring on the sense of a dizzying plunge to the blackest depths of ocean trenches.

Where else was left for her to go but here, to Innsmouth, the place that time seemed to be trying hard to forget.

And the more days she kept watch from the widow's walk, the longer at a time she could do it, even while the fire below dwindled to embers, and so the more it seemed that her blood must've been going cold in her veins.

"I don't like it here," Tabby would say. "You never used to yell in your sleep until we came here."

How could she even answer that? No one could live like this for long.

"Why can't I go stay with Daddy?" Tabby would ask. *Daddeeeee*, the way she said it.

It really would've been complete then, wouldn't it? The humiliation, the surrender. The admission: *I can't handle it anymore, I just want it to stop, I want them to make it stop*. It still mattered, that her daughter's father had

once fallen in love with her when he thought he'd been charmed by some half-wild creature who talked to animals, and then once he had her, tried to drive them from her life because he realized he hated to share. He would never possess all of her.

You got as much as I could give, she would tell him, as if he too could hear her whisper. *And now they won't let go of the rest.*

"Tell me another story about them," Tabby would beg, and so she would, a new chapter of the saga growing between them about kingdoms under the sea where people lived forever, and rode fish and giant seahorses, and how they had defenders as tall as the sky who came boiling up from the waters to send their enemies running.

Tabby seemed to like it.

When she asked if there were pictures, Kerry knew better, and didn't show her the ones she had, didn't even acknowledge their existence. The ones taken from Colonel Escovedo's office while the rains drenched the wreckage, after she'd helped the few survivors that she could, the others dead or past noticing what she might take from the office of their commanding officer, whom nobody could locate anyway.

The first eight photos Tabby would've found boring. As for the ninth, Kerry wasn't sure she could explain to a six-year-old what exactly it showed, or even to herself. Wasn't sure she could make a solid case for what was the mouth and what was the eye, much less explain why such a thing was allowed to exist.

One of them, at least, should sleep well while they were here.

Came the day, at last, in early February, when her binoculars revealed more than the tranquil pool of the harbor, the snow and ice crusted atop the breakwater, the sullen chop of the winter-blown sea. Against the slate-colored water, they were small, moving splotches the color of algae. They flipped like seals, rolled like otters. They crawled onto the ragged dark stone of Devil Reef, where they seemed to survey the kingdom they'd once known, all that had changed about it and all that hadn't.

And then they did worse.

Even if something was natural, she realized, you could still call it a perversity.

Was it preference? Was it celebration? Or was it blind obedience to an instinct they didn't even have the capacity to question? Not that it mattered. Here they were, finally, little different from salmon now, come back to their headwaters to breed, indulging an urge eighty-some years strong.

It was only a six-block walk to the harbor, and she had the two of them there in fifteen minutes. This side of Water Street, the wharves and warehouses were deserted, desolate, frosted with frozen spray and groaning with every gust of wind that came snapping in over the water.

She wrenched open the wide wooden door to one of the smaller buildings, the same as she'd been doing every other day or so, the entire time they'd been here, first to find an abandoned rowboat, and then to make sure it was still there. She dragged it down to the water's edge, plowing a furrow in a crust of old snow, and once it was in the shallows, swung Tabby into it, then hopped in after. She slipped the oars into the rusty oarlocks, and they were off.

"Mama . . . ?" Tabitha said after they'd pushed past the breakwater and cleared the mouth of the harbor for open sea. "Are you crying?"

In rougher waters now, the boat heaved beneath them. Snow swirled in from the depths overhead and clung to her cheeks, eyelashes, hair, and refused to melt. She was that cold. She was *always* that cold.

"Maybe a little," Kerry said.

"How come?"

"It's just the wind. It stings my eyes."

She pulled at the oars, aiming for the black line of the reef. Even if no one else might've, even if she could no longer see them, as they hid within the waves, she heard them sing a song of jubilation, a song of wrath and hunger. Their voices were the sound of a thousand waking nightmares.

To pass the time, she told Tabby a story, grafting it to all the other tales she'd told about kingdoms under the sea where people lived forever, and rode whales and danced with dolphins, and how they may not have been very pleasant to look at, but that's what made them love the beautiful little girl from above the waves, and welcome her as their princess.

Tabby seemed to like it.

Ahead, at the reef, they began to rise from the water and clamber up the rock again, spiny and scaled, finned and fearless. Others began to swim out to meet the boat. Of course they recognized her, and she them. She'd sat with nearly a third of them, trying trying trying to break through from the wrong side of the shore.

While they must have schemed like fiends to drag her deep into theirs.

I bring you this gift, she would tell them, if only she could make herself heard over their jeering in her head. *Now could you please just set me free?*

One Last Year Without a Summer

I had a dream, which was not all a dream.
The bright sun was extinguish'd, and the stars
Did wander darkling in the eternal space,
Rayless, and pathless, and the icy earth
Swung blind and blackening in the moonless air;
Morn came and went—and came, and brought no day,
And men forgot their passions in the dread
Of this their desolation; and all hearts
Were chill'd into a selfish prayer for light . . .
—"Darkness," Lord Byron (1816)

The days reach across time, two hundred years and more, and they are all the same. Then and now, this day and tomorrow. None of it is a dream.

It's what I wake up to, instead. I'm always the first one up by at least an hour, slipping out of bed, never knowing why I'm so careful to avoid waking Aurora. No matter how fetal she might've been when we turned in, by morning her face is buried in the pillow and she looks as if she crash-landed through the ceiling. Never a peep out of her.

At the other end of a long hall, Clark and Riley slumber on, too.

In the kitchen I put the coffee on, meeting the dawn from the bleak side, still biologically bound to a schedule that's lost its meaning. It got me this far, though, so it might as well carry me through to the end. Plus the cats

appreciate it. They want their food ten minutes ago. They will not be denied. They love me above all others. You have to take your master plans where you can find them now.

That first fresh steaming cup is my reward, and, shrouded in a heavy flannel robe, I take it out onto a deck that isn't mine, my favorite feature of this house I never earned. The day lightens, from starless black to shades of gray, a sky the color of faded slate. It's been weeks since we've seen a legitimate sunrise.

At least they went out on a high note. Millions of tons of volcanic debris in the atmosphere can create spectacular dawns and dusks, the low-angle rays of the sun scattering into horizon-spanning smears of red and pink, lavender and orange, in luminous shades and intensities that painters can only dream of capturing.

They were glorious while they lasted . . . but even then, something seemed off. These were the first sunrises and sunsets I'd seen with vivid streaks of emerald and sapphire and teal. No matter how gorgeous something is, when it's wrong, you know it.

Down the incline to the lake's lapping water, the grass is pale with frost. In the trees, the birds are confused—or confus'd, Byron would have written. Should they sing? Should they keep quiet? Should they fly off now and come back to roost in the early afternoon, when peak light has passed and the day starts going dim again?

July in the Rocky Mountains isn't supposed to be like this.

I sip my coffee and watch the lights wink on in the houses around the shore, yellow spots of warmth in a dawn whose dominant feature is the chilly sighing of slow wind through a mountain range of pines.

When the day has lightened as much as it's going to, I down the last of my coffee and set up my RED camera. I've daubed three circles of paint onto the deck so the tripod is in the same spot every time, marked the tripod itself to keep the angles and elevation consistent. I aim west, across the lake and down its length, at whatever is going on at Roper Forsyth's place. He still has the giddy instincts of a showman, and keeps the work hidden from view behind makeshift walls, a towering scaffold tied with tarps. But sometimes the scaffolding expands, or the tarps shift position, or the work crew rolls them up before the worst of the storms blow in so the tarps don't turn into sails, and I can tell they're making progress, whatever they're constructing.

There aren't many people in the world who could afford to make concrete the way the Romans did, or be willing to go to the trouble of it, but Forsyth is one of them.

I grab a few more frames of the site. Soon, I'll upload them to my laptop, dated and cataloged, so I can piece together a time-lapse video after Forsyth's project is complete. It's part of the deal here. Although it's not that he orders things done, more that he wonders aloud about them—wouldn't it be nice if they happened?—and that's somebody's cue to get on it.

Aurora is next to trudge upstairs. Coffee and cats for her, too. The way they beg, you'd think they hadn't eaten an hour ago. Aurora gives me a hug and a burrowing kiss on the neck, and I remember to be grateful for her, that the universe was once kind enough to direct me to someone who took me as a work-in-progress and made life better in every way.

I'm the kind of guy drawn to high, prominent cheekbones.

I'm also the kind who can't shake the dread of some inevitable day when I'll look at her and see that now there's too much of a good thing showing.

▽

I can hear the questions now: How can you be so resigned? What happened to raging against the dying of the light?

Nobody would ask if they'd had a Scotty Tremayne in their lives.

He was my best friend for close to half my life. We met early, in preschool, and clicked, and didn't drift. With other boys and girls, floating in and out of one another's orbits is a part of natural selection. They get older, their personalities morph and gel, they diverge. One heads for the basketball team, the other, the chess club. One lands in the academic express lane to pre-med, the other *really* loves smoking weed. One accepts Jesus as her personal lord and savior, the other thinks Lucifer had a point in rebelling.

Not Scotty and me. We ran parallel the whole time.

But he was a short kid. When he got to be fourteen, his genes told him, "Huh uh. Five foot four, that's it for you." Strike one.

When he was fifteen, barely into our sophomore year of high school, he woke up with Bell's Palsy, everything to the right of his nose yanked into a droopy sneer. "Stop making that awful face," his mom told him when he walked into the kitchen that morning. Strike two.

At first, the blowback was limited to words. Oliver Twisted, that was one of the more clever names someone came up with for him. Then there was Frankenscott, hah hah, because he was such a monster now. The one they really had fun with was Scotty Skidface. A bunch of classmates emailed around a video clip from some midget-wrestling match of a dwarf

getting drop-flipped heels-over-head by another and face-planting across the width of the ring. How Scotty Skidface got his start.

Then some of them decided, okay, since he doesn't fight back against the words, let's crank this up a notch. They made a game of it. Two games, actually: Let's See If We Can Smack Scotty's Face Loose, and its inverse, Let's See If We Can Make the Other Side Match.

When you're fifteen, it doesn't matter how many times you hear the promise that it's not a permanent condition. That it will run its course. For one thing, the ordeal still seems eternal, and release will never arrive. Worse, you know nothing will change when it does. Once you've been Scotty Skidface, you'll always be Scotty Skidface. When something's been this much fun, people don't just let it go.

Strike three.

He never left a note, but when he hanged himself, the *why* was obvious.

Here's the bigger point: Those last couple days before he did it, Scotty seemed happy. Relaxed and happy and no longer stressing over anything. You'd think he woke up six inches taller and could fly.

How could he have done this, people asked. Just when he seemed to be doing so much better. He really appeared to have turned a corner.

Well, he had. Just not in the direction we assumed.

He'd made up his mind. He'd known what he was going to do and when he was going to do it. So of course he was happy. He'd known the pain was about to end.

As went Scotty Tremayne, so go those of us here on the dark and frosted summer shores of Lake Wapiti. The difference is, for us, the underlying condition is permanent.

But we're good with that. We have to be.

As the unlikely residents of this ad hoc colony around the lake, we go about the day doing our various things, the saving graces that got us here. Or just thinking about doing our things. Or stepping away to deliberately *not* do our things, because a day of hiking the hills and the spongy tundra that's been made of the meadows and valleys between them will leave us in a better frame of mind to do our things tomorrow.

We have painters here, and photographers—that's where Aurora comes in—and sculptors. We have writers and a poet laureate. We have musicians, including a Chinese pianist wunderkind and a world-renowned string quartet from Vienna. Composers? Those too, including a Hollywood effects designer whose medium is sound itself. This would be Clark, who met Riley on the job when she was scoring my second movie.

It's a high-altitude convention of insufferably needy pricks, really, everybody here because we spent our lives driven by a hunger for validation so fierce it drove us to achieve things that actually got us noticed. We all get along for the most part. There's a time and a place for ego, and the end of the world as we know it ain't it.

I do sometimes wonder why I'm the only film director that Forsyth brought in, because, as far as the label is concerned, I've barely been at it long enough to become a footnote on a minor blip. I'd think Forsyth could've had his pick from higher up the food chain. But maybe Steven Spielberg was busy, and he knew James Cameron would've mostly screamed at people for disappointing him, and Werner Herzog had dropped everything and immediately gone to Iceland for a front-row seat at the opening of the void.

So it's just me, and, as the only director, I'm honor bound to be at Forsyth's beck and call. By default this makes me the resident documentarian, whether I'm cut out for it or not.

Learning on the job—it never stops.

Later in the morning, I take one of the rowboats to the other side of the lake, the prow slow-cutting the still water like a V-shaped warp in the black glass surface of time. From down the shore, whenever the wind carries it right, the sound of a violin floats over the water. I wish I could freeze the moment instead of the moment freezing me. By the time I'm across, the sky is spitting a stinging cold rain. I tie off at Forsyth's dock, then climb onto the boardwalk with my camera bag slung over one shoulder and carrying a tripod like a club.

From my left, behind the tarps, I can hear the labors of the workers he's brought in, people who've probably forgotten more about concrete than the rest of us will ever know. I should interview them, too, asking if it's different this time, formulating concrete the way the Romans did. If that's a dream come true for a concrete expert, or if they don't think much about it, and it's just a way to keep their families intact a little longer.

Forsyth has brought in volcanic ash by the ton, in steel cargo containers. That was the strength of Roman concrete: using pulverized rock that they could reconstitute back into solid rock again. That's why so many Roman arenas and aqueducts are still standing 2,000 years later, while the average driveway is crumbling after a decade.

As always, Forsyth greets me warmly. He greets everyone warmly, and after a few years in Los Angeles, I've seen enough phony warmth I can spot the difference. He means it. It helps that he's Australian by birth, and has kept most of the broad, amiable accent.

He's wearing a bulky, roll-neck sweater, and with his shaggy hair and a day of graying stubble on his square face, he looks like an adventurer who should be out climbing the Matterhorn. That's among the ones he's missed. Everest and Denali and Kilimanjaro and several others, he's already ticked those off the checklist.

Colorado alone has close to sixty peaks topping 14,000 feet, and he's summited over half of them. Somehow the man also found time to start nearly 220 companies. He ran a bunch, sold a bunch, closed down the stinkers and walked away wiser, a track record that's left him worth six billion dollars. I still don't get how such a thing is possible, even in his sixty-odd years of living. There are days when I feel my biggest accomplishment has been putting together a matching pair of socks.

"What should we talk about today?" he asks as I set up the camera.

I've been working up to this. Like all good documentarians, I aspire to be a disembodied voice that gets out of the way as quickly as possible. "Why aren't you saving yourself?"

He seems surprised. There's nothing he can do that the camera doesn't love. He's ruddy and weathered and deeply comfortable in his skin. He's never tried to hide the lines—if it's not a fight, you can't lose it.

"What makes you infer that I'm not?" he says.

I keep mum a few moments because the weather has become a major player in the scene. We've been joined by the crack and rumble of another storm that's blown in with the fury of a marauder, bringing cold rain to beat at the windows.

"Exposure. You're a lot more vulnerable up here than you would be if you really put your money to it."

"Oh. The bunker mentality," he says. "I've seen the floor plans. I know of two companies that build them. I know seven tall poppies who've had them made, and I'd be surprised if I didn't know more but they kept their mouths shut about it. But they were all doing this years before Iceland happened. They look prescient now, but what they really were was scared of everything."

You could say he looks prescient now, too. He has five residences around the world, from Sydney to Seattle, but this one, south of Vail, lakeside at 8,200 feet, has always been his favorite. Over the course of fifteen years, he bought out his neighbors around the lake. Sixteen homes, and every one of them is his now. Guesthouses, perks for employees, favors for vacationing friends, investments—they're whatever he wants them to be.

"One of the builders tried to sell me on one, once. On paper, the places are very nice. I was just never interested. You can have an underground complex so well-appointed it has a theater that seats twenty-four, and a garage for all the cars you think you'll get to drive up topside again someday." He comes off as amused and bemused. "But it's still a hole in the ground, isn't it?"

Although I get this, it still seems to me that Forsyth is taking an unusual middle path with how he's chosen to finish out what, in all likelihood, remains of his life. He's not selfish, but here beside Lake Wapiti his thinking seems uncharacteristically small.

"Then why aren't you putting your considerable resources to use trying to help the rest of the world out of this crisis?" *Instead of making a few dozen privileged guests as comfortable as possible in the most expensive hospice on the planet*, I could add, but don't.

The question makes him laugh, but there's only about 20% humor in it. The rest is pure, unadulterated fatalism, a rare display from someone whose public persona has always struck me as that of an unbridled optimist.

"Resources have to be administered by people who know what they're doing. But projects on the scale I sense you're talking about really only can be taken up by governments. So you can see the problem already."

Outside, lightning cracks so loud I'm afraid it may have clipped our audio.

"Do you remember when Miami Beach was starting to have a regular problem with flooding?" he continues once the rumble has ebbed. "It was a canary in the coal mine moment. The response of the Florida governor's office was to ban the use of the phrase 'climate change' in state documents. I've met too many drongos like that, in positions they should never be in, to have much faith left in what they can manage . . . especially with something they didn't have years to see coming." He shakes his head, and there's tremendous sorrow in it. "These aren't people who rise to the challenge. They assign blame. They're experts at that."

Now the grin. The familiar Roper Forsyth grin. He can get away with saying nearly anything as long as it comes with that disarming grin.

"I didn't accomplish a single thing in my life alone, and I definitely didn't do it by associating with no-hopers. I'm too fixed in my ways to start now."

He peers more intently at the camera—beyond it, actually, at me, the resident documentarian who's failing miserably at keeping out of the way.

"Do you not want the responsibility for it, whatever you're afraid it is that I'm denying the world?" he says. "You have to realize by now that all this didn't come from me. It came from you."

Context—we have to place what we're doing up here in its proper context.

Documentaries are forced into an unwinnable struggle against the reality that nothing happens in a vacuum. Nothing ever begins, nothing really ends. We just put brackets around arbitrary points in time and look at the people and events inside them under the illusion that they're contained.

What my wife and friends, my partners, this tiny in-house production company we comprise, have to do next is concede history's cyclical side. How sometimes we're doomed to repeat it because we didn't learn, or yearn to repeat it because we did. We have to provide structure to chaos.

My raw material: a bunch of fragments of video and audio, and despair. I have no idea how to fit it all together. The best I can do is trust that if I shuffle various chunks into enough configurations, a few will start making sense.

Like Clark and Riley, doubling as narrators. Both sound-people, each in their way, they've also been blessed with appealing voices.

There's Clark, reciting the beginning of Byron's poem, underplaying it, a weary witness to the end of a world.

I had a dream, which was not all a dream . . .

I'm coming to see it as the perfect voice-over for snippets I've shot of the sun's losing struggle to break through what Iceland has spewed into the sky. First, the flamboyance of those early dawns and dusks, saturated with the colors we expect, as well as the streaks that shouldn't have been there at all, the jeweled greens and blues slashing through the glow. It was caused, we now know, by a profusion of boron and copper compounds in the atmosphere, proving that even poison can be beautiful.

As the sky continues to fill, a drifting dark haze supplants the stained glass glory, giving way to a dulling gray.

The bright sun was extinguish'd, and the stars
Did wander darkling in the eternal space . . .

A grainy kiss of software reverb adds some murky distance, the voice of God if God didn't care anymore, talking over his shoulder on his way out the cosmic door.

Rayless, and pathless, and the icy earth
Swung blind and blackening in the moonless air . . .

I don't have to tweak anything in post-production to prove the point. The world has already desaturated itself.

Morn came and went—and came, and brought no day,
And men forgot their passions in the dread
Of this their desolation . . .

Slow-panned shots of fruit trees and fields in submission, of withering green apples and brittle leaves falling months too soon, of naked branches raking at the slate sky. A Memorial Day seashore deserted by people driven back by the cold, by the rain and lightning of wrathful black storms. Half-grown corn whose stalks slump toward the soil under the weight of their rotting ears. Los Angeles and Denver streets turned to gutters by the backed-up drains, and people sloshing along them, first in soggy overcoats and then in parkas.

This is summer now. Imagine what winter will bring.

I shuffle the pieces and find a flow, the last of the contemporary shots doing a slow dissolve into paintings from the early 1800s. It predates photography. All the visuals we have are paint on canvas. It's the same thing, lurid beginnings and endings to the day, then the cold color-bleached starkness of landscapes leached of warmth.

The score, too, fading in. We can't forget the musical score. Most of it will be original, because Riley is working on that and God knows we've got a top-notch string quartet and pianist to play whatever elegiac chamber music she composes, and Clark has the gear to record them at their best.

However, for this sequence we'll borrow from history. It wasn't only painters and poets who reflected the spirit of their age. Composers had at it, as well. So I think Riley will approve. I've already downloaded the recordings, never mind acquiring rights to the performances. I would actually welcome being sued for ignoring that part.

First, beneath the more colorful depictions of early 1816, we drop a few bars of Beethoven's Piano Sonata No. 28 in A Major, op. 101. It's light, gentle, pastoral . . . but it can't last, so as the paintings turn somber we cross-fade into the chillier minor-key piano that opens Franz Schubert's *Winterreise*, and stay with it long enough for the tenor to come in, so delicate he sounds ready to snap in half.

Riley, too. Now we need what her clear-eyed, throaty voice brings to the table.

"This isn't the first time this has happened," she says. "It's happened before. The same, only different. Not as bad, but to people who had no idea why it was happening.

"In 1816, what captured the morbid side of Lord Byron's imagination, and the imaginations of so many writers and painters and composers of his day, was the plunge in global temperatures. The northern hemisphere came out of spring and went back to snowfalls and iced-over lakes. By autumn, harvests had turned to famines. Today, we call 1816 'the Year Without a Summer.' At the time, people called it 'eighteen-hundred-and-froze-to-death.'

"The world was bigger then. Nobody in the northern hemisphere was aware that, the year before, thousands of miles away, in what would be called Indonesia, a dormant volcano named Mount Tambora came roaring back to life, blew itself into a huge crater, and spent the next two weeks in a constant eruption."

Graphics, too. This is where Aurora and her Photoshop skills come in. Context, remember. Everything is about context, and everything is relative.

It's almost cute, what Aurora makes—a row of cartoon volcanoes, identical except for a puffy fart of smoke at the top. Mount Vesuvius, that buried the Roman city of Pompeii in the year 79; Indonesia's better-known Krakatau eruption of 1883; Katmai, Alaska, 1912; Mount St. Helens, 1980; Mexico's El Chichón, 1982 . . . if the smoke from their mouths were toys, they'd be marbles and golf balls.

Next to them, Mount Tambora 1815 is belching up a big fat softball.

If there's any doubt, Riley clears it up: "It was the worst volcanic eruption in known human history . . . since the Stone Age."

We pull back. Surprise! You think you've seen the worst? No, the worst is still to come, a volcano to dwarf the rest. Indonesia again. If Tambora is a softball, this is a beach ball, and a monstrous one at that, spewing into the stratosphere.

"Seventy-five thousand years before Tambora, the Toba supervolcano nearly became an extinction-level event," Riley says. "It's theorized to have caused such a die-off that human evolution reached a bottleneck, with as few as 10,000 individuals left to carry on our species."

It's not a bedtime story, but she still makes it sound almost okay. You don't want a man's voice telling you this. You want to hear it from your sister, your mother, your friend, your lover. Riley is all of them at once, whoever you need her to be. Her voice is a soft hand cupping your cheek, so tender you want to reach into the audio realm and press her hand to your face a little firmer, to keep her from leaving a while longer.

No mercy, though. Fuck you. What do you think this is, the History Channel? We glide over and pull back again. There's no surprise now. This one you already see coming: the rift volcanoes that have ripped open the Icelandic interior. To contain this much cartoon smoke, our perspective is so far back now that Vesuvius and Krakatau and Tambora are jagged little bumps on our make-believe horizon.

And that's how it comes together—in fits and starts, bits and pieces, with good ideas and bad, and ideas that sound good until we see them executed, and then try not to think about how much time they've cost us.

It's strangely therapeutic, even fun. We laugh when we mess up, and celebrate each creative victory. We bicker when we disagree, and gloat when we're right and someone else was wrong. We're so caught up in making this from scratch that you'd think it was someone else's demise we were documenting.

Still, we have our limitations. There's a hurdle here that I'm not sure how to clear, and it's beyond our team's abilities to solve. When we show the darkened skies, the brutal storms, the frosty ground, the famine-in-the-making that our fields have been reduced to . . . no matter how well shot, they're still just effects.

They aren't *causes*. Nothing ever begins, remember.

Ultimately, even Iceland's rift volcanoes are another batch of effects. Behind them there's a deeper cause, and I don't know how to show it, or what it should look like if I did.

There are destinations that, even if you possessed unlimited funding, there's no practical way to get a camera there. Like the Jurassic Period. Or deep space, in case there really were attack ships on fire off the shoulder of Orion.

Or way way waaaay deep down inside the earth.

On the plus side, Forsyth has high-level contacts. He may not think much of government officials, but they'll take his calls, regardless. He got his hands on some visuals composited from number-crunching reams of seismic readings, classified satellite data, and some experimental new form of ground-penetrating radar. Even then, the images are hardly revelatory. I couldn't make much of what I was looking at until he pointed out the subtle geometries.

Still, as the money-shot payoff for our build-up of humankind's oppression under volcanic winters, it falls flat. It's the realest, truest thing we have about our fate, and I can't use it. Because it doesn't make for good TV.

So it's a good thing Forsyth added a few painters and digital artists to our stable at the end of time. I'll have to tap them. Theirs is the kind of

imagination you rely on when you have no way to depict what's going on in the Jurassic or off Orion . . . or with immense, interconnected machines many miles beneath the surface of the earth.

They're all going to have their own ideas of what these contraptions looked like once. And what it looks like now that they're breaking down.

Undoubtedly, they'll all be wrong.

But maybe, as with a living body made from the parts of dead ones, their ideas will yield enough pieces that can be stitched together into something close to the truth.

Growing up, I never thought about the origins of the Frankenstein story. I was too young to care, or realize there even was a story behind the story. I was too young to be spellbound by anything but the notion of a corpse assembled from other corpses being revived by captured lightning, then getting off the table and, not being the most articulate of brutes, lashing out at everything around him, even when he meant well.

At first I didn't know the monster came from a novel, much less that the novel had an author, still in her late teens when she conceived of him. I didn't know that Mary Wollstonecraft Godwin Shelley had made her monster more erudite than the filmed depictions I'd seen allowed him to be. I didn't know she'd made him more thoughtful than anyone I'd grown up listening to, or, worst of all, given him the capacity to ponder his place in creation and strive to make sense of his sufferings, and understand how desolate he truly was.

That came later, after classmates mocked my best friend as Frankenscott, and I began to see what a priority it was to get away from that wretched town and its people.

The original Year Without a Summer was made for me back then, waiting for when the time was right for me to discover it. When I was ready to be spellbound by the Lake Geneva of the early 1800s, and a scandal-ridden coterie of poets and lovers heading for Switzerland to flee the provincialism of home, the stodgy twats who disapproved with one side of their faces and leered in tittering fascination with the other.

I yearned for a season's retreat to work and think and explore as the mood and muses compelled, and to meet someone who could trek up to an alpine glacier and see in it, as Byron wrote, "a frozen hurricane." As an often-derided devotee of all things wintry, I was captivated by the notion of a summer that never came, with crackling fires and a well-stocked larder and good companionship to keep warm.

It's the sort of thing you can romanticize when you're young and selfish, blind to the harsh fact that your reverie means that down other roads, people are losing their livelihoods and livestock and maybe life itself. Starvation happens too slowly to see it play out in a glance.

Still, I spent years gripped by an obsession with retelling the story of those months by Lake Geneva, in the Year Without a Summer. I'd already discovered I had a knack for pointing a camera at people and getting them to act things out in front of it. That came from the Scotty Years, the result of spending so much free time goofing with my best friend, and how when you're twelve there's no such thing as a stupid idea. The last thing that mattered was how ridiculous our movies turned out, sixth-graders fighting terrorists and Nazis and aliens and were-collies—the point is, *we made them.*

When the time came to make something for real, the Year Without a Summer wouldn't let go. I wanted to bring it to life as my first film whose cast and crew got paid in something other than comic books or pizzas. But at least three others had beaten me to it. Some of their films I'd even liked. All of them I watched with a painful awareness that the world didn't need a fourth.

Not with Byron, anyway. Or Mary Shelley. Or Percy or Claire Clairmont or Dr. Polidori. Not a period piece. Definitely not another nineteenth-century costume drama at a lakeside villa whose rental fees would eat up the single biggest chunk of whatever budget I could scrape together.

When all else fails, I guess, make it post-apocalyptic. *The Ice House* was five friends on the cusp of a nuclear winter, a summer rental beside a lake, and enough survivalism, moral quandaries, salvation, sexuality, and impinging psychoses to last anyone a shortened lifetime.

Somehow it worked. It didn't just work, it got me to the Sundance Festival, then to Cannes. It got me a second movie, then a third.

It got me here, to another lakeside house 8,200 feet above sea level, with up to three guests of my choosing.

Because, as I was to learn, *The Ice House* counted Roper Forsyth among its fans.

＊

Despite its gloomy atmosphere, that cold, wet summer beside Lake Geneva, which gave birth to one of the world's enduring monsters, was a mostly happy time for the people there. They enjoyed themselves and

each other's company, and they could afford to . . . because they didn't know what was coming.

Within eight years, all three men were dead. Polidori went first, by suicide. Percy Shelley drowned in a boating accident. Lord Byron succumbed to a series of maladies and fevers made worse by medicinal bloodletting with dirty instruments. Claire finished the summer pregnant, prompting Byron to wonder, "Is the brat mine?" Their daughter lived just five years. For Mary Shelley, only the last of her four children with Percy survived, and her future held a fatal brain tumor. Claire lived longest, but came to bitterly regret the bohemian spirit of free love that had shaped her youth. It only worked out well for the men, while warping them nonetheless. Even as she praised Shelley and Byron as the two finest poets England had produced, she damned them as "monsters of lying, meanness, cruelty and treachery."

What had I ever seen in these people?

Or maybe I'm giving myself too much credit, and it's the clarity talking. All of us know very well what lies beyond this summer.

So when after weeks of living and working under the same rain-hammered roof, my genes make me wonder what it would be like to sleep with Riley—a year from now, what's it going to matter?—I let it go. I don't want to be that guy. Don't want to start feeding the monster now. I've done enough thoughtless things that I'd rather finish this life trying to be something better than the sum of my ill-fitting parts.

It's enough to savor every dinner. It's enough to put off clearing the table until morning and sit before the bank of windows with people I love, stoking the fire and sharing wine as we face a brooding lake whipped to whitecaps by the howling mountain wind. And when we tip our glasses and talk of regrets, what I did or didn't do with Riley isn't one of them.

For Clark, who's always loved space and its exploration, his regret is the album of electronic music for planetariums that never made it beyond fragments and notation. For Riley, it's the symphony she couldn't convince herself she had the chops to write. For Aurora, it's the photo book of ghost towns and abandoned vehicles scattered across the Southwest deserts that remained strewn across various hard drives.

We're the type of people who most regret the things we never made.

For me? There's a bagful of them, projects of commerce and labors of love, all stuck in Development Hell, but when it's my turn to lift my glass in a toast to the Great Undone, I surprise myself by popping out with an idea I've had only since we've been here at Lake Wapiti. This unexpected turn as a documentarian has made an impact.

The kooks and the nutters and the crazies . . . that's who I wish there was time to seek out and interview. The hikers and cavers and amateur explorers mocked after claiming they'd stumbled across pipes and other metal structures jutting from ancient strata of rock. The retired old miners who'd found similar wreckage jumbled with the coal far below. The geologists pressured into forgetting about some rogue anomaly if they didn't want it destroying their careers.

They're out there. I would like to hear them tell their stories of loneliness and humiliation. I'd like to ask them how it feels to be vindicated.

It wasn't that they were up against a conspiracy. Nothing that grandiose or organized. Just resistance and hostility. Whether driven by logic or faith, the average person has unshakable beliefs about terra firma. You contradict them at your peril. Even the idiots plodding along under the conviction that the sun revolves around the earth have no patience for anyone suggesting that this giant ball of rock underfoot is anything other than *their* rock. There was no room for any implication that, however natural the origins of our water-slicked rock may have been, in some unfathomable antiquity at least a portion of it had been pressed into service as a geothermal-powered machine.

I'd have to expand the interview pool beyond the wrongly convicted lunatics. I'd have to assemble a panel of experts and let them fight it out, beating each other to death with their pet theories while shredding the other guy's.

No answers, just assigned blame, right up to the very end—what *were* we sitting on this whole time? Was it some unknown advanced race's remote chemical factory? Someone's off-world fueling station? A weapons depot? And whatever it was, why was it seemingly forgotten?

Or maybe it was more related to our development than we would ever want to believe, a time bomb engineered on a geological scale, triggered by accident or design. A test we failed because we were too caught up in our own small lies and meanness and cruelty and treachery to find the problem, recognize it, and solve it.

That's my regret. I can see it playing in my mind, but will never see it anywhere else.

Even an imaginary documentary needs a title.

Skidding Into Oblivion—I like that.

I would dedicate it to a ghost named Scotty.

The great unveiling gets moved up a week ahead of schedule, but we don't have much choice. There's no dishonor in it. Many renowned works of art came to posterity unfinished. The worst you can say about it is that their creators were human, working against circumstances and a clock.

The moment comes in the middle of a late August morning as cold and gray as the rest. The more observant among us already suspect something's up. The birds know before we do, those of us on the ground waking up to a screeching southeast migration going on above our heads.

Whatever it is, it's coming from the northwest, and can't be good.

Later, the ground quivers and windows rattle, and the slopes around us shudder with spills of dislodged rocks. It's tempting to hope that's all there is, a half-hour of calm settling our rattled nerves before the sound catches up . . . and when it does, there's no mistaking it. A faraway roar fills our world with a noise not heard for 75,000 years, since the event called Toba.

There's a supervolcano underlying Yellowstone National Park, too, the engine that powers its geysers and hot springs and smelly blorping mud pots. Forsyth has allowed for this possibility. It's what he does, considers possibilities, even if he hasn't talked about this one much. Because what could we do about it?

If you have to find one bright spot in Yellowstone blowing—I mean gun-to-your-head have to—it's that it completely eclipses people's overuse of that worn-out term *game-changer*. On our part of the continent, if it's bad enough, and by this point why wouldn't it be, there won't be any game left at all.

We were already living in the past and didn't even realize it. Five hundred miles . . . the speed of sound . . . we're listening to something that occurred forty minutes ago.

It brings everybody out at once, the lakeshore as alive and busy as I've seen it this entire time. This isn't something you stay in for, to hear about later. This is what we've been here for the whole summer.

With Aurora and Clark and Riley in tow, I shoot it all on the run. To whatever extent I'm an artist, I feel like the least among them here, but by my ordained role, I'm the last one standing. A documentary needs an end, the second bracket to contain its people and events, and now we've arrived at it.

Deadlines—you're always up against them sooner than you wish.

Walking, rowing, sprinting . . . people get to the construction site at Forsyth's house however they can, bundled into overcoats and scarves.

A few have the foresight to carry umbrellas in case it starts to rain ash, a good idea with a short life. It doesn't take much ash coming down before it's like a layer of concrete.

Another day or two, and roofs are going to be collapsing.

Even now, Forsyth has the giddy instincts of a showman, clambering up the levels of scaffolding to hack the ties apart and let the concealing tarps fall. Whatever they were doing in there, around-the-clock for months under terrible conditions, we've seen it only in fragments, a glimpse of this and a peek at that. Never the whole. We've known only that it's enormous, easily taller than Forsyth's house, four stories and maybe more.

The man has made billions of dollars and thousands of headlines, he's climbed mountains, and from the exuberance of his smile—a smile I don't need to zoom in to see—I'm thinking none of that has mattered to him as much as this.

I'm thinking it's the greatest moment of his life, and he's shared it with so few. If he's spent any time toasting his regrets, he doesn't show it. If there was more work to do on this mighty statue, it doesn't matter. You unveil the statue you have, not the statue you wish there'd been time to complete.

The scaffolding is next to fall, and I don't even hear it crash. Does anybody? Vision is all the sense we have the bandwidth to process.

Finished or not, it's still a colossus. No other word will do.

And . . . I get it now. I get his desire to conceal it until this moment. Because it's us. In spirit, it's every single one of us.

The base is enormous, as big as the foundation of a moderate house. It will never topple, and looks exactly like what it is: rock. Reconstituted rock.

Two figures rise out of it, titans both of them. The sculptor is to the right, in the foreground. She emerges from the stony base on one knee, rendering the other figure with a massive hammer and a chisel worthy of the job. Her progeny strains for the sky, and in his agonized, ecstatic form I see echoes of Michelangelo's David, da Vinci's Vetruvian Man, Rodin's Thinker, the Zeus of Greeks whose names were never known.

The base is as much a character in the tableau as the other two, like something grown out of the mountains around us. Behind the figures, a pyramidal peak rises, and in the middle is an open doorway, the only feature with a normal human scale. It's not for the titans. It's for us. Every single one of us.

Because nobody has come empty-handed.

We are painters and photographers. We are musicians and technicians and scribes. By ones and twos, by trios and quartets, we ascend the stairs

227

and wind past goliaths who could crush us if they were alive, and make our way to the door and the deep stone chamber it accesses. We bring photos and paintings. We bring words. We bring music in as many formats as we can think of. We bring the sights and sounds of the world we knew, born of the love-hate relationship it's always had with us. We bring them exactly as we perceived them or as we interpreted them to be. We bring who we were, and what we saw and heard and felt, and we lay it in its tomb and then we let it go.

And it's possible, if not easy, to grieve and celebrate at the same time.

Forsyth watches from off to one side, sitting on the foot of a giant. He has a hug for whoever wants it, a smile or nod or wink for who doesn't. Mostly, he seems content to watch.

My turn, though? Not yet. Not yet.

I'm still participating through a viewfinder.

Someday, someone will come here. That's the idea. Someone will come. Even in the middle of a mountain range, along the spine of a continent, someone will come, and discover they were not the first. Maybe the far-future descendants of our next genetic bottleneck. Maybe whatever has become of whoever it was that took a planet and made a factory, then let it idle. Or maybe it will be someone with no context to know what to make of any of it.

But we've left them as much as we can.

A century from now, the houses may be heaps of rubble, but these guardians will still be standing. In five hundred years, there may be no trace that anyone lived here at all, but our magnificent monsters will be standing. A thousand years from now, the lake may be gone and their stone eyes may be looking out over a glacier or a desert, but they'll still be standing. . . .

Instilled with as much heart and knowledge as we were able to give them in so short a time as we had before the rain of ash began.

△

I end as I began, adding the last frames to the time-lapse sequence of a season's shots across the lake, only now there's a greater sense of urgency. It's all down to this, having returned to the workroom of our communal home, for one more session— from importing the concluding raw video to the final cut, in one last sprint.

But I have help. Everybody has a say. A house that isn't going to stand much longer is no place for tyrants.

From Aurora: Why not let that shot linger a few beats longer?

From Riley: This is where we should bring in my threnody, not there.

From Clark: Dude, what are you thinking? The last thing you need here is sound. You can't make out any of it and it takes the focus away from everybody's faces.

It's a group effort, and I might as well be twelve again, because there's no such thing as a bad idea.

When the power goes off, the countdown begins—we have only as long as the batteries hold out. I suppose that's a good incentive, because there's been this part of me thinking if we never finish, if we keep putting it off with one more edit, one more change in transition, one more minuscule shift of the last voice-over Riley recorded yesterday, that's fine, the time will always be there for us.

I'd rather still be arguing with these people six months from now.

Instead, as the last documentary takes its final form on our table, I have to come to peace with everything it isn't. The seams that show. The color palettes that aren't consistent. The jerky way it moves sometimes.

Beyond the walls, the August winter wind howls its fury and the black clouds descend and the lightning strikes so often that one crash of thunder overlaps the next. And for a moment that stops us all—maybe for no better reason than that we want to, need to—we hear from across the lake, and over the lightning, what sounds like the Promethean hammer of a god striking a chisel fit to split the world.

Endnotes: Because Black Holes Have Emissions After All

What you've just finished reading, unless you're cheating, is my fifth story collection . . . the 2.0 version. For most of its inception it had a different title, a slightly different running order, and was headed to a very different final destination.

Be of good cheer. We're all better off that it's ended up the way it has.

There's even a little magic afoot here, too.

I couldn't tell you why, exactly, but when the stars aligned and the time seemed right to put the thing together, I obeyed a compulsion to return to an approach that served my first two collections well.

The Convulsion Factory and *Falling Idols* were both gathered around a broadly unifying theme, and concluded with what I regarded as an anchor piece: a new novella designed to echo and further play around with a lot of the concepts and motifs of its companion stories.

Which turned out to be the right thing to do. When it was just me and the computer monitor, those hefty new pieces were valuable learning experiences. When they were published, they, and the books they lived in, were well received. I suspect that "Liturgical Music for Nihilists" was what cinched it for critic Stanley Wiater when he ranked *The Convulsion Factory* among his roster of the 113 best books of modern horror. The *Falling Idols* capstone, "As Above, So Below," eventually held down the year 1998 in the massive two-volume *The Century's Best Horror Fiction* anthology.

By the time the next two collections happened, that approach was no longer feasible, although *Lies & Ugliness* at least had thematic subgroups. But *Picking the Bones*? That roamed widely and at will, because so was I by then.

As a writer I've tended to go through phases . . . periods whose work has ended up characterized by a particular approach in aesthetics or topicality or both. Not exclusively—even Picasso did other things during his Blue Period—but they have a definite trend-line. There was the industrial phase. There was the religion phase, with an offshoot phase or two of its own. There was the era where I leaned heavily toward crime fiction. Lately I've been getting drawn toward fantasy.

Over the past few years, I've primarily been in a cosmic phase. Much of what I've written has skewed that direction. Sometimes it's of a more overtly Lovecraftian nature; sometimes not. I've found it as creatively rewarding as anything I've explored. There's no bigger canvas to paint on than the cosmos.

So I got after it with rocket-fueled enthusiasm, an ambitious piece that would also give the collection its title: *The Immaculate Void*.

Roughly 300% of my projected word count later, I'd accidentally written a novel.

Triumph? There was that. Dismay? That, too. The book-to-be was now . . . wrong. It *felt* wrong. Nothing is lopsided in quite the same way as a story collection bolted onto the front of a novel is lopsided. Months of planning and work had resulted in a mutant desperately hoping you wouldn't notice its giant deformed leg.

When publisher Brett Savory suggested splitting things up and putting out both a novel *and* a collection, my sigh of relief registered on that evening's local weather report. *The Immaculate Void* and *Skidding Into Oblivion* . . . they could stand as companion pieces, separate, each book allowed to be its own entity.

Alas, that left the collection right back where it started: with a vacancy where the journey should culminate. I didn't necessarily *have* to fill it. But it still felt wrong.

And here's where the sweet kiss of serendipity comes in.

As it happened, I had a newish piece that had spent most of the previous year in a kind of limbo, after the project I wrote it for went into a limbo of its own. The more I got to thinking about "One Last Year Without a Summer," for everything the closer needed to do, it was . . .

Ideal. What felt like the perfect terminus was already under my nose. I'd written it ten months before understanding what it was truly meant for.

"Time is a flat circle," said *True Detective*'s Rustin Cohle. "Everything we've ever done, or will do, we're gonna do over and over and over again."

From where I sit now, *The Convulsion Factory* and *Falling Idols* and their anchor pieces are early works from an irretrievable past. They were written in another place and time, by a prior custodian of my byline. He and I still say hello to each other on occasion, but are mostly content to keep to our respective time zones.

Even so, I wanted to see what would happen if I circled back to an approach he came up with. It didn't turn out the way either of us expected, but we managed to put aside our differences and work together pretty well, regardless.

Because, above all else, the thing we've done over and over and over again is trust the process.

It's the surest route to magic that I know.

♧ **Roots and All.** Around the time I read Steve Rasnic Tem's debut novel, *Excavations*, I also read an interview with him in which he quoted somebody saying that you had to be gone from a place you'd once lived for a lot of years before you could really write about it. At the time, in my twentysomething naïveté and arrogance, I couldn't see the validity of that. For proof, I might have waved in your face the first couple of novels I was working on. "Look! Parts of them are set in my hometown, and I'm still here."

Now I realize the distinction. Setting events there was the only thing I was doing. I wasn't actually writing *about* the place at all.

As for the fallen rural hamlet of "Roots and All," I didn't come from there. But my father did. My grandparents lived out their entire lives there, and so, growing up, I spent a lot of time there, too. Chunks of the summer. Weekends. Sunday afternoons. For the story, I made the house different, but nearly everything else was pretty much as described. Once upon a time.

My grandfather died when I was graduating from junior high. My grandmother lived until I was in my twenties. Sitting in her reading and sewing chair, glasses in hand—she really did go out that way.

By then, though, my visits were fewer and further between, infrequent enough to ask myself about the general area, "Did it always look this junky, or is it legitimately getting worse?" The wilderness lying outside their doors already seemed to be, not in retreat, but beaten down by encroaching new neighbors. Woodland had been cleared, and the A-frame hog shelter torn away. The little vineyard was gone. Land had been parceled and sold, and a trailer sat where the far gardens used to be.

Not long after my grandmother's death, I was summoned for jury duty at the county courthouse and ended up as one of the twelve who would determine the fate of the defendants in a civil lawsuit over a stabbing that had occurred in her community. This was my first prolonged look at how the area was changing. How it was rotting from within. It saddened me in ways I couldn't explain, but I knew I would have to weave it into a story someday.

Years passed. Moving to Colorado helped ensure that if I ever wrote it, whatever resulted might have the perspective that comes from looking back after being gone long enough. The urge lay dormant longer than expected, rekindled only after a visit back, and a mention from my uncle that the place had continued its sorry decline, having degenerated into a haven for meth cookers and addicts, and a number of convicted sex offenders who had chosen to settle there after doing their time.

Much of the rest you might call wishful thinking.

⁂ This Stagnant Breath of Change. There's a message that comes through loudest and clearest from horror and crime fiction and whatever it is that David Lynch does: While small towns may look placid on the surface, even idyllic, they're festering underneath.

Awhile back, I read the summary of a study that concluded that, despite all the fears directed at urban areas, you're statistically more likely to be murdered in a small town. The worst murders I've ever heard about took place in a tiny town twelve miles from the place I grew up, and still lived at the time. They haunted me for the twelve years they went unsolved. They didn't happen in a vacuum; they were the worst in an aberrantly bloody span of about sixteen months. Several years ago I wrote an essay about them, and the era they emerged out of, for a book benefiting the since-freed West Memphis Three, scapegoated victims of another multi-layered small-town nightmare.

So when the invitation came, I found the idea of placing a Lovecraftian story in a retro small-town setting instantly appealing. I loved the potential for juxtaposing the comfortably familiar and the unfathomably alien.

The more I tossed around ideas, the more I felt compelled to not merely *use* the small-town setting, but pry away at the reverence American culture has for it in the first place.

We excel at polishing a Golden Age nostalgia that celebrates what's genuinely good about small towns by overlooking or downplaying aspects about them that were never worth preserving. For instance, the legacy of what have been called "sundown towns": *If you have the wrong color skin, you may get away with walking our streets in daylight, but make sure the sun doesn't set on you here.* I grew up a few miles from one of those, too, and spoke to people who remembered seeing the sign along the road in.

Just as crucial was getting at how the good old days were really the province of good old boys, with their vested interest in preserving the status quo, to make sure everything stayed ripe for the picking.

I tapped many memories of where I came from to weave into this, and they were good ones. I hope that comes through. Just the same, I was reminded of Hemingway's subtly barbed comment on St. Louis: that it was a good place to be *from*.

☫ Scars In Progress. The title came first, by a wide margin. One day I was skimming some technical material and misread the phrase "scans in progress," which jolted me out of what I was semi-focusing on at the time. I knew I had a keeper and had to jot it down. Happy accidents, a photographer friend called things like that.

It would be great if I could say those three words suggested an entire narrative, but they did no such thing. Instead, they sat around for two or three years on a scrap of paper, freeloading, not lifting a finger to earn their keep. Until John Skipp invited me to add some pages to a big doorstop of a book about demons he was editing. I wasn't that far into the story before I realized that this was the piece the title had been waiting for.

I have a deep, abiding thing for ruins, both ancient and modern. It's been there, a favorite aesthetic flavor, for as long as I can remember. So our modern ruins struck me as the kind of locales where contemporary demons would hang out, in the guise of the sort of people we try to avoid engaging with eye contact.

That last bit seemed especially important. There's something about the classical representation of demons that now seems more quaint than anything. Their images are used for marketing. I kid you not: As I'm writing this, I've been tipping back a bottle of Avery Brewing Company's White Rascal, a Belgian-style wheat ale whose label is ruled by a pale, sharp-faced imp with red talons and a spiky tail. He never scares me. He makes me happy every time I see him.

Other storytellers have faced this conundrum.

A prime example: *Jacob's Ladder*, with Tim Robbins, from . . . holy shit, 1990 already? For years, Bruce Joel Rubin's screenplay was one of those legendary properties that floated around Hollywood, beloved by nearly everyone who read it, yet it was widely considered unfilmable because of the ambition of its visuals. The depiction of demons it called for could hardly have been derived from a more classical source—creatures and infernal vistas inspired by Gustave Dore's woodcut illustrations for a lavish 19th-century edition of Dante's *Divine Comedy*.

When the film finally went into production, director Adrian Lyne went a different route, embedding his demons in New York as a part of the everyday cityscape, in its cracks and crevices and lesser byways and shadowed hallways. I can understand why, even without the budgetary restrictions in an age when rampant CGI effects were still years away. It made the demons feel so much closer to home. They were just human enough for their otherworldly aspects to seem all the more inhuman. For their look, Lyne traded in Dore for the work of photographer Joel-Peter

Witkin, whose tableaux and grotesques have, for me, the same kind of weird beauty that I find compatible with all the finest ruins. With some influence from painter Francis Bacon, too, if I recall correctly.

My own go-to guy, however, was the late Polish surrealist Zdzislaw Beksinski. I discovered Beksinski more than a decade ago, and have gotten a lot of inspirational mileage out of his work ever since, both in fiction and when recording ambient soundscapes. The paintings from his more fantastical years are often macabre, often disturbing, often dark and dismal and full of his own take on ruins. Yet to Beksinski—who was a child in Nazi-occupied Poland during the Second World War and no doubt saw enough horror to last lifetimes—his only intention was to create what he regarded as beautiful paintings. They're that, too.

I can identify with his longing. I just want to write beautiful stories.

⚜ Just Outside Our Windows, Deep Inside Our Walls. It's rare for me to write an extended fragment of something, then leave it indefinitely, without knowing the larger narrative it connects to, but that's how this got its start. I wrote the sequence about the fantasized magic show, plus the earliest bit about Roni moving in, after rereading Thomas Ligotti's first collection, *Songs of a Dead Dreamer*. It may not be apparent to anyone else, but some flavor of his lingered in me and needed an outlet, and the magic show was the result.

This orphan then sat idle for three years before I knew what more to do with it. Maybe because I had to shake loose of its conception and pick it back up after feeling like myself again.

I identified with the isolation of the narrator. Because I never had siblings, and the neighborhood where I grew up had just a handful of other kids, I spent a lot of time in solitude. Lately, in bios, I've taken to describing myself as one of those people who must always be making something, and this is where it got its start: models, dioramas, drawings, stories, sound experiments with tape recorders, weapons, black powder explosives, and invasion plans, if only I had an army. The house directly faced the city park, and when I wasn't playing there myself, I found it interesting to spy on people at a distance.

To an extent, I also shared the narrator's disgust with particular adults. Some of them were fine—some of them were beloved—but a great many of them seemed to me ponderously big, gratingly loud, and smelly, with breath to make you recoil. They seemed like some other species, and I couldn't imagine growing up to be like them. I emphatically didn't want to, and don't think I have.

There's a certain amount of integrity in that, I like to think . . . but then again, it means that I'm also familiar with what it's like to be, ehh, not what your parents had in mind.

ℙ **Eternal, Ever Since Wednesday.** As a writer, I got my start, my *real* start, in the pages of a small press magazine called *The Horror Show*. Since my junior year of high school, I'd been winning or placing in academic contests and publishing in student literary magazines and newspapers. But *The Horror Show* marked the beginning of sending off a manuscript to someone across the country and waiting for a verdict. After a couple of near misses, with entreaties to try again, a postcard arrived to inform me of my first story acceptance.

The Horror Show was the brainchild of an earthbound saint named David B. Silva. He wore many hats—writer, editor, publisher, mentor—and shone brightly at all of them. Maybe mentor most of all. Dave provided a place where I was able to learn and grow and discover like-minded others. He freely gave encouragement and feedback and constructive criticism. He loaned books by mail. In total, he published eight of my early stories, and featured me in one of the magazine's two Rising Stars issues. That first story soon grew into my first novel, *Oasis*.

Dave's impact on my life is inestimable, and I'm far from alone in that. He did such things for many fledgling writers.

And a few years ago, he died.

So when Dave's friend and colleague and co-editor on various projects, Paul F. Olson, hatched the idea to edit a new anthology as a tribute to him, he began by rounding up a roster of writers who became fixtures in the magazine and gauging their interest. I didn't have to think about it. *Count me in. I am so in.*

I viewed it as an opportunity to look back. I wanted whatever I did to reflect that heritage, to feel directly connected to it. My ultimate intention, if such a thing were even possible, was to write the kind of story I might have written during those early years of the magazine, but at my current level of craft.

Which sounds good, but I'd written 100+ more stories since then, and a number of books, and didn't feel much like the same human anymore, let alone the same writer. But, at minimum, I could attempt to work the same way. Back then, that meant latching onto a bonehead simple idea—often drawn from some recent observation or experience—and running with it. This time, all I had to do was look out the window. It was late winter and had been snowing for days.

Hence the question: *What if it didn't stop? What if what began as that favorite thing of grade-school students everywhere, the snow day, had no end?*

That's all it took, and it really did feel like revisiting the past.

I still love snow days, when the weather discourages going any farther than you can trudge by foot. They just pass a lot faster than they used to.

⚡ Let My Smile Be Your Umbrella. Whenever editors invite me into a project that has the potential to involve obvious tropes, I try to ricochet in the opposite direction. Such was the challenge when Stephen Jones asked me into *Psycho-Mania*, which would evoke the spirit of Robert Bloch, who will always be best known as the father of Norman Bates.

In context, then, what could be more counterintuitive than happiness and positive thinking?

There's something creepy about people who strive to be so relentlessly upbeat and cheerful that they wear their happiness persona like a shiny suit of armor. It feels as if it's shackled in place to keep something contained, rather than projected. Sometimes you can sense the pressure, and know that eventually something's going to blow.

Most therapists worth their diplomas will tell you that to be an emotionally healthy, psychologically integrated person, you need to go through the down days, the dark times, without any filters in the way. I'm not talking about clinical depression, just the lows and blows of everyday life. Western society, particular here in the U.S., has developed an aversion to this. Which no doubt helps explain the title of a 2011 entry from Harvard Medical School's Health Publications: "Astounding Increase In Antidepressant Use By Americans." This sits side-by-cultural-side with a multibillion-dollar positivity industry that often preaches an end goal of 24/7 bliss, with implications that any failure to lock it down is a personal defect that needs to be fixed.

The story was intent on having the last laugh. Its final word count came in at 5150: California's law enforcement code for an involuntary psychiatric hold.

Halfway through, I started working on it while listening solely to the Cure's *Disintegration* album, maybe the greatest paean to gloom ever recorded. It helped me get in touch with HungryGirl234 better. My second favorite track is called "The Same Deep Water As You," and because I knew, once this story was done I was going to jump straight into a piece about Lovecraft's Innsmouth, it felt like I was ahead of the game by at least realizing I'd found the perfect title to steal.

▽ **We, the Fortunate Bereaved.** Two-for-one day at the story mill. For what seemed like forever, I wanted to write a story set on Halloween, but never had. For nearly as long, I'd wanted to write a story involving scarecrows, and had never managed to come up with an idea for that, either . . . at least one that didn't fail the five-minute test:

Minute one. *Hmm, this could be a cool idea.*

Minute five. *We shall never speak of this again.*

Then I picked up an out-of-print, nonfiction British import—*The Scarecrow, Fact and Fable*, by Peter Haining. While interesting, it wasn't the gold mine of idea fodder I was hoping it would be. Still, all you need is one. It wasn't like I had a master plan to corner the market with an extensive line of scarecrow stories. So one was enough. I read the entire book for the single line that referred to an old folkloric belief that scarecrows could come to life on Halloween.

I had never heard this before. The book didn't elaborate, which was just as well, because that meant I wouldn't have any prior associations getting in the way as I tried to figure out the W-questions. Why? And why just this one night of the year? What do they want? What's the life force that animates them, and where is it the other 364.5 days of the year? Who are they when they're alive?

In the end, I decided to cap the scarecrow quota at one, and the less it did, the better. Because it's a still a flimsy scarecrow, after all. They don't make for durable foes.

⛤ **One Possible Shape of Things to Come.** This piece came straight out of one of those junk food list articles that seem to comprise a third of the Internet: "The 20 Creepiest Things Kids Ever Said" . . . something like that. Everything appeared copied verbatim from various boards and forums. Several entries involved children being precociously morbid. With others, the implication was that the kids were seeing ghosts or spirits. Some knew things they shouldn't have.

Then there was the one from a babysitter who recounted checking on her charge after bedtime, to find the boy standing in the corner. When asked what he was doing there, the kid turned his head away from the corner and slowly raised his finger to shush the babysitter: "Shhhh. It is the punishment."

That was the pick of the litter. That was the sticky one.

It's an odd comparison, but maybe you remember Gary Larson's *The Far Side* cartoons. They're still around, in one form and another. I've always found the funniest ones to be those that depict more than an isolated instant in time. They work by forcing you to imagine either something that has happened the moment before, or what's going to happen a moment later.

For me, this babysitter's anecdote operates in the same way. It's part of a bigger sequence of events, only you—now the babysitter by proxy, standing mystified and creeped-out in the bedroom doorway—have no idea what they are.

But think it through: A punishment suggests there has been a transgression. A transgression means that something's rule or sense of propriety has been violated. A punishment is most often imposed from a greater system of authority and order upon a transgressor of lesser power, with an implication that even worse consequences will follow if it's not fulfilled. Or, worst of all, it may be arbitrary, punitive measures for someone or something's entertainment.

From the doorway, you don't know. You can only imagine.

So I tried to think as big as I could, looking at something as small as a child standing in the corner and finding in it an extinction event.

△ **Cures for a Sickened World.** A few people have, I know for certain, assumed that I wrote this as a reaction to having gotten a bad review. There are probably many more that I don't know about who concluded this. Why, what other explanation could there possibly be?

They're half right. It was indeed inspired by a vicious review. Just not a review of anything I'd done, or even cared about.

While spending too much time on Facebook one afternoon, I saw a link posted by author Steven Savile, with this observation, more or less: *No matter how bad a review I might ever get, it could never be this bad.*

It was a full-bore assault on a then-new Coldplay album. Scathing doesn't begin to describe it. I've seen plenty of bad reviews, but never one like this. I looked up a few other pieces by the same "reviewer"—a term to be used in the loosest sense possible—and he appears to have been at this a long time. His shtick seems to be that he decided years ago that he hates everything and everyone, and in justifying this foregone conclusion strives to be as insulting as possible, even if he has to bring your family into it. Apparently it's supposed to be comedy, rather than anything that would land within pissing distance of that pitiful dying creature known as journalistic integrity.

Not a lot of people actually seemed amused. But in the age of clickbait, hate-readers are every bit as good as genuine fans.

Truthfully, I don't give a shit about Coldplay. I don't think I've ever heard one of their songs in its entirety. So the review would've bubbled back down into the tar pit of Internet ooze within a day or two, if not for an unrelated factor of such impeccably timed synchronicity I can only conclude the muse was working extra hard to line things up.

At the time, I happened to be happily plowing through Dayal Patterson's big, fat, encyclopedic book *Black Metal: Evolution of the Cult*. I may not care about Coldplay, but I love me some black metal, and as I was reading that review, the thought arose: *How might one of those crazed Norwegians from black metal's early years react to this? What if someone decided to take this reviewer's hyperbole at face value?*

Black metal is another topic I'd wanted to write about forever. For darker speculative fiction, it seems a natural fit. Its world is full of extreme personalities. Its aesthetics are nightmarish, its metaphysics grim. If anything can lay claim to the title of the devil's music, this is it.

The tricky bit? It can also be riotously cartoonish. On those few occasions I'd read the work of someone else bringing in black metal, they never confronted this stumbling block. They sidestepped it and played everything straight, as if this weren't a factor.

It was a eureka moment. In the Coldplay review, here was the solution: Put the cartoonishness front and center, at the heart of the entire conflict. Instead of ignoring it or pretending it doesn't exist, go straight at it, in order to go *through* it into something else.

In the aftermath, the few fellow black metal fans I've talked to about it seemed to pick right up on the real-life character who served as the loose model for Tomas/Ghast. Amusingly, all the reviews I saw were complimentary, with *Locus Magazine* going so far as to put the story on their Recommended Reading List for 2014. I choose to think they all took it as a warning.

🜐 **The Same Deep Waters As You.** Any time seminal editor Stephen Jones gets in touch to ask me into something is a great day. But his invitation to contribute to the final volume of his trilogy of Innsmouth anthologies was one of the high points of recent years.

Innsmouth, of course, is the decayed seaport setting of one of H.P. Lovecraft's most highly regarded tales. I'd read *The Shadow Over Innsmouth* several times since I was in college, when I rounded up those ubiquitous Del Rey paperbacks collecting much of Lovecraft's work. Not once, though, had I wondered what had happened to all those Innsmouth residents taken prisoner during the raids of early 1928. Not until I sat down to read the novella once again, this time with the specific intention of looking for entry points from which I could spin off something of my own. Then it jumped right out at me. It seemed *too* obvious, yet I was unaware of any other work that had explored this thread. It at least hadn't come up in either of Steve's prior Innsmouth books, and for me, that was the only green light necessary.

I wasn't only intrigued by the question for its own sake, postulating an answer within the parameters of Lovecraft's universe. It also occurred to me that the Innsmouth prisoners might well constitute the original precedent for the terrorism-era U.S. policy of endless detention without due process.

The anomalous ocean recording in the story was a genuine, real-world event, and another of those things I'd kept sitting around for years, itching to play with it. In an irresistible coincidence, the Bloop was triangulated to have originated close to where Lovecraft located the sunken city of R'lyeh.

In another bit of synchronicity, a few weeks after I finished this piece— fifteen years after the event, mind you—the National Oceanic and Atmospheric Administration announced that they'd concluded the sound was similar to the sonic profile of icebergs recorded in the Scotia Sea. They would know, although I'd love to learn more about how there would've been enough ice around Polynesia that August that its calving was picked up 3,000 miles away. It's more fun living in a world where this remains a mystery.

As I finalize these notes, the same is happening with a contract to option this story for adaptation into a TV series by a London-based production company. Much yay.

♂ **One Last Year Without a Summer.** By this point it's starting to feel like a clearance sale at the idea warehouse. That whole overly romanticized mystique around Lake Geneva, summer 1816? Yeah, that's had a grip on my imagination for a long time, too, yet another bottle waiting to be uncorked after blowing off a thick coat of cellar dust.

After I returned the cap and gown from the last graduation ceremony I would ever attend, and the phrase "summer break" would no longer have any relevance to my next eighty or so years, the season ceased to offer much of anything I craved, except for its movies. I tolerate heat, but only to get to the good stuff on the other side. Give me fall and winter, and plenty of them. I like rain. I like storms and clouds and thunder. I like snow and ice, fires and fleece.

So, the idea of trading in the sun's cruelest months for more of that, with good company, spectacular scenery, and all the time, space, and conducive atmospheres to write that anyone could want . . . ? Sounds like paradise.

It's not really about the thermometer, though.

There has always been more behind the peculiar appeal of 1816 than granting spring an extension and getting an early jump on autumn, until they join seamlessly in the middle. It's the backdrop of anomaly that's always stirred my imagination the most . . . the underlying sense that something exceptionally strange was going on in the world, even if you didn't know why, and maybe things would sort themselves out and maybe they wouldn't, so best to not take a single day for granted, and to live with the intent of squeezing the most out of each one that you can.

The times we remember most vividly, and assign the most meaning, are the ones that break the mold.

If I couldn't live such a summer, I could at least write about it and experience it vicariously. Except no scenario ever seemed right for going there.

Not until I decided it had to be the very last one. For the urgency.

It's never been put better, or more starkly, than by Samuel Johnson, thirty-eight years before the eruption of Mount Tambora: "When a man knows he is to be hanged in a fortnight, it concentrates his mind wonderfully."

Final Credits Where Credit Is Due:

Big thanks to the editors and anthologists who asked me to write for them and were happy enough with the results to run with it: Stephen Jones; John Skipp; Shane Ryan Staley; Paul F. Olson; Mark Morris; Doug Murano and D. Alexander Ward; and Christopher Jones, Nanci Kalanta, and Paul Tremblay. Thanks, too, to Ellen Datlow and Paula Guran, plus Steve Jones again, for seeing fit to give five of these pieces extended lives in their respective year's-best and additional anthologies, and *Locus* magazine for naming three of them to their annual Recommended Reading lists.

Thanks, magnified, to Brett Savory and Sandra Kasturi of ChiZine Publications—first for thinking this book would be a good idea, and then for seeing their way clear to splitting the baby in two and still having two beautiful healthy babies.

And if you've made it this far, thanks to you, too, the reader. I'd do this anyway, but as long as you're there, that makes it so much better.

—Brian
October 2017

xiv

Publication History

"Roots and All" © Brian Hodge 2011. First published in *A Book of Horrors*.

"This Stagnant Breath of Change" © Brian Hodge 2015. First published in *Shadows Over Main Street*.

"Scars In Progress" © Brian Hodge 2011. First published in *Demons*.

"Just Outside Our Windows, Deep Inside Our Walls" © Brian Hodge 2010. First published by Darkside Digital.

"Eternal, Ever Since Wednesday" © Brian Hodge 2015. First published in *Better Weird*.

"Let My Smile Be Your Umbrella" © Brian Hodge 2013. First published in *Psycho-Mania*.

"We, the Fortunate Bereaved" © Brian Hodge 2013. First published in *Halloween: Tales of Magic, Mystery, and the Macabre*.

"One Possible Shape of Things to Come" © Brian Hodge 2015. First published in *Eulogies III*.

"Cures for a Sickened World" © Brian Hodge 2014. First published in *The Spectral Book of Horror Stories*.

"The Same Deep Waters As You" © Brian Hodge 2013. First published in *Weirder Shadows Over Innsmouth*.

"One Last Year Without a Summer" © Brian Hodge 2019. Original to this edition.

"Endnotes: Because Black Holes Have Emissions After All" © Brian Hodge 2019. Original to this edition.

About The Author

Brian Hodge is one of those people who always has to be making something. So far, he's made eleven novels, around 130 shorter works, and five full-length collections.

His latest titles include the novel *The Immaculate Void*, and *I'll Bring You the Birds From Out of the Sky*, a novella of cosmic horror paired with folk art illustrations. More of everything is in the works.

He lives in Colorado, where he also likes to make music and photographs; loves everything about organic gardening except the thieving squirrels; and trains in Krav Maga and kickboxing, which are of no use at all against the squirrels.

Connect through Brian's web site (www.brianhodge.net), Twitter (@BHodgeAuthor), or Facebook (www.facebook.com/brianhodgewriter).

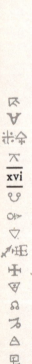